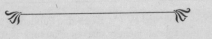
"Ready?" Mr. Dare inquired.

"Actually, no," Clara said, releasing Bear's hand and leaning back in her chair. "It's very warm in here, and this cape feels restrictive." Pulling open the ribbons that tied the cape in front, she smiled up at Ben Dare. "Would you?"

"It would be my pleasure." Stepping behind her, Ben lifted the cape from her shoulders.

The audience released a hissing noise like the sound of escaping steam, followed by a stunned silence. Bear's eyes widened and his jaw dropped and he didn't even try to disguise the direction of his gaze.

"Oh—my—God," he whispered hoarsely, staring down into her cleavage. It was impressive cleavage indeed. The good Lord hadn't given her big hips without balancing her out with glorious breasts.

Clara gripped his hand hard, putting her strength behind the clasp. They leaned into each other over the corner of the table, gazing deeply into each other's eyes. Then Clara slowly and deliberately licked the tip of her tongue around the edges of her parted lips.

And bang, she had him. . . .

Also by Maggie Osborne
Published by Ivy Books:

SILVER LINING

I DO, I DO, I DO

Maggie Osborne

IVY BOOKS • NEW YORK

An Ivy Book
Published by The Ballantine Publishing Group
Copyright © 2000 by Maggie Osborne

www.randomhouse.com

Library of Congress Catalog Card Number: 00-105284

ISBN 0-449-00517-8

Manufactured in the United States of America

First Edition: October 2000

10 9 8 7 6 5 4 3 2 1

Prologue

———

September 10, 1896
Linda Vista, California

"Do you, Jean Jacques Villette, take Juliette March for your lawfully wedded wife?"
"I do."

January 2, 1897
Sandy Hollow, Oregon

"Do you, Jean Jacques Villette, take Clara Klaus for your lawfully wedded wife?"
"I do."

April 30, 1897
Seattle, Washington

"Do you, Jean Jacques Villette, take Zoe Wilder for your lawfully wedded wife?"
"I do."

Chapter 1

"I know Jean Jacques would send word if he could. Something must be terribly wrong."

"What's wrong is Mr. Villette seduced you, stole your money, and then he abandoned you." Aunt Kibble lowered her embroidery hoop to her lap and reached for the palmetto fan to swat at a cloud of gnats. "Everyone in the county knows this except you. You refuse to admit the truth."

Juliette folded her arms across her chest and leaned against the porch post, fixing her gaze on the dirt road that curved past Aunt Kibble's house. Nine long months ago, Jean Jacques had ridden away at one o'clock. Therefore, he would return at one o'clock, but only if she was waiting for him on the porch.

And he would return only if she set a place for him at every meal.

Only if she brushed her hair one hundred strokes.

Jean Jacques would come back if she always wore the blue garter that she'd been wearing when they met.

Heaven help her. Raising a hand, she rubbed her forehead. When had she started performing these silly rituals? What lunacy made her believe that standing on the porch at one o'clock possessed some kind of magic that would bring Jean Jacques back to her?

"He's my husband, not a seducer. He didn't steal anything, I lent him money because he was temporarily embarrassed. And he didn't abandon me. He rode out of

2

here with the intention of finding and buying us a home of our own."

Aunt Kibble waved the fan so rapidly that tendrils of brown and gray hair fluttered up from her forehead. "This is what comes from marrying in haste. I know you don't want to hear it, Juliette, but there are scheming men who marry women for their money."

"So you've been telling me for years." Juliette held her gaze on the road. A wagon had passed, and two riders. But no Jean Jacques. He wasn't coming home today.

"This time you lost your head." Setting aside the fan, Aunt Kibble frowned and ran her thumb along a line of embroidered rosebuds twining across the pillowcase hem. "Villette is a confidence man, and confidence men are smooth talkers. He talked you into such a fever that you wouldn't listen to reason."

Each time they had this conversation (which was more and more frequently of late) Juliette felt like screaming and tearing her hair and hammering her fists against something breakable.

But her mother had always said: *If you can't be a beauty, you must strive to be an impeccable lady.* Juliette's self-worth depended on being a lady, so she didn't have tantrums.

She didn't speak to strangers, didn't associate with the wrong sort of people. She didn't rush about or act in haste; her movements were restrained and graceful. She wouldn't dream of being loud or assertive or immodest. She was always kind to those less fortunate than herself; she put the wishes and comfort of others before her own needs. She considered herself a perfect lady, one whom the other women in Linda Vista could seek to emulate.

In the tradition of the gently bred, she had spent a lifetime doing what she ought and squelching any selfish impulse to do what she wanted. When a conflict arose between her personal desires and the proper course, she set her wishes aside and never failed to act in the proper manner.

Once only had she closed her eyes to propriety and followed her heart. And she hadn't regretted her marriage. When Jean Jacques placed his hands on her waist and gazed into her eyes, the *should*s and *ought*s evaporated like fog in the rays of the sun.

"Never in a month of Sundays would I have believed you'd fall prey to a man's sweet talk. Or that you'd agree to an impulsive marriage."

Juliette waved a hand at the gnats that pestered her now. Usually a cooling ocean breeze flowed down the slopes of the Klamath Mountains and carried away the insects, but today the summer air hung still and shimmered with heat.

"Is it so hard for you to believe that a man could love me?" She twisted her wedding ring on her finger, the ring that had first belonged to Jean Jacques's grandmother and then to his mother. He wouldn't have given her an heirloom if he hadn't intended to return.

"Oh, Juliette!" Distress widened Aunt Kibble's eyes. "You have many, many fine qualities. But you didn't know Mr. Villette long enough for him to discover your qualities. Therefore, his insistence on rushing to the altar must have been motivated by a reason less noble than love."

Juliette noticed that her aunt did not define those many, many fine qualities. And far from being reassuring, Aunt Kibble seemed to underscore the notion that any man who proposed a swift marriage must be in love with Juliette's inheritance.

Despite a determined resistance on Juliette's part, her aunt's oft-stated condemnation had begun to carve small inroads on her mind. Was it really possible that Jean Jacques had been more interested in her money than in Juliette herself? Could she have been a victim rather than an angel as he had claimed?

She let the questions torment her all afternoon, as she

had done so often of late. It seemed that all she did anymore was perform the stupid rituals that she hoped would bring Jean Jacques back to her—and think about every minute they had spent together.

The thing was, Jean Jacques couldn't have known about her inheritance. He had been in Linda Vista for only two days when Juliette collided with him in the doorway of the post office. Meeting him had been the result of serendipity, not of calculation.

All right, he *might* have somehow learned about Linda Vista's wealthiest spinster, but she couldn't imagine how that would have happened. And yes, he *might* have lain in wait for her at the post office—as Aunt Kibble believed—but Juliette had no regular time when she called for the mail. Moreover, Mr. Albertson, the postmaster, would have noticed a man loitering for any length of time and would have ordered him to leave.

It wasn't the money.

Jean Jacques claimed that he fell in love with her the minute he steadied her after the collision, and Juliette believed him. She had gazed up and observed an expression she had never before seen on a man's face. He looked dazed, confounded. His dark eyes had glowed with desire and—dare she say it?—love. As astonishing as it seemed, already he had begun to love her.

She had to believe it was love at first sight exactly as Jean Jacques claimed. The alternative was to accept that she had been tricked and manipulated, lied to and used.

After tidying her hair for dinner, she studied her pale face in the vanity mirror.

Jean Jacques had whispered that her gray eyes reminded him of shining pewter. He had made her feel pretty. Now, as she looked into the glass, she remembered herself as she had become in the glow of her husband's admiration.

During the brief period of their marriage, a constant smile had curved her lips—lips made rosy by kissing.

He'd made her laugh. And oh, how he had teased her, poking fun at the ladylike restrictions that defined her life. In bed, he had swept away all modesty and inhibitions and made her forget they had ever been important. In bed she had been anything but a lady.

A rush of heat scalded her throat, and she pressed her palms to her cheeks.

It couldn't have been just the money.

Following dinner, Aunt Kibble resumed the afternoon's conversation. "How long are you going to pretend that Mr. Villette will return? A year? Five years? The rest of your life?"

Juliette placed her hands in her lap and turned her wedding ring around her finger. "Maybe he was struck on the head. I read a book in which that happened. When the man regained consciousness, he had no memory of the heroine."

"Amnesia occurs very rarely in real life, Juliette. I sincerely doubt that Mr. Villette is off spending your money with no memory of how he got it."

"But it *could* have happened," she insisted, leaning forward and wanting Aunt Kibble to agree.

"He's a confidence man. That explains his absence and his silence." Aunt Kibble waited until after Howard had served coffee and withdrawn from the dining room before she continued. "For the sake of discussion, let us suppose there are three possibilities. Mr. Villette may be dead. He may be wandering about with amnesia. Or he may have abandoned you and is now wooing his next victim." She lowered a lump of sugar into her coffee. "Where does that leave you?"

"I don't know," Juliette whispered, twisting her hands.

Aunt Kibble leaned back in her chair. "The truth is, you don't know much about this man."

"But I do! First, he's second-generation French." When he whispered her name his soft accent made the word sound like a thrilling endearment. "He has no surviving family. He's a successful businessman who owns an import-export company." When Aunt Kibble's expressive eyebrows soared, Juliette waved her hand in an exasperated gesture. "Large amounts of his fortune are tied up in inventory. That's the nature of the import-export business."

"Is it really?"

Juliette ignored her aunt's raised eyebrow. "Jean Jacques owns two companies, one in San Francisco and one in Seattle. He felt we should locate our home in Oregon, midway between his business interests."

"And how did you feel about that decision? To my knowledge, you've never stepped foot beyond the county lines. But you were willing to pack up and move to Oregon? Frankly, Juliette, this astonishes me."

The notion of leaving everything safe and familiar had alarmed and frightened her. A great deal of persuasion had been required for Jean Jacques to overcome her resistance.

But Jean Jacques possessed a gift for persuasion. "Darling, there is a big world out there, and you have seen none of it. You haven't walked on a beach and felt the sand between your toes. You've never caught a snowflake on your tongue. You have never listened to the noisy heartbeat of a large city or ridden in a streetcar." He had placed his hands on her shoulders and gazed into her eyes. "I want you to experience all these things and more. Seeing a bit of the wide world will change you in ways you cannot now imagine."

He intended to begin her transformation by building her a magnificent home overlooking the ocean. It was time to leave Aunt Kibble. Every woman needed a home of her own. Every couple required privacy. A new marriage deserved a new beginning. It would be difficult to manage his business from a small town like Linda Vista.

Gradually, the weight of reason toppled her objections. She had agreed to a home perched on the coast of

Oregon. And then she had written a bank draft—a loan, he insisted—and he had ridden away.

"Moving to Oregon will be difficult," she conceded. Jean Jacques had worn away her protests, but not her anxiety or her fear of travel and the unknown. Even Jean Jacques could not completely convert her timidity to boldness.

"Is it necessary to point out that nothing he told you about himself has been verified? You have only Mr. Villette's word that he's a wealthy businessman, and that his fortune was tied up in—what was it?—inventory. He could have invented everything he told you."

She didn't believe that. In any case, she knew the important things. She knew that Jean Jacques was a man who savored every minute, who lived each day as if it were his last and best. She'd never known anyone who took such joy in small things. He rhapsodized about the shine of sunlight in her hair, saw poetry in her earlobe. He could recite in two languages, and he liked to read aloud before sleeping. He teased about her attention to etiquette, but she hadn't minded.

Their wedding night proved his capacity for patience and tenderness. In the ensuing weeks, she had observed his unselfish commitment always to put her pleasure before his own. Most important, Jean Jacques Villette had made her feel cherished and loved, pretty and interesting and desirable, and younger than her twenty-nine years.

These were the truths that mattered. Not whether his background and his bank account measured up to the impossible standards that had turned Juliette into a spinster.

"I wish he would come home."

"He never will, darling. The sooner you accept that, the sooner you can get on with your life."

But she couldn't go on as if her marriage had never happened. She had to do something. Waiting for him was driving her crazy.

"It's time to begin divorce proceedings," Aunt Kibble

said, pouring more coffee. "As I've been advising you to do for weeks."

Juliette drew a breath and stiffened her backbone.

"Respectable people do not divorce." She paused and then made herself state her decision aloud. "I've considered what to do for weeks, and I've reached the conclusion that my only course is to search for Jean Jacques. Perhaps he wrote, sending for me, but his letter was lost. Or he may be lying in a hospital bed, horribly injured, wondering why I haven't come."

Aunt Kibble's mouth dropped, and she stared. "Are you saying that you intend to travel to Oregon?"

Juliette shrank from the word *travel* and the images of change it conjured. She didn't like new experiences. "I'll follow my husband's most likely route. If that takes me all the way to Oregon, then I suppose that's where I'll end." Merely talking about leaving all that was safe and familiar made her feel slightly ill.

"I can't agree to this foolishness," Aunt Kibble said after a moment. "If your mother were alive, she would strenuously disapprove."

"With due respect, Aunt, I don't require permission to search for my husband." Aside from announcing her marriage, this was the bravest thing she had ever said to Aunt Kibble.

"You do require a companion," Aunt Kibble reminded her sharply. "But I'm too old to go traipsing around the countryside on a fool's errand. I won't do it, Juliette."

She had anticipated this response and steeled herself for what must follow. "I can't stay here and do nothing because I lack a traveling companion. If I must, I'll search for my husband alone." Everything in her shrank from this decision, but there was no longer a choice. She had to know what had happened to Jean Jacques.

Aunt Kibble gasped and pressed a hand to her mouth. "You're making another dreadful mistake. Haven't you learned that following the dictates of your heart instead of the rules of propriety only leads to disaster?"

Juliette couldn't bear not knowing. When she stood on the porch at one o'clock watching the road, she felt as if she were losing her mind.

As for what her mother might have said . . . She had worried over that question for weeks. Certainly a respectable woman did not chase after a man, not even if the man who needed chasing was her husband. She suspected her mother would have advised her to hold her head high and live out her days pretending that her husband would return at any moment.

Over the last nine months Juliette had done just that, but she couldn't follow that path any longer. Her bone-deep need to know gave her the daring to flout propriety and travel alone.

But, heaven above. The world beyond Linda Vista was alien and frightening, peopled with strangers who didn't know or care about Juliette March Villette.

The outside world wouldn't know that her needlepoint had won a blue ribbon at the fair last Fourth of July. Strangers wouldn't care that when she was twenty, she'd been chosen to carry one end of the memorial quilt in the Founder's Day parade. No one would give a fig that she kept the milkweed off her parents' graves or that every week she dutifully dropped fifty cents in the Cup for Charity.

Moving among strangers would shake her very foundation. How could she know who she was if no one around her knew?

For the occasion of Juliette's departure, Aunt Kibble wore her best at-home dress and powdered her nose.

Juliette touched gloved fingertips to her aunt's cheek while Aunt Kibble fussed with Juliette's traveling suit, straightening her collar, adjusting her hat, picking imaginary lint from her sleeve.

"Thank you for taking me in." Aunt Kibble had rescued her from the yellow fever epidemic that carried away her parents.

"You sound as if you'll never come back!"

"I don't know why I said that." Nerves made her hands shake. The instant she found Jean Jacques, she'd bring him home and use her own powers of persuasion to convince him to stay and never leave Linda Vista again.

"You know why I won't go with you. It's a matter of principle." Aunt Kibble drew a deep breath. "This is so unlike you. Why won't you send a representative?"

Juliette didn't trust a representative to keep her secrets if he discovered the worst. She had her pride after all. Not that she believed for a moment that Jean Jacques had abandoned her.

But just in case.

All things considered, it was better that she found him herself.

Aunt Kibble lifted a handkerchief to her eyes. "It isn't too late to change your mind," she said, shooting a glare toward the carriage driver.

"I have to do this," Juliette insisted.

"You don't even know where you're going!"

"I have a general idea." She'd consulted maps, plotted the route she guessed Jean Jacques had taken. He hadn't said anything about the Northern Pacific, so she wouldn't travel by train. He'd mentioned wonderful views of the ocean, so she would stay along the coast. The route was sheer speculation, but it was the best she could do.

"I'm going to miss you so much!" The admission appeared to surprise and annoy Aunt Kibble.

Juliette studied her aunt's dear face, committing to memory the stubborn jaw, the tiny lines, a sweep of silvery brown hair. Then she clung to Aunt Kibble in a fierce embrace, murmuring good-bye as if this were, indeed, the last time they would see one another.

The driver had to clear his throat a third time before

Juliette wiped tears from her eyes and climbed into the carriage.

"This is my duty," she called, leaning out the window. "I must find him."

"Oh, Juliette." Aunt Kibble stood on the bottom porch step, twisting her handkerchief between her fingers and shaking her head as if Juliette had taken leave of her senses.

Juliette waved from the window until the carriage curved out of sight of the house, then she collapsed against the seat back and squeezed her eyes shut. The leave-taking had exhausted her—as did thinking about the journey ahead. Mr. Ralph would drive her to the coast, where she would spend the first night. In the morning, she would take the stage along the coast road to Oregon.

Her heart thudded painfully against her rib cage. Tonight she would sleep among strangers on a bed that others had slept in. She couldn't have been more apprehensive of what lay ahead if she'd known for a certainty that she traveled to her doom.

Abruptly it occurred to her that she had never really been tested on life's road. Until Jean Jacques vanished, nothing disastrous had happened in her adult life. All her bumps had been small ones, and she was thankful for that.

For one terrible disloyal moment, she stared down at her hands and burned with resentment that Jean Jacques was putting her to the test. She didn't want to be in this carriage traveling to heaven knew where. She detested the necessity of speaking to strangers and revealing that her husband had gone missing.

Snapping down the window shade, she leaned back and pressed her fingertips to her temples.

She would find him. It was unthinkable that she would endure this ordeal without being rewarded. And when she was once again in the arms of her husband, she would find the courage to ask if he'd married her only for the money. Then he would look astonished and assure her that he loved her, and that he had never given her inheritance a single thought.

Jean Jacques loved her. It wasn't the money.

Chapter 2

Peterson's coast-road stage was late today, so Clara had time to dash upstairs and inspect the rooms. On the floor near the bed in number four she found a lady's hairpin and tucked it into her pocket. The curtains were not aligned properly in number six, and a pot of ivy was dying for lack of water in room number seven.

Here was proof of the very thing she had feared from the moment she decided to sell the inn. The new owners would run the place into the ground. Mrs. Callison would never have overlooked the hairpin or the curtains or the ivy—no, sir. But the new owners had insisted that Clara dismiss her regular help and hire new employees before they arrived to take possession of the property. They wanted employees whose loyalties were to them, not to Clara or to her late father.

Well, it wasn't easy to hire good help. Clara had interviewed five applicants before settling on Miss Reeves, who was the best of a bad lot.

If it were up to her—if Miss Reeves had been *her* employee—Clara would have torn into the girl, given her what-for, waved the hairpin under her nose, then dismissed her without a reference. But the new owners expected the inn to be fully staffed when they arrived. So the slatternly Miss Reeves was their problem. That is, if they considered haphazardly cleaned rooms a problem. She had her suspicions about that.

Biting her lip and refusing to feel guilty about selling,

she hurried downstairs to the kitchen to make sure dinner would hold until the stage arrived. An inn could offer the most comfortable beds in creation, but if the food was mediocre or served late or less than stove-hot, guests would not return. Repeat business paid the major bills.

"Get out of my kitchen," Herr Bosch shouted as Clara rushed into a haze of fragrant steam.

"*Guten Tag* to you, too," Clara called cheerfully. She dipped a spoon into a simmering meat broth that was almost ready for liver dumplings. "Perfect," she breathed with a sigh of pleasure.

The new owners weren't entirely crackbrained. They had kept Herr Hugo Bosch and, at his insistence, his two assistants and the potboy. For tonight's meal, they prepared Wiener schnitzel, roasted potatoes, and red cabbage slow-cooked with apple slices and caraway seed. The baked bread and strudel hot out of the oven filled the kitchen with the scents of heaven.

Herr Bosch took the spoon from Clara's hand and made a shooing motion. "Out, out, out." But his voice expressed no pleasure with their customary banter. "I cannot bear that you are leaving tomorrow," he added in a low tone meant for her ears alone. Absently, he patted the pockets of the starched white tunic he wore over white trousers. "I've been waiting for you. Come outside with me."

To her knowledge, Herr Bosch had never left the kitchen this close to serving time.

They stepped outside the back door, walked around the kitchen garden, then stood beneath the shade of a spreading maple, where they could see the road and the stage when it arrived.

Herr Bosch lit a cigar and waved out the match. "You're making a mistake, Clara."

"What's done is done," she said with a shrug. "I know Papa wouldn't have approved, but the time is right to sell. The railroad passed us by, and if you ask me, I think horseless carriages will eventually put the stage out of business. Then where will the guests come from?"

"You know that isn't what I meant," he said, glaring at the end of his cigar. "I meant *him*. It's a mistake to leave everything behind and go running off after that husband of yours. He isn't treating you right. Not a single letter since he's been gone? Is this how a man treats his new bride?"

"I haven't written to him," she answered lightly. Even if she knew where to address a letter, she wasn't much for writing. Clearly, her husband wasn't either.

"I'll never understand why you chose him. Together you and I could have built the inn into an attraction so grand it wouldn't matter about the railroad or the stage."

Bosch, like all her suitors, had really wanted to marry the inn. She was merely the workhorse who came with the inventory.

Curious, she closed her eyes and lifted her face. "What color are my eyes?"

"What?"

"My eyes. What color are they?"

"They're . . . black?"

She knew he was annoyed and frowning before she looked at him again. "Light brown." An unusual shade, near the color of coffee with cream. Certainly not black.

Her husband would have answered correctly and without hesitation because he was the only man who had looked at her and seen a woman instead of the owner of a prosperous inn.

The first thing Jean Jacques had said when he approached the registration counter was, "*Mon Dieu!* Never have I seen such beautiful skin!"

No one had ever said anything remotely similar to Clara Klaus. The compliment was so amazing, so enthralling, that she didn't care that it was delivered in a French accent. In fact, she had secretly yearned to meet a Frenchman. Her German parents had despised the

French so much that anything French seemed mysterious, exotic, thrillingly forbidden. And suddenly, a handsome Frenchman was standing before her, admiring her skin and looking at her in a way that made her feel hot and funny inside, looking at her as if she were the most dazzling creature ever to appear before his eyes.

"It was *his* idea to sell the inn, wasn't it?"

Distracted by memories of that first meeting, Clara shook her head and tried to recall when she had originally considered selling the inn. She didn't remember now who first had made the suggestion, Jean Jacques or herself. But she did recall long discussions about the booming town of Seattle, Washington. So many men poured into the area bound for the gold fields in Alaska that there weren't enough hotels and boardinghouses to accommodate them. Jean Jacques told her that men slept on boardwalks and lawns with newspapers for blankets. Not because they couldn't afford a bed, but because few beds were available.

Clara recognized opportunity when it came knocking at her door. She'd sent Jean Jacques to Seattle with her nest egg and instructions to purchase a place that could be converted into a boardinghouse.

"We made the decision to sell together, but it was my decision to sell the inn now instead of waiting." Jean Jacques would probably be annoyed that she hadn't delayed the sale until he wrote that he'd purchased a new place. That was how they had agreed to handle things. But it was taking him so long to find the right property that she'd grown impatient. She missed him more than she could possibly have imagined and wanted to be in his arms again.

Hugo Bosch looked shocked. "You're a married woman now. You should not have made such a decision, much less acted upon it, without your husband's knowledge! If he's half a man, he'll beat you for disobedience."

Uh-huh. She saw now that if she had married Hugo

Bosch, they would have spent the next fifty years plotting to kill each other.

"Seattle is a big city. You do know where Villette is staying, don't you?"

Well, no. But she would find him. She and her Jean Jacques were like two magnets exerting an irresistible attraction that would sweep aside all obstacles. Theirs was a joyous, exuberant marriage welded by two people wildly, madly, passionately in love. If they were in the same hemisphere, she had no doubt they could find each other.

Like most redheads, Clara blushed easily and violently. When Herr Bosch stared at her with raised eyebrows, she turned away from his gaze.

"Well. Here comes the stage."

"Clara, I beg you. Divorce this Frenchman."

"Divorce?" She considered herself a modern woman, but she wasn't modern enough to consider divorce. The idea horrified her.

"I could make you happy. I would feed you tortes and strudels, paprika noodles. Sauerbraten." His eyes glowed as he continued to list her favorite foods and desserts.

Clara sighed. She was big, but not as big as she would be if Hugo Bosch had his way. She was big shouldered, big breasted, big hipped, and she had big hands. But she curved in where she should and out where she should; she wasn't fat. Her papa had said she was a good German girl, big boned and a beauty. But, as far as she knew, no one else had thought her a beauty until Jean Jacques Villette.

"I have to meet the stage," she said gently, placing her hand on Hugo's sleeve. He meant well, she knew that. And who could say? Maybe if Jean Jacques hadn't swept her off her feet . . . maybe she would eventually have married the best strudel she'd ever tasted and Hugo Bosch would have married her inn. Maybe she would have persuaded herself that it didn't matter that he couldn't recall her eye color or that he thought wives deserved an occasional beating.

She left him standing under the maple tree biting on his cigar and hurried inside to remove her apron, smooth her skirts, and pat down her flyaway hair. Then she arranged a smile on her lips and stepped out on the front veranda to greet her guests.

Only one woman climbed down from the stage, which made Clara decide that she had sold the inn not a moment too soon. In her papa's time, the stage had arrived twice daily and deposited a half dozen guests on the inn's doorstep at each stop.

Suppressing a sigh, she examined the slender woman who had turned to look beyond the inn toward a sweeping view of the sea. The woman impressed Clara as anxious and nervous, but she didn't know why. Her guest was smartly turned out in a well-cut traveling suit that appeared to defy wrinkles. Beneath a small, neat hat, every hair was perfectly in place, her gloves were immaculate, and she didn't fidget.

"She's the only one?" Clara asked Ole Peterson after he'd placed the woman's tapestry bags on the veranda.

"The rest of the passengers are continuing on," Ole said. He sounded apologetic.

Clara nodded and wished him a safe trip, hesitated, then walked across the lawn to join her guest. "It's beautiful, isn't it?" she asked pleasantly, glancing toward the ocean.

"It's amazing. Wonderful. Magnificent. Words fail me." She glanced at Clara, then back at the ocean. "The colors are so vivid here in Oregon. The blues aren't as blue nor the greens as green in California, I'm sure of it. And the ocean! My husband promised I would love the sea, but I never imagined it would be so big, so overwhelming, or so fascinating."

As the Pacific had always been in Clara's backyard, she tended to take it for granted. Seeing the landscape anew through her guests' eyes was always a refreshing experience.

"This must be your first trip to the coast."

The woman's slender figure stiffened, and her spine pulled ramrod straight. She folded her gloved hands one over the other at her waist and frowned straight ahead.

Clara had seen this before. Stuffy little women who mistook friendliness for prying because the silly books on etiquette said a person didn't discuss personal matters with strangers, didn't reveal anything of themselves.

"Well," Clara said, watching dots of color burning on the woman's cheeks. "Please come inside. I have a room I think you'll find to your liking. Dinner will be served in the dining room promptly at seven. You'll have time to freshen up."

"You are the proprietor?"

"Yes." Until tomorrow when the new owners arrived. She paused on the veranda to collect the woman's tapestry bags.

"Shouldn't you call someone to handle the bags?"

"There's no need," Clara said brightly. "I'm not a little thing like you." She could almost hear Papa saying: *My Clara, she's as strong as an ox*. He'd been gone for almost two years, but she still missed him. She wished they could sit down together over steins of beer and she could explain why she'd sold the inn.

She led the way past Papa's cuckoo clocks and Mama's collection of tiny china cups into a homey lobby where she set down the tapestry bags and stepped behind the counter.

Apparently the woman from the stage hadn't arranged her own accommodations often enough to be comfortable with the process. She blushed deeply and didn't meet Clara's gaze.

"I wonder . . ." The color deepened in the woman's cheeks, and she blinked rapidly, her words coming in an anguished rush. "I know this will sound like a strange request, but I wonder if I might examine your guest book from nine months ago. You see, there's someone who might have stayed at your inn. It would be helpful to me to know if he did stay here."

All was explained. Clara would have wagered the money in the cash drawer that the woman's husband had left her and that she was attempting to find him. She had heard this sad tale before. There wasn't much that she had not seen while growing up in the hostelry business.

Sympathy softened her gaze. The poor soul wasn't a beauty, but who was? She was pretty in a cautious sort of way, as if she felt it more virtuous not to turn men's heads. Clara thought the woman's eyes were her best feature. She had lovely, heavily lashed gray eyes—one might even say soulful eyes. Certainly she had a sense of style. Her traveling ensemble was well coordinated and the quality of workmanship was good. But Clara sensed her guest's timidity and discomfort. This woman traveled alone out of necessity, not by choice. And asking after her husband was clearly agony for her.

Carefully suppressing any hint of pity, Clara turned the register to face the woman and extended a pen, saying, "Of course you can examine the register from last year. I'd be happy to show—" She stopped talking and stared.

The woman's horrified gaze had fixed on Clara's wedding ring. She gripped the edge of the counter as if to hold herself upright and the color abruptly drained from her face, leaving her as white as a new towel.

"Your ring!" She sounded as if she were strangling.

"It's my wedding ring," Clara explained slowly, wondering if the woman was having some sort of fit. "It's a family heirloom. My husband's grandfather designed the ring, and his grandmother wore it all her married life. Then his mother wore it."

The woman shook her head. "No. This can't be. No."

"Ma'am? Can I get you something? A glass of water?"

"You don't understand. But look." She tore at her gloves, clawing at her left hand. "It has to be a coincidence. Yes, that's it, it must be a very strange coincidence." She thrust out a shaking hand and the counter lamp gleamed down on her wedding ring. Clara gasped, and her heart stopped beating. Her eyes widened until they ached.

The woman wore the same ring. Two bands of twisted silver enclosing filigreed silver hearts. But how could the rings be identical? Jean Jacques had said the ring was one of a kind, an original design.

"Oh!" The word became a wail, stretching on and on until Clara ran out of breath. She reeled backward a step, vigorously shaking her head in denial. "No. This cannot be. I won't believe this."

"Please," the woman whispered. "Tell me your husband's name."

"Jean Jacques Villette." The name choked her because one look at the woman's sickly ashen face confirmed an unfolding nightmare. "*Mein Gott!* We're married to the same man!" The words came from a great distance. Her ears rang and her knees shook. She felt nauseated.

If ever a situation had called for someone to faint, this was it. So Clara was glad to see the other Mrs. Villette sink below the countertop and hit the floor.

Somehow Clara stumbled through the dinner hour, seating her guests, overseeing the service, smiling and nodding good night as the guests exited the dining room. When everyone had departed, Clara discovered she couldn't recall a word she had spoken or anything she had done since Juliette March Villette fainted on the lobby floor.

She found herself standing in the middle of the dining room, staring stupidly at Hans and Gerhard as they set the tables for the breakfast service. Now and then they slid a glance toward her, then lifted eyebrows at each other as if she had gone daft and they didn't know what they should do about her.

Abruptly, she turned on her heel and returned to the lobby to pace in front of the counter.

What should she do now? Was there any point in going to Seattle as she had planned? But she couldn't stay here. The new owners would move into the personal quarters tomorrow, and her belongings were already in storage. The only items left to pack were the cuckoo clocks and Mama's tiny cups.

But wait. Stiffening, she stared into space. Why was she worrying about where she would lay her head? Her shocked mind had stopped on the questions: How can this be? Where will I go? But there were other equally important concerns.

Was she the first or the second wife? Was she married or not married? And what about her money? The money! Jean Jacques, her passionate, dearly beloved, no-good thieving scoundrel of a husband, had taken her nest egg.

Was it his thievery that made her so furious? That in the end, Jean Jacques had been like all her suitors, enamored by what she owned?

But that could not be true. Jean Jacques had chased her all over the inn, swearing that he would make love to her in every bed. And, laughing, she had let him catch her, and they had indeed made love in every bed. Closing her eyes, Clara swayed on her feet. A man couldn't fake desiring a woman. Jean Jacques had loved her. He must have loved her. But if he loved her, then surely he couldn't have loved Juliette March Villette.

Turning, she gazed toward the landing at the top of the staircase. She'd put it off long enough; they had to talk. And Miss March should be recovered by now.

She poured two steins of stout German ale strong enough to numb pain and carried them upstairs to room three. At first she thought Miss March wouldn't respond to her knock, then she heard a resigned voice bid her to enter.

Miss March was already in bed, wearing a plain, un-adorned nightgown that circled high around her throat. She'd brushed out her hair and braided it for sleeping, but Clara doubted either of them would sleep tonight.

"Are you feeling better?"

"I'm sick at heart." The other Mrs. Villette's face re-mained waxy white, making her eyelids appear more red and swollen. "I can't move. I can't think. It's like my mind is paralyzed and my body is too heavy to lift. I've never hurt this much in my life. I can't bear it that Aunt Kibble was right."

So much for not revealing oneself to strangers. Shock and devastation had eroded Juliette March Villette's re-serve. Unhappily, Clara foresaw that she and her hus-band's other wife would become intimates before this evening ended. "I brought you some ale."

She simply could not think of this woman as Mrs. Vil-lette. It was repugnant, impossible. And she couldn't con-tinue thinking of her as Jean Jacques's other wife. That was too painful. She decided to think of her as Miss March.

Miss March's eyebrows arched, and she sniffed in dis-taste. "I don't drink spirits."

"Well, it's time you started. I can promise you, this ale will make you feel better than the tea did," Clara stated, looking at the teapot Miss Reeves had brought up ear-lier. She set one of the steins on the edge of the bed and watched Miss March lurch forward to grab the handle before the ale toppled, then pulled a chair next to the bed.

Now that she was here, Clara couldn't remember the questions she had intended to ask. She was too distracted by the inevitable misery of comparing herself to Miss March. Judging by the way Miss March stared back, she, too, was making comparisons.

As far as Clara could see, they didn't share a single physical likeness. Where Clara was sturdy and big-boned, Miss March was slender and delicate. Clara's hair was curly auburn red; Miss March's hair was a smooth medium brown. Miss March had gray eyes; Clara's eyes were light brown. She was apple-cheeked and quick to laugh, whereas Miss March was fashionably pale and slow to smile. Clara sensed their backgrounds would prove as dissimilar as their personalities and appearance.

"It was the money," Miss March blurted in an anguished voice. Fighting tears, she sipped from the stein, then gasped and pursed her lips with a shudder. "Aunt Kibble warned me, but I didn't want to believe it."

"The second swallow goes down smoother."

"He said he was temporarily embarrassed. He said he only needed a loan." She gave her head a shake and swallowed another draft of the ale. She gasped again, but not as loudly. "Did Mr. Villette take money from you, too?" Her gaze pleaded with Clara to say yes.

Reluctantly, she nodded and explained about giving Jean Jacques her nest egg to buy a boardinghouse in Seattle, and how she had sold the inn to follow him. Then Miss March told her about giving Jean Jacques money to buy them a home in Oregon.

Finally they discussed dates and established the order of events.

Clara lowered her head. "So he married you first." Her mind felt numb, insulated from the pain that would knock her down later.

"I just can't believe this is happening." Unshed tears glistened in Juliette's eyes, and she bent her head over the ale stein. "I thought he loved me."

"I thought he loved me, too. I never doubted for a minute that every word my Jean Jacques uttered was true and sincere." Clara frowned down at her wedding ring. Jean Jacques had claimed it was an heirloom. One of a kind. And she had swallowed every word like a lump of sugar, had never dreamed that he could be lying. The bastard.

"He told me he was in the import-export business. His money was tied up in inventory."

"He told me he was in the hotel business," she said. "His money was invested in an inn in California that he was trying to sell."

"All lies. But ... I keep remembering ..." Scarlet flooded Juliette's cheeks. She spread her hands in a helpless gesture. "I don't know how he could have been so convincing if it was all a lie. I keep thinking I would have known. I would have sensed something. *Something.* Maybe I'm deceiving myself, trying to find one small thing to cling to. But I can't believe that he didn't love me. At least a little. It couldn't have been entirely the money."

The same argument unwound in Clara's thoughts. Jean Jacques couldn't have married her just for the money. He hadn't known that she had a nest egg tucked away for her old age. And he hadn't married her to get the inn. He'd specifically told her not to sell until he wrote. Now she knew he would never summon her, had never intended to contact her again. He was gone.

The anguish of knowing she would never see him again sliced through her heart like a blade, made worse by the shock of discovering she'd been taken in by a handsome and charming womanizer.

When Clara looked up, she saw that Miss March had covered her eyes with a lacy handkerchief. "I can't possibly address you as Mrs. Villette," she stated abruptly. For the first time in her life, Clara experienced a deep bite of jealousy. Sharp fangs poisoned her mind when she imagined her Jean Jacques making love to Juliette. And she couldn't push the hateful images away.

Juliette shuddered behind the handkerchief covering her expression. "And I can't possibly call *you* Mrs. Villette!"

"Call me Clara, and I'll call you Juliette. Or we can call each other Miss Klaus and Miss March."

Juliette automatically extended her little finger as if she drank from a teacup instead of a stein. Clara had never seen that done before. How on earth could Jean Jacques have married this prissy woman? He couldn't have loved her. He simply couldn't have.

"Mr. Villette married me first," Juliette said after a period of silence. Her chin came up. "I'm glad you concede that point."

Her tone surprised Clara. Perhaps a real woman existed beneath the brittle veneer of ladylike reserve. "My marriage is as authentic and as legal as yours," Clara answered sharply.

"I don't see how it could be since he was married to me when you seduced him."

"When I seduced him? I'll have you know that my Jean Jacques took one look at me and fell deeply in love! From that moment on, he pursued me relentlessly until I agreed to marry him! He was the seducer, not me."

"He called me his angel; he said I made him happy! I don't know what wiles you used to snare my husband, but when he rode out of Linda Vista, he was a happily married man!"

"Well, that didn't last long. By the time he walked into this inn, he'd forgotten that you ever existed!"

Juliette stared, then turned swimming eyes to the ceiling. Clara finished her ale and angrily told herself that she had no cause to apologize. Then Juliette apologized and made her feel as small as a mushroom.

"I'm sorry." Juliette wiped her eyes and her nose. "You must think I have the manners of a fishwife considering how I've behaved. I apologize for being angry at you. It's just that I want this nightmare to be someone else's fault, not my husband's." Blinking, she glanced at Clara. "We should be sympathetic to each other. We've both been betrayed."

Clara considered pointing out that Juliette had a foam mustache drooping across her upper lip. But she liked the idea of Juliette discovering the mustache later and being mortified.

Usually Clara thought of herself as a good woman, but

Jean Jacques's other wife brought out her low-down, mean-as-a-cat wicked side.

"I'm sorry, too," she said finally. "I guess at some point we're going to have to put this mess in the hands of the authorities and let the law sort everything out."

Juliette looked horrified. "Put my husband in jail?"

"I'm starting to think that's where my husband belongs. I'm starting to think he stole my money. And I'm starting to get mad about what he did to me."

They stared at each other.

"I think it's possible that Mr. Villette has amnesia," Juliette said. This time she tactfully chose not to refer to Jean Jacques as *her* husband while she explained her theory. "Since he couldn't remember, he thought he was free to fall in . . . to marry you."

"That is the stupidest idea I've ever heard," Clara said after a minute. "And it doesn't explain identical wedding rings."

They looked down at their left hands.

"There has to be a reasonable explanation," Juliette insisted stubbornly. After a long silence, she sighed, "I've thought about everything, and I'm going to continue searching for him. Whether it's amnesia or not, I need to know why he did this to me."

Clara studied the foam mustache on Juliette's upper lip. The little bubbles were starting to dry. "The reason is money. He stole our money. I know what I'm going to do. I'm going to go to Seattle and get my nest egg back!" When she found Jean Jacques she knew she would burst into tears and love him and hate him and pray that he could somehow make everything right and wonderful.

Standing, she stared down at Juliette's slender fingers gripping the ale stein and glared at her rival's ring. No, her world would never be right and wonderful again.

Juliette handed her the stein and then rubbed her forehead. "I can't think of a ladylike way to say that I'd prefer not to travel to Seattle with you."

"Because we detest each other?"

"It might be more tactful to say that we don't know each other and don't wish to."

"Unfortunately, there's only one stage tomorrow. Unless you want to dawdle here for another day, that stage is your only way north to Seattle." Clara lifted her head and walked to the door. "I'll be on that stage." At the door she turned and looked back. Immediately she wished she hadn't.

Juliette presented a picture of abject misery: sad reddened eyes, the unadorned virginal nightgown, a slumped posture that cried pain and defeat. Clara wondered how she had managed to get this far in her search for Jean Jacques.

Sighing, she shook her head. She didn't need to lay out Mama's cards to read the future. Like it or not (and she didn't like it), she and Juliette would be traveling together.

First, there was only the one northbound stage. Second, she didn't want Juliette to find Jean Jacques before she did. And third, Clara was cursed with a caregiving nature. On some idiotic but basic level she felt it her duty and her obligation to look after her husband's other wife. Jean Jacques would expect her to take Juliette in hand because clearly she was stronger and more wise to the world than Her Ladyship.

Shaking her head, she covered her eyes. She didn't want to take care of Juliette. She wished Juliette would step off a cliff. Or get run over by a freight wagon. She would cheer if a huge rock squashed Juliette. Would love it if a swift-acting disease carried her away before morning.

In Clara's defense, she hoped Juliette's death was instantaneous. She didn't wish any painful suffering on the woman, she just wanted Juliette to vanish and never return.

"Breakfast is at seven." She sighed heavily, and did the

right thing. "You have a foam mustache on your upper lip. You look ridiculous."

Closing the door behind her, Clara walked down the staircase and made it to her quarters before her heart collapsed and a flood of anguished tears streamed down her cheeks.

Chapter 3

The town of Newcastle filled the depression below a steep hillside that had been logged off to provide lumber for the small, weathered houses ranged along Coal Creek. Stumps littered the ridge like wharf pilings.

Unpainted fences defined minuscule front yards, and here and there a drooping azalea struggled to survive, but most of the yards were dirt and weeds defended by skinny roosters and a few tired hens.

These things Zoe remembered, but the soot and coal dust always surprised her. Yet if someone had inquired, the ubiquitous coal dust would have leapt to mind before anything else. It crept beneath sills and coated floors and furnishings with a layer of dark grit. Outside, the coal dust soiled wet laundry and settled on hats and shoulders and plants and rooftops.

Before she sat down at her mother's table, Zoe shook out her skirts, knowing better than to brush at the dust and leave a smear. She'd wiped the table after breakfast, only two hours ago, but already a fine layer of grime had accumulated on the surface.

Ma pushed a cup of coffee across the table and glanced at the clock above the stove. "I wish you could stay longer."

"I do, too," Zoe said, but her answer wasn't true. Four of her six brothers still lived at home, in a house with two bedrooms. Creating space for Zoe inconvenienced every-one when she came to visit.

She castigated herself for not coming more often, but she'd been spoiled by living in Seattle on her own, reveling in the one thing she had never known in this house. Privacy. In her two rooms at the boardinghouse she didn't have to dress behind a screen, didn't have to listen to the rude noises six brothers could make, didn't have to fight for a seat at meals. Best of all, she didn't have to share her space with anyone except her husband. And she didn't mind that.

"You're happy, aren't you?" her mother asked, studying Zoe in the hazy light filtering past grimy windowpanes.

"Yes," Zoe answered softly, smiling down at her coffee. Ma had given her the last of the real cream instead of using the skim.

"I used to think you never would get married. I guess you broke every male heart in Newcastle." Alice Wilder smiled, and some of the years softened on her face. "When I was twenty-four, I'd already buried two babies and had two more hanging on my skirts."

That was the life Zoe had escaped, thank heaven. She didn't want to be stuck in a tiny, crowded house slaving after males who always had a dark line embedded beneath their fingernails no matter how hard they scrubbed. She didn't want a half dozen babies wearing her out before her time. Most of all, she wanted a few nice things in her life, something more than a coal miner's wife could expect.

"I was right to wait, Ma." If she had married a Newcastle man, she would have been stuck here. Instead, she had bided her time and used the wait to improve herself. Her reward had been Jean Jacques Villette. Zoe hadn't dared to dream that men like him existed.

Her mother smiled. "I used to tell your pa if you ever lost your heart, it would happen just like that." She snapped her fingers. "And you'd be married before we even knew you'd met someone special."

Zoe smiled. "The week I met Jean Jacques was the

most exciting week of my life. First I saved the Van Hooten boy after he fell in the tide marsh, then came the award ceremony."

"And the newspaper article. Don't forget that. I clipped it out and saved it inside the family Bible. They called you a heroine." Pride restored the color to her mother's faded eyes.

"Three days after that article, Jean Jacques walked into Uncle Milton's store. Did I tell you the first words he said to me?" Lord, she would never forget. "I was working in the back, sacking dried peas, and I heard a man's voice talking with an accent that made everything he said sound like music. And he said this, Ma. 'Your hair reminds me of midnight spun into silk.' "

"Oh, my!" Her mother gasped and slapped a hand over her chest. "He said *that*?"

Zoe touched the glossy coil on her neck, trying to imagine silk. "It was like lightning flashed out of the ceiling and struck me to the heart. There he was, the handsomest man I'd ever seen, and he had clean fingernails, and he was standing in front of me saying I had hair like midnight silk."

"Well. I guess I understand why you'd marry a man with no calluses on his hands. I thought for sure you'd made a mistake." Her mother stared across the table. "Did he say other pretty things?"

Oh, yes. She'd heard poetry from her husband's lips, but never a coarse word. He believed she was a real lady. She, who had grown up fighting with six brothers, scrapping for a few feet of space that she could call her own. She'd tried so hard to rise above her background, but she hadn't known if she had succeeded until Jean Jacques Villette came into her life and treated her as if she were made of eggshell, as if she'd never bloodied her knuckles standing her ground.

"When do you expect your husband to return?"

"After he finds gold, I expect. And Ma, we have such

plans!" A sparkle jumped into her eyes, and she leaned forward. "When Jean Jacques comes back from the Yukon, we'll either buy Uncle Milton's store or design our own. And we're going to build a big house on Denny Hill like all the swells."

"But Zoe, what if your husband doesn't strike it rich up there in the Klondike?"

"There's something I didn't tell you, Ma." She'd feared she would pop her dream bubble if she talked too much about the wonders of her new life. But enough time had passed that she felt secure now. "Jean Jacques comes from a rich family. Prospecting for gold is just a lark for him. An adventure. He'd like to scrape up a fortune so he doesn't have to depend on family money, but if that doesn't happen," she shook her head, marveling, "it won't matter."

"You married a rich man?" Her mother leaned back and frowned. If Ma had said it once, she'd said it a hundred times. *Stay with your own. If you marry above or below yourself, you'll wed heartache and sorrow.*

Ma's expression said it cost her dear not to repeat the warning. Instead, she fell silent for several minutes and then asked, "But didn't you mention that you paid for your husband's outfit and his passage with some of your reward money?"

"Something went awry with the transfer of funds from Jean Jacques's accounts back East to his account in the Seattle bank. First it was a problem with his accountant, then the wire service. Everything that could go wrong, did go wrong. Rather than delay his journey I paid for the outfit and passage."

Her mother's gaze sharpened. "You do have access to his funds now, don't you?"

"Actually Jean Jacques sailed before the problem was solved. He had to leave when he did, or the weather would have made reaching the gold fields impossible."

She didn't like the way her mother stared, didn't like the way her explanation sounded a bit airy, like something out of a storybook. The longer Zoe talked, the more inexplicably naive she sounded. Irritated, she lapsed into silence.

"I'm suspicious by nature," Ma said finally. "So you can take this with a grain of salt. But it doesn't sound right that this rich husband of yours would go off for months and months without leaving you any money to live on."

"I have my employment at Uncle Milton's store, and I still have some of the reward money. Plus, I've saved a nice nest egg." And she had married a wealthy man. Never again would she worry about money. Never again would anyone look down on her. It was a miracle.

But from Ma's viewpoint, she admitted it did seem peculiar that Jean Jacques would sail away without an apparent worry as to how his new bride would fare. On the other hand, it hadn't seemed odd at the time. Zoe remembered urging him to go, assuring him that she would manage nicely on her salary from Uncle Milton. She had felt proud when Jean Jacques praised her independence and self-sufficiency.

Ma refilled their coffee cups from the scorched pot on the stove top. "You have time for one more cup before you leave."

The coal train would take her back to Seattle. Mr. Cummings, the engineer, wasn't permitted to transport passengers, but he looked the other way if a miner or his family wanted to climb into the caboose.

"I'm sorry I didn't warn you about the Owner's Day Parade before you came. I know you've never enjoyed the festivities."

Zoe turned her face to the window, and her lips thinned. She'd been five or six when she realized the elegantly dressed men and women in the carriage parade looked at the people lining the lanes of Newcastle with a mixture of superiority and contempt. That was the year she had overheard one of the men say, "They're so dirty. And look how they live." As if they were animals. As if they had a choice about the coal dust and the small company houses.

The following year she had promised herself that she would not scrabble in the dirt for the candy the ladies threw from the carriages. She'd stood upright, her spindly body stiff with pride while pieces of candy pelted her skirt. But it was the only candy she would have until the parade next year, and in the end she had dropped to her knees and snatched at the pieces before someone else got them.

She was eleven before her pride grew stronger than her longing for the candy. But her pride was crushed anyway. She might as well have fought for the candy.

The rich people in the carriages observed the children and people of Newcastle with laughter and nods and occasional pointing, the way they might have viewed dumb beasts in a zoo. As if the visitors were members of a superior species that had never seen or imagined such distasteful creatures or the hovels that furnished their habitat. They looked at Zoe as they passed, and she felt ashamed of the dress she had outgrown, ashamed of her bare feet and the unpainted small house behind her. Their laughter diminished her and made her feel like weeping.

"I hate Owner's Day," she said quietly, keeping her eyes on the window. "They come here like feudal lords to view the peasants."

"Just ignore them like the rest of us do." Her mother shrugged. "It's a holiday. The men have a day off. There's the picnic and dancing afterward. When something nice comes along, Zoe, you grab it."

"I suppose so," she said for her mother's sake.

Ma studied her until Zoe felt heat rise in her cheeks. "You worry me sometimes."

"Don't you worry about me, Ma. I've got my head on straight."

"Do you, Zoe? I hope so. Those people in the parade

aren't any better than you and me. The people in New-castle aren't rich, they don't have fancy manners, and they don't talk pretty, but they're good, decent, hard-working folks."

Sometimes Ma layered meaning in her words, and Zoe wondered if this was one of those times. "Are you hinting something about Jean Jacques?"

"I haven't met the man, and I don't know him. But I'm wondering if it's possible that your husband is taking advantage of you."

Shock widened Zoe's eyes, and it was hard not to take offense. "How can you say that?"

"Think about it, Zoe. Your pa would never go off and leave me without access to our money."

"This isn't the same thing at all. I don't need to depend on Jean Jacques's funds. I earn enough from my job to pay my expenses. You couldn't support yourself on your egg money."

"Way back, I offered to buy your pa some decent boots and pay his union dues so we could get married sooner. But he wouldn't hear of it, wouldn't take a cent from a woman. We didn't tie the knot until he'd hired on with the company and had a place for us to live. I'd feel better if I saw that sort of thinking in your man. He should have straightened out his affairs and taken care of his wife before he went traipsing off on his Yukon adventure."

Anger deepened the color in Zoe's cheeks. "I didn't turn down all those proposals and wait all these years to end up marrying badly. I'm not dumb, Ma. If you'd met Jean Jacques, you'd know that he's wonderful and he loves me. He'd never treat me wrong."

"I worry, Zoe. That's all."

"Rich people do things differently. They don't think like we do. Jean Jacques never had to scrape pennies, money just appears when he needs it. I doubt he thought about leaving me without access to his money. I doubt it entered his mind. Rich people don't think about paying rent or buying food or things like that. They've never had to."

"One more question, then I won't say any more about it."

"Good."

"How much of your reward money did you spend on outfitting Mr. Villette?"

"A lot," she admitted eventually, resenting the implications behind her mother's question. "I would have spent it all because a man like him is used to the best of everything, but he wouldn't hear of it. In many ways, he's like regular people, Ma. You'll see when you finally meet him."

Inside she cringed at the thought of bringing Jean Jacques here to meet her family. She didn't think he'd look at her home and the people in it the way the swells in the carriages did. He wasn't like that. But still, he'd see the grime and the chipped dishes and all the rest. In fact, she couldn't imagine Jean Jacques in this tiny house at this dusty table focusing his charm on a tired woman who didn't place much value on charm.

"One last thing. Did you tell Mr. Villette about us? About your family?"

Standing, Zoe looked around for her hat and gloves. Ma had placed them atop her small overnight bag. Taking up her hat, she pinned it on before a cloudy mirror framed next to the window where the light was good.

"I told Jean Jacques about Newcastle and Coal Creek and about the family." She'd never been able to look into her mother's eyes and lie, so she kept her gaze fixed on the mirror. "He knows I didn't grow up with advantages." That much was true, but she had kept the details vague. She would confess her complete history eventually. Feeling guilty, knowing she hadn't done right, she avoided turning toward her mother.

"Will his family accept you? Are you worried about meeting those rich folks?"

The inevitability terrified her. She pulled on her gloves

and smoothed down the fingers. Jean Jacques had promised that his family would love her as much as he did. But she felt certain they would have preferred that he marry in his own class.

"That's a bridge I'll cross when I reach it," she murmured, giving her skirts a twitch to shake dust from the folds.

Her mother stood and came around the table. "I'll walk to the train with you." She didn't mention Jean Jacques again until Zoe was about to climb onto the narrow porch behind the caboose. Then she caught Zoe's face between chapped hands and looked into her daughter's eyes. "I'm so proud of you. I know you're too smart to let some scoundrel bamboozle you, but I can't help worrying about my chicks. I just want you to be safe and happy."

"I know, Ma. Don't worry."

"I trust your judgment. I'm sure Mr. Villette is as wonderful as you say he is or you wouldn't have married him."

Zoe stood on the little porch of the caboose waving her handkerchief until she saw Ma turn up the road toward the company store, then she stepped inside to get out of the wind and the blowing soot and smoke.

A visit home always left her with a disturbing mix of feelings. It was good to see everyone, but no one in her family could talk without shouting, and the house seemed smaller each time she came. Though it made her feel guilty, she felt relieved when the coal-laden train rolled away from Newcastle and she left behind the black dust and the chickens scratching for treasure in dirt yards and men scratching for coal under Cougar Mountain while their women waited and worried.

Thank heaven she had escaped all that. And she had done it by working hard to better herself through evening classes to improve her education and by taking Miss Lydia's weekly classes in decorum.

Bending her head, she closed her eyes and touched her wedding ring through her gloves, thinking about the conversation with her mother. She wished they hadn't talked about Jean Jacques. Decisions that had felt perfectly reasonable at the time seemed odd and puzzling when examined through her mother's hard-eyed skepticism.

Since Zoe didn't doubt her husband for an instant, she could only conclude that she had explained things poorly. Still, she hoped Jean Jacques would write soon. A letter would go a long way toward putting to rest a strange niggling restlessness that she couldn't define.

The stage driver informed them that forty thousand people resided in the Seattle area. If anything, Juliette believed the driver might have underestimated the number. Every shop, every restaurant, every street, every place she went to or saw teemed with people. She'd never seen so many folks in one place, and it awed and frightened her.

Fortunately, she and Clara had found rooms at the Diller Hotel, which was jam-packed to the rafters. Actually, the registration clerk had informed Juliette there were no rooms, but Clara spoke to the same man, and in five minutes she had rooms for them both. It annoyed her to the bones that Clara could obtain rooms and she could not.

The hotel was situated too near the railroad depot and the docks, but they were lucky to have found a room at all. One of the positives was discovering the business district lay within walking distance. That's where she began her search for Jean Jacques's import-export shop.

Within a day she recognized the futility of the task. The city was too large, too far-flung. She would never find his company. After forty-eight hours of searching followed by agitated pacing and wringing her hands, she came up with the idea of checking city and county records. A visit to city hall and then to the King County

Courthouse verified what she desperately did not want
to admit.

"The city didn't issue a business license for a Villette
Import and Export Company. And no Jean Jacques Villette owns property anywhere in King County."

Clara lowered a fork full of lemon pie. "You actually
wasted time checking?"

There was virtually nothing about Clara Klaus that
Juliette admired or liked or enjoyed. And Clara exhibited
innumerable traits and habits that Juliette deplored. At
the moment, she would have liked to scream across the
dining-room table that she was sick and tired of Clara's
implied criticism. Naturally she did no such thing. The
more life crumbled around her, the more she retreated
within, relying on the manners and standards that made
civilized life possible.

"It would have been unjust to assume that my husband lied about everything," she said coolly. "I prefer to
keep an open mind." It irked her to realize that she had
hoped for a little praise for going to city hall and then to
the courthouse all by herself.

"So now you know that he did indeed lie about everything." Clara finished her pie.

Here was another thing that Juliette despised. Clara
brought no grace or delicate niceties to the table. She appeared to know which fork and spoon to use, but chose
to employ them correctly only about half the time. She
ate with unbecoming gusto and cleaned her plate, which
no true lady would think of doing.

"I refuse to believe that Jean Jacques lied about everything," she insisted. She couldn't let herself believe that.

"He didn't lie about going to Seattle," Clara said, leaning back in her seat so the waiter could whisk away her pie
plate while another waiter poured coffee for them both.

The waiters scrupulously treated Clara the same as
they treated Juliette, even though Clara lacked even a
semblance of style. Clara wore a straw boater squarely

on top of her flyaway red hair, and she squinted when she was outside because the hat brim didn't shade her eyes and she never remembered to carry a parasol. She insisted her plain, ugly boots were sensible for walking, but Juliette thought they looked like men's boots. In between the poorly trimmed hat and chunky boots, Clara wore a dark skirt, a white shirtwaist, and a cape that might have been modish during a distant ancestor's lifetime.

For the life of her, Juliette could not fathom why a discriminating man like Jean Jacques Villette would have taken up with a common creature like Clara Klaus.

After a deep sigh, she broke the silence. "All right. How do you know that Jean Jacques came to Seattle? You couldn't possibly have called at all the hotels and boardinghouses."

"There are six banks in the area. I started with the one nearest the hotel and told the manager that Mr. Villette wished to rent commercial space from me and had named the bank as a reference. I wished to verify that he had an account and inquire if he was known to the bank personnel."

"You misrepresented yourself!" Juliette could never have done such a thing. But she grudgingly conceded the scheme was clever.

Clara rolled her eyes, then continued the story of her triumph. "I found him at the fourth bank."

Juliette clapped a hand over the sudden racing of her heart. "He's here?" she whispered.

"He was. The manager said Jean Jacques closed his account two weeks ago." She ground her teeth together. "We missed him by two weeks."

"Oh, no." Juliette stared across the table. "And we have no idea where he might have gone from here!" Tears burned her eyes, and she blinked them back rather than cry in a public place or in front of Clara.

Clara stirred cream into her coffee. "Ask yourself this question. Why would a man come to Seattle? What's happening here as opposed to—" She shrugged. "Chicago, for instance?"

Juliette had seen enough of Seattle to notice the lines of grimly determined men crowding the outfitters' stores. Since the hotel was near the wharf area, she'd even strolled to the piers to watch the crowded Alaskan steamers sail off for the Klondike.

"Are you suggesting that Jean Jacques went to the Yukon to search for gold?" she inquired, forming the words slowly.

"I'm starting to think it's certainly possible. What I don't understand is why he didn't sail immediately. Why would he wait until late July?"

"Men are still sailing to the Yukon. Steamers leave for Alaska every day."

"True. But the stampeders are taking a risk by leaving this late. Winter comes early up there. So why didn't Jean Jacques sail in April or May?"

"Maybe he didn't have enough money to pay for his passage and his outfit? Someone told me the Canadian customs won't allow anyone into the Klondike unless they have a year's worth of supplies."

Clara's lips thinned into a bitter twist. "He had plenty of money, believe me."

It was small comfort to realize that Clara also felt foolish. Juliette wished that she had never met Clara Klaus. Clara was living, breathing proof that Jean Jacques was not the man she had so totally believed him to be. Lowering her head, she gazed into her lap at her wedding ring, hating that Clara's ring was identical to hers.

In fact, Clara Klaus brought out the worst in her. Her mother and aunt would have been appalled by the unladylike thoughts tumbling through her head and the sharp words that occasionally shot from her lips like barbs aimed at Clara.

"So what do you suggest we do now?" she said, looking away from the curly red strands falling out of Clara's hat.

"I don't know what you're going to do, but I'm going to visit every outfitting store until I confirm that Jean Jacques bought supplies for the Yukon."

"Couldn't we just ask down at the piers? The ship companies must have passenger manifests." But they didn't know the date he had sailed or even if he had sailed. Didn't know which ship company he might have chosen or if he had used his correct name.

Juliette nodded to the maître d', and he hurried to hold their chairs so they could rise and leave the dining room. As they did every night, she and Clara stepped outside and took a turn around the terrace. A damp fish scent reminded Juliette of the nearby Sound. And they could hear street noises, the rush and rattle of harness-drawn vehicles, the cough and bang of an occasional horseless carriage. The wonders of electricity were evident as here and there bright lights flickered on across the city. Power poles and telephone wires were strung along every street like giant clotheslines.

A hollow space opened inside her. Never had Juliette felt so out of place and so completely alone as she did this minute with Clara by her side and dozens of people within sight.

Not a single person, certainly not Clara, cared about Juliette March. No one gave a fig that the noise and bustle of this enormous city unnerved her or that she grieved for the man who had left her behind.

Homesickness swamped her like a wave rearing out of the gathering darkness. She yearned to run home and hide herself away in Aunt Kibble's house. She belonged in small sleepy Linda Vista, where crossing a street didn't terrify her, where strange men didn't tip their hats and pretend a small courtesy gave them the right to run their eyes over her figure. She didn't have the temperament for travel and new places. She wasn't that brave. It did, in fact, astonish her that she had come as far as Seattle.

But going home would be a mistake. Sooner or later,

everyone in Linda Vista would hear their suspicions confirmed: that she had been victimized by a confidence man. Such stories had a way of surfacing; they didn't remain secret.

And she couldn't face the scandal and gossip, not after she had once been a role model of decorum. So she wouldn't go home.

But she had no idea what to do next.

Sighing again, she slid a sideways glance at Clara. Only a lifetime of rigid adherence to good manners made it possible for her to endure the intolerable necessity of traveling with a woman her husband had dallied with. She detested Clara Klaus because Clara had known Jean Jacques's touch, and imagining them together made Juliette's bones ache.

"You're quiet tonight," Clara commented, pausing to examine a riot of blossoms stuffed into a stone urn. "Not that I care, you understand, but what are you thinking about?"

"I'm thinking about what you said at the table." Juliette touched the back of her glove to her forehead. She absolutely did not want to dwell on Clara lying naked in Jean Jacques's arms. It was better to suppose such an outrage had never happened. "If we find the outfitting store where my husband purchased his supplies, what do we do then?"

Clara halted at the corner of the terrace and faced her with narrowed eyes. "Every time you say 'my husband' I want to slap you silly."

Such statements no longer shocked her. Which was shocking in itself. "How utterly vulgar to threaten a person!" Truly Clara was common and base.

"Jean Jacques is *my* husband, too. He is not exclusively *your* husband."

Juliette's lips went as stiff as her spine. "He was *my* husband first!" That was important. Hers was the legal marriage. At least that was her assumption, and she believed she was correct.

Clara puffed up, and her face pulsed red. "You know what I think? I think *my* husband got tired of your prissy superior attitude and left you to find a real woman he could laugh with and be himself with! That's what I think!"

"I'll have you know that Jean Jacques and I laughed all the time!" Juliette refused to be intimidated by a person who slurped her coffee. Pulling to her full five feet two inches, she glared up at Clara. "If I weren't a lady, I would point out that my husband left *you* quicker than he left me! Apparently sinking to a common level wasn't as fulfilling for him as you'd like to believe!"

"If being common means not putting on silly airs or extending my pinkie when I sip from a cup, then I'm common and proud of it!"

Furious, both Clara and Juliette turned in a spin of summer skirts and strode toward the lobby door. At the foot of the grand staircase, they faced each other again.

"Breakfast at seven," Clara snapped.

"You never said what we'll do if we find where he bought his supplies."

"I don't know, all right? You can go home to California. I wish you would. Maybe I'll buy a boardinghouse with the money I got from selling the inn." Lifting her plain dark skirt, Clara started up the staircase. "I can't wait to see the back of you and your stiff-necked ways!"

"And I you," Juliette said, raising her chin. Even to her own ears she sounded prissy. And she was so weary of this conversation. Every night they exchanged a variation of the same words and sentiments. My husband; your husband. No, *my* husband.

Juliette didn't tell Clara what was constantly on her mind. She didn't say, *I hate you because he touched you and lay with you and held you in his arms. I hate you because you laughed with him and because he said beauti-*

ful things to you. I hate you because jealousy is tearing me apart and because I need to know that he loved me better and more than he loved you.

Frowning and blinking hard, she lowered her head and stared at the brooch pinned to her lapel. If she wore this brooch and her blue garter every day, Jean Jacques would come back to her.

Waiting, she gave Clara time to reach her room and go inside so they wouldn't have to encounter each other in the corridor.

Had he ever loved her? Even a little bit?

Blinking rapidly at the liquid burn in her eyes, she lifted her skirts with shaking hands and ascended the staircase. She had never dreamed that a person could hurt so much.

Most of the outfitting stores were strung along First Avenue South, not far from the piers. Mountains of goods spilled onto the sidewalk and into the street, presided over by eager-eyed men checking lists against receipts.

Clara didn't spot any women near the corner of First and Yesler except herself and Juliette. Even so, they didn't attract much attention. Dreams of riches stuffed the heads of the men crowding the walkways and stores, not thoughts of women. Many seemed unaware of the noisy chaos around them; they concentrated solely on packing a year's supply of food into as small a space as possible.

Clara and Juliette began at the top of the street and moved slowly toward the Northern Pacific ticket office, stopping at each of the outfitting stores to interrupt feverishly busy salesmen with questions about a handsome Frenchman. No one recalled the name Jean Jacques Villette.

Discouraged, they silently entered the next store and then stopped abruptly. Juliette gripped her arm. "Good heavens! There's a woman working in this store."

Clara fully supported a woman's right to work if she must, but she, too, was shocked to discover a female working in a store catering exclusively to a male clientele. That the woman was young and attractive made her presence seem even more inappropriate. On the other hand, Clara reminded herself, some people believed it was scandalous for a woman to hand a man a key to a hotel room.

Drawn like magnets, Clara and Juliette passed two harried salesmen and moved directly toward the woman at the back of the store. She watched them approach with cool eyes.

"Can I help you?" she asked, stepping back from her worktable and wiping loose cornmeal off her hands.

Sacking cornmeal was respectable enough, Clara decided. "We'd like to inquire if—"

"Oh!" Juliette sat down hard on top of a flour barrel. Her hands flew to her mouth, and her eyes widened until they must have ached. Shock blanched the color from her cheeks.

Frowning, Clara stared at her. "What's the matter with you?"

"Her hand. Clara, look at her wedding ring!"

"Oh, no!" This time it was Clara who examined a wedding ring and felt like fainting from the pain of recognition. Confusion altered her breathing. How could this be? How many women had Jean Jacques married? Blinking to clear the fog from her vision, she steadied herself on the table in front of her. There was no question. The woman wore Jean Jacques's grandmother's silver heart ring.

The black-haired woman looked back and forth between them with grave apprehension as if she expected them to start foaming at the mouth any instant. "Uncle Milton?" she called, not taking her gaze off Clara and Juliette. "I need some assistance."

"We're not having fits, and we're not crazy," Clara whispered. From the corner of her eye, she saw Juliette yanking at her glove. "Look." She and Juliette held out their left hands.

The woman reeled backward as if they had struck her a punishing blow. Stunned by shock, she stared at her own left hand, then again at Clara's and Juliette's hands.

"My God." Disbelief and bewilderment made her face go slack. She raised trembling fingers to her lips. "The rings. How can this be possible?"

"We both married Jean Jacques Villette," Juliette stated in a toneless voice. "Apparently you did, too."

"My God," the black-haired woman said again. "He had two other wives?" She raised swimming eyes to the tin ceiling. "I trusted him. I . . ." In the silence that followed, Clara could almost see the woman working it through. "Everything was a lie, wasn't it?"

"I'm sorry," Clara said softly. "We know how hard this moment is for you. It's a shock to us, too, believe me."

"All the time he . . . but he was married to you two. And I . . ." Her eyes snapped down into slits. "That son of a bitch! He told me all the things I wanted to hear and played me for a fool."

"Zoe?" A bearded man wearing a long apron emerged from a back room. "Is everything all right here?" He swept a curious glance over Clara and Juliette.

"I'm sorry, Uncle Milton, but I have to leave now." The woman threw off her apron and ran her hands over her skirts, then looked around as if she couldn't remember where she'd put her hat and gloves. "I need to talk to these ladies."

Zoe Wilder shoved a hat on her head and snatched up a small wrist bag. "Follow me," she snapped at Clara and Juliette, then she almost ran out of the outfitting store.

"I feel sick," Juliette whispered. Her face had turned the color of whey. "We're in the center of a nightmare that just gets worse and worse."

Clara understood. A sense of unreality made her feel

dizzy as they followed Zoe outside and climbed back up the steep incline to First and Yesler.

Grimly, Clara watched wife number three veer into a small park, fling herself down on a wooden bench, and fall forward, burying her face in her hands.

Clara and Juliette silently waited, once again subjecting themselves to the misery of comparisons.

Chapter 4

⊰꙰———————————————꙰⊱

After punctuating Juliette's and Clara's tales of woe with little moans and cries, Zoe related her story. As she finished on a half-sob, drops of warm summer rain splattered her hat brim and spotted her skirt. Jumping to her feet, she dashed toward her boardinghouse, beckoning the other Mmes Villette to follow.

Once inside she recognized her mistake. Pain pinched the faces of her rivals as they gazed around her small sitting room and then stared at her bedroom door. Oddly, until now Zoe hadn't noticed how little Jean Jacques had left behind.

Her gaze swung to the book of wildflowers on the small round table near the window. Between the pages she had pressed the roses from the bouquet Jean Jacques had given her on their wedding day. She had one of his handkerchiefs, a cuff link she'd found beneath the bed, and a book of poetry. These items could have belonged to anyone.

Fearing her knees would collapse, Zoe sagged against the wall and covered her eyes. How could she have been so stupid? Why hadn't she looked beyond that handsome face? There must have been signs if she'd had the eyes to see, small slipups if she hadn't been too dazzled to notice.

"We're not permitted to cook in our rooms, but everyone does. I'll make some coffee." If Ma were here she'd throw up her hands. Not only had Zoe brought home her husband's other wives, she was about to serve them refreshments like the perfect little lady that Jean Jacques had believed she was. Or had he?

Opening her eyes, she stared at Juliette. Juliette perched on the edge of the divan, her spine not touching the back cushion. Her knees were modestly pressed together, her hands folded in her lap. With a sinking sensation, Zoe suspected Juliette was the genuine item. And they could not be more unalike. Zoe didn't possess Juliette's quiet stillness, nor her sense of style. She would never have sat as Juliette was sitting. Everything about Juliette March Villette proclaimed her pedigree. Her posture, her clothing. The way she spoke, the way she walked and carried her head. And the reverse must be true as well. Everything about Zoe Wilder Villette announced that she was a Newcastle girl with a chip on her shoulder and calluses on her palms. She knew how to work and fight and swear, and she suspected her background was as obvious as Juliette's.

Aching inside and no longer sure of anything, she went through the motions of making coffee atop the potbelly stove. At once the room became unbearably hot, so she opened her window, not caring if rain dripped inside. For a long moment she gazed at her watery image reflected in the upper panes. The face of a fool.

She should have known that Jean Jacques couldn't be real. Handsome princes didn't appear and lay a kingdom at the feet of someone like Zoe Wilder. What craziness had made her think she deserved to have her dreams come true?

"Oh, Ma," she said softly, pressing her forehead to the cool window glass. She had betrayed the people she loved most. Jean Jacques's aristocratic tales of wealth and the exalted life they would lead together had made her feel ashamed of her family. She had actually felt humiliated when she anticipated what the servants would think when Ma came to visit wearing her crushed hat and mended stockings. Shame almost dropped her to her knees.

She would never forgive him for making her feel embarrassed about her family.

"Thank you. This is good coffee," Juliette murmured after Zoe poured. She balanced her cup and saucer on her knees, making the feat look comfortable and easy.

Clara's eyebrows lifted toward a fringe of red hair. "What are you doing? This is the worst moment of our lives, and you're making polite comments about the coffee!" Disgust pursed her lips as she set her saucer on the floor beside her sensible shoes.

Zoe wished she had splurged and purchased the table she wanted to place before the divan. Later, Jean Jacques's other two wives would probably laugh and make cutting comments about how they'd had to place their cups and saucers on the floor.

"We needn't abandon proper manners because we're upset and distraught," Juliette announced, raising her chin. "Manners are the armor of civilized people. Manners will see one through the most difficult situations."

Clara sighed heavily and rolled her eyes.

First Zoe listened in disbelief. Then outrage stretched her skin tight across her cheekbones. Jean Jacques must have secretly chuckled every time he referred to her as a lady. Mortification flamed bright on her throat. She, who always believed herself too smart to be flimflammed, had been taken in completely. What stuck in her craw was how easily and quickly she had lost her senses. A few besotted glances. A few flattering honeyed words. Clean fingernails. And she had fancied herself in love.

"I am going to find him," she said furiously, speaking between her teeth. "And when I do, I swear I am going to put a bullet between his lying eyes!"

"I'd appreciate it if you didn't make me a widow before I get my money back," Clara said in a short, terse voice.

"And not before he explains everything," Juliette added.

Clara threw out her hands and gave Zoe an exasperated look. "She refuses to believe that he married us for the money!"

"If it was only money, then why didn't he take more?" Juliette glared at them. "I would have given him twice the amount he suggested. He could have waited until you sold your inn, Clara, and taken those funds, too. And you would have given him all your reward money plus your nest egg, wouldn't you?"

"Yes," Zoe admitted, hating the truth of it.

"But I guess I do know it was mostly the money," Juliette admitted softly, blinking down at her cup and saucer. "I want to believe it wasn't only that. I want to believe he loved me a little, too. Maybe that's why he only took part of my money. In any case, he owes us an explanation. I need to hear the truth from his own lips."

At the mention of Jean Jacques's lips, they all fell silent, remembering feverish kisses on sweat-dampened skin. And all three were bitterly aware that the others shared identical memories.

Zoe decided she had never hated anyone or anything as much as she detested the two women staring at her across her inadequately furnished sitting room. Logic informed her it was not their fault that Jean Jacques was a lying, thieving, womanizing son of a bitch. But her heart insisted otherwise.

Jumping up, she crossed the room and gripped the doorknob. "I want you to leave. Right now."

She desperately needed to crawl into bed and wash his scent out of her pillow with her tears. And then, when no more tears would flow, she needed to put herself through the miserable ordeal of reviewing his every word and action, and fully consider the extent of the worst disaster in her life.

Juliette pulled back in disapproval, twitching her lips. After glancing about, she carefully set her cup and saucer on the floor, then rose gracefully and smoothed down her skirts as if dusting Zoe's rudeness off her person.

Clara also stood, appearing more disappointed than offended. "We know how you feel. We—"

"You don't know me, and you don't know how I feel! I can hardly bear to look at the two of you! I don't know how you can stand each other." Aware that the walls were thin and she had shouted, Zoe forced her shaking voice lower. "You've had your say, you've ruined my life, now get out! I don't ever want to see either of you again!"

"Thank you for the coffee," Juliette said in a flat tone as she brushed past Zoe and into the corridor.

Clara paused. "We didn't discuss what we're going to do."

Zoe stared. "There is no *we*. You can fall off the edge of the world for all I care! I hope you do." She slammed her door, no longer minding what the other tenants would think. Shaking with pain and fury, she collected the cups and saucers and threw them out the open window, leaning from the sill to watch the porcelain shatter two stories below. Then, flying through her two rooms, she collected Jean Jacques's handkerchief, his cuff link, the book of poetry, and the dried flowers from her wedding bouquet, and she flung those items out the window, too. She would have sent her wedding ring sailing after the rest if her fingers hadn't swollen in the heat and humidity.

Cursing under her breath, she twisted and tugged at the offending ring, then gave up and burst into deep shuddering sobs. Sinking to her knees before the window, she covered her face and rocked back and forth, hot tears scalding her eyes and cheeks.

She had loved him. But she'd loved a person who didn't really exist. He'd only been a mirror reflecting her dreams.

When the tears and self-flagellation passed, and after she had remembered and considered all that she could endure to remember and consider, the light had faded and Zoe sat on the floor in shadow. But anger directed her toward decisions that needed to be made.

She knew she ought to go home to Newcastle and confess how she had been wronged and let her father and brothers find Jean Jacques. There wasn't a doubt in her mind that her pa and her brothers would avenge her honor. They would beat the living hell out of Jean Jacques, maybe kill him, and it would serve the bastard right.

But three things stopped her from seeking comfort in the bosom of her family. First, the company did not grant time off unless a man had broken bones. If her father or brothers went to the Yukon in search of Jean Jacques, they would lose their jobs at the mines. Zoe couldn't let that disaster happen on top of everything else. Second, she had her pride. Eventually she'd have to tell Ma and the others how dumb and foolish she had been. But it didn't have to happen yet. Third, she didn't deserve her family's support, not after she'd betrayed them in her mind.

No, if she was to have retribution, she'd have to see to it herself. She would be the one traveling to the Yukon.

Near daybreak she understood that she'd made yet another mistake by sending the other wives away with a hearty good riddance. If they also intended to seek Jean Jacques in the Klondike, then it would be smarter and more efficient to travel together. They could take one set of cooking utensils instead of three. One clothes iron, one curling iron. One tent to share.

Zoe desperately needed to do something smart to salvage a fraction of her self-esteem and feel worthy of Ma's faith.

A deep sob gurgled up from her despair, and she fell back on the floor, staring at a stain on the ceiling just visible in the predawn light. Admitting to Ma that she'd been played for a sucker would be the hardest thing she ever did.

* * *

It seemed to Juliette that she'd done nothing for months but wring her hands and search for guidance. First she had looked to Aunt Kibble for answers, then she had transferred her hopes to Clara. For a few minutes yesterday she had believed Zoe Wilder would know what to do.

Looking to others to make her decisions disgusted her. She had gotten herself to Clara's inn on the Oregon coast, hadn't she? And then to Seattle. True, she had been fearful every step of the way, dreading the new experiences sure to fall in her direction. And rightly so. Thus far, nothing good had come from this painful journey.

So. What should she do now?

No matter what the answer was, she knew she would hate it. There were no comfortable answers in this situation.

"At least we know where he is," she stated glumly after the waiter had removed her breakfast plate. "I suppose we've achieved our objective."

"I haven't. My objective was and is to get my money."

She and Clara sat back to back at separate tables in the hotel's dining room. They had stepped out the door of Zoe's boardinghouse yesterday, taken a hard look at each other, then marched off in different directions. There was no point trying to be polite about it. Juliette loathed Clara and Clara loathed her. They both loathed Zoe.

She took a sip of coffee, extending her little finger. "How do you intend to get your money?" she asked, gazing across the dining room.

From behind her, she heard Clara sigh. "He has to return to Seattle sometime. I'll wait here and meet every ship that returns from Alaska."

She could do the same thing. She had no other pressing business. Heaven knew she wasn't ready to return to Linda Vista, face Aunt Kibble, and confess the truth.

"Well, glory be, look who's come calling!" She couldn't believe her eyes.

Zoe Wilder stood in the doorway scanning the hotel dining room until she spotted Juliette staring back at her. Then, grim-lipped and determined, she stepped forward.

Clara swiveled in her chair to look. "She's very pretty."

Indeed she was, Juliette thought, feeling a sharp bite of jealousy. A crisp straw hat trimmed with cloth daisies held Zoe's abundant black hair in place. She wore a snowy summer shirtwaist with a black ribbon at the throat and a dark skirt that appeared freshly brushed and ironed. Her snapping blue eyes were not as soulful or melting as Juliette's nor was her skin as glowing and fine as Clara's, but many heads turned to follow her progress.

Before a waiter could rush to assist her, Zoe pulled out a chair at Juliette's table. "Clara, come over here."

"If you want to speak to me, the two of you can come to my table."

Zoe's eyes narrowed, and she muttered something about being childish, then she motioned Juliette to her feet and they moved to Clara's table.

Juliette detested Clara's triumphant smile. She caught the waiter's eye and ordered fresh coffee for the three of them and then fixed a look on Clara. "Since we're at *your* table, *you'll* be charged for the coffee," she mentioned in a steely sweet voice. "I'm sure you won't mind since sitting here is *your* demand."

Clara ignored her, turning to Zoe. "This is certainly a surprise. I believe you said you couldn't stand us and never wanted to see us again. Correct me if I'm mistaken, but didn't you shout this as you were ordering us out of your rooms?"

"And I meant every word. I think we can agree that we hate each other and with good reason," Zoe stated in a businesslike tone. "But hating each other needn't prevent us from doing the smart thing." She nodded to the waiter as he placed a cup and saucer before her, then watched Juliette take a sip. She, too, extended her little finger, then made a sound of disgust and set her cup back in the saucer with a hard rattle.

Juliette watched with interest. Zoe Wilder was not a lady and never would be, nor was Clara. Jean Jacques had made only one marriage worthy of him. "And what do you consider the smart thing?" she inquired.

"Most outfits run between eight hundred and a thousand pounds," Zoe explained, leaning forward and looking back and forth between them. "If we travel as a common party, we can eliminate duplications. That will bring down the poundage and make moving our goods more manageable. But we can't omit anything essential because we could get stuck up there. That's possible, even likely, since we're leaving very late in the year."

Juliette stared, feeling the start of a headache behind her eyes. "What in the name of heaven are you talking about?" She knew as sure as she was sitting here that she was going to despise the answer.

Clara frowned as understanding dawned. "I take it you're suggesting that we all go to Alaska?"

Surprise lifted Zoe's eyebrows. "Isn't that what you intended to do? You said you were going to find Jean Jacques."

Clara stared into space for a moment, then slowly nodded. "*Ja.* That's exactly what I intend to do."

"It is not," Juliette objected. "You were going to wait here for my—for our—" She threw up her hands. "For Jean Jacques to return to Seattle."

"This is a better plan." Clara stared at her.

The air rushed out of Juliette's chest, and she thought her heart would pound right through her rib cage. "Me? Us? Travel to the Yukon?" She gasped. She couldn't believe they were serious. "Do decent women go to the gold fields?"

"More do than you might suppose," Zoe answered. "It's not common for women to join the stampeders, but it isn't rare, either." Her gaze traveled over Juliette in critical appraisal. "Frankly, I don't think you should go. Clara looks strong enough to withstand the rigors of the journey, and I've worked hard all my life. But you don't appear fit or strong enough to undertake a difficult and demanding trek."

Juliette reared back in her chair, a burst of anger sending hot streaks across her cheeks. "If the two of you can go to the Yukon, then so can I!" They were not going to find her husband without her. "I'm going!" She could not believe what she was saying. Hearing the words made her feel sick to her stomach.

"We'll camp in a tent after walking miles every day. You'll be colder than you've ever been. You'll be in danger of frostbite and you'll have to keep a lookout for bears. No one will coddle you. You'll have to do your share of the work. Does the journey still sound appealing?"

Of course not. But who was Zoe Wilder to take such a superior tone? Or Clara Klaus, who looked at Juliette as if she had about as much substance as a lint ball.

"Don't you worry about me! I can take care of myself!"

Oh, my Lord. What was she doing? Instant regret nailed her to her chair. Her knees would not have supported her if she had tried to stand. All she could think was that someone else was speaking out of her mouth.

Zoe shrugged and fished a notebook out of her purse. "This late in the summer, the waiting list for the steamers is shorter than it was, but still. We should get on the list first thing." She wrote a note, then studied Clara. "Can you be trusted to book our passage?"

"I beg your pardon. I'm as reliable as the day is long," Clara stated angrily. "Who put you in charge?"

"Do *you* know anything about Alaska or provisioning?"

"I can learn."

"Well, I already know!"

"Continue, please. What else do we have to do?" Juliette asked. Her voice had risen an octave and emerged in a squeak. Her headache grew worse by the minute.

"I'd suggest you walk up and down Seattle's steepest hills and strengthen your legs," Zoe advised, giving Juliette a look of doubt that irritated Juliette down to her marrow.

"What else?" she snapped. If Jean Jacques could see her now he wouldn't recognize her. He wouldn't compare her eyes to shining pewter. He'd think of steel balls. And when she glared at Clara, Clara's skin wasn't beautiful as Clara had claimed Jean Jacques had said. Her skin flushed an angry scarlet that clashed with her hair. As for hair, Juliette didn't think Zoe's mass of hair looked like silk. What a ridiculous notion.

"I'm sure my uncle Milton will sell us provisions at his cost. Nevertheless, passage and provisions aren't cheap." Zoe made a notation in her notebook. "Plus, we'll have to pay a customs charge when we cross into Canada. Can you afford to go?"

"Can you?" Clara demanded.

Juliette listened to the story of Zoe's reward. This time Zoe shared more details. "It must have been a substantial sum," she said at the end of the tale.

"The Van Hootens are among the wealthiest families in King County, and Mr. Van Hooten was very grateful that I rescued his grandson. Plus I have a small nest egg." Zoe swallowed a sip of coffee. "But I won't have much left after this journey."

Grudgingly, Juliette conceded it was courageous of Zoe to wade into the tide marsh and rescue the little boy. She wondered if she would have done the same thing in Zoe's place.

For another hour they talked about what needed to be done and what they would take to the Yukon. Then Juliette excused herself and returned to her room. She clapped a damp cloth across her forehead, then dropped on the bed and stared at the ceiling with dulled eyes.

Oh, lordy. She was going to the Yukon. The shock of it paralyzed her.

* * *

Sun slid across the window of Wilder's Outfitting Company and reflected a sensibly clad tall woman with excitement glowing in her eyes. Clara could hardly believe it. In less than a week, she would sail to Alaska. This journey would be the most thrilling event in her entire life.

Since her early teens she had catered to the needs of travelers on their way to strange and exotic places. San Francisco, Canada, Mexico, Missouri . . . But she had never been anywhere nor had she expected to go anywhere. Now everything had changed. She had observed the bustle and glory of Seattle and she would explore the mysteries of Alaska. It would be something wonderful to tell her grandchildren.

The image in the glass sagged, and she watched her lips turn down. She would never have grandchildren because she would never have children because her husband was not really her husband after all.

Pained by the injustice, she shifted a frown to Juliette's and Zoe's reflections. They stood behind her in the street inspecting mounds of goods, discussing methods of packing and arranging. At least that's what Zoe appeared to be doing. Juliette wrung her hands and gazed at the packs with a dazed look of confusion and disbelief.

Clara sighed. Next to the other two Mmes Villette, she felt like a Saint Bernard plodding along beside two sleek greyhounds. In the last week she had stopped thinking of herself as merely substantial and had started thinking of herself as unbecomingly big and clunky. Secretly she wondered what her Jean Jacques had seen in her since two out of three of his wives were petite. She was the unfortunate anomaly.

She wasn't skinny like the other two. Her hair wouldn't stay put. She preferred comfort to fashion. She'd rather scrub a staircase than pick up an embroidery hoop. She liked to grow vegetables and she liked to polish silver.

Mostly she liked to eat a perfectly prepared and abundant meal. She was a peasant.

Sighing again, she gazed into the reflection and watched Juliette and Zoe bend their heads over Zoe's list. After a minute she noticed a man leaning against a mound of goods and smoking a cigar on the far side of the street. He observed Juliette with narrow intent eyes, his gaze following as she paced beside Zoe.

Clara's attention sharpened and she turned from the reflection to study him directly. Like most of the stampeders buying outfits at Wilder's, this man wore a beard, but his was new, just beginning to fill in. He wore denims with plain suspenders running over the shoulders of an open-collared shirt, had tilted his hat to shade the late August sun. He was tall and good-looking, but it was his attitude that set him apart from the other men in the street.

Whereas the others had an air of frenzy and perhaps desperation about them, this man did not. He wasn't focused on his outfit to the exclusion of all else. And he was more aware of his surroundings than the others seemed to be. Certainly he was aware of Juliette. He hadn't looked away from her in several minutes.

When Clara was certain she wasn't imagining his interest, she moved between the piles of foodstuffs and camping equipment.

"Juliette," she said in a low voice. "There's a man across the street who's watching you like you're a dumpling and he's starving."

Juliette did not glance up from Zoe's list. "Is he broad-shouldered and handsome? Smoking a cigar and wearing a green scarf twisted around his hatband?"

Clara hadn't noticed the scarf until she turned sideways and shot him a suspicious look. The man smiled slightly and tipped his hat to her, then returned his attention to Juliette.

"Do you know him?"

"Certainly not." Juliette glared from under her hat brim. "But we keep running into him. He was in the park last week when we talked to Zoe, and I think he's staying at our hotel."

Clara could swear she had never seen the man before, but apparently she had. "Well, he sure seems interested in you."

"If you're implying that I've encouraged him, I assure you I have not. I am a married woman!" Juliette straightened and sniffed, her shoulders stiff with insult.

"Oh, for heaven's sake. I didn't imply anything, I only . . . Just forget it!"

Throwing up her hands in annoyance, Clara turned in a huff to walk away and crashed into the biggest man she'd ever seen.

Huge hands steadied her. "I beg your pardon."

"No, no. It was my fault."

As he was easily six feet six inches tall, she had to tilt her head back to see his face. Shaggy masses of golden hair tumbled around his jawline since he carried his hat instead of wearing it. No one would have described him as handsome. His face was too lived in, and there were reminders of too many brawls in the once-broken nose and a scar that cut through one eyebrow. It was a craggy, intimidating face until he smiled, then Clara saw that some might consider him handsome after all.

"Did I stomp your toes?"

Like an idiot she peered down at her sturdy shoes. "I don't believe so."

"Excellent." Bowing slightly, he made a flourish with his hat. "Bernard T. Barrett at your service." A grin revealed teeth as white as baking soda. "Everyone calls me Bear."

Clara could see why. His voice seemed to growl out of a barrel chest and he had twinkly brown-bear eyes.

She would have told him her name, too, but she suddenly heard the silence behind her and realized Juliette and Zoe were watching and listening. Juliette at least would be shocked to her toes if Clara, a married woman, offered her name to a stranger.

Smiling down at her, he made another flourish, then tapped his hat onto the back of his head. "Well, then. If you're sure I didn't injure you."

"It was nothing. Really. I turned too fast and wasn't looking where I was going." Clara dipped her head. Mr. Barrett kept gazing at her. Staring, actually.

"You sure are a pretty little thing," he remarked in a booming voice, causing several men to look up and give her the once-over. Before she could take offense, Bernard T. Barrett grinned, bowed slightly, then moved away from her through the piles of boxes and sacks, his strides as big as the rest of him.

An hour later, during a demonstration emphasizing the dangers of camp stoves, Clara gave up trying not to think about him. She couldn't get over the fact that Mr. Bernard T. Barrett had complimented her as a pretty *little* thing.

In twenty-six years, no one had ever described Clara Klaus as little. The word ravished her and sent a shiver of delight coursing through her body followed by a pang of regret. Where had men like Bernard T. Barrett been when she was single? She just knew that he didn't have a string of Mmes Barrett trailing out behind him. Her heart understood with rock-solid certainty that he wasn't that kind of low-down, good-for-nothing man.

"Clara, are you paying attention?" Zoe glared at her. "We all need to know how to operate this stove, because we'll each have our turn at using it."

"Wait a minute." Juliette's gray eyes rounded in horror. "You don't expect me to cook. Oh, my heavens. You do."

Clara listened to Zoe's sharp reply with half an ear. As far as Clara could discern, Juliette had not acknowledged the man across the street. Judging by Juliette's demeanor, she was entirely indifferent to a handsome man's intent interest.

Which meant that Juliette was a far better person than she, Clara thought with a sigh of irritation. She cast another surreptitious glance in the direction Bernard T. Barrett had taken. She would never see Mr. Barrett again, and that was just as well. After all, she was sort of married.

Bracing herself, she thought of her thieving husband and waited for the anvil of pain to squash her as it usually did when she grieved over Jean Jacques.

The pain came, but it didn't quite squash her. For the first time since Juliette had appeared and ruined her life, Clara sensed that a moment might come when she could think about Jean Jacques without the anguish of wanting to hold him or kill him.

Possibly. Maybe.

Chapter 5

The piers at the foot of First Avenue were crammed with men jammed shoulder to shoulder trying to shout or push their way on board the *Annasett*. Hoping to catch the attention of an armed crew member guarding the bottom of the gangplank, Zoe waved her ticket above her hat. It was useless to shout as everyone was yelling. And, she realized, she was too short for her waving ticket to be noticed in the chaotic melee.

Peering over her shoulder, she screamed at Juliette and Clara to stay right behind her. Then she lowered her head and went to work with her elbows, opening a path. When one man stepped back in surprise or anger, she slipped in front of him and jabbed at the next one. By the time she reached the gangplank, her hat was askew, splatters of tobacco juice soiled her skirts, and her elbows were bruised from banging against ribs, but she presented her ticket with a triumphant flourish.

The crewman's eyebrows soared at the sight of three ticketed women, but he grinned and waved them on board with a look that said he thought they were crazy.

Once on deck, Juliette gripped the railing and stared down at the crush of men shouting and shoving on the pier, all hoping to be the one chosen to fill a last-minute vacancy.

"What if our outfits didn't get loaded?" she asked, speaking next to Clara's ear to be heard.

"That's why we had them sent to the dock yesterday. To make certain no mishap occurred," Clara reminded her.

"How safe is this boat?" After straightening her hat and cape, Juliette gazed up at the stack, then scanned the deck. "I was told the *Annasett* has room for sixty passengers, but there's twice that many standing at the rail."

"I'm guessing we'll share the trip with three hundred fellow travelers," Zoe said with a shrug. "Can't blame the owner for making a profit while he can."

Juliette gasped and her face turned pale. "We'll sink!"

Zoe raised her eyes to the hills of Seattle and fervently wished that Juliette were standing on one of them. All she had heard for the last week was: "I can't do this." "What if we don't have enough food in the packs?" "What if we freeze to death?" What if, what if, what if, until Zoe felt like screaming.

She truly did not understand why Juliette undertook a journey that so clearly terrified her. She must have loved Jean Jacques very much to do something she desperately did not want to do in the hope of finding him.

Jealousy whipsawed down Zoe's spine. For several days now, she hadn't imagined Jean Jacques kissing Juliette and Clara every time she looked at them. But at odd moments the images rose with tormenting power, blindsiding her as now.

It made her furious. She wanted to feel nothing but hatred when she thought of Jean Jacques, wanted to imagine no scenes except that of herself firing a bullet into his black heart. Unlike Juliette, Zoe had no questions she wanted to ask, and she didn't care about getting her money back as Clara did. She just wanted revenge, just wanted to kill his butt.

Glaring down at the docks, she watched Bear Barrett stride through the yelling throng, knocking aside smaller men—which included everyone on the pier. She knew him by sight because he came into Uncle Milton's store once or twice a year, ordering supplies to be sent to his place in Dawson City. Coming up the gangplank behind him was the man who had shown an interest in Juliette the day they assembled their outfits. Today, the green scarf he'd worn around his hatband was tied to a belt loop.

Zoe slid a glare toward Clara and Juliette, noticing they watched the gangplank, too. And it suddenly occurred to her that they would find other men, other loves, once she had made them widows. But what about her? What man could possibly interest her after Jean Jacques? Men like him came into the life of a Newcastle girl only once, if ever. Except he hadn't been real.

"I'm going to find our stateroom," she announced abruptly, turning from the rail.

Stateroom was a grossly grandiose term for what she discovered. Deep in the bowels of the steamship, she entered a closet-sized cubicle barely large enough to contain a cot and a two-decker bunk bed. As a concession to gender, they'd been issued a cracked chamber pot painted with daisies and a cloudy mirror that hung above a shelf supporting a lone washbasin.

"Oh, my heavens," Juliette breathed, appearing in the doorway. Her gray eyes widened in an expression of shock and dismay that was becoming annoyingly familiar.

"This would be cramped for one person, let alone all of us," Clara observed tightly, stepping past Juliette and blocking the light from a single smoky oil lamp.

Making little whimpering sounds, Juliette collapsed on the bottom bunk. "Three weeks of this? I can't endure it!"

Maybe she'd give herself the pleasure of shooting Juliette, too, right after she shot Jean Jacques, Zoe decided. Then she'd shoot Clara, just for good measure. Of course, if the other wives were dead, maybe she wouldn't shoot Jean Jacques after all. Maybe they could . . .

What was she thinking? Giving her head a disgusted shake, she set her bag on the plank floor. Inside were her toiletries, a couple of nightgowns, a change of clothing, a warm coat, and heavy underwear because the temperatures would dip as they neared the coast of Alaska.

Juliette said it first. Naturally. "There's no place to lay out our things."

"We can shove our luggage under the cot and bunks," Clara noted briskly. Bending, she removed a hammer from a side pocket on her bag. "I'll put up some nails to hang our hats and capes."

Zoe's mouth dropped. "You packed a hammer and nails for the voyage?" Grudgingly, Zoe conceded she was impressed. There were depths to Clara that she hadn't suspected.

"Be careful you don't drive a hole in the side of the boat and sink it!" Alarm widened Juliette's eyes. "I can't swim."

"If a single nail hole will sink this ship, then we're done for anyway," Clara said around the nails in her mouth. In minutes, she had completed the job. "It's an inside wall," she assured Juliette, inspecting the row of nails. "Now get off that bed. I need one of the slats. If we take one slat from each of the bunks, I don't think the beds will collapse."

Immediately Zoe grasped the plan. "Extra shelves."

Nodding, Clara laid the edge of a slat against the lip of the wainscoting. A few hammer whacks and they each had a shelf.

"Are we going to get in trouble for this?" Juliette asked. "I'm grateful for the innovations, but—" She broke off speaking and placed a hand against her stomach. "Are we moving?"

"Not yet." With a sinking heart, Zoe studied her face. "Why? Are you feeling ill?"

"I'm not sure," Juliette said slowly.

Clara leaned against the wall and covered her face with one big hand. "I don't even want to think about sharing this tiny cell with someone who's seasick."

Far above them, the ship's whistle blasted and the ship rocked and lurched, and the floor slid beneath their feet.

Juliette gasped and gripped the edges of the bunk bed. "I've never been on a boat before."

It turned out none of them had.

"Don't you dare get seasick," Zoe hissed. The room was so tiny and cramped that the smell of the tobacco juice on their skirts overwhelmed every breath. Body heat generated by the three of them had already raised a damp sheen across her forehead. And the greasy smell wafting from the lamp made her feel queasy inside. "I swear, Juliette, if you throw up one time, I'm going to toss you overboard!"

"I'll help you," Clara promised firmly.

An odd rocking, sliding motion told Zoe the *Annasett* was drifting out of her slip. Never in her life had she felt such a strange loss of bearing and gravity. The cape she'd hung on one of Clara's nails swung slightly back and forth. The oil in the lamp base gently sloshed from side to side. As the contents of her stomach were undoubtedly doing.

Cold sweat popped out on her forehead. A nasty taste scalded the back of her throat. Panic flared in her eyes when she heard another blast of the whistle. They were under way.

Something heaved in her stomach. "Oh, God!" Dropping to her knees on the floor, she frantically yanked their bags from under the bunks in a desperate search for the chamber pot.

She found it in the nick of time and gave up her breakfast while Juliette and Clara watched in horror.

There was time for humiliation to crush her before the next wave of nausea sent her back to the chamberpot.

As they did whenever they could escape the cubicle, Juliette and Clara strolled round and round the decks of the shockingly crowded steamship. Oily black smoke blew into their faces when the wind shifted, and when it wasn't actually raining, a good possibility existed that flying sea spray would mist them with tiny annoying droplets. Another irritation was enduring the unending scrutiny of bored men with nothing to do but inflame tempers by staring at fellow passengers.

Juliette paused by the rail rather than approach the crowd of men gathered around a fistfight at the far end of the deck. As usual, the onlookers appeared more interested in wagering on the outcome than in breaking up the brawl. Frowning in disapproval, she tried to imagine Jean Jacques involved in such brutish behavior. He was far too refined.

"You have that Jean Jacques look," Clara commented, shaking her head.

"I wish you'd stop calling it that. Of course I think about my husband, don't you?"

"I try not to."

They gazed down at the water, still choppy from this morning's rain. The sea was never the same, although Juliette had expected it would be. Instead, the color and movement constantly changed. Sometimes the water was green and glassy. Other times, saucy blue waves spit foam at the sky. On three occasions she had watched dolphins arching through the sea like big gray needles stitching an invisible thread.

"It's your turn to check on Zoe."

Clara made a face. "Lordy, I hate going down there!"

Their cubicle trapped the heat, stench, and dismal ambience of a nightmare. Sleep was next to impossible because of Zoe's continual retching and moaning. Never in her life had Juliette seen anyone as sick as Zoe Wilder. Zoe begged to die, and Juliette believed it likely that she would.

"You know what the captain said. We have to get some food into her."

"I don't mind that part," Clara said unhappily. "It's

emptying the chamber pots." They had three now. "And cleaning up. And bathing her. And just trying to breathe in there." Tossing back her head, she inhaled deeply, pulling the fresh sea breeze deep into her lungs before she squared her shoulders and marched off with firm but reluctant steps.

When she reflected on it, Juliette experienced a thrill of triumph that it wasn't she who was sick and begging to die. If someone asked at the end of her life what her proudest moment had been, she would think: Zoe Wilder got seasick, and I didn't. Ha!

Halfheartedly castigating herself for feeling superior at Zoe's expense, Juliette considered going to the mess hall to escape the blowing smoke and the noise of the fight. But the mess hall would be crowded with men. Most were respectful and tried to curtail swearing and coarse language in her presence, but she knew she made them uncomfortable. Moreover, they believed she had no business going to Alaska. She believed it, too.

"Beautiful," a voice said softly at her side.

Stiffening, she straightened abruptly and glanced at the tall man who appeared next to her on the rail, noting a corner of the green scarf sticking out of his shirt pocket. His beard was fuller now, coming in the same luxuriant brown as his hair. But what she noticed most were his eyes, a brilliant blue that made her think of Aunt Kibble's bright prizewinning delphiniums.

"The sea. It's beautiful, isn't it?"

Ordinarily she would not have dreamed of striking up a conversation with a stranger. But these were not ordinary circumstances. After two weeks packed together as tightly as a paper of pins, no one was really a stranger anymore. All the faces were familiar.

"Indeed," she murmured uneasily. She had never excelled at conversing with strangers, particularly men. She always imagined a tiny Aunt Kibble sitting on one shoulder and a tiny version of her mother perched on her other shoulder, both listening and observing with critical expressions, waiting for her to err.

"Permit me to introduce myself. I'm Benjamin Dare, from San Francisco, California." Removing his hat, he held it against his chest and studied her face with an expectant expression.

The tiny Aunt Kibble *tsk*ed in disapproval as Juliette hesitantly offered her own name, giving it as Miss March. For the duration of the journey, she and the others had agreed to call themselves by their maiden names rather than raise gossip and scurrilous speculation by identifying themselves each as Mrs. Jean Jacques Villette.

"Do you mind if I smoke, Miss March?"

So he didn't intend to leave immediately. And she couldn't continue her stroll since the fistfight was still in progress. "Please do." Her father had smoked cheroots. The scented smoke was her strongest memory of him. Besides, it seemed churlish to protest when the stack's black smoke hung thick across the decks.

"We seem to run into each other rather frequently," he said, waving out a match.

"I beg your pardon?" She would have set herself on fire before admitting that she, too, had noticed.

In view of her ongoing experience with chamber pots and retching fellow wives, his clean soapy scent pleased her enormously. And she liked the pleasant rumble of his deep voice. He wore the ubiquitous denims and flannel shirts favored by the majority of passengers, but on him the prospector's uniform seemed exotic and appealing.

"We stayed at the same hotel in Seattle," he explained. "And I saw you in the Yesler Park and again at the outfitting store. Now we're aboard the same ship. It's an interesting set of coincidences."

She thought so, too, but made no comment, keeping her gaze on the sea while she watched him from the edge of her eyes. It was flattering that he had noticed and remembered her. Surprising that she had noticed and remembered him. But she definitely had.

"I'm puzzled to find a lady such as yourself traveling to the Yukon. If you'll pardon a personal observation, you don't seem the type of person to seek your fortune in the gold fields."

"Good heavens!" She met his blue eyes directly. "You can't think that I . . ." The notion was hilarious. "No indeed, Mr. Dare, I have no intention of panning or digging for gold."

Most people looked at others without really seeing more than an overall impression. But Ben Dare looked at her with an intensity that made her think he saw deep inside her. Flustered, Juliette resisted an urge to pat her hair and wet her lips. Even Jean Jacques had not gazed at her with such total absorption. An odd warmth spread through her stomach and she hastily lowered her eyes, frowning and biting her lip.

From atop her shoulder her tiny mother advised her to nod politely and walk away, and Aunt Kibble warned that it was no one's business but her own that she traveled to the Yukon in search of a philandering husband. Either caution was unnecessary. She would no more have confided in a strange man than she would have adjusted her corset in public. Not even if the man had intent blue eyes and a well-shaped mouth and made her feel strangely tingly.

After coughing into her hand, she asked, "Do you intend to search for gold, Mr. Dare?"

Despite the beard and clothing, he didn't impress her as a prospector type. If he were clean-shaven and dressed differently, she would have guessed that his air of easy authority suggested he moved in the business world. He seemed too well spoken to be a laborer. And he lacked the feverish nervousness common to the other stampeders, that odd blend of eagerness and desperation.

"Certainly."

"Oh." Disappointment sharpened the word. Without being aware, she had set him above the other passengers. She had wanted his objectives to be loftier than the pursuit of fortune. Discovering that she had thought about him at all startled her.

Her sudden frown caused him to laugh, and she was struck by the rich timbre of his voice and how handsome he was. Dark hair, blue blue eyes, broad shoulders, a tall lean body. Such observations flooded her cheeks with hot pink, and she abruptly turned aside, pretending an interest in a coil of rope.

"With the exception of yourself and presumably your companions," he said, "everyone here intends to make his fortune in the Klondike."

"Intends or hopes?"

"Hope is the more accurate word. And most will be disappointed. I've heard that nearly every foot of Klondike creek front has already been claimed." He leaned his forearms on the rail and blew a smoke ring into the sea breeze. "It's the original discoverers who reap a bonanza, and the first claimants to follow. But a year later . . . Well, I doubt those who make it to Dawson will find enough gold to justify the journey."

Surprise arched her eyebrows. "But . . . if that's true, then why are you going?"

Instantly she wished she could withdraw the question. Direct and personal questions were an embarrassing breach of good manners. She didn't know what had come over her, or maybe she did. She was picking up disgraceful habits from Jean Jacques's other wives.

"A year ago my wife died of meningitis." His fingers rose to brush the green scarf at his shirt pocket.

"I'm sorry," Juliette murmured.

In her experience this conversation was unprecedented. People did not share personal details on such brief acquaintance. While she felt wildly flattered that he had taken her into his confidence, it simply was not done.

However, she had read books about long voyages and instant intimacy was portrayed as rather common. Being contained for long periods within a small space led passengers to confide in one another, the suggestion being that intimacy was possible and permissible as they would part ways at the conclusion of the voyage, never to see one another again.

"The only thing that's interested me in over a year is the Klondike." Straightening, he looked down at her. "I need to test myself and find the man I used to be." His raw honesty appeared to make him uncomfortable because he shrugged and abruptly smiled. "Maybe I'll even stumble across a nugget or two."

"I hope you do," she said earnestly, feeling a kinship. They had both lost a spouse dear to their hearts. His wife had died. Her so-called husband had run away and betrayed her. Though she couldn't say so, they had grief in common. Except Mr. Dare was now moving forward, while she was stuck in place.

"Well," he said, tossing the cigar into the sea. "Is Miss Wilder feeling better?"

My, my. He'd made inquiries and had known her name and the names of her companions before he spoke to her. His interest raised a fluttery warmth in her stomach.

Drawing a deep breath, she strove mightily to look sorrowful about what she had to say. "I fear Miss Wilder is dying."

No one could recover from such violent illness. To her shame, Juliette couldn't bring herself to mourn Zoe's imminent demise with any real distress. She hadn't liked Zoe to begin with, and she liked her less now that she'd wiped vomit from her lips, had bathed her, and repeatedly washed her nightgowns. Granted, a woman was not at her best when ill and dying, but Zoe had displayed a shocking lack of gratitude for Juliette's and Clara's ministrations. She had shouted at them, sworn at them, sobbed at them, and ordered them out of the cubicle. Twice she had thrown up on them. Though the thought revealed how swiftly Juliette's character was deteriorating, it would not break her heart to have one less wife to deal with.

Ben Dare's laugh brought her back from a recurring dread of her upcoming turn as nursemaid. "People rarely die from seasickness, although Miss Wilder probably wishes she would. She'll recover almost instantly next week when we dock at Dyea."

It didn't seem possible that Zoe would survive, or that Juliette and Clara could endure another week of sleepless nights and the long, awful stretches struggling to put up with Zoe and her ill-tempered dying, and trying not to breathe in the cubicle.

"I've enjoyed meeting you, Miss March," Mr. Dare said as they both spotted Clara emerging from the staircase. A large wet spot darkened the front of Clara's skirt, and she didn't look happy. "May I visit with you again?"

"Oh, but I'm—" Juliette bit off confiding that Miss March was actually Mrs. Villette. She had promised not to tell a soul.

She wasn't certain how to handle this situation. She was such a novice in matters between men and women that she didn't know, couldn't be sure if Mr. Dare's request was improper. After all, he believed she was unattached. And really, there was nothing unseemly about exchanging a few words. They were no longer strangers, so a conversation wasn't exactly out of line.

Flustered and blushing, she thanked heaven that Clara reached them before she had to decide how to respond.

"She's still alive," Clara snarled. "But only because I didn't have a weapon." She nodded to Benjamin Dare. "I'm Clara Klaus, and you're Mr. Dare. I've heard the captain address you." She turned a stare on Juliette. "It's your turn in hell."

"Clara! Such language!"

"Mr. Dare, I apologize for requesting a favor on short

acquaintance, but do you know if there's any liquor on this vessel? And if there is, will you help me get some?"

A rakish grin widened the area where his mustache ran into his new beard. "I believe we could find some whiskey hereabouts."

"Excellent. Due to a certain violently ill viper with whom I am sharing a cubicle very much against my will, I am desperately in need of a drop of fortification. Lead on."

Laughing, Ben Dare offered his arm to Clara, and they started toward the mess hall, leaving Juliette behind.

Bewilderingly, she felt a hard twinge of something like jealousy as she watched Mr. Dare walk away with Clara on his arm. And the thought crossed her mind that by heaven Clara Klaus was not going to take another man away from her.

Good grief. Where had that thought come from? Shaking her head, she stiffened her resolve and headed for the staircase.

Now that landfall was predicted for the day after tomorrow, growing excitement replaced the boredom that had stretched tempers and patience. Drawn by a buzz of loud male voices, Clara turned her collar up around her cheeks to block a chilly breeze and wandered toward the mess hall, looking for something to occupy her until it was again her turn in Zoe hell.

Even before she stepped into the large overheated room, she heard Bear Barrett's booming shout rise above the others. Surprising herself, she hesitated about going inside.

She and Mr. Barrett had passed each other on deck at least a dozen times, and each time he had tipped his hat to her and stared like she was a sight for sore eyes, but he'd made no effort to speak nor had he sought her out in a solitary moment as Mr. Dare had done twice now with Juliette. Naturally she was relieved by Mr. Barrett's reticence as she had nothing whatsoever to say to him because of

Jean Jacques, her thieving no-good sort-of husband. But still, it would have been nice to converse with someone who wasn't complaining or vomiting.

Slipping inside the door, trying unsuccessfully to make herself small and inconspicuous, she took a seat at one of the long tables near the back and listened to Mr. Barrett speaking to the crowd of men gathered around him.

"We'll have as many rounds as it takes to get down to two contenders." His brown-bear eyes flicked to Clara, held a moment, then he leaned against a chalkboard mounted on the wall. "We'll put all names in a hat and draw them two by two until everyone has a partner for the first round of the tournament."

"What kind of a tournament is he talking about?" Clara asked the man nursing a cup of coffee on her left.

"Arm wrestling, ma'am."

She thought about that. "Is there a prize for the winner?"

"One hundred dollars and free drinks for a month at the Bare Bear Saloon." When she looked puzzled, he explained, "That's Bear's place in Dawson City."

So he owned a saloon. In her opinion that was a lot smarter than digging for gold he might never find. You couldn't go far wrong selling food, beds, or whiskey.

Interested, she watched as a man drew names from his hat and Bear wrote the match pairs on the chalkboard.

One hundred dollars.

It was a lot of money for a little bit of labor. Hugo Bosch would stand over a hot skillet for two months to earn a hundred dollars. In Seattle, the average man would work three months to earn the same amount. Throw in free drinks, and the prize probably doubled. Just for winning a silly arm-wrestling contest.

After thinking another minute, she stood and stared at Bear Barrett until he felt her concentration and turned in her direction. Then she mouthed the words, "Can I ask a question?"

"All you cheechakos shut up. The little lady wants to say something."

Little lady. Clara loved it.

Judging by the frowns and mutters wafting her way, interruptions were not appreciated. But Bear Barrett didn't seem to mind. Those brown-bear eyes narrowed and traveled to the open strip between the edges of her cape, then touched at her hips before rising back to her face. He was a bold one all right.

Clara took a good look at him, too. He wore denim trousers held up by red suspenders that crossed the shoulders of a white shirt made from enough material to upholster a wing chair. He was a big, big man, but she could see that most of him was muscle. She could have bounced a cannon ball off his chest.

When the mutual inspection had continued a beat too long, she asked, "Can anyone on board enter this match?"

A grin spread his lips, revealing big strong teeth. "You have someone you want to sponsor?"

"*Ja*. Me."

Laughter erupted, then abruptly ceased when the men realized she was serious. Then two dozen heads swiveled toward Bear.

"She's a woman!"

"It wouldn't be fair! It would be like handing her opponent a free pass to the next level."

"I ain't gonna arm-wrestle no woman."

Bear's gaze locked to hers during the torrent of objections, and she watched him thinking about it. When she saw a twinkle appear, she knew she was in.

"There's a five-dollar entry fee," he said finally, watching to see if the hugely expensive entry fee would discourage her.

The objections erupted into a firestorm of protest while Clara counted the names on the chalkboard and realized Mr. Barrett could offer the hundred-dollar prize and still make money on the tournament. She wished she had thought of this before he did.

Bear shoved a mass of shaggy gold curls back from his face and lifted his lip in a sneer. "Are you sissy boys afraid of going one-on-one with that itty-bitty woman over there?"

Itty-bitty. Clara almost swooned.

At the end of a heated discussion, the men fell silent and glared at her. She'd heard enough to know they resented her for interjecting herself into their contest. Either they figured her for a pushover or feared being beat by her. Neither outcome mattered since none of them would agree to be her opponent.

"Guess that leaves me, Miss Klaus." Bear gave her a confident grin. "With apologies in advance for taking your money and whupping you."

"You weren't going to enter," someone groused, spitting on the floor in disgust.

Another voice agreed. "You can't enter your own tournament!"

"Well, I'm going to." He raised huge hands to calm the protests. "After I beat her, I'll withdraw."

She'd hoped for one of the little skinny ones. But all right. She could deal with drawing the strongest opponent.

Tilting her head, she squeezed down her eyes and studied him. Strength was part of it, but so was strategy. He was big and powerful and confident, but he was a man. He could be had.

"When's the match?" she asked. It was flattering to notice that he continued to size her up, too.

"The first round starts tomorrow morning after breakfast."

Excellent. She'd have the time she needed.

The cubicle looked and smelled as hideous as it had when she left it. Zoe sprawled on the bottom bunk, moaning, gagging, and looking like death. Tuckered out, Juliette half dozed on the cot.

"I need your help," Clara announced, dropping to her knees to pull out her bag. She told them about the tournament and that her first match was in the morning.

"You did *what*?"

Even Zoe sat up to stare. "You're crazy," Zoe muttered before she flopped down again.

Clara found her extra dress and shook out the wrinkles, holding it to the sputtering lamp. It would do nicely.

"Whatever you have in mind, Zoe can't help. She's still dying," Juliette said in tones of long-suffering patience.

"It will look good on her tombstone to say that she died with a needle in her hand. Get up, Zoe. We need to pool our brains and our belongings, and we need to alter this dress."

Chapter 6

As if by magic, Alaska's coastline materialized during the chilly night. Thin cool sunlight glittered on the snowcaps of mountains that appeared to rise directly out of the sea.

Goose bumps thrilled up on Clara's skin. She was going to see and do things in Alaska that she'd previously never dreamed of seeing and doing. She just knew it. The majestic coastline represented the great adventure of her life, and she wanted to fling out her arms and embrace all that she saw.

After drinking in another long draft of Alaska's glorious coast, she cracked her knuckles, flexed her fingers, then raised her head and strode into the smoky overheated mess hall.

The first round of matches was well under way. Several names on the chalkboard had already been lined out, winners declared. Men battled arm to arm at nearly every corner of every mess table, critically observed by those whose matches were finished or hadn't yet begun.

Bear Barrett's craggy gold head rose above the other men, making it easy for Clara to spot him at once. Since yesterday he'd found time for a hair wash and trim, and none of the golden whiskers that had sparkled on his jaw yesterday remained today. He'd spiffed up his attire, too, wearing dark wool trousers and a dark gold-striped waistcoat beneath a black bow tie.

As no one else had chosen to set aside their denims,

Clara wondered if he'd gussied up for her sake, or if hosting a tournament called for a more formal image than he'd affected yesterday. No, if formality were an issue, he would have worn his jacket instead of standing about in his shirtsleeves.

She watched him remove a cigar from his lips, then kneel to critically study the distance between the table and the arm of a sweating, straining man.

"We have a winner!" he shouted, and the observers at that corner of the table cheered. A man at the chalkboard added another name to the list of second-round contenders.

Then Bear spotted her. His mouth fell open, and he did a double take. As well he might, because Clara didn't look like her usual plain and practical self. She didn't look like a woman should look at this hour of the morning.

For starters, she wore no hat over a coiffure suited for evening. Juliette and Zoe had dressed her hair in an updo that resembled a fountain spouting red curls. They had crimped her bangs and made curlicues in front of her ears. Then they topped off the arrangement with a black ostrich tip held in place by a fancy hairpin set with brilliants.

The black cape belonged to Juliette and fit too snugly, but the stiffened collar stood up to frame her face and set off dangling eardrops of flashing Ceylon brilliants that also belonged to Juliette.

What showed of her dress belonged to her, but the shoes beneath now sported clever cloth roses created by Zoe that matched the cloth rose pinned to Zoe's best handbag.

Blushing a little at Bear Barrett's intent scrutiny, Clara opened the handbag and removed a five-dollar gold piece. "Do I pay you my entry fee?" she asked as he strode up to her.

"There's a rule that waives the entry fee for ladies." A slow glance traveled over her hair, the flashing eardrops, and slid down her throat to the first ribbon holding the cape closed.

"That rule didn't exist yesterday. In fact—"

"It's a new rule," he interrupted, gazing down at her. "You sure do look fine this morning, Miss Klaus. Mighty, mighty fine."

"Why, thank you, Mr. Barrett." She dropped the five-dollar gold piece back into Zoe's best purse.

He continued to stare at her with a flattering warmth of admiration. "You might be wondering why I haven't spoken to you until yesterday."

"Not at all," she lied, hoping her tone conveyed surprise that he would think for an instant that she might welcome a word from someone to whom she had not been properly introduced. Well, they hadn't been introduced now either, but still.

"Until someone told me your name yesterday, I assumed you were a married woman."

"Really?" So that was the message he'd been giving her with the intense silent stares. *I'd like to talk to you, but you're married.* Immediately her spirits soared.

"What I mean is, you're obviously a respectable woman, and I didn't see you talking to any men. You seemed unapproachable."

Now she recognized the dilemma that Juliette had mentioned. She wasn't actually married, but she wasn't actually single either. She couldn't encourage Mr. Barrett, and shouldn't want to. If she did want to. She wasn't sure. But regardless of her wishes in the matter, he now looked at her as a single woman. It hadn't occurred to her or the others that placing a Miss before their names might create new difficulties.

"I don't mean to say that looking like a married woman is a criticism," Bear hastened to add. "I just mean that you didn't seem open to . . . Oh hell, I don't know what I mean." He grinned down at her. "Are you ready for our match?"

"I believe so, *ja,*" she said, dropping her eyelashes and drawing off her gloves one finger at a time. The wedding ring she had once been so proud of didn't impress her as unique anymore. Besides, wedding rings should be gold, not silver. This one was as much of a sham as her marriage.

Proving her thought, Bear noted the ring without a ripple crossing his brow. To his eye it was decorative, not evidence that she had a husband lurking somewhere in the background.

"Are you right-handed?" he asked, leading the way to a table where a crowd of men waited, eyes fixed on her approach.

"*Ja,* I am right-handed."

Lordy, lordy. Walking beside him actually made her feel small. Even wearing dress shoes with an elevated heel brought the top of her fountain curls only a little above his shoulder. Never in her life had she met a man who made her feel almost little.

The audience for their match stared as Bear made a point of introducing her to Ben Dare, who would judge their contest.

"Miss Klaus and I have met," Mr. Dare said, smiling beneath eyebrows that soared when he looked at her hairdo and the flash of brilliants in her curls and at her ears.

Juliette was going to be appalled when she heard that Ben Dare had been the judge for this match. Well, that wasn't Clara's fault. He held out a chair and she sat down, facing Bear across the corner edges of the table.

"Hey, Bear. You ain't never going to live this down if she beats you," someone said to a burst of laughter.

Bear grinned and winked at Clara. "I'm big enough to accept defeat with grace."

His tone and the wink informed her that he didn't believe for one minute that he could lose this match. Such a possibility had not entered his mind. And now she saw the concessions he was making for her. No one else's entry fee had been waived. None of the other contestants were being introduced to their judge. No one explained any rules at the other table corners; the contestants just sat down and went at it.

"What rules?" she asked Benjamin Dare. "There aren't any rules for arm wrestling."

"You can place your elbow on that book," he said, nodding to a thick dictionary. "That will raise your hand to the height of Bear's. But you can't lift or move your elbow once it's set."

Anyone who didn't know that had never arm wrestled, Clara thought with disgust. But she said nothing. She crossed her legs, something else that would have appalled Juliette, and she let the movement hike up her skirt enough to expose a black-stockinged ankle. A very nice, comparatively slim ankle, if she did say so herself. That ankle and the shoe with the cloth rose looked positively dainty next to Bear's massive leg.

He cast an involuntary glance at her ankle as she had known he would. Then he quickly raised his eyes to hers and she saw *that* look. *That* look was the look men got when they had glimpsed a woman-part they were not supposed to see and the woman knew they had looked and knew they wanted to look again. It was a look of surprise and guilt and pleasure and discomfort overlaid by a flash of happy triumph that they had ogled a seldom-seen item of feminine pulchritude.

"All right, back up," Benjamin Dare ordered the onlookers. "Give the contestants room to concentrate and breathe." It was all for show. No one took this match seriously enough even to wager on it. Mr. Dare nodded at Bear and Clara. "Get set."

She raised her arm up under the cape, leaned forward, and planted her elbow atop the dictionary. She'd feared her hand would disappear within Bear's massive paw, but she had big hands, too, and the disparity wasn't as great as she had imagined it might be. But her reaction to his touch was electric.

His hand was warm and solid, and she felt his quick pulse where their wrists touched. His sleeves were rolled up and the overhead light turned the mat of thick hair on his arms to a fascinating sheen of burnished gold. And she could smell him. The starchy scent of his shirt, a tweedy soap smell, a whiff of cigar smoke, and the pleasant fragrance of brilliantine, which she would have sworn he wasn't wearing because his hair looked naturally shiny.

His eyes weren't six inches from hers. "What is that perfume you're wearing?" he asked in a growly voice.

"Hoyt's Genuine German Cologne." Her own, not borrowed. Jean Jacques had claimed the scent drove him mad with desire. Now, as she analyzed the heat in Bear Barrett's stare, she decided the cologne affected other men as it had Jean Jacques. Excellent.

This close, she spotted gold flecks in his brown-bear eyes and admired a thick curve of gold lashes. Saw a light dew of perspiration collecting at his temples as he stared into her eyes and thought his thoughts and felt his impressions, which she hoped were concentrated on trim ankles, the pulse at her wrist, the flashing eardrops swinging toward her cheeks, and the scent of a cologne guaranteed by the maker to drive men wild.

"Ready?" Mr. Dare inquired.

"Actually, no," Clara said, releasing Bear's hand and leaning back in her chair. "It's very warm in here, and this cape feels restrictive." Pulling open the ribbons that tied the cape in front, she smiled up at Ben Dare. "Would you—?"

"It would be my pleasure." Stepping behind her, Ben lifted the cape from her shoulders.

The audience released a hissing noise like the sound of escaping steam, followed by stunned silence. Bear's eyes widened and his jaw dropped and he didn't even try to disguise the direction of his gaze.

The bodice that she and Juliette and Zoe had all taken a hand in altering now scooped so indecently low that it skimmed the tops of her nipples. Even to her it seemed that acres of full creamy skin lay thrust up by her corset and exposed to view. And she knew she had skin as smooth and inviting as a peach. Big beautiful breasts that begged to be stroked and kissed. Jean Jacques had said so a hundred times.

Leaning forward, giving Mr. Barrett a full heart-stopping view, she planted her elbow on the book again, and clasped his limp hand. His bones appeared to have dissolved.

"Oh—my—God," he whispered hoarsely, staring down into her cleavage. It was impressive cleavage indeed. The good Lord hadn't given her big hips without balancing her out with big glorious breasts.

"We're ready," Clara said pleasantly, nodding to Ben Dare.

With great effort, Ben wrenched his gaze up from her bosom, checked their elbows, then swallowed hard. "On your mark."

Looking dazed, Bear blinked and stiffened his wrist. "The match is starting?"

"Almost," Clara murmured, fluttering her eyelashes.

"Get set."

"That perfume is making me . . . and those . . ."

"Go!"

Clara gripped his hand hard, putting her strength behind the clasp. They leaned into each other over the corner of the table, gazing deeply into each other's eyes. Then Clara slowly and deliberately licked the tip of her tongue around the edges of her parted lips.

Bear sucked in a sharp breath, stared hard, and a drop of sweat rolled down his temples. But Clara wasn't finished with him. She inhaled, letting her breasts swell and swell until he couldn't resist, and he dropped his gaze down the front of her dress for a direct look.

And bang, she had him. Seizing the exact moment, she slammed his forearm down on the table and held it there until he looked up into her eyes with a hot brown gaze that set all her exposed skin aflame. A searing gaze that made her tingle where decent women weren't supposed to tingle. Nose to nose, eye to eye, neither of them made a move to unclasp their hands.

Later, when she thought about every little detail, Clara supposed there must have been an uproar from the audience. But she didn't hear a thing except her pulse roaring in her ears as she and Bear leaned toward each other, hands locked, faces close enough to feel the warmth of each other's rapid breath. It was like they were utterly alone in a bubble of scents and gazes and heat and pulses racing where their wrists met. He ravaged her with a smoldering stare and she ravaged him right back.

Heaven help her, but if Jean Jacques had walked into the mess hall, she wouldn't have given that Frenchman a second look.

"For heaven's sake, get out of that dress. You're practically naked!" Juliette snapped, while Clara counted eighty dollars into her outstretched hand. According to Clara's triumphant account, the extra money came from the wagers Clara had placed on her succeeding matches. "I still can't believe you exposed yourself to a roomful of men. It's indecent."

"It was practical. A person does what she has to do, and I won the tournament, didn't I?" She started to relate the story again, how she had pinned five other male arms after beating Bear and had won each match in under thirty seconds.

"It's disgraceful what you did," Zoe interrupted, thrusting her arm past the edge of the bottom bunk to receive her share of the win. She managed a wan smile. "And very clever."

Juliette tucked the money into her wrist bag. Clara had left her all morning with Zoe, and she was desperate for some fresh air and an escape from the fetid atmosphere of their cubicle. After glancing into the mirror at the tired dark circles under her eyes, she pinned on her hat and took the cape Clara returned.

"Her majesty is in particularly bad humor today," she warned, marveling that she could refer to Zoe so rudely. But after living in cramped quarters for three seemingly endless weeks, they were no longer strangers and no longer polite.

"Well damn it, you'd be in a temper, too, if you were dying!"

Juliette ground her teeth. Zoe had picked up bad habits while growing up with six brothers. She considered pointing out that swearing was unbecoming behavior, but her advice would only fall on deaf ears. Instead, she silently glared at the two of them, then sailed out the door and up the staircase into cold clean air that smelled and tasted like ambrosia.

The coastline caught her by surprise. Though she should have, she hadn't anticipated the mountains. Even when she was purchasing heavy woolen underwear, she hadn't been able to imagine snow and cold. Well, here was her first glimpse of snow, and the afternoon air was cold enough to pink her cheeks.

And there was Mr. Dare, loitering beside the railing within view of the staircase as if he'd been waiting for her to emerge. A tiny frisson of pleasure skittered down her spine, accompanied by a damper of guilt.

Thank goodness the voyage ended tomorrow and with it her great pleasure in Mr. Dare's company. She and Mr. Dare would go their separate ways and she could stop lying awake nights listening to Aunt Kibble and her mother lecture about the dangers of married women spending time with handsome, engaging single men. Aunt Kibble muttered about playing with fire. Her mother reminded her that a respectable lady would rather die a painful lingering death than open herself to the slightest suspicion of impropriety.

"Good afternoon, Miss March." He removed his hat with a smile. "May I accompany you on your stroll?"

Shamelessly, she didn't even pretend to consider. "Please do." She hoped she was not begging for a painful lingering death.

"By now you know that Miss Klaus won the arm-wrestling tournament." His smile widened. "The story making the rounds is assuming the proportions of a legend."

Fire invaded her cheeks. She deeply regretted helping Clara alter the bodice of her dress. "It's a fine day," she murmured, changing the subject. She refused to spoil her final encounter with Mr. Dare by imagining him observing Clara's indecency.

"So," he said, "does your journey end at Dyea? Or are you traveling farther?"

"We're going to Dawson City." My, the air was invigorating today. On the other hand, she always felt invigorated when she spoke to Mr. Dare. Her heart beat faster, and she smiled more often. And recalling every word of their conversations had helped pass the time when she was stuck below with Zoe. Moreover, his flattering attention helped soothe the battering her self-esteem had taken since learning of Jean Jacques's betrayal.

"But not to seek your fortune," he said in a teasing voice. "You'll join a traveling party in Dyea?"

"We're not meeting anyone, no."

Stopping abruptly, he turned to her with a frown. "You're traveling to the Klondike alone?"

His expression raised a kernel of alarm in her chest. "Why does that surprise you?" she asked when his stare deepened.

"Has anyone explained the trail from Dyea to Dawson City?"

"I've been told it will be an arduous trek."

"It certainly will."

For a moment she was distracted by trying to decide exactly what shade his eyes were. She'd thought delphinium blue, but now the color had darkened, forming a thrilling contrast to his suntanned forehead and cheeks. And his voice roughened when he spoke seriously, something she hadn't really noticed until now.

"You do know, don't you, that you'll make the journey on foot, transporting your outfit?"

"We aren't going on foot. We'll hire a stage."

His beard was filling out, Juliette noticed. Zoe had shocked her by remarking that full thick beards were a sign of virility. It wasn't proper to think about such things, especially with him standing so close. Still . . .

"Damn." Taking her arm, the first time he had touched her, Ben led her to the rail.

Startled, Juliette frowned at her arm as if she could see the hot tingle that raced from his hand to her shoulder. How was it possible that his touch sent her nerves shooting to the surface? She didn't recall anything like this happening when Jean Jacques touched her.

When they stopped at the rail, Ben noticed that he still held her arm, and he dropped his hand immediately. It occurred to Juliette that they were not parting company any too soon. This man was dangerous. She was becoming entirely too fond of him.

"Miss March. There is no stage, no train, no carriages. Even horses can't make it over Chilkoot Pass."

His words disturbed her uneasy concentration on his mouth. Disbelief widened her eyes. "That can't be correct." She rubbed her tingling arm. "If what you say were true, then how would anyone get their outfits over the pass and down to Dawson City?"

"By carrying them on their backs."

She laughed. "The outfits can weigh a thousand pounds apiece."

"You carry as much as you can as far as you can, then you return for the next load and the next load and the next until you've assembled your outfit, then you start the process over. You'll cover each piece of ground at least ten times or more."

The smile faded from her lips. "But it would take forever to get there, doing it like that."

"It will take several months, working at it seven days a week," he agreed. "That's why I assumed you must be traveling with a larger party. A large party can pare duplicates and add sleds and dogs." He gazed down at her with a concerned expression. "And are you aware that you may have to winter over at Lake Bennett? Living in your tent," he added, watching her.

She gasped, and a hand flew to her throat. "Camp in a tent for a whole winter?" The question ended on a squeak. Trying to live in the outdoors was unimaginable enough. Doing it through a winter was inconceivable. From what she'd heard about snow and frigid temperatures, she didn't think she would enjoy either.

This was not one of their better conversations. She didn't like what he was saying or the images he placed in her mind.

"Some folks wait until the river freezes, then push on with dogs and sleds," he said slowly. "Others wait until the river thaws and go by boat. There are pros and cons to both approaches."

Juliette wasn't seeing any positives to any approach. The headache that signaled unpleasant choices began to build behind her eyes, and she picked at her gloves.

"You've given me a lot to think about," she said finally, speaking in a faint voice. Zoe had argued there were no stages, but she and Clara hadn't believed that Alaska would be too uncivilized even for stages. Zoe's experience was with men preparing to sail to the Klondike, not with those who had returned, so clearly Zoe didn't know everything.

But Zoe had a way of stating things that made it sound as if she were an authority. If they had known of the impossible hardships Mr. Dare listed, Juliette felt certain none of the Mmes Villette would have departed Seattle. The obstacles Mr. Dare described were insurmountable for women.

Suddenly she felt like weeping. Once or twice she had experienced a euphoric view of herself as an intrepid traveler braving the perils of a hostile land to reach her poor deluded husband. She had liked that image.

Now she grasped the impossibility. Alaska had defeated her before she ever set foot on shore. "Are there others who turn back when they learn of these hardships?" she asked in a whisper.

"The *Annasett* won't return to Seattle empty." He waved toward the mess hall. "Some are already talking about going home."

"I see." She, too, would be on the *Annasett* when the ship turned around. And all she would have accomplished was treating herself to a late-summer cruise, which she had spent confined in a stinking tiny room with two women she wished she'd never met.

She had to tell them what she'd learned. "Excuse me," she murmured, feeling an urgency build in her chest. "I must speak to my companions."

It wasn't fair. For two days she had occupied nearly every moment considering what her bittersweet parting words would be, and speculating how he might say goodbye to her. Now all she could think about was the horrifying knowledge that they were expected to carry their outfits on their backs.

She did the math in her head. If it was approximately seven hundred miles from Dyea to Dawson City—and they had to cover that ground at least ten times to move their outfits—then they would walk a trail that was seven thousand miles long.

Her eyes glazed in shock. She thought of Zoe and for the first time in her life understood the term *crime of passion*. At this moment she could happily have fallen on Zoe and strangled her. Juliette should never have listened, should never have agreed to undertake this wasted voyage.

"I have to go," she said abruptly, blinking at the headache rising hot behind her eyes. "It's been . . . I've enjoyed . . ." Abandoning any final tender words that he could remember her by, she turned in a swirl of skirts and rushed to the staircase.

When the little broomlike bristles adorning Miss March's hat had vanished into the stairwell, Ben frowned, then lit a cigar and turned toward the sea to watch the coastline drawing nearer.

His instinct was correct. She hadn't the faintest notion of the hardships that lay ahead, which made him wonder why she was traveling to Dawson City in the first place.

She was an interesting woman. Her delicate patrician face and trim figure had been first to catch his eye. He admired her sense of style and her thoroughbred carriage. He knew she'd led a sheltered life of genteel privilege. Yet, here she was in a place few ladies would ever go.

She lacked male relatives to look after her, but someone should have told her what to expect or stopped her from taking this journey.

Most likely she would turn around and return to Seattle now that he'd explained the realities of what lay ahead. On the other hand, maybe not. When he'd observed her in Yesler Park, she had clearly not wanted to be there, had appeared to want to jump from the bench and rush away from the two ladies he now knew as Miss Klaus and Miss Wilder. But she hadn't.

The same odd behavior had recurred in front of Wilder's Outfitting Store. She'd paced before the piles of goods in the street, wringing her hands and making faces that suggested a desperate desire not to proceed. But she had.

On board she kept saying, "I can't go back down there," meaning the cubicle and Miss Wilder. But she did return to her cabin and to her nursing duties.

Miss March sold herself short. He suspected she resisted challenges because she didn't believe she could succeed or because the goal frightened or worried her. Then she stiffened her shoulders and went ahead and did the thing.

Therefore he couldn't predict whether she would return to Seattle or if she would attempt the trail to Chilkoot Pass with her companions.

They, too, were a mystery. He didn't understand the relationship between the women, and Miss March hadn't offered an explanation. He'd searched for a family resemblance during the one visit Miss Wilder had managed on deck, but no resemblance existed. Nor did similarity of nature or interest bind them. That Miss Klaus had entered and won the arm-wrestling tournament didn't surprise him. But it was beyond imagining that Juliette would do such a thing.

Granted, he knew the ladies only superficially, but even their motivations for this journey appeared vastly different. From what he'd gathered from Juliette and Miss Klaus, Miss Wilder was determined to reach Dawson City to achieve some personal goal of a dark nature. Miss Klaus had said with a laugh that she was going to the Klondike looking for her fortune like everyone else. He had no grasp of why Juliette was going.

Frowning, he flipped the cigar toward the waves, and wondered if she knew how puzzling, amusing, contrary, and mysterious she seemed. And he surprised the hell out of himself by wondering if her shining dark hair was as soft as it looked.

Damn it. He wasn't ready for another woman in his life.

Chapter 7

"I am *not* going back to Seattle," Zoe said firmly, staring at herself in the cloudy mirror above her shelf. "I swear I will never set foot on a ship again. Unless there's an overland route home, I'm going to live and die in Alaska."

The face in the glass was gaunt and drawn, and for an instant she didn't recognize herself. Her skin, pulled tight over her cheekbones, emphasized deep half circles that made her eyes look bruised, and her lips were pale and dry. When she pinned on her hat, her fingers brushed brittle lifeless strands. To complete the dismal picture, she'd lost so much weight that her clothing hung on her like the castoffs of a much larger person. She looked a hundred years older than she had three weeks ago when she'd begun this hellish voyage.

Clara shoved their communal crimping iron into her bag, then stood and dusted her hands together. "I'm sick of hearing about how we can't get ourselves to Dawson City! Other people have gotten there. We can, too."

First to be dressed and ready to disembark, Juliette sat on the cot, wringing her hands. "Why can't I make you understand? I must not be explaining the perils well enough."

"You have explained at stupefying length," Zoe said, still studying her pathetic reflection in the mirror. "You've been explaining since yesterday afternoon. And all last evening. And every minute since we woke up." If she hadn't been weak and half-dead, she would have stuffed a scarf down Juliette's throat. She made a face of disgust at the mirror, then turned to Clara. "I detest asking another favor, but I tried and I'm too weak to carry my bag. Would you take it upstairs?"

"If I have to." Clara turned to Juliette. "Are you going to get off this ship or are you going to stay on board and go back to Seattle when the *Annasett* turns around?"

By now Zoe knew her companions well enough to predict what Juliette would do. Juliette would join them in the tender to Dyea, fully intending to return to the *Annasett* before it sailed. But in the end, after a lot of whimpering and hand-wringing, she would decide to go with them to Dawson City, pissing and moaning every step of the way.

She glared at the cot where Juliette sat. "If you decide to continue to Dawson City, then by God you better not give up at the halfway point! You better be prepared to go the full distance. Because I'm not going to bring you back to Dyea. I'll just leave you on the trail and go on."

Juliette stiffened, and her expression turned cold. "Well! Your gratitude and sentiment overwhelm me. Hearing that you'd abandon me makes me so happy that I spent three weeks nursing you, washing out vomit buckets, and bathing and feeding you."

"You two don't want gratitude, you want everlasting servitude and groveling! How many times do I have to thank you?"

"Once would be nice," Clara snapped, staring at her.

Ordinarily Zoe would have argued and defended and walked out feeling triumphant, but she was too weak to rise to the challenge. The damned ship rocked at anchor and she felt only marginally better than she had during the voyage. She yearned for terra firma with a need that was visceral, longed to stand on solid ground as she would have longed for a missing limb. She could hardly think of anything else.

"All right," she said between her teeth. "Thank you for caring for me while I was dying. I'm sure I said it before, and now I've said it again. I'm not going to keep saying it."

Truly, she appreciated everything they had done. In her heart she felt certain she'd be dead now if they hadn't fed her and nursed her. But she was not going to fawn over them or anyone else for that matter. Trusting Clara to follow with the bags, she glanced about to make certain she hadn't forgotten anything, then lifted her head and wobbled out of the cubicle.

A shock of cold air braced her the instant she stepped on deck. The deck itself she didn't look at, as she suspected the slant would lead to the humiliation of throwing up in front of the men staring at her. She supposed she didn't blame them for staring. Clara had reported they referred to her as the mystery passenger whom few had glimpsed since Seattle.

By the time Clara appeared, carrying her bag and Zoe's, cold perspiration had appeared on Zoe's forehead, and she swallowed repeatedly, beginning to feel desperate. She needed to get off this ship and right now, but a line of men stretched down the deck, impatiently awaiting their turn in the tender.

That's when Bear Barrett appeared, a golden giant coming to the rescue. He took the bags out of Clara's hands, studied Zoe, then walked to the head of the line and knocked aside the man about to descend the ladder leading down to the tender.

"These ladies go first, gents," he boomed at the men scowling back at him. He winked at Zoe. "In ten minutes you're going to feel like a new woman."

To her vast relief no one argued. Some under-the-breath grumbling occurred, but the line stepped back as Bear handed her down the ladder. At the bottom, another man caught her by the waist and helped her sit.

The small rocking, bobbing, tilting, tipping tender was

too much. She managed to gasp, "Excuse me," before she leaned over the side and embarrassed herself. Lord, would it never end?

When she straightened, Juliette pushed a handkerchief into her hands so she could wipe her mouth. "You decided to come." Guessing correctly didn't especially make her happy.

"I might as well see Dyea before I go back."

"Look at those mountains!" Clara said as the tender floated away from the *Annasett* and headed toward a rocky beach.

Before Zoe groaned and closed her eyes against the waves, she spotted a tide of white tents pitched around a raw town that had obliterated the original Indian fishing village. The snowcapped mountains that interested Clara rose sharply from a flat valley floor, but Zoe could not have cared less.

Then finally, finally, finally, thank God, a man helped her out of the tender, and she walked through frigid calf-high seawater to the beach, so thankful to reach land that she hardly cared that no one had told them they would have to walk through water. When she stood on the rocky beach, she dropped her skirts and closed her eyes while the water ran out of her shoes.

A blessed stillness spread through her stomach. Her brain didn't rock from side to side. Her legs felt shaky and her knees unsteady, but that was a result of her long illness. Nothing inside her was sloshing, churning, slipping, or sliding.

Tears burned her eyes, and she felt like falling down and kissing the unmoving earth.

"Feeling better?" Clara asked. Setting down their bags, she planted her hands on her hips and looked toward town, a distant collection of unpainted storefronts.

"It's a miracle." And it happened swiftly, almost instantly. Cold bright air poured strength into each breath. She could feel color returning to her cheeks and throat.

The sour scald at the back of her tongue had already faded, and she knew with marveling confidence that she would not vomit in the next two minutes.

"I knew this would happen, I just knew it," Juliette said, hurrying up to them. "Can you see over there? Those tenders are bringing the outfits to the beach. The stevedores are dumping our goods on the shore and we have to move them somewhere else!"

"To where?" Clara asked, frowning.

"Well, look around you!"

Now Zoe noticed that the men scurrying around them were staking out spots to pitch their tents, then rushing off to begin transporting their goods. Caches of supplies piled up in front of tent stakes driven into the ground to mark each man's territory.

Juliette pressed gloved hands to her temples. "They said we have to move our goods immediately to make room for the outfits coming in on the next tenders. I forgot to tell anyone not to bring my outfit ashore. And now . . ." She turned a plea to Clara. "I don't know what to do. Do you think Mr. Barrett would help us move our outfits?"

"He'll be moving his own things." She slid a frown toward Zoe. "And I see some handwriting on the wall here. You aren't going to be any help. We'll have to move your outfit, too."

"I'd love to tell you that I can be gravely ill for weeks, come within minutes of dying, and then bound out of bed bursting with energy and vigor. Unfortunately, I can hardly stand up."

"This is terrible, just terrible," Juliette moaned. "They should at least let us do something about wet shoes and stockings. My hem got wet, too. It will be a miracle if we don't catch our death of cold. My feet already feel like lumps of ice."

Zoe sat down hard on top of someone's crated goods. If she'd seen any possibility whatsoever of doing it, she would have carried her outfit farther ashore. But she felt exhausted. Steady inside, but too bed-weak to stand comfortably, let alone make twenty trips back and forth carrying heavy supplies.

"I need your help again," she stated grimly, looking at Clara and Juliette. The request cost her dearly. The Wilders had never been people to ask for help or favors, refused to be beholden to anyone. But here she was dependent again on the two people whom she detested most in the whole world.

"Oh!" Juliette bent at the waist and turned in a circle, striking her hips with her fists. "You don't know what you're asking! Or how long . . . I can't possibly carry . . ."

It was the first time Juliette had lost control so totally, and even Clara watched the performance with an interested eye. Then she pulled back her shoulders and narrowed her eyes into hard brown beams focused directly on Zoe.

"Moving three outfits is going to take a long time. Especially with one of us able to carry only about two pounds a trip." She jerked her head toward Juliette, who was still turning around and around. "You find us a place to put our things. Surely you can do that much."

Tents and piles of goods stretched out as far as Zoe could see. "I'll find us a place," she snapped.

"How will we know where it is?"

"My body's weak, not my mind." Zoe thought a minute. "I'll tie a scrap of pink on our marker." The sea of pole markers all looked alike. A spot of pink would stand out.

"And you're responsible for supper." Clara stared at her. "You can take your time and do it slowly. But at the end of this, neither Juliette nor I are going to feel like cooking. We're going to want to eat and then collapse. You can set up the tent and organize it, too."

"Why don't I just chop down the trees left on that mountainside and build us a cabin?" Zoe returned her stare.

"All you have to do is find us a place and get us set up. Come on, Juliette. The sooner and faster we get moving, the sooner and faster our shoes and feet will dry out."

Without another word, they walked toward the piles of goods accumulating like hills at the water's edge. Juliette stumbled along beside Clara, looking like a woman about to fall over with shock. Clara plowed forward with a grim set to her shoulders.

Swearing beneath her breath, Zoe sat slumped on the crate, the only still person in a mass of rushing humanity, struggling to find the strength to get up and search out a campsite. All the close-in spots were already claimed and staked out.

She was going to have to walk at least a mile to find a scrap of space not already occupied. On the other hand, her shaky legs would have to make the trip only once, instead of dozens of times like Clara and Juliette. She was too exhausted to feel much gratitude for this boon.

"Zoe? Zoe Wilder?"

Hundreds of men swarmed the beach, so she didn't immediately spot the man calling her name. When she did, she recognized him at once.

Tom Price. From Newcastle. He was a friend of Jack's, her second-oldest brother. If she had felt better, she might have smiled at meeting a Newcastle boy this far from home. Instead, she wondered how he had recognized her, considering that she looked worse than she remembered ever looking in her life.

And he wasn't a boy anymore, she realized, watching him dodge hurrying men and step around supply piles, smiling as he made his way toward her. He must be about the same age as Jack, thirty-three. When had she last seen him? It must have been about ten years ago. She couldn't be certain, because she hadn't paid a lot of attention to her brother's rowdy friends. She'd had nothing to do with them, and even then had known she never would. Not a boy from Newcastle.

"This is a surprise," he said, sweeping off a wide-brimmed hat and swinging it against his thigh. "Did you come in on the *Annasett*?"

People said such silly things on greeting someone they hadn't seen for a long while. If she wasn't fresh off the *Annasett* why would she be sitting on a crate on a beach with seawater dripping out of her shoes and hem?

"Were you on the ship, too?"

Oddly she didn't remember Tom Price as an especially good-looking youth. But he'd grown into a strikingly handsome man with strong square features and a solid, confident air about him. The men charging back and forth took care not to bump or jostle him as if a quick glance warned that here was a man it would be unwise to offend. Her pa and her brothers had that air about them, too, as did most Newcastle men. Miners worked hard, drank hard, took offense easily, and fought hard. It showed.

Lifting his boot, he propped it against the crate beside her, then leaned forward and rested his forearm on his thigh, studying her face. "I've been up here for a couple of years. Maybe Jack told you that I started my own packing business."

"No, he didn't." First she noticed that his eyes were dark green, then she noticed his flicker of disappointment. "I'm sure it slipped Jack's mind. I'm living in Seattle now, working for my uncle. There's so much to talk about when I go home, that we don't always have time to cover everything. And sometimes I don't see Jack at all. He's married now, you know."

"Jack? Married?" A grin lit his face and made him look more like the boy she remembered. "That old son of a gun. Did he marry the Snodgrass girl? Do they have any children?"

"He married Abe McGraw's youngest daughter. They have a boy who's almost two, and they're expecting another around Christmas."

"My sister married one of the McGraw cousins. He died at the mine last year."

"I heard about that." Zoe nodded. "Ma mentioned a dance the ladies gave to raise money for Mrs. McGraw and her children. So that was your sister?"

"Carrie's living in Seattle now, working at one of the hotels. She's a Newcastle girl—she'll make her way." The comment seemed to remind him that Zoe was sitting on a crate in the midst of chaos when she ought to be doing something. "Am I keeping you from—?"

"I felt a bit under the weather aboard ship," Zoe said lightly. "So my companions were kind enough to offer to move our outfits to our site. As soon as I find us one."

A fleeting frown shadowed his brow, and he moved his boot to the ground. "I heard you got married," he said slowly.

Zoe had known Tom Price most of her life. As recollections flooded her mind, she could picture him sitting at the Wilder supper table shouting as loudly as her pa and brothers, and coming by the house to join her brothers on the trek to the mine. She remembered that he'd lent her a book once, and once he had given her a handful of summer wildflowers.

Her instinct was to pour out her heart and tell him about Jean Jacques, her rotten husband. Tom would understand how a Newcastle girl could be dazzled by a Frenchman who glittered like the end of the rainbow.

But he would also wonder why a hardheaded Newcastle girl hadn't opened her eyes and asked more questions. He might not say it outright, but he'd know she had been foolish and stupid.

Worse, the next time he wrote home, he'd tell his ma that he'd run into Zoe Wilder, and the poor thing was married to a bigamist and she was traveling with the bigamist's other wives and wasn't *that* something. The gossip would be too titillating for Mrs. Price to keep to herself, so she'd head straight to the company store to ask if anyone else had heard the news, thereby spreading it around. In the end Zoe's ma would hear a smeared version of the gossipy details and be humiliated that she had to learn the truth from a neighbor instead of from Zoe.

Zoe drew a deep breath and tilted her head to look at the mountain peaks rimming the valley. "I was going to marry, but it didn't work out." God forgave lies that protected mothers.

Something moved in his eyes. "So you don't have a husband."

"No." That much was certainly true.

"Damn it, Zoe! You're still sitting right where we left you!" Clara rolled a wheelbarrow up beside them and gave Zoe a scowl and Tom a nod. "Excuse me for swearing, mister, I don't usually, but what's happening down there on the beach would try the patience of a wooden saint." She wiped her forehead. "No one knows what they're doing, they don't understand the concept of organization, and the outfits are getting mixed together."

"Where's Juliette?" Zoe didn't see her anywhere.

"You'd think pushing a wheelbarrow would be a simple thing, wouldn't you? It should be. I don't know what in heaven's name she's doing, but the wheelbarrow keeps tipping over and dumping out her load. After the third time of helping her repack, I left her to pick up the mess and repack it herself." Clara flopped down on the crate beside Zoe and fanned her face. "I'm Clara Klaus," she said to Tom, "the only healthy, sensible person among the three of us."

Laughing, Tom inclined his head. "I'm Tom Price, a friend of Miss Wilder's family."

"Where did you get the wheelbarrows?" Originally Zoe had wondered what had drawn her husband to Clara. Despite Clara's glowing skin and impressive curves, Clara just didn't seem the type of woman to attract a man of the world. But Zoe was beginning to see Clara as a fount of resourcefulness. It occurred to her that she could have done far worse in choosing a companion for a journey into a hard land.

"It was easy." Clara laughed. "I arm-wrestled one of the men off the ship. He wanted a rematch." Her eyes sparkled. "He got whupped again, and I got his wheelbarrows."

Zoe stared. "What did you wager?"

"You don't want to know."

"You're the arm-wrestling Amazon that I've been hearing about?" Tom asked, grinning.

Zoe groaned, picturing the indecent bodice and Clara's breasts burgeoning like peachy mountains. The story was going to follow them the entire time they were in Alaska.

Tom smiled with admiration. "Congratulations. I've met some men who became legends up here, but you've managed to do it before you got off the ship. I'm pleased to make your acquaintance."

"Help! Help me!"

Through the crisscrossing of hurrying men, Zoe spotted Juliette. As she watched, the stacked wheelbarrow began to lean and would have tipped over except that Juliette dropped the handles and darted to the side, catching the load on her back. For a moment Zoe thought Juliette would go down under the weight of the load now balanced on her small shoulders. But she clamped her teeth and dug her heels into the churned-up ground.

She wasn't strong enough to push the load upright. And she couldn't jump out from under fast enough to avoid the heavy load falling on her. She was stuck in place.

Tom strode forward, catching the toppling load as the weight began to push Juliette to her knees. She went down anyway. Her skirts pushed into the wet ground, and she covered her face with her hands as Tom shoved the load and the wheelbarrow upright.

"I can't do this! Women aren't supposed to do this!"

"Well, you did do it, ma'am." Tom helped her up, then clasped the handles of the wheelbarrow. "You brought this load where you wanted to bring it."

"Well, my heavens." She stared up at him. "It took me a while and a few mishaps, but I did get it here, didn't I?" A thunderstruck expression dazed her eyes.

Grudgingly, Zoe granted her a thimble's worth of credit. But she also took an inordinate amount of pleasure in Juliette's disheveled appearance. Her Ladyship's hat hung over one ear, she'd lost a glove, muddy knee prints soiled the front of her skirt. She didn't look like the trim, crisp Juliette that Zoe had come to know and wanted to kill.

Adding to Zoe's guilty pleasure was the surprised look Ben Dare fixed on Juliette as he wheeled a handcart up next to them. And Zoe found it interesting that Juliette blushed bright and instantly set about fixing her hat and slapping at the mud drying on her skirts. So, Clara was correct, and Miss Propriety had spent rather a lot of time with Mr. Dare on board ship. But the confirmation wasn't too interesting.

The conversation going on above her head was. Clara had made introductions in her perfunctory way; it had been discovered that the crate Zoe sat on belonged to Ben Dare, and now the men were taking the ladies in hand.

While Tom and Mr. Dare discussed the logistics of how and where to move the ladies' outfits, Zoe closed her eyes and breathed the good scents of the sea and wood smoke. She listened to male shouts and curses and a faint tinkle of saloon music floating from the distant town of Dyea.

She wanted to manage this journey without depending on others, and tomorrow she would hate it that she was beholden to Tom and Mr. Dare. But right now, she was too exhausted to care. If the men wanted to move their outfits and set up the tent, God bless them for it. All she wanted to do was fall into her collapsible cot, rest, and regain her strength.

When she opened her eyes again, Clara had dug some dried fruit out of the pack, and Juliette was asking if she should make tea on Mr. Dare's camp stove. In the middle of the off-loading process, Zoe's companions were having a social occasion.

Well, why not? The men had offered to assist them, after all, and there was odd comfort in discovering they weren't entirely alone in a strange new place. They knew people here.

Her gaze traveled to Tom. The folks in Newcastle talked about leaving, talked about going to Seattle or somewhere else where life wasn't as stark and hard. But few actually left, and those who did were likely to return having discovered that cities could be harsh and uncaring.

She knew why Tom Price had left Newscastle and the mine, that was a given. But she wondered why he had fetched up in Alaska instead of someplace closer to home. And owning a packing company, too. Whatever that was.

When she noticed him watching her as he talked to Mr. Dare, she turned her head toward the haze of wood and coal smoke overhanging the town. Nothing had changed. She didn't want an involvement with a Newcastle man even in a small way. Besides, she was still married to The Bastard.

But oh, my, it was good to see someone from home.

Sliding a sidelong look toward the men, she noted dark curls lying against the collar of Tom's heavy coat. Faded denims snugged around his thighs, and he wore lace-up work boots. Mr. Dare was clad similarly, but Mr. Dare's clothing looked new, whereas Tom's garments were comfortably worn and familiar.

After Tom and Mr. Dare strode off to do whatever they intended to do, Zoe wondered if she would see Tom Price again. There was no reason to do so. On the other hand, Ma would have her hide if she wrote home and mentioned that she'd run into him but had no news to report. She would have to make a point of meeting him again and asking a few questions. For Ma's sake.

She chose not to examine why that decision improved her spirits so greatly.

Chapter 8

Bear leaned against a post inside Tom Price's stable, watching Tom load the panniers draped across a big jack mule. It was a pleasure to watch a man who was good at his job. When Tom finished, there wouldn't be half an inch of wasted space, and the well-padded liquor would arrive in Dawson City without a single broken bottle, having gone from Dyea to Skagway, over Dead Horse Pass, then another six hundred miles by boat or sled.

"Fifty-one cents a pound is highway robbery."

Tom shrugged. "Nose Malley's Indians will pack you in cheaper." He buckled down the pannier straps. "Your liquor's leaving for Skagway in about two hours, so if you want to hire Nose Malley, say so now. I'll have to charge you a loading fee."

Nose Malley was notorious for dumping one man's load beside the trail and continuing on with someone else's if the newcomer offered a higher price. Most of the packers played that game, except Tom Price. After Tom Price shook your hand, the deal was set in stone. Your goods arrived, intact, and for the cost originally agreed on. And Price didn't shy from big jobs. He'd taken a piano over the pass for Bear and gotten it to Dawson without busting the cabinet all to hell or dunking it in a river.

When Bear didn't instruct him to start unpacking the mules, Tom stepped back to run a critical eye over the jack's load. "Are you going to Skagway with the pack train?"

The load looked balanced to Bear's eye. "This time I

think I'll go over Chilkoot. Are you leading the Skagway train or is Davidson in charge?"

"Davidson's a good man. He'll get your liquor to Dawson."

Bear nodded. "Have the ladies hired you to pack their outfits over Chilkoot?"

It wasn't necessary to explain which ladies he meant. First, there weren't many women in Dyea, and fewer still were ladies. Second, Ben Dare had mentioned that Price was a friend of Miss Wilder's family.

"Miss Wilder said we'd talk this morning."

"When you talk to her, tell her you'll pack her and her companions all the way to Dawson for thirty cents a pound." When Tom's eyebrow soared, Bear bit down on his back teeth. "I'll pay the extra plus a bonus if you get all their goods to Dawson."

"Your saloon must be doing very well indeed," Tom commented. "This will cost a pretty penny."

Bear kicked at the dirt and frowned. "Don't tell them it's me doing the paying."

The words falling out of his mouth astonished him. He was as surprised and mystified by his anonymous generosity as Tom appeared to be. He didn't owe those women anything. He didn't even know them except for Miss Klaus, and he didn't know her except to nod and say howdy do.

But everyone in Dyea had linked their names. Clara Klaus, the redheaded Amazon, had whipped Bear Barrett in about thirty seconds flat with twenty men looking on. The unthinkable had happened. Bernard T. Barrett had been publicly bested by a mere woman, and everybody knew it. He couldn't walk a dozen steps without someone giving him a knowing grin or laughing right out loud. Already he'd fought five men in defense of his manhood, and he'd only been in Dyea for two days. Miss Clara Klaus had brought him a potload of aggravation and trouble.

Yet, here he was turning strange and chivalrous not

only toward her, but toward her companions, too, paying out a king's ransom just to make their journey a little easier. He had no idea why he was doing this. And not even taking credit for it.

"Civilization's coming our way," Price commented, stepping up beside Bear at the open end of the stable. He offered Bear a cigar and lit one himself.

"When genteel ladies start showing up on pleasure excursions, civilization has definitely arrived."

Twice today, Bear had done something without knowing why he'd done it. Ordinarily he'd accompany his goods to Dawson. It wasn't necessary, but that's what he usually did, packing out of Skagway instead of Dyea. But he'd made an impulsive decision to climb Chilkoot instead of Dead Horse. And then he'd spent a chunk of money to assist three women he hardly knew. Maybe his manhood really was in danger. He was going soft. "Who's shooting out behind your place?" he asked abruptly, jerking a thumb toward the sound of shots.

"Miss Wilder is doing some target shooting."

"She's shooting? These are very interesting ladies, damned if they aren't." These three didn't behave like most ladies, but like most men, Bear knew at a glance who was a respectable woman and who wasn't, and Miss Klaus, Miss Wilder, and Miss March were as respectable as they came.

"So you think they're going to Dawson City on a pleasure excursion?" Tom asked, studying the glow at the end of his cigar.

"Why else?" Since Tom was a friend of Miss Wilder's, Bear had hoped Tom would know why the women were traveling to Dawson. "I can't picture them prospecting."

"Well, there isn't a brain among them if they think getting to Dawson is going to be a mild lady's adventure."

"So why do you think they're going?"

Tom shook his head. "I don't know."

The stable sat at the end of the muddy ruts scarring Dyea's main street. From where they stood, they had a

long view of the horses, carts, and foot traffic flowing in
a constant stream past hastily erected storefronts and
tents large enough to accommodate boisterous saloons,
gambling halls, and primitive lodging. In front of Hanra-
han's Supplies, Bear spotted a bright redhead wearing a
little hat without enough brim to keep the northern sun
off the wearer's marvelous skin.

Lord almighty. If Bear lived to be a hundred, he'd never
forget the moment Ben Dare lifted away her cape and
Clara Klaus's magnificent breasts filled his vision. In his
time, he'd seen some breasts, he was happy to say, but none
like hers. First they were respectable breasts attached to a
respectable woman, meaning they were not meant to be
seen. This fact alone was enough to drive a man half mad
with guilty joy. Next they were beautifully stupendous,
large enough to fling a man's imagination toward peaks
and valleys and images of losing himself in soft yielding
mountains of womanly warmth. And finally, her satiny
pink skin glowed with such health and beauty and exuber-
ance that only a dead man could be exposed to the sight
and powdery scent without breaking into a hot sweat.

He'd been seeing those breasts in his dreams and day-
dreams, and he wouldn't mind seeing them again in
reality. But that wish was a pipe dream. It wouldn't happen. Clara Klaus was a clever woman who had figured
out how to win the tournament. In the days before and
since, no one could claim to have glimpsed a scrap of the
woman's flesh other than her face.

Shoving his hands into his pants pockets, he watched
her lean to examine the items displayed in the supply
store window. She wasn't the most beautiful woman he'd
ever met, but she ranked as one of the most appealing.
He liked her direct, clear-eyed gaze, and his impression
that she could accomplish whatever she set her mind to.
He liked that she had some meat on her bones and was
full-figured. He even liked the way she didn't back down,
didn't let her sex set limitations.

"Tell your boys I'll be leaving in the morning. I'll meet up with them at Sheep Camp." He'd pack light as far as Sheep Camp, where he'd catch up with Price's Chilkat Indians who would bring the bulk of his supplies.

When he saw Miss Wilder coming around the corner of the stables carrying a Winchester at her side, he tipped his hat to her, exchanged a few words, then set off down Main Street. If he happened to run into Miss Klaus, he might offer to buy her a cup of coffee or tea. He suspected she would prefer a mug of hearty German ale, but there wasn't a saloon in Dyea fit for a lady.

Ordinarily he wasn't an introspective man. He did whatever felt smart or right or good at the time and he didn't question it later. But Clara Klaus had him examining his thoughts and behavior and searching for reasons to explain both.

She had humiliated him before a roomful of companions and shipmates. In the stories making the rounds, she was either an Amazon or a wisp of a little thing, but in both versions, Bear was depicted as being half the man he used to be.

By the time he reached her, he was mad as hell that she'd put a dent in his reputation.

"I didn't know you enjoyed shooting," Tom commented, taking the Winchester and hefting it for weight, then sighting down the barrel before he handed it back to her.

"My brother Pete taught me."

"It's a good idea to have a shooter in your party. You never know what you might run into."

When he'd spotted Zoe on the beach, he'd been shocked by her haggard appearance. Since then he'd learned how seasick she had been, and since then she had improved miraculously. Today her cheeks were a healthy pink, and her hands were steady. She still looked too thin, but her eyes had the flash and blue sparkle that he remembered. And he remembered her well.

Jack Wilder's little sister had been the prettiest girl in Newcastle. When Tom was twenty-two, he'd beaten up Harv O'Day for daring to suggest that Tilly White was prettier than Zoe Wilder. No girl could hold a candle to Zoe; she outshined them all.

She still did, he thought, gazing down at her. No other woman had lashes so long they cast shadows on her cheekbones. He'd never seen a prettier mouth or lips that so invited kissing. And he'd always liked her hair, which was glossy black with red in the depths that could be seen when she stood in the sun. He used to look at her across the Wilder supper table and imagine drawing the pins out of the knot on her neck and then watching her long black hair spill through his fingers.

"Is something wrong?" she asked, frowning up at him. "You're staring, and you seem a hundred miles away."

"Sorry." He still wanted to loosen the heavy twist on her neck and wind the strands through his fingers. After coughing into his hand, he drew back his shoulders. "I believe you wanted to talk about my men packing you into Dawson."

"I've done some checking. You have the best reputation among the packers, but you're also known as the most expensive."

He smiled at her raised eyebrow and the way she paused. She was a Newcastle girl, all right, ready to negotiate the price of anything and everything. It was a trait he shared and admired.

"Some speculators are feverishly building a railroad in Skagway, to go over Dead Horse Pass. And someone will figure out how to make Chilkoot easier. Or the gold fields could play out." He shrugged. "My motto is, make as much money as I can as fast as I can, because this boom isn't going to last forever."

A flicker of esteem brightened her gaze and made his chest swell with pride. There were few things as satisfying as standing tall in the eyes of someone from your hometown.

"I've heard you charge fifty-one cents a pound." She'd never been flirtatious, and she wasn't now. But she tilted her head and gazed at him from beneath her hat brim with a quizzical expression that he found wildly appealing. "I can't pay that much."

He flicked his cigar toward a muddy puddle, then looked back at the jack mule. "I'm prepared to offer you and your companions a deep discount. My Chilkats will pack you into Dawson for thirty cents a pound."

The quick breath she sucked between her teeth told him that she knew the price he named was unusual and outrageously low. "I understood the fifty-one-cent fee was for packing someone up Chilkoot Pass. I didn't realize it covered the trail to Dawson."

"Ordinarily it doesn't." He'd lose money packing them an extra six hundred miles. But if Bear was willing to help them financially, he could do no less. "Old friends get a discount and special consideration."

Pride stiffened her spine so abruptly that the edges of her cape fluttered. "I can't accept your offer," she said flatly. "Even if it wasn't improper to accept an expensive gift from a man, I don't want to be beholden to anyone." Circles of high color burned on her cheeks, and she turned to leave.

"Wait a minute, Zoe." She stared up at him with eyes like blue glass, but she stopped to listen when he grabbed her elbow. "First, a discount isn't a gift. You still have to pay. And if you accept this offer, you're not beholden in any way. This is a business arrangement." Some of the hard glitter eased out of her gaze. "Second, I'm going to Dawson anyway, ramrodding a short load for another customer. It's no problem to add your goods to the roster. And finally, I'm not losing money by discounting my rate. Someone else is paying the additional twenty-one cents."

"Oh?" She frowned as he released her elbow. "Who's paying the extra money?"

"The person insisted on anonymity. I probably shouldn't have mentioned it at all." He hadn't handled this well.

"It's Juliette, isn't it?" Anger snapped in her eyes, and she pressed her lips in a furious line. "Well, tell her no thank you. I don't want her charity!"

At once he understood that he couldn't deny her guess. If he took that path, she'd start listing names until she reached one that he couldn't deny without lying.

"I wouldn't jump to conclusions if I were you," he said lamely. Damn it.

"Who else could it be?" she snapped. "You might discount your fee a few cents to help a family friend, and that's what I'd hoped for, but I don't think you'd cut your fee almost in half." Her gaze narrowed and swung to the sea of white tents surrounding the town. "So who's left? The heiress."

"Zoe—may I call you Zoe?"

"That's how you addressed me when you practically lived with us."

"I guess I did spend a lot of time at your house, didn't I?" he said with a laugh. Then his expression sobered. "Don't turn your back on an offer that is going to make this journey a hell of a lot easier. Don't let pride do you an injury. Someone wants to offer you and your friends a little help. Take it."

"You don't understand," she said, frowning at the ground.

"I've been told I'm a good listener. . . ."

For a moment he thought she would talk to him, really talk to him, then her expression closed, and she gave her head a shake.

"I just don't want to be in another person's debt. Especially not Juliette's."

That was undoubtedly why Bear had chosen to remain anonymous. He didn't want them to feel obligated. "If your benefactor wanted you to be beholden, that person wouldn't have insisted on anonymity."

"Juliette has to know that Clara and I will guess it's her. And I hate it," she said fiercely. Her grip on the Winchester tightened until her knuckles turned white. "I have half a mind to throw her offer back in her face!"

Tom stared. If he hadn't known Zoe was traveling with Miss March, he would have taken her expression and her anger to mean that she and Miss March were mortal enemies.

"Before you do something foolish, think about climbing Chilkoot pass ten or twelve times while Miss March and Miss Klaus climb it once," he said, his voice sharper than he'd intended. "Think about walking ten or twelve times as far to reach Dawson than they do. That's a high price to pay for pride."

"I'm not stupid—in the end I'll accept her offer," she said angrily. Even the little feather on her hat brim quivered with indignation. "But I'd rather refuse her charity!"

"Suppose your benefactor isn't Miss March," he said, giving it another try. "You should think about that."

She gazed up at him as if he had disappointed her, then she sighed. "All right. What's the protocol? When do we leave, and do we have to do anything special with our goods?"

There hadn't been a woman in his life since he'd come to Alaska. He'd forgotten how frustrating females could be.

"Since every minute of delay brings you closer to bad weather, I'd suggest you and your party leave tomorrow morning. Figure you'll carry on your backs whatever you might need immediately. My men will transport the rest. But they don't pack and unpack. So be sure your goods are organized in a way that you can easily get to your tent, stove, foodstuffs."

She turned to leave, carrying the Winchester comfortably in a manner that confirmed she knew how to use it. Tom doubted anyone would get in her way.

"Zoe?"

She glared back at him over her shoulder.

"You used to smile a lot. What happened in your life that you don't smile much anymore?"

The chip flew off her shoulder, and her chin quivered. "Oh, Tom," she said softly. Then she rushed away from him, almost running toward the tent city.

Puzzled, he watched her go. He was wrong to think she was the same girl he'd known when they were younger. She was a woman now, and she'd changed. Secrets and pain lay at the back of her gaze. He wished he knew why she was going to Dawson City.

"Why are you staring at me? What have I done now?" Both Zoe and Clara had returned to the tent in bad moods. Well, Juliette wasn't in a good mood either.

The *Annasett* had sailed this morning without her, and no one knew when another steamship might arrive. But she couldn't wait for another ship in any case, since she and Clara and Zoe owned the tent jointly. Clara and Zoe would take the tent on the trek to Dawson City, and then Juliette would have no place to live and sleep if she remained behind in Dyea. Fate was pushing her toward Dawson City, which was acceptable, she supposed, but getting there scared her to death.

Low temperatures had intrigued her at first. She'd told herself the chill on her cheeks was invigorating. But she'd had enough of the cold now. It was no longer interesting to lie shivering in her camp cot. Even without the cold, it was hard to sleep on the narrow cot. But the worst was living in a tent. Two days of coping with the inconveniences of camping out had obliterated any allure roughing it might have originally held. If it ever *had* held any allure.

These discomforts would only worsen as the journey progressed. It seemed that everyone in Dyea had told her a half dozen horror stories about incidents along the trail. It was enough to make a grown woman whimper.

Clara ladled out three bowls of the thin soup Juliette had prepared, and she stared hard at the burned crust on Juliette's bread before she tore it into chunks.

"I told you I don't know how to cook!" Tears of frustration floated near the surface. She hated the stove. First she had to build a fire on the ground, then place the camp oven over the fire, then fit the cooktop over the oven. But of course it wasn't that simple. The fire kept going out. Neither the oven nor the cooktop heated evenly. Consequently, the bread got scorched but the vegetables in the soup were crunchy and half-cooked and the soup hadn't thickened.

"Tomorrow I'll cook," Clara announced.

"I have some news to share." Zoe sat on one of the folding camp stools, balancing the soup bowl on her knees. "I spoke to Tom Price today. And you'll never guess. *Someone* is paying almost half of our packing fees. Tom's company will pack our goods over Chilkoot Pass for thirty cents a pound. And that includes packing us all the way to Dawson." She stared at Juliette while she spoke.

"Glory be!" Clara blinked hard. "I was getting a bit depressed thinking about how many times we were going to have to climb the pass to get our goods to the top. But I can afford thirty cents. And all the way to Dawson!"

Zoe glared. "It's charity, Clara. *Someone* pities us. *Someone* who feels superior has condescended to make our journey easier."

"I'd already decided to hire a packer," Juliette said. After the experience with the wheelbarrow on the beach, she'd decided it was simply impossible for her to transport her goods herself. "I think it's very nice that someone already made the arrangements and saved us a lot of money."

"Really. And who do you suppose that nice someone might be?" Zoe asked in a furious tone.

"I have no idea." Juliette didn't understand Zoe's tight expression and snippy attitude.

"I think you do have an idea."

Clara frowned. "Wait a minute. It almost sounds like you think Juliette is paying the extra."

"Oh, my. Now why would you imagine that?" Zoe asked, arching an eyebrow. "Could it be because Juliette has more money than anyone we know and can afford to give the little people a handout? Or is it because we don't really know anyone in Alaska except each other, so it must be one of us?"

"Well?" Clara asked. "Are you paying Tom Price to pack us in for a ridiculously low price?"

Dumbfounded, Juliette looked from one face to the other. "It isn't me. Admitting this makes me sound selfish and thoughtless, but it never entered my mind to pay a packing company to pack you two all the way to Dawson."

They were traveling to the same destination at the same time, but they weren't companions and they weren't friends. The best that could be said was that they were related by marriage. And they loathed each other for that relationship.

"If you didn't make the arrangements, then who did?" Zoe demanded.

"Your friend, Mr. Price?" Juliette had no idea who would do such a generous thing.

"I haven't seen Tom in years. And he wasn't my friend, he was my brother's friend. Tom's doing well up here, but I don't think he's rich enough or foolish enough to squander his money helping three greenhorn women."

"The only other people we know are Bear Barrett and Ben Dare," Clara pointed out. "Is Mr. Dare rich?"

"I doubt it." Juliette seriously considered the question. "Mr. Dare is going to the Yukon to prospect for gold. I don't think a rich man would do that."

"And I don't think Bear Barrett would subsidize two

women he doesn't know and one who humiliated him in public," Clara added. A frown pulled at her brows. "He's angry that I bested him in the arm-wrestling tournament. I ran into him today, and he didn't even say hello. He just leaned down and growled at me. He said, 'There will be a rematch. And the next time you aren't going to win.' "

"So who does that leave us with?" Zoe asked in a hard voice, scowling at Juliette.

She couldn't believe this. "I promise you, I'm not the mysterious benefactor. But if I were, why would that make you so angry?"

"Because I know what you're doing! You want to tell Jean Jacques if it wasn't for you, we would have worn ourselves to a nub carrying goods back and forth. You want him to think it was your idea to find him and you made it possible. And, you want to feel superior to us! Like you're better than us!"

Juliette gasped. "That isn't true! Until the *Annasett* sailed without me, I was planning to return to Seattle!"

Zoe rolled her eyes. "You don't plan anything, Juliette. You just let yourself get carried along. I suspect you've known all along that you wouldn't be on the *Annasett* when it returned to Seattle. You want to find Jean Jacques as much as we do."

To her dismay, most of what Zoe said was true. She did allow herself to be swept along by events and people. Moreover, she couldn't argue that she didn't feel superior to Zoe and Clara, because sometimes she did. Sometimes she thought that Jean Jacques had married beneath himself when he wed those two.

"I'll accept your charity," Zoe continued, her eyes as glittery and hard as blue ice. "I'll accept because I'm worried about how long my money will last and because using a packer will make the journey a hundred times easier. But I'll never thank you for this handout. And I detest you for hiding behind anonymity and for putting me in a position where I have to accept your charity or feel stupid and suffer great hardship."

After setting her soup bowl on the ground, Zoe strode into the tent and threw down the flap behind her.

Juliette blinked at Clara. "Truly, I didn't pay Tom Price any part of our packing fees. It's someone else."

Juliette couldn't eat either, she was too upset. Life with Aunt Kibble had not been a fraction as turbulent and draining as life with her husband's other wives. And no one had ever spoken to her as directly or as insultingly as Zoe and Clara did. Nor had she ever addressed anyone as directly and, yes, occasionally insultingly as she sometimes addressed Zoe and Clara. It was a terrible thing to be forced to endure the company of people one loathed. The circumstance brought out the very worst in her.

"I don't know why Bear's so angry," Clara said, studying the chunk of black crust that she turned between her fingers. "Before the match, he said he could accept defeat gracefully." She frowned at Juliette. "Surely he knew it was possible that I'd beat him. Even if he believed it would take a miracle, he must have known it could happen."

"So who could it be?" She scanned the closed flap of the tent, upset that Zoe was so angry at her. "Ben, that is Mr. Dare, speaks well and he has nice manners. But I just don't think a rich man would travel all this distance to dig around in frozen sand. He doesn't even believe he'll find gold."

Now that she thought about it, Ben's trip to the Yukon didn't make much sense. Unless he didn't want her to know that he was as desperate as the other stampeders.

Clara dropped the bread crust into her bowl. "I never meant to humiliate or embarrass him. I didn't think about that. I just wanted to win the prize."

Last night Juliette had dreamed about Benjamin Dare. They had been walking along the shore, except in her dream, the shore had been white sand instead of pebbles.

Overhead was the twilight sky of an Alaskan spring, but she could see stars anyway. There was no tent city in her dream, no town, no mountains. Just the shore and the sky and Benjamin. He had turned her in his arms, kissed her, then they had sunk to their knees on the sand, and she had swooned as he began to open her shirtwaist.

Lowering her head, she swallowed and blinked at the cooling surface of her soup. For months she had wanted to dream about Jean Jacques, but she never had. She didn't want to dream about Ben Dare, but this was the second time he had made love to her in her dreams. It didn't feel decent or right.

After a while, she looked at the closed tent flap and wondered what Zoe was doing inside. "Do you think Zoe will really kill Jean Jacques?" she asked Clara.

"What? Oh, *ja*. I think she will."

For a moment Juliette felt disoriented. Surely she was not in Alaska, for heaven's sake, dreaming about a handsome man she had not known five weeks ago and sharing a tent with a would-be murderess and an arm wrestler. How on earth had such an improbable thing happened?

Tilting her head back, she stared up at the pale night sky and wished she could go home to California, where the nights were warm, the days boringly tranquil, and where she had never heard of a disturbing man named Ben Dare.

In her dreams there was no Jean Jacques, there was only Ben, his intent blue eyes filling her vision before he crushed her in his arms.

Guilt made her touch her wedding ring. How could her dreams be filled with such longing for one man when she was married to another? What kind of person was she?

Chapter 9

The Chilkoot trail, or the Poor Man's Trail as it was also called, twisted through twenty-five miles of steep, tangled terrain. But the first five miles hadn't been too difficult, Clara decided, stopping to swing the pack off her back.

The day was bright and crisply cold, a grand day for new beginnings, a day to absorb nature. The ragged beauty of abruptly rising mountains awed her, and the flow of humanity ascending toward the pass made her feel part of something momentous.

Choosing a rock beside the trail, she sat down and rummaged in her backpack until she found the sandwiches she'd made early this morning out of canned ham. She also had an apple, a piece of hard cheese, and a bottle of her carefully hoarded German ale, but she would save those items for her lunch.

While she unwrapped a sandwich to eat now, she watched the steady stream of men trudging past her. Some pushed wheelbarrows piled high with boxes and crates, most carried huge loads on their backs, and others led pack animals even though the actual pass was too steep for horses or mules to climb. Clara wondered what happened to the animals when the prospectors reached Sheep Camp at the bottom of the pass.

"Well, well, if it isn't Miss Klaus."

Bear Barrett stepped out of the stream of foot traffic and approached the rock where she sat. His shaggy golden hair hung below a well-worn hat with a brim large enough to keep the sun off his face. He wore a heavy green sweater over loose trousers and sturdy walking boots.

"Mind if I join you?" he asked, already sliding his pack to the ground beside her. "What have you got there? Ham? I've got fried egg and bacon. Would you like to trade one of your sandwiches for one of mine?"

Clara accepted his offer and then pulled her corduroy skirt to the side to make room for him on her rock.

"How many of those cheechakos do you think will make it all the way to Dawson?" Bear asked before he bit into one of Clara's ham sandwiches. His sharp gaze studied the men hiking past them.

"I keep hearing that word, *cheechako*. What does it mean?"

"It's the Chinook word for newcomer."

"I suspect it means a bit more than that. Like stupid greenhorn. Or, idiots. Something not too complimentary."

When Bear grinned, his craggy almost-menacing face relaxed into near handsomeness. Looking at him, Clara tried to imagine him without the broken nose and minus the scar through his eyebrow, but she couldn't. His crooked nose and dented face were part of who he was, and part of the reason her skin flushed when she gazed at him too long.

"After you've been in the Yukon a year, you're entitled to call yourself a sourdough," Bear explained, "but not before."

She smiled and nodded, feeling his physical presence as she felt the chill wind on her cheeks—as a tangible thing. He enveloped people with his size and his energy, overwhelmed most, Clara guessed. He didn't intimidate her, but she felt his warmth and size and vigor, and she responded strongly to the challenge he represented. He was a mountain, and mountains were there to climb, or to whittle down to size.

They ate in companionable silence, watching the tide of prospectors struggle up the trail. "I behaved badly yesterday," Bear said suddenly. "I don't know what happened. Hell, I wanted to buy you a cup of coffee. Instead, I got mad." After a minute he added, "I'm always explaining myself to you. I don't do that with anyone else. But whenever I see you, I feel like I need to explain whatever I did or said the last time I saw you."

"Explaining spares a lot of misunderstandings." Clara didn't dare turn her head, or she'd be looking directly into those brown-bear eyes and then her stomach would flip over and fall to the ground.

"If I'd asked, would you have let me buy you a coffee?"

"I don't know." She was playing with fire here. "I might have." Surely no one got burned sharing a simple cup of coffee. She couldn't see any harm in it, not really.

His teeth flashed in a smile, and his eyes narrowed down in a crinkly way that made it impossible not to smile back at him. "Then I'll ask you again sometime."

They ate their midmorning snack and watched the cheechakos, and Clara tried not to feel the heat of him against her side. Tried to ignore the clean outdoor scent of his hair and clothing.

"How long have you been in Alaska?" she asked, mostly to focus her thoughts away from wanting to lean against him.

"Sometimes it feels like I've been living in one wilderness area or another for as long as I can remember. I like the raw vitality of the boomtowns. And the opportunities. Men have gotten rich chasing prospectors."

"Then you search for gold, too?"

He laughed. "No, ma'am. I make more money selling one bottle of liquor than most miners earn in a week. I guess you could say I mine the miners."

Clara nodded approvingly. She understood this thinking. Providing food, drink, and shelter would lead an ambitious person to prosperity. That's what her papa had always said.

But Papa was a man to stay put, not a man like Bear

who followed opportunity wherever it led. As for herself, she'd been willing to sell the inn and chase opportunity to Seattle, so she guessed she was more like Bear Barrett than like her papa.

Feeling him stiffen next to her brought her thoughts back to the present in time to notice a scowling man who had halted on the trail. He stared at Bear with such hatred that Clara gasped.

"Who's that?" she asked. The man spit on the ground as if the sight of Bear had left a bad taste in his mouth, then he snarled something beneath his breath and moved on.

Bear frowned at the clouds gathering to the west. "His name is Jake Horvath. I won the Bare Bear off him in a poker game. He claims I cheated."

An odd expression tightened his face as he paused and studied Clara. After a minute she realized he was waiting for her to ask if Horvath's accusation was true. When she said nothing, he nodded, then intensified his gaze and looked deep inside her.

How long they sat on the rock staring into each other's eyes was anyone's guess. Finally Clara blinked and turned her face toward the trail, pressing her palms against fiery cheeks. "Oh, my," she murmured in a breathy voice.

"You know, things would be a lot easier if you weren't a respectable woman."

"I beg your pardon," she said, abruptly coming to her senses. Surely she had not heard him correctly.

"There are things I'd like to say to you, but it's hard to talk to respectable women. I have to be careful what words I choose and where I look."

The fire continued to blaze on her cheeks as she imagined the kind of women he must usually speak to. "Well! I'm sorry that my respectability inconveniences you." The idea. She shrugged her arms through the straps of her backpack, not allowing him to assist her. "If you'll excuse me," she said coolly.

"Wait a minute."

Striding forward, she fell into the line of cheechakos hiking over terrain that steadily worsened and became more difficult to cover. Once she looked back and saw Bear standing to the side of the trail, glaring after her with an expression of annoyance and exasperation. That's how she felt, too.

Much of the time he had an infuriating way of disappointing her or making her angry. She didn't know why she thought about him so often anyway. Well, yes she did.

Whatever spark flared between them was strictly superficial. She wouldn't have admitted it to another soul, but a large part of his enormous appeal was purely physical. Her skin tingled where she brushed against him. When their eyes met, her chest tightened and an earthquake shook her stomach. Sunlight shining on the golden hair on his hands and wrists made her mouth go dry.

Jean Jacques had caused a similar reaction, but not as strong, and she knew where that mistake had taken her. Frowning, she grabbed hold of a cottonwood branch and pulled herself up a steep incline. The ground was a damp tangle of exposed roots.

Ironically, after years of zealously protecting herself from fortune hunters, that's whom she had impulsively married. And she'd done it largely because Jean Jacques made her itch somewhere deep down inside. It was enough to make a cat laugh.

Well, it wouldn't happen again. Tingling nerves and hot shivery stares were not going to lead her astray this time. But she almost understood Bear's comment about wishing that she was a woman of loose virtue. If that were the case, she and Bear could spend a rollicking night together, she could get him out of her system, and that would be the end of it.

But since she was a respectable woman, his comment had to be viewed as insulting. Quivering with moral indignation, she hardly noticed how the trail had deteriorated.

* * *

If Juliette died, and she thought she might, it would be Jean Jacques's fault. If it wasn't for him, she wouldn't be here, struggling up the steep slope of a mountain, panting like a dog and perspiring as no lady ever should.

Stepping out of a quagmire of churned earth and animal droppings, she leaned into the hillside, placed her hands on her knees, and fought to fill her lungs with enough air to survive.

This was madness. There wasn't even a trail. Men and animals picked their way up as best they could, climbing around boulders ranging from skillet size to the size of carriages. Hemlock and spruce grew thick enough to snatch at hats and clothing. And she'd overheard someone say they were only halfway to the first night's camp.

Easing herself down on a fallen tree trunk, she yanked off her pack and rubbed sore shoulders. The pack couldn't weigh more than fifteen pounds, but after three and a half hours, it felt as if she carried a block of marble on her back. She didn't know how the men bore it, those who carried towering packs that must have weighed near a hundred pounds. And when the men reached Canyon City, the first night's campsite, they would turn around and return to Dyea to fetch another hundred pounds of their goods and continue back and forth over this hellish trail until their outfit was reassembled. A shudder rippled down her spine.

"You're shivering? You can't possibly be cold," Zoe gasped, climbing around a boulder and staggering toward Juliette. She doubled over and gulped huge mouthfuls of air. When Zoe's skirt tipped up in back, Juliette noticed that Zoe's legs were twitching as badly as her own.

"It starts to feel cold after you rest for a minute."

Perspiration had dampened Zoe's collar, and her cheeks were bright pink from the sun. Juliette supposed she looked equally disheveled. For once she didn't care. "If I had to walk this horrible so-called trail a couple dozen

times like most of those men, I'd give up and go home."
She thanked heaven for their mysterious benefactor.

Zoe nodded and dropped on the log beside Juliette.
"For once I agree with you. Right now I don't care that
you paid for us. I'm just grateful that I don't have to pack
one more ounce than the two tons I'm already carrying."

Juliette didn't waste breath denying she was the benefactor. Nothing she said would convince Zoe. She closed
her eyes and sighed. "I don't think I have the energy to
eat lunch."

"Me neither. I'll tell you one thing. Tomorrow I'm not
wearing this corset. I don't care if Ma hears about it from
a dozen sources, I'm not lacing tomorrow."

Juliette wished she could fall asleep and wake up in
Linda Vista with all this behind her. She wished she had
never met Jean Jacques Villette. "Sometimes I think I could
shoot Jean Jacques myself. If it wasn't for him, I'd be warm
and comfortable at home." But she could never shoot anyone. Not even the man who had ruined her life. At the moment this seemed like a character flaw. "Could you really
shoot someone you love?"

Zoe didn't answer immediately. "I'm not sure anymore
if I actually loved him. Maybe I loved the kind of life he
offered. I'm not proud of that, but maybe that's how it
was." She fished around in her backpack and pulled out
a hard-boiled egg, but cracking and peeling it seemed beyond her.

Juliette picked bits of bark off the log they sat on. "Sometimes I remember how fast everything happened, and it
shocks me. How could I have married someone I knew
so slightly?" She shook her head. "Was I that afraid of
ending on the shelf?"

She kept circling back to that question. Maybe Jean
Jacques had been a desperate last attempt to save herself
from spinsterhood. She was beginning to wonder if love
had even been involved. How could she love someone
who had never existed? He was none of the things she

had believed him to be, but he was many of the things Aunt Kibble had taught her to despise.

He was a thief who preyed on women. That was the unvarnished truth. A man who cared nothing for the marriage sacrament. He was a hollow wisp wrapped in charm and possessing a gift for saying what women wanted to hear. A liar and a fraud.

"If I ran into Jean Jacques right now, I'd give him a piece of my mind that he'd never forget!" The muscles in her calves still twitched, her shoulders ached, and she was damp with perspiration. She deeply resented how she looked and felt. "I wish I'd never come here."

"I wish you'd never come here, too," Zoe said with a sigh.

Maybe it was the improbable circumstance of sitting on the side of a boulder-strewn mountain in Alaska. Maybe the altitude had made her giddy. Maybe switching from the heat of laboring uphill to sitting still in cold air had affected her mind. Maybe Zoe's acerbic comment broke the spell of confiding in each other. But Zoe's remark struck her as humorous.

"I don't want to be here, and nobody wants me here, yet here I am." A decidedly unladylike laugh shook her body and burst out of her like a cork under pressure. "I hate this, I truly hate it! So why on earth am I here in Alaska?"

Zoe stared at her. Then her lips twitched and a faint smile brushed her lips. "You're here for the same reason I am. Because of that son of a bitch, Jean Jacques."

"He is a son of a bitch, isn't he?" She'd never said such words in her life, had hastened away in offense from men who used coarse language, had never known women who spoke such phrases until she'd met Zoe and Clara. But by heaven, it felt good to say the words herself. It felt good to let the fury and resentment finally boil out of her.

Struggling to her feet, she cupped her hands around her mouth and shouted down the mountainside. "Jean

Jacques Villette is a rotten son of a bitch!" There. She'd told everyone in the world what she thought of him.

Zoe burst into laughter.

"You used us and threw us away, and I hate you! I hate you, I hate you!" Juliette's face was hot and her hands shook, but she had admitted her own truth. The words exploded up from deep inside, burning the back of her throat. And she didn't know if she wanted to laugh or cry because she had finally conceded that Jean Jacques was an unscrupulous scoundrel just as Aunt Kibble had insisted he was. There were no excuses for what he had done, no justification. No explanation she could accept.

She turned to Zoe. "I don't think I've heard you laugh before. You're very pretty when you smile."

"Being pretty never did a thing for me," Zoe said, her smile curving down into a frown. She tapped the egg against the log and then peeled away bits of shell. "I used to think that being pretty would somehow save me from a life of work and babies. Instead it brought me a no-good bastard who ruined me for any other man. So yes. I'm really going to shoot him. And if they hang me for murder—so what? I have no plans beyond shooting Jean Jacques, so they might as well hang me. I don't care."

"I don't have any plans either." After they found Jean Jacques and Zoe shot him, what would she do? Spend the rest of her life listening to Aunt Kibble remind her what a fool she'd been?

"Are you all right?" Ben Dare pushed through a tight growth of thick spruce and scanned the clearing where they sat. His legs braced and his muscles tensed as if he were spoiling for a fight.

"Of course." Hastily Juliette patted her hair and brushed loose bark from her skirt. Strands of hair fell around her face, and she must have smelled of perspiration. There was nothing she could do about it.

"I thought I heard you screaming," he said, running a quick gaze over her body, checking for injury.

Circles of pink flared on her cheeks. Jean Jacques had given her a long slow look before they made love, just as Ben was doing. Jean Jacques's eyes had been a paler blue than Ben's, and Ben was taller. But the way Ben stared at her made her remember making love. The same fluttery, chaotic tingling raced around her body.

Zoe glanced up from the log. "Perhaps you heard Juliette shouting to me. Telling me where to find her."

"It didn't sound like that." He walked up to her. "But I'm glad you're all right."

"I'm fine," Juliette insisted. Except for being confused, exhausted, detested by her companions, and abandoned by her husband. "Perfectly fine."

Then she collapsed against his chest and burst into tears.

Clara had a stew bubbling and coffee perking by the time Zoe spotted the tent pole with the pink ribbon and made her way through a tent city set up in no particular order.

"We don't have our tent or camp stools yet," Clara announced cheerfully, "but there are tree stumps all over the place. Pick one and sit down. You look all tuckered out."

"I am." Zoe's feet ached, the backs of her legs were so sore that every step was a trial, and her backpack had rubbed a raw spot on one of her shoulders. "Has our medical kit arrived?"

"I don't know." Clara waved toward a tumbled mound of boxes and crates. "I thought I'd get the stew started before I began sorting things out."

Zoe had never been this tired in her life. "Where's our tent?" she asked when she'd summoned a small burst of energy. All she wanted to do was fall into her cot and try to relax her tight throbbing muscles.

"One of the pack mules went down," Tom Price said, walking up to the camp stove. Clara gave him the cup of coffee she'd been about to hand to Zoe. "My men are bringing that load up on their backs. They should be here soon."

"Did you know the Indian men can carry a hundred pounds and the women carry seventy-five pounds?" Clara spoke in the same cheerful tone that made Zoe want to hit her with a rock. "Look at this scenery," she said, waving at the narrow canyon's walls. "Isn't it spectacular? And smell the air!"

To Zoe the air smelled of wood smoke, tobacco, mule and dog droppings, and various cooking odors.

"Did you see the glaciers hanging in the high valleys to the west?" Clara's enthusiasm seemed boundless. "And wasn't it beautiful when the trail dipped down to the river?"

Tom smiled at Clara's high spirits and Zoe wanted to hit him, too. "Tomorrow you'll see the snowfields." He gazed at the clouds advancing across the sky. "It will be cold tonight. The Chilkats say it will snow before morning."

Zoe groaned, and Tom and Clara laughed at her.

Then a silence opened, but Tom showed no signs of leaving. Abruptly Clara straightened and looked back and forth between them. "Well," she said, stepping backward. "I guess I'll go see if I can spot Juliette or find out where our tent is." She straightened her cape and smoothed the brim of her hat. "Don't forget to give the stew a stir every now and then."

"How did the first day go?" Tom asked after Clara had bustled off. He smiled at her over the rim of his coffee cup.

Zoe couldn't believe this was only the first day. "I didn't think it would be this difficult." When his eyebrow rose, she lifted a hand. "I know, I know. Everyone talks about how hard the trail is. But I expected to take it in stride as Clara apparently has." She glanced up, noting the easy way he stood, with his legs apart and braced for whatever might come. He didn't look like a man who had just

kicked and coaxed a pack of mules over god-awful terrain, most of which was steeply angled, heavily treed,
and littered with boulders.

"It won't get easier. A person has to be truly motivated
to endure this journey."

The way his voice invited her to talk about motivation
told her that he was curious about her reasons for going
to Dawson City. And for one crazy moment, she considered confessing the truth. But then he'd feel obligated to
try to talk her out of shooting Jean Jacques. Or maybe,
as a long-standing family friend, Tom would insist on
killing Jean Jacques for her. She didn't want to talk about
it. Nothing he said would change her mind about killing
Jean Jacques, and she didn't want someone else to pay
the price for doing her job.

When Tom noticed that she didn't have coffee, he
poured her a cup. Jean Jacques had been thoughtful, too,
but in the end his thoughtfulness hadn't mattered for
squat. She would a lot rather that he'd been truthful. In
that case she would never have married him. Would
never have ruined herself. Wouldn't be here in Alaska eager to make a murderess of herself.

"Why are you going to Dawson?" she asked, gazing
up at him. She liked the way he wore his hat tilted at a
rakish angle. "Is it really worth your while to pack anyone all the way to Dawson?"

Sipping his coffee, he gazed out at the stovepipes sticking through hundreds of tents. "My primary competitor
is a man named Nose O'Malley. He and I have gotten
into it enough times that it seems prudent to put some
distance between us. So I've decided to winter over in
Dawson City."

The news pleased Zoe, who was beginning to realize
she would be stuck in Dawson for the winter. It would be
nice to have a friendly face nearby. She glanced at him
and then looked down at her cup. "It's funny how things

work out. I never thought you'd leave Newcastle. I figured you'd stay in the mines like your pa."

"I always knew you'd leave," he said in a soft voice, keeping his gaze on the tent city. "I knew fate had something special in mind for Zoe Wilder."

His comment flattered and saddened her. "It didn't work out that way."

"You're being too modest. One day you're going to tell your grandchildren that you were part of the great Klondike gold rush." Green eyes sparkled down at her. "Not many women will be able to say that."

The comment made her feel a little better. "Tom? I'm glad we ran into each other again."

"So am I."

For a long moment they studied each other, acquainting themselves with the man and woman they had grown into. Zoe saw a confident man with an inner stillness that she didn't recall him possessing as a boy. Stubbornness defined his jawline, and she saw determination in his brow. She liked what she saw. And part of her hoped that Tom liked whatever he saw in her.

Then she spotted Juliette and Ben Dare winding a path through the tents toward the pink ribbon that identified their site. Zoe blinked; she could not believe her eyes. They were walking arm in arm as if enjoying a leisurely Sunday stroll.

Immediately her confidence plummeted, and so did her mood. She rubbed her eyes, and looked again. There was no mistake.

Something had to be very wrong with her. Every inch of her body ached and was beginning to stiffen in the cold air. She was so exhausted she felt like weeping over the prospect of setting up their tent. She didn't have an ounce of energy left.

Yet Clara was bouncing around as if she could hike another five miles, like she wished they didn't have to stop and wait for their goods to catch up. And here came

Juliette, chatting and smiling and strolling along as if she hadn't just fought her way through clutching trees and roots and nine miles of steep rocky ground that left even the pack animals heaving for breath.

Maybe Zoe should rethink this journey.

She had supposed herself to be best suited for an arduous journey, but she was proving to be the weakest of the three, a fact that utterly astonished and humiliated her.

"Good evening, Mr. Price." Juliette nodded to Zoe, then released Ben's arm, lifted the pot lid, and glanced at the stew bubbling atop the camp stove. "Where is our tent?"

Zoe decided if Juliette invited Tom and Benjamin to share supper with them, if Juliette had the energy to set up a social evening, then Zoe would take it as a sign from above. She would hand Clara her Winchester and show her how to kill Jean Jacques. Then she would return to Dyea and forget about Dawson City.

But Juliette didn't mention supper. She waved to Clara, who appeared leading two of Tom's Chilkat Indians. "The tent has arrived," Clara called.

Juliette made a fluttery movement with her hands and gave Tom and Ben Dare a roll of her eyes. "I guess we'll get better at putting up our tent. . . . It just takes so long."

To Zoe, Juliette's blatant manipulation appeared obvious, but neither of the men seemed to notice. They knelt beside the boxes the Indians unloaded and assured Juliette they would have the tent up in no time.

Now Juliette would gush, thank them, and invite them to supper. Then Zoe would find the Winchester and give it to Clara. But Juliette didn't gush a single word. She glided around the boxes, finding and setting up the camp cots, pulling blankets out and shaking them open. She moved slowly, gracefully. If Zoe hadn't known better, she might have guessed that Juliette had spent the day in idle repose.

Clara caught Juliette's eye, nodded to the stew pot and

then to the men before she raised a questioning eyebrow. Like Zoe, Clara looked to Juliette to lead them in the social graces, such as extending invitations.

Juliette returned Clara's long look, but she said nothing to the men about supper even after they had the tent erected and secured and both of them glanced expectantly at the stew pot. Tom even mentioned how good the steam smelled.

Zoe couldn't wait another minute. Now that the tent was up and the cots unfolded, she was going to collapse. Groaning, she stood, wincing in pain and hating that she was the only one of them with sore muscles. She said good night to Tom and Ben, and limped toward the tent, leaving Clara and Juliette to properly thank them. Somewhere in the boxes of goods was a medical pack and some liniment, but she was too whipped to look for it.

Falling into her cot, she stared at the ceiling of the tent and decided she really and truly detested Clara and Juliette.

Then the flap flew backward and Juliette staggered inside. "Lordy, lordy, I thought they would never leave!" She dropped on her cot like a rock. "I'm dying. My back hurts, my legs hurt, I hurt everywhere." A long moan blew against her pillow. "I won't be able to walk tomorrow, or move. I'm so sore, I could just cry, except I don't have the energy for tears. If you want to shoot someone, shoot me. You'd be doing me a favor."

Zoe heaved up on one elbow and stared. "You weren't even wincing when you came strolling in here! You set up the cots like you weren't even tired!"

Juliette lay facedown, her arms dangling off the sides of the cot. She looked like she was paralyzed. "I didn't want Ben to think I was weak or unfit," she said, speaking into her pillow. "You can't imagine how hard it was."

The remark told Zoe that Juliette cared a lot about what Ben Dare thought of her. More to the point, Juliette had demonstrated an astonishing iron will and steely discipline that Zoe suspected she could not have replicated. She eased back on her cot, struggling against a grudging flash of admiration. She didn't want to admire anything about Juliette.

Clara threw back the tent flap and stepped inside. "All right. You're not going to sleep in your hats and shoes. Get yourselves undressed and I'll rub liniment on your shoulders and legs."

"I can't move," Juliette groaned.

"Why aren't you sore and aching?" The prospect of standing and stretching to get undressed made Zoe feel like weeping.

"I am. But it isn't as bad for me as for you two." Clara shrugged. "I guess running up the inn's staircase a dozen times a day strengthened my legs. Who knows? Before you get undressed, you should come outside and see the snow. It started a few minutes ago."

Chapter 10

Juliette considered the snow pretty for a scant half a day, then boots and hooves churned it into a muddy broth of offal, food scraps, and tobacco juice. Makeshift privies froze before they thawed and overflowed. The temperature edged above freezing during the day and then plummeted at night.

Already Juliette was sick to death of the constant cold and damp and wearier still of striving to be cheerful about it. "I just want to find Jean Jacques and get this over with," she said at the end of their third day in Canyon City. Earlier, ground fog had wafted through the tent city. Now it was snowing again. California had never seemed so far away.

Zoe stepped closer to the camp stove and held her hands over the rising heat. "Tom said his men will have the last of the goods moved up here by tonight. We can leave for Sheep Camp tomorrow morning."

They didn't have to make a few dozen trips to Dyea and back to move their goods, but they had to wait while Tom's Indians made the relay. On the positive side, the Indian teams could move their crates and packaged goods in three twelve-hour days, whereas the prospectors moving goods on their own backs would spend two or three weeks moving their outfits from Dyea to here.

The delay wasn't entirely wasted. Rest and a strong liniment had given Juliette's muscles an opportunity to recover. Also, the powerful astringent scent of the liniment blocked many of the unpleasant camp odors.

Every few minutes she peered into the steady fall of snow, half hoping to see Ben, though she knew he probably hadn't yet returned from Dyea. He'd paid to be packed over the pass and then on into Dawson, but he insisted on doing some of the packing himself. Juliette supposed this saved him money, and heaven knew it must put a strain on his finances to pay Tom Price's rates. Not many of the prospectors paid to be packed. She wondered if Ben had sunk all his money into this venture.

"I've been meaning to ask—what reason did you give Mr. Dare for bursting into tears?" Zoe brushed snow off her hat and shoulders.

Clara looked up from feeding wood into the fire beneath the camp stove. "You burst into tears?"

Trust Zoe to make sure Clara knew about the incident. "I told him it was one of those days," Juliette said irritably.

Men hastily changed the subject when a woman explained odd behavior by saying it was "just one of those days." They didn't want to hear more.

"What was the real reason?" Clara asked, arching an eyebrow.

"I was tired and every muscle hurt and I absolutely didn't want to be on that trail. I was furious at Jean Jacques."

"It's about time."

"Then Mr. Dare rushed out of the trees thinking I needed help." She looked into a swirl of snowflakes. Everything was pale and colorless—the sky, the snow, the ground. "I was so angry. And so sad that I hadn't met Ben before . . . furious that I'd married someone who lied and took my money and then left me." She lowered her head. "We don't talk about it much. But I think about Jean Jacques a lot. I've decided that I don't like him anymore."

"You know something?" Clara looked at Juliette and Zoe. "Sometimes I still get jealous and angry when I look at you two and imagine you being with my husband. But even if Jean Jacques begged me, I wouldn't want him back. All I want is my money."

"I don't want him back, either," Zoe said firmly. "But I haven't changed my mind about shooting him," she added. "My family . . . He made me feel . . . I don't want to talk about that, but he has to pay for what he did."

"*Ja*, he has to pay."

For the first time Juliette conceded that she, too, had crossed a line. She didn't want Jean Jacques either. Weeks had passed since she had last performed the silly rituals she had once hoped would bring him back to her.

"He has to pay," she agreed.

"It's your turn," Zoe said, looking at her through a swirl of snowflakes.

To pass the time, they had taken turns talking about their families and growing up. Tonight, Juliette told them about losing her parents, about growing up with Aunt Kibble. Pride prompted her to mention the suitors that Aunt Kibble had disapproved of since Clara had talked about beaux and so had Zoe. She also mentioned her embroidery circle, and choir, and calling on friends and acquaintances, and serving tea at Aunt Kibble's at-home days.

"Women mend in Newcastle," Zoe said when Juliette had finished her story. "No one has time for embroidery. And every day is an at-home day since there's so much work to do."

"Why do you sound so bitter when you speak of Newcastle?"

"Weren't you listening when it was my turn? Ma works her fingers to the bone, and she still can't keep the house clean. The coal dust gets into everything. Everyone's life is tied to the mine. And always, always, everyone is listening for the whistle that signals a cave-in or gas in the shafts or a man down for some other reason. No one has much leisure in Newcastle, and the women don't pour tea for each other. If I sound bitter about Newcastle, it's because I hated growing up there."

"Your growing-up years sounded wonderful. I would have loved to have had parents like yours," Juliette said softly. "And brothers." She adored hearing about the loud raucous mealtimes in the Wilder household, with everyone laughing and shouting to be heard and being reprimanded and teasing. And she liked to hear about the rough escapades of Zoe's brothers. And how Pete had taught Zoe to shoot and Jack had taught her to fish and Cal had helped with schoolwork. The twins had protected Zoe from bullies and later from unwanted suitors. Jimmy had been the prankster.

Zoe stared at her. "You've lived the life I always wanted. You had your own bedroom and privacy, and servants to do the cooking and cleaning and washing. You aren't ashamed to tell anyone where you're from!"

"I would have traded it all for a mother like yours."

Color rose in Zoe's cheeks, and for a moment Juliette thought Zoe would cry. Astonished, she blinked and spread her hands. "Did I say something to upset you?"

"It's late. I'm going to bed."

Juliette watched her enter the tent, then turned to Clara. "What did I say?"

"I think sometimes it's harder for Zoe than for you or me." Clara frowned toward the tent flap. "We don't have to struggle with how we feel about our family. Or worry that people we love think we were foolish or stupid about Jean Jacques."

"Aunt Kibble certainly believes I was foolish and stupid."

"But your Aunt Kibble would have disapproved no matter how lengthy an engagement you had, and no matter who you chose to marry. Isn't that correct?" Clara asked shrewdly.

"It's true that Aunt Kibble never approved of my suitors," Juliette admitted slowly.

"It sounds as if your aunt didn't want you to marry and leave her. I suspect she saw you as a companion for her old age."

"Oh, my heavens."

Not once had Juliette considered that Aunt Kibble might have had selfish motives for emphasizing the flaws in Juliette's would-be beaux. Over time Juliette had accepted Aunt Kibble's inferences that no man would be interested in her—he could only be interested in her money.

Clara stood and stamped her boots to shake the snow off her skirts. "Now I've upset you."

"No," Juliette said, drawing out the word. "But you've given me some things to think about."

Aunt Kibble had used Jean Jacques as proof that a man would only be interested in Juliette's inheritance. Unfortunately Aunt Kibble had been correct about Jean Jacques Villette. But had she been correct about Robert Wright? And Forrest Braithwaite?

Chewing her lip, Juliette stared into the falling snow and thought about her only two serious suitors. She had relied on Aunt Kibble's judgment and had scorned Mr. Wright and Mr. Braithwaite, making it clear she did not welcome their attentions. In retrospect, she understood that she had acted on Aunt Kibble's recommendations, not her own inclinations.

Only when she was looking spinsterhood squarely in the face had she defied Aunt Kibble and made her own decision. And Aunt Kibble had not let her forget for one moment what a disastrous decision she had made.

Here was one more reason not to return to Linda Vista. Juliette did not doubt that her aunt cared for her, maybe loved her. But Aunt Kibble's decisions would benefit Aunt Kibble first and Juliette second.

But if she didn't return to Linda Vista, where would

she go once her marriage difficulties were resolved? With all her heart she wished she could tell Ben the truth and request his advice. Most of all she wished she could forget how good it felt when his arms had closed around her and he had pressed her to his chest.

· She remembered the starchy scent of his shirt and a whiff of cigar smoke. A hint of male perspiration. These scents and his arms around her cast her memory back into childhood and raised feelings of safety and comfort. And other feelings, too, that made her squirm on the camp stool and that were anything but childlike.

The so-called trail followed the Taiya River out of Canyon City and toward a cleft in the rocky walls that opened into an area someone had christened Sheep Camp. Perhaps two thousand tents crowded Sheep Camp, each marked by piles of goods mounded before the flap. A choking haze of wood smoke overhung the camp.

While waiting for Tom's Chilkats to bring up their outfits, Zoe wandered toward the river to escape the smoky camp and to watch weary men trudging back and forth along the snow-wet trail, their eyes on the ground, their backs bowed from the weight of heavy, bulky loads. Occasionally, though not often, she noticed a woman following a man, toting what she could. Two of the women she saw carried babies bundled in their arms.

By now Zoe knew that she wasn't with child. But the possibility of pregnancy had kept her awake nights after learning about Clara and Juliette. Thank heaven she didn't have the complication of an infant to add to the disaster wrought by Jean Jacques Villette.

"A penny for your thoughts . . ."

When she looked up from the rock where she was sitting, she saw Tom Price seated atop a roan gelding, his arms crossed on the pommel as if he'd been watching her for a while.

"Have you ever killed a man?" she asked abruptly.

Surprise lifted his eyebrows and then his smile hardened. "I've busted up a few, but I haven't killed one yet. Why do you ask?"

"I just wondered." She turned her head toward a field of rocks poking through wind-drifted snow. The snow had stopped falling earlier in the morning, leaving the world brushed in strokes of white and gray. The river resembled molten slate rushing to reach the sea, reflecting the gray sky overhead. Gray stones scarred the snowy landscape. Even the men trudging past seemed gray today, gray-clad, gray-faced. The reddish sheen of Tom's horse struck Zoe as a jolting splash of color in an otherwise drab landscape.

"There's something I was wondering about, too."

"What would that be?" Damn, he was handsome. Occasionally Zoe caught him looking at her in a way that shot an electric spark burning down her spine. It was a narrowed speculative look that kindled fire in the depths of those green eyes. That particular look and her response troubled her greatly.

"My teams are working smoothly, everything's under control. It seems I have a free afternoon." The horse shifted beneath him, and his body moved as if part of the animal. "I wondered if you'd like to join me for a picnic up near the glaciers."

Men didn't picnic by themselves, so inviting her wasn't a last-minute impulse. He'd planned this, had packed a lunch.

Was she free to accept his invitation? A frown tugged Zoe's mouth and brow, and she pressed her wedding ring through her glove. Exactly how married was she? She didn't know what the legalities might be, but the facts were that she had exchanged marriage vows with a man who was not dead and whom she had not divorced. She had a husband looking for gold somewhere out there in the Klondike wilderness.

"Zoe?"

"I'm thinking about it."

A slow smile lifted one corner of his lips. "This isn't a difficult decision."

"Actually, it is."

"Do you have other pressing matters? Appointments? Engagements? Urgent tasks?"

He knew she didn't have a thing to do except wait for his Indians to finish relaying the outfits from Canyon City to Sheep Camp. "Are other people going with us to view the glaciers?"

"No."

She pushed at the fingers of her gloves and then brushed at her skirt. Certainly she was beyond the age and innocence of needing a chaperon. But a married woman didn't go off in private with a single man, not if maintaining her good name and reputation were important to her.

But no one except Juliette and Clara knew that Zoe was married. And no one knew exactly how married she might be. All three marriages couldn't count. So did Jean Jacques's first marriage to Juliette count the most, or did his last marriage to her count the most?

"I brought fresh fish pulled out of the Taiya this very morning. Potatoes for roasting. Biscuits made with my secret recipe. And for the finish, bread pudding with raisins. Will that help you make up your mind?"

When she saw his grin, she laughed at how silly she must appear from his viewpoint. Tom was a family friend; they had known each other since childhood. Where was the harm in spending an afternoon together? He might well have invited her to accompany him to examine the glaciers even if he'd known that she was Mrs. Jean Jacques Villette. His invitation was a gesture of friendship, not courtship.

"I'd love to see the glaciers," she said.

"Good. What finally made up your mind? Was it my legendary biscuits or my devastating smile?"

"Neither," she said, laughing up at him. "I've started a letter home, and I'm telling Ma that I've run into you.

She'll want to know all about your packing business, how long you've been in Alaska, and what are your plans for the future. I don't dare mail my letter without including your news."

She hoped that mentioning Tom would soften Ma's shock at learning that her only daughter was in the Yukon chasing after a no-good husband. She hadn't mentioned the no-good part, but Ma would read between the lines and suspect that all was not as it should be in Zoe's marriage. A few hints would prepare the way for future shocks and revelations.

"Be sure to post any mail before you leave Sheep Camp. From here on, mail delivery will be spotty at best and more likely nonexistent." Tom nudged the gelding close to the rock and instructed Zoe to stand and jump on behind him.

Zoe hesitated only a minute, then raised her skirt high enough to swing a leg over and plop herself behind him. He kept his gaze steadfastly forward, and if he caught a glimpse of the heavy woolen knickers beneath her skirt, he gave no sign.

They rode away from the river and up a sparsely wooded slope. Once this side of the divide had been thickly forested, but now the trees had gone up in smoke, having fueled thousands of campfires since the gold rush began.

After almost sliding off the horse, Zoe stopped being silly and wrapped her arms around Tom's waist and hung on. He stiffened when she first touched him and then relaxed as if having her arms around him was the most natural thing in the world. In truth, she really didn't feel much of his body—mostly she felt and pressed against the heavy weatherproofed duster he wore.

They zigzagged up and up and up until the tents and telegraph poles were lost to view beneath layers of smoke and low-lying clouds.

"Can you hear the glaciers?" Tom asked after a while.

"I think so." A faint, eerie creaking made gooseflesh stand up on her skin. And she knew she would never be able to describe the ghostly groan of the glaciers grinding forward at a slow, inexorable pace.

Awed by the sheer frozen mass, Zoe didn't speak when Tom reined inside the blue shadow of an ice wall and then helped her to the ground.

"How long has this glacier been a glacier?"

"Why are you whispering?"

"I don't know," she said, taking a cloth from him and spreading it over the flattest boulder she could find. One day years and years from now, this boulder would be engulfed by the glacier. No memory of their picnic would remain.

While Tom built a fire with wood he'd brought from below, he told her what he knew about glaciers, and Zoe listened carefully so she could tell Ma in her letter.

"Are you cold?" he asked at the finish.

"A little," she admitted.

"Pull on your nose, that will warm it."

Laughing, she did as he suggested. "Would you like some help preparing our lunch?"

"Nope. I invited you." After explaining that the two large potatoes were partially cooked already, he pushed them into the coals beneath the flames. "There's hot beer in my canteen."

She didn't think she'd like hot beer, but it turned out she did. She suspected she would have welcomed anything warm.

They touched their mugs together, and Tom said, "Here's to old friends, the best friends." He gazed into her eyes and continued looking at her while he took a swallow of the beer. "You're still the prettiest girl in Newcastle."

"This isn't Newcastle," she said. But she blushed with pleasure. "Ma used to say, 'that Price boy could talk an angel out of her wings.'" Zoe smiled. "It was a compliment to you and maybe a warning to me."

Immediately she regretted passing along Ma's comment, which seemed to link them together in a way she hadn't intended. Uncharacteristically flustered, she set out plates and utensils.

"Did you bring salt?"

"Salt and butter for the potatoes are in my saddlebags."

"Butter?"

"Enjoy it. Butter is going to get very scarce, and it will cost the earth if you do find any."

While they waited for the potatoes to finish baking, they sat on rocks in the shadow of the glacier and drank hot beer.

"Tell me what you're doing in Alaska, Tom Price."

"You probably know that I went into the mine about the same time as your brother Jack. I worked there for a few years," he said, refilling their mugs from the canteen. "I told myself I'd get out, leave Newcastle and seek my fortune elsewhere, but I didn't do it. My friends were in Newcastle, and that was more important. Eventually I moved into one of the houses on Shaft D Lane, and I started accumulating debt at the company store."

"My family knows about *that*."

"You remember Saturday nights."

"Payday."

"The night for drinking, fighting, and carousing." He smiled and shrugged. "Well, a bunch of us were at Ned's place, and I'll admit I'd had a few. Some company men came in, and after a while they asked if we were the skags who were talking strike. One thing led to another and—"

"—And a brawl erupted," Zoe finished for him. She'd heard depressingly similar stories every weekend during her growing-up years. And helped Ma doctor the black eyes and split lips, cuts and bruises, and scraped knuckles.

Tom nodded. "Turns out I gave better than I got. Seems I damned near killed one of the company men. Which meant the end of my days at the mine. I had to forfeit my last pay packet, got tossed out of the house on Shaft D

Lane, and I was given thirty days to clear my debt at the company store or go to jail."

"I think Jack told me about this." The story was coming back to her as Tom related it.

He sat with his legs apart, an elbow on the flat boulder, and his hat thumbed to the back of his head. Dark curls dropped on his forehead.

"Times were hard, and people talked about a national depression. I couldn't find work in Seattle. At the end of thirty days, I stowed away on a Russian trawler. I thought I'd end in the Orient somewhere, but the Russians came up here." He shrugged again. "I fished with the Russians for a while, made enough money to clear my debt back home. Eventually I bought a boat and started fishing for myself."

Zoe tried to imagine him as a seaman, captaining his own outfit. She had no difficulty picturing him at the helm of a fishing boat. Tom was the type of man who would be successful at whatever he undertook, particularly if he was the man in control. She suspected he made a better employer than employee.

"When the stampede to the Yukon began, I saw an opportunity. Not to join the prospectors, but to help them get where they're going. So I leased out my boat and started packing." He met her gaze. "I've made a fortune, Zoe." He shook his head and laughed.

"A fortune," she repeated in a low voice.

"Well, not a fortune like the Van Hootens have. I wouldn't say I'm wealthy, but I've put aside enough to buy a house and business when the stampede ends or after they get the train over the pass at Skagway, probably next year. I own a boat, a business, and I have investments. I'm proud of that."

"I'm proud for you," she said softly, staring at his fingernails. His nails were clean; there was no black miner's line. He had broken away from Newcastle, and he had prospered. Maybe fate had placed him in her path to underscore the extent of her pride and stupidity. She had waited for dross when gold had been right under her nose.

"Stay here while I check on the potatoes. Sorry to bore you with the long version of the Tom Price story."

"I wasn't bored." She watched him prepare the fish for grilling and supposed his cooking expertise came from camping. "Tom? Do you think you would have gotten out of Newcastle if the brawl with the company men hadn't happened?"

"I doubt it. Why would I? Everything and everyone who's important to me is in Newcastle." He shrugged, turned the fish on the grill over the fire. "Ma and two of my sisters still live in the hollow. My pa is buried on the hill. Given my druthers, I would have stayed in Newcastle."

Zoe gasped, and her spine snapped upright. "With all your prosperity and your accomplishments—you'd rather be working at the mine in Newcastle?"

"Conditions at the mine improve a little every year. Still, it's a hard life, I know that. But no man works alone. You have your mates there with you. And friends to share a pint after the whistle blows the shift change. There's Saturday nights at Ned's Place and sometimes a dance. And Sunday morning in the Price pew or explain to the Reverend Greer why not." He smiled.

"I don't believe this. Everyone in Newcastle wants out except you." She stared at him.

He studied her face with a curious expression. "Do you really believe that?"

"Of course I do! You're a perfect example of why people want to leave. You couldn't have made your fortune in Newcastle!"

Tom placed the fish on plates, added the potatoes, and heaped biscuits on the side. After serving Zoe and emptying the canteen into their beer mugs, he sat across from her at the flat rock.

"I'm glad I've prospered," he said after a minute. "I'll have things and I'll live a life I couldn't have lived if I'd remained in Newcastle and worked at the mine. But I've paid a price, Zoe. These have been lonely years. I don't have a wife and family like Jack does or like other friends do. I know a lot of people up here, but I don't know any of them well enough to tell them the story I just told you. Or to expect they would care if they heard it."

"But you've made something of yourself," Zoe argued. "You're better than you would have been if you'd stayed home."

His brow lifted, and he tilted his head. "I'm different, not better. I'm different because I've had experiences I couldn't have had in Newcastle. But I'm the same person I was, and I'd be that person no matter where I lived. Same as you."

That's what she hated and what she fought against. The idea that Newcastle was part of her, like ground-in dirt, and it always would be. "Don't you remember the Owner's Day Parade? They still have that parade, Tom. All the owner's friends and colleagues driving past in their fancy carriages, looking at us like we're trash, like we're there for their amusement." A long violent shudder shook down her spine. "I want to be better than trash. Better than someone to pity and laugh at."

"Why do you care what those people think? No one can make you feel diminished, Zoe, unless you let them do it."

"You're wrong," she said flatly. "But that isn't the point. The point is to improve yourself. I believe that people can overcome their backgrounds. I believe people can better themselves through education, or hard work, or . . . marriage." Her cheeks grew hot. Marrying to improve her lot hadn't worked out for her, but for some it might be a successful tactic. Tactic? No. She had married Jean Jacques because she'd believed she loved him. She felt sure of that.

Tom considered her comments. "You might better your finances or your position, but I don't think you make yourself a better person by accumulating money or learning more or by marrying well. We are who we are, and that's a mixture of the values we grew up with and our experiences and what we believe in and what we think is important. These values don't change with more education or harder work or a brilliant match."

He looked at her across the cloth spread atop the boulder. "And a person's values don't change with the scenery. If you're a loyal person in Newcastle, you'll be a loyal person in New York City. If you're honest in Newcastle, you'll be honest in Alaska." His gaze met hers. "You and me, we're never going to welcome debt, Zoe. We'll always remember our families scraping to pay the company store. That's going to be true no matter where we are in life or what we're doing or who we're married to. That's just one example of who we are, and an example of the Newcastle in us. And it's not a bad thing. You'll find good people and solid values in Newcastle. I don't see Newcastle as a background we have to 'overcome,' as you put it."

"Are you telling me that you didn't care about those people looking at you like you were a worthless piece of trash?"

"I'm telling you that I don't accept their opinion, if that's what their opinion is. I know the people at home. Those swells in the parade don't know anyone in Newcastle except the mine owner. When it comes to my friends and neighbors, I trust my own opinion more than anyone else's."

"Since you're so enamored of the place, maybe that's where you should buy a house and business when the Yukon boom goes bust and you return to the outside." Her voice snapped and crackled in the cold air. "But I'm never going back to Newcastle."

Tom laughed. "I'll always have ties to home, but Newcastle is strictly a company town, and I don't aim to buck the company again." They finished their lunch in silence, then he said, "So, Zoe Wilder. Why are you in Alaska?"

She wished he hadn't said that a person who was honest in Newcastle would be honest in Alaska. The best she could offer was a half-truth. "I'm looking for a man," she said after a pause.

"Ah, I see," he said in an offhand tone. But she knew he didn't see. "Would that be a specific man? Or do you mean you're looking for a man in the sense of seeking a husband?"

"A specific man," she said reluctantly, knowing she couldn't reveal much more without betraying her promise to Juliette and Clara. And she didn't want Tom to know that she had lied about not being married or that she was hunting a runaway husband.

"What's the man's name? Maybe I know him."

For Tom to know Jean Jacques, Jean Jacques would have had to go to Dyea instead of Skagway. He would have had to hire packers to get him over Chilkoot, and he would have had to choose Tom's company from the dozen or more packing companies in Dyea. Finally, he would have had to speak to Tom instead of one of Tom's employees. Certainly, such a chain of events could have happened, but Zoe thought it unlikely. She hoped it was.

"I doubt you know him," she said, wishing she had evaded his question in the first place.

"Zoe? Look at me." When she glanced up, his green eyes were clear and steady. "You can trust me."

"It isn't that I don't trust you," she said, rising from the rock she sat on. "I don't care to discuss this subject with anyone, not just you."

"You're saying it's none of my business." A grin widened his mouth, and then he laughed. "Now there's a reason I understand."

"I'm getting cold, and I'm concerned that my traveling companions are worried that I didn't turn up for lunch."

Rising, he picked up their plates and utensils. "We

don't see things quite the same, do we? It's funny. I felt certain that we would."

Oddly, she had also assumed they would agree on everything. She felt let down. Disappointed. Tom's expression told her he felt the same way.

They scattered the wood ash in front of the glacier, almost like an offering before they packed away the plates and mugs. Zoe waited beside the gelding while Tom buried a handful of food scraps.

When he returned, he walked toward her with a purposeful stride, his gaze on her face. Before she understood what he intended, Tom had placed his cold hands on either side of her face and tipped her mouth up to his.

"For years I've promised myself if I ever had a chance to kiss Zoe Wilder, I'd do it or kick myself forever after. I never thought that chance would come."

He gave her a moment to understand, a moment to pull away. But surprise and—curiosity, perhaps?—rooted her to the frozen ground. Her gaze locked to his, and her eyes widened—her lips parted.

He didn't hurry. When he realized she wouldn't step free, he stroked the back of his hand across her cheek, traced his thumb along the curve of her lower lip.

Gently he pulled her past the edges of his duster and into his body, reached beneath her cape to circle his hands around her waist.

Zoe drew a quick sharp breath. This was wrong. She knew it, knew she should pull away before they crossed a line they could not uncross. But his green gaze trapped hers and held her powerless to resist.

His hands on her waist pressed her tighter against the hard length of his body, slowly, deliberately. There was no awkwardness, no need for adjustment. They fit together easily, magically. Tom held her close until they began to feel each other's heat along their hips and stomachs, and he gazed into her eyes while nerves ignited and two mouths dried.

Finally, when Zoe feared the tremble building inside would erupt into outer shaking, when she thought her heart might pound through her chest, he lowered his mouth to hers.

The hot thrill of his lips shot through her body, and she forgot that they stood in the shade of an ice wall. The heat of his mouth and body enveloped her, set her skin aflame. And an unexpected jolt of yearning brought her arms up around his neck.

What began as a gentle, tender kiss deepened into something Zoe could not have predicted. Sudden, overwhelming desire rocked her body. Tom's hands tightened on her waist, then he cupped the back of her head in his palm, kissed her hard, and moved against her as if he needed to be closer, closer. And heaven help her, that's what she wanted, too.

When they pulled back to look at each other, their breathing was quick and ragged.

"My God," Tom said softly.

Zoe couldn't speak. She sagged in his arms and lowered her forehead to his shoulder. Tears choked her.

Everything about this moment was wrong. Tom was a Newcastle boy who prided himself that he would always be a Newcastle boy. Zoe was a married woman. She had lied to him about her status, could not confide the truth about coming to the Yukon to find and kill the man she had married.

"Please," she whispered, stepping out of his arms. "Please don't do that again."

It seemed that a lifetime passed during the time he stared at her. Then his expression stiffened, and he apologized.

Quickly, she placed a finger across his lips. "No, don't. I'm as much to blame as you. I could have stepped away. I could have said no. I should have."

"Why?"

Right now it didn't matter that she had agreed with the others not to tell anyone they were all married to the same man. Right now, pride stopped her tongue. Her battered self-esteem wanted Tom to believe she was desirable. She didn't want him to know how blind or deluded she had been, or that her husband had abandoned her without a backward glance.

"I'd like us to remain friends," she said, turning from him.

"We'll always be friends."

"Friends don't kiss like that. It's better to pretend it didn't happen."

For a full minute he remained silent. Then he touched her shoulder. "Something happened, Zoe. I didn't imagine it, and neither did you. Pretending isn't going to change what I felt."

"I think we should leave now," she insisted, blinking hard as she walked toward the gelding. He wanted her to admit that she'd felt something, too. But she couldn't.

Maybe she still felt a minuscule dollop of loyalty toward the man she had married. Maybe it felt indecent to press her body and her lips to one man while she wore another man's wedding ring. Maybe she simply did not want to admit she could desire a man from Newcastle.

Silently Tom mounted the gelding, then extended his hand to swing her up behind him. After a tiny hesitation, Zoe wrapped her arms around his waist and leaned her cheek against his back.

Tears burned her eyes. If Jean Jacques Villette had appeared right now, she could have killed the bastard without a pang of remorse.

Chapter 11

The trail bent sharply upward from Sheep Camp toward an area known as the scales. Clara made the three-mile ascent in a thick snowfall that didn't thin out until she reached the scales, where she had agreed to meet Juliette and Zoe.

Once she caught her breath, she raised her eyes to Chilkoot Pass and her heart sank. A single file of men struggled up one thousand feet at a forty-five-degree angle. The barren treeless snow-covered slope looked a straight perpendicular from Clara's vantage point.

Here and there a spent form dropped out of the line, and the man giving up came tumbling down the snowy incline in a dangerous uncontrolled fall. The controlled descent lay on the far right of the climbing men. A trough called the grease trail had been worn into the snow by those who had reached the summit and were now sliding down on the seat of their pants to fetch another load of goods before they made the nearly impossible climb again.

"It takes from three to six hours to reach the top," a growly voice said at her side. "Unfortunately, the pace is set by the slowest climber."

Clara pulled a heavy scarf away from her mouth and nose and refused to notice that her pulse accelerated when she heard his voice. "How do the men keep their footing?" she asked, holding her gaze on the climbers. They made her think of a line of dark ants steadily advancing up a steep and snowy anthill.

"See those sourdoughs standing at the bottom? They cut steps in the ice. Fifteen hundred steps. If you want to use their staircase—and everyone does—you have to pay a toll."

She nodded. Opportunists abounded in this wild inhospitable land, most of them seeking to profit from the prospectors' desperate push to reach the gold fields. Governments profited, too. At the top of Chilkoot, Canadian Mounties would collect customs duty on all supplies before the cheechakos were permitted to enter Canada. One needed a fat purse to survive this journey.

The ragged mountain peaks that surrounded them were as craggy and intimidating as Bear Barrett's face, Clara decided without looking up at him. She edged away, but he stepped forward, moving closer this time.

"All right," he said after a minute. A long breath expelled vapor from his lips. "I apologize for saying aloud that it would be easier if you were a woman of loose virtue, or whatever it was I said. I didn't intend to offend you, and that's the truth."

She stood in unmoving silence so long that her feet started to chill despite thick stockings and heavy boots. "I accept your apology," she said finally, as they had both known she would.

"Just once I would like to get through a single damned conversation without one of us getting mad."

She shifted to look at him through the diminishing fall of snowflakes and sucked in a breath. "What in heaven's name have you rubbed all over your face?"

"Bacon grease and wood ash. I recommend it to you and your companions to protect against wind and cold."

Immediately Clara felt the raw fire in her cheeks raised by altitude-frigid temperatures and the steady wind blowing off the glaciers. But she couldn't quite imagine herself smearing that mess on her own face.

A twinkle appeared in the brown-bear eyes peering out of ashy gray holes, and she noticed the defined contours of his lips since they, too, were outlined in grease and ash. Feeling her own mouth go dry, she swung her gaze back to the line of men struggling up the ice steps.

"Have you thought about our rematch?"

"I don't recall agreeing to any rematch," she said, feeling the bulk of him immediately behind her.

"I think we should go for the best two out of three."

The vapor from his breath puffed above and to the side of her hat, trailing away while she watched. "Maybe," she said, smiling. "I'll consider it."

"Excellent!" His pleasure made her wonder if he'd been in more fights, defending himself from snickers or snide comments. "So. Are you ready to make the ascent? I'll follow behind you."

If he did, she would feel his gaze on her bottom for the next three to six hours and agitate herself wondering what he was thinking—and thinking unseemly thoughts herself. Now a stream of vapor sighed from her lips. This huge shaggy man was driving her crazy. An example of her craziness was her embarrassing desire to shove him down in the snow and then jump on top of him. And it was shameful how Bear's presence obliterated all remembrance of Jean Jacques, her thieving no-good stinkbug of a husband.

Suddenly her gaze sharpened, and she peered hard through the diminishing snow. "Is that Juliette standing in the ascent line?"

Bear narrowed his eyes and nodded. "It looks like her."

"We agreed to meet at the scales and make the climb together."

She and Bear reached Juliette in fifteen minutes, ignoring shouts of "get in line," and "wait your turn."

"What are you doing?" Clara demanded. "You were supposed to wait for Zoe and me." Juliette continued to astonish her. Clara would have wagered all she owned that she and Zoe would have to drag Juliette up Chilkoot

Pass. But here she was. The first among them to join the climb line.

Juliette raised liquid eyes and an ashen face. She tugged at a frost-white scarf wrapped around her throat and mouth. "If I stop to think about this, I'll never do it. I need to keep going." She gripped her gloved hands together. "Oh, Lord. I'm just . . . I'm so . . . Oh, Lord. This is going to be . . ."

The line inched forward, pushing Juliette closer to the men collecting the toll. Clara considered Juliette's petite form and delicately boned face. Already her hem was caked with heavy ice, and her cheeks burned red with cold. The shoulder pack containing a bite to eat and a canteen of hot tea looked too big, like the pack would topple Juliette at the next step. It seemed inconceivable that such a small fragile creature could make a climb that was defeating men twice her size.

As if to underscore Clara's thoughts, a yell caught her attention, and she turned just as one of the men who had stepped out of line hurtled down the slope, bouncing from snow-covered rock to snow-covered rock. He landed at the bottom near the line waiting to ascend. When someone rushed to help, it became apparent that his fall had broken several bones.

There was nothing to say except good luck. And, "I'll meet you at the summit." She gazed up at Bear. "That goes for you, too," she said, before leaving to search for Zoe.

"I'll buy you that cup of coffee at the top," Bear called, giving her a jaunty wave. He focused a doubtful scowl on Juliette before he, too, strode away.

Clara found Zoe at the scales staring up toward the summit with shock and dread. "I'd rather sail around the world than make that climb," she whispered when Clara asked if she was ready.

Clara knew how to get her moving. "Juliette is already in line."

"What?" Zoe swung around, squeezing her eyes into

a glare. She swore for a full minute and then sighed heavily. "Damn it. Is she with Ben Dare? Is she attempting this to impress him?"

"I didn't see Mr. Dare."

"Damn," Zoe said again, infusing a volume of feeling into the word. She stamped her boot in the snow and ground her teeth together. "I cannot tell you how much I detest Jean Jacques! I hope he goes straight to hell after I shoot his butt."

"Before you can shoot him, we have to find him. That means we have to climb Chilkoot Pass."

Clara fixed her gaze on the antlike line toiling upward, and her heart fluttered. A word of encouragement from Bear would have been welcome. But like Juliette and Zoe, he appeared to assume that Clara had no fear. Sturdy ole Clara, that apple-cheeked workhorse, she would make the climb, don't worry. Well she was scared to death that her legs would give out midway, or that she'd lose heart, or slip and slide to the bottom in a pile of broken bones. Heights had never been her forte.

Silently, she watched a man walk toward the line with a dog draped around his neck and shoulders. The incline was too steep for animals, the sled dogs had to be carried over the pass. Most of the men would make that horrible climb seven or eight times with at least a hundred pounds on their back.

"All right," Zoe said, her teeth and fists clenched in determination. "Let's climb that bastard."

"Go ahead. I'll be along in a minute," Clara promised, as Zoe stomped away from her toward the toll line.

She would have run naked through the snow in front of everyone before she would have admitted that right now she had less courage than Juliette and Zoe. Reaching deep, she searched for the willpower to make herself join the line.

*   *   *

Climbing Chilkoot Pass was the worst experience of Juliette's life. The absolute worst. Altitude thinned the air she fought to suck into her lungs. Her feet and hands were so cold they tingled. All she could see was the seventy-five-pound pack carried by the Indian woman directly in front of her. She couldn't see ahead and didn't know why the line stopped moving every now and then. Like everyone else, she seized those moments to rest and try to regain her breath. But then she became aware of her calf muscles knotting and twitching in violent protest against the grueling climb. When the line moved forward again, her legs were shaking and her back ached. Her throat hurt, her chest heaved, she couldn't breathe.

She couldn't do this.

Staggering, she stepped out of the line and sat in the snow, digging her heels in to prevent an undignified slide to the bottom. Lowering her head over her knees, she gasped for breath, trembling in every limb.

She had no idea how long she'd been sitting, guiltily aware of the line struggling past her, before Zoe dropped into the snow at her side. But it was long enough to get thoroughly chilled even though she had drunk all of her hot tea.

"I'm dying," Zoe gasped between gulps for air. "I ache all over. This pack weighs a million pounds. I swore I wouldn't thank you for paying Tom the major share of our packing fees, but I thank you. If I had to climb this again, I'd shoot myself."

"I tell you, I didn't—"

"Just remember I said I'm grateful."

It was hopeless to argue. "At least it's stopped snowing."

She didn't know why she said that. Whether it snowed or not wouldn't make the ice stairs shorter or less steep. She didn't say anything more for five minutes, silently praying that Zoe would say, "Let's slide to the bottom and go home. Let's forget about Jean Jacques Villette."

What Zoe said instead was, "Look. There's Tom, carry-ing a dog on each shoulder."

When Tom spotted them resting, he stopped, halting the men behind, and wordlessly beckoned them back into line in front of him. Zoe muttered under her breath and then stepped onto the ice stairs. Tom looked at Juli-ette and waited.

Pride brought her to her feet and reluctantly back into line. It cheered her somewhat to climb past men who had fallen out to catch their breath. She wasn't the only one experiencing grave difficulty. But she began to doubt that she could reach the summit. Her lungs couldn't pull in enough air, her leg muscles burned, and her feet steadily became too heavy to lift to the next step.

She went as far as she could, then she fell out of line again, giving Tom an apologetic look as she dropped down in the snow, sweaty and gasping hard for breath, half be-lieving that she was having a heart attack. Now it was a long way to the bottom and the possibility of sliding down frightened her, but she decided she could do it. She had to do it because she simply wasn't strong enough to make it to the summit.

"On your feet, woman," a voice boomed. "You'll catch your death if you let yourself get too cold after sweating."

For a minute she thought she was looking at a mon-ster. Then she recognized Bear's eyes peering out of a gray greasy mask.

"I can't," she whispered, shaking her head. Exhausted tears of defeat glistened in her eyes.

"I'll help." Catching her hand, he jerked her to her feet and back into line. Then she felt his huge hands on her buttocks, pushing her up to the next step.

Embarrassment scalded a face already red from the wind and cold. She was too frozen to feel his hands through her petticoats, her skirt, her coat, and his gloves. Still, it was indecent. But she didn't say anything, she just let him help her up one step and then another and another. But eventually, even Bear's assistance wasn't enough to keep her going. She was simply tuckered out, done in from exhaustion and strenuous effort.

"I'm sorry," she muttered, stumbling out of the line.

He frowned through the monster mask, then shrugged and moved on. And she felt like crying. The slide down terrified her. But she could not go another step farther, her feet were chunks of lead, her lungs burned, she shook all over. And now she was stuck two-thirds of the way up Chilkoot Pass, unable to go on up and too frightened to slide down. She no longer believed she could slide to the bottom without enduring severe injury.

Weeping, she ate her sandwich and the last of her apples, not because she was hungry but in an effort to lighten her pack.

"You miserable weakling."

Choking on hopelessness, she opened her eyes and discovered Clara standing on the ice steps glaring at her.

"Get up and get back in this line," Clara hissed. "Every man who passes you is feeling vindicated. Women don't belong in the Yukon. We're the weaker vessel. We aren't tough enough." She gasped between the words, sucking air into her chest. "Get in this line before you totally disgrace your sex. Be a man."

"I'm not a man," Juliette protested weakly, blinking hard. Teardrops had frozen on her lashes. "And I admit I'm not tough enough. They're right."

"If I can do this, so can you. Get the hell back in this line! And I mean right now!"

Ice caked her scarf and coated her skirts almost to the waist. She hardly had enough strength to get up and step back into line, let alone climb more steps. But Clara's scorn got her moving again. For one bitter moment, she couldn't endure the thought that Zoe and Clara would succeed where she could not; that notion gave her a tiny motivating burst of energy. Anger pumped her muscles and stiffened her determination, and she scraped together enough willpower to fight upward. This time she labored behind Clara, listening to ragged breathing, watching Clara's legs tremble with fatigue when the wind caught her skirt. The line moved forward at an excruciating and inexorable pace.

But the moment came when she could not lift her foot up one more step. She simply could not. Over the hours, the muscles she needed to climb had played out. Her throat was dry and burned from the effort to draw in enough icy air to fuel her lungs. The weight of her pack threatened to pull her over backward.

Like a dumb animal seeking relief, she turned out of line and sat hard on a rock buried beneath inches of snow. And she cursed herself for not sliding to the bottom when the bottom was a short distance away. Now she stared down nine hundred feet and knew the fall would break every bone in her body if not kill her. But she could not make it to the summit. Fresh tears of fear and panic froze on her cheeks.

"Resting a minute is an excellent idea," Ben said, dropping down beside her.

She hadn't seen him step out of the line, it was as if he magically appeared. And she was so glad to see him. Turning blindly, she dropped her head and pressed her forehead against his chest.

"I can't go farther," she gasped between shuddering sobs.

He held her tightly as if he feared she would go careening down the mountain side if he released her. "We're almost to the top. It's only another fifty feet or so."

It might as well have been a mile. She couldn't do it. She said so, sobbing until no more tears would come. Then she realized she was sitting in the snow with a man's arms around her and his lips against her hair in full view of the hundreds of men dragging themselves up the ice steps. The impropriety of it rocked her, and she pulled back.

"Don't move too suddenly," Ben warned, concern darkening his eyes. Vapor fanned from his lips and bathed her cheeks in warmth. "You don't want to set off a snow slide. Or fall. There'd be no stopping if you begin to slide." He gripped her arms through her coat sleeves, steadying her on the buried rock.

His beard had completely filled in and he wore it a bit shaggy like the other prospectors did. And like them, he wore sturdy all-weather trousers today, a loose sweater, and a drill-cloth coat with the heavy lining removed for the climb.

She brushed the fingers of her gloves across the green scarf tied through a buttonhole of his coat. "Would your wife have made this climb?" she asked. Good heavens. Where had that question sprung from? She tried not to think of his late wife just as she tried not to think of her present husband.

"Helen? I doubt it." Smiling, he carefully swung his pack around to his chest, then found his canteen and opened the lid. "It's hot coffee," he said, handing her the container.

Ignoring the line moving to the side of her and the steep life-threatening fall below her boot tips, Juliette lifted the canteen. She hated that they had no cups and had to drink directly from the mouth of the container, but she wanted a hot drink more than she needed to stand on proper manners.

"Helen would have researched every detail about Chilkoot, about the Yukon, about gold prospecting. She would have loved learning about it, would have loved the idea of being here, but she would never have actually come."

"Whereas I hate the idea of being here, but I did come," Juliette said unhappily. She accepted the canteen for another sip of coffee, feeling the warmth travel from her throat to her stomach. "Tell me about Mrs. Dare," she said, her voice almost conversational now that she'd caught her breath. "That is, if you're comfortable talking about her and don't mind."

At the moment it didn't strike her as improbable or strange to be sitting in the snow less than a hundred feet from a windswept Alaskan summit, staring down at a sheer drop while hundreds of men trudged past not three feet away. This was the only place she could be: she lacked the energy to go up and the fall down would probably kill her.

"Helen was an admirable woman," he said after a moment. "She was tireless in her efforts to promote women's suffrage, and she helped expose the suffering of Chinese women forced into slavery and prostitution."

Juliette's mouth rounded as he spoke. He had said the word *prostitution* in her presence. And he spoke in an even tone as if he didn't realize her proper response should be to clap her gloves over her ears and depart, never to speak to him again. Or was that indeed the proper response? Could it be that Aunt Kibble's notions of propriety were more rigid than what the rest of the world imposed? It was something to think about. Later.

"Do you have children?" she inquired, staring at him in fascination. She envisioned Ben and his wife engaged in stimulating discussions about taboo topics. Obviously he didn't think less of his wife for her interest in subjects proper ladies were not supposed to know about. The freedom of such a relationship staggered her mind.

"No children."

Juliette glanced at the green scarf while they sipped coffee and Ben spoke about his late wife. When his voice trailed, they sat in silence.

Juliette thought about Helen Dare. Juliette knew nothing about prostitution and couldn't have discussed the practice if her life depended on it. As for women's suffrage, she didn't know enough about it to have an opinion. The only thing she could do to earn Ben's admiration was to climb the rest of this damned staircase and reach the summit. Lordy.

Bowing her head, she touched her fingertips to her forehead and grimaced. Now she was silently swearing. What next? Drinking liquor, smoking cigars, and cursing in public? She was keeping bad company, that was clear. She was picking up egregious habits from Clara and Zoe.

"Well," she said, drawing a deep breath as he replaced the canteen in his pack. "Are you ready to finish the climb?"

What a hypocrite she was, conveniently forgetting her earlier tears and protests and making it sound as if she was eager to resume the torture. She refused to consider that she was willing to push her limits to the point of peril in order to compete with a dead woman.

"If you are," he said, meeting her gaze.

It seemed they looked into each other's eyes for an eternity, unconsciously leaning toward each other, lost in pools of escalating speculation. Then Juliette turned aside, her cheeks flushed with more than cold. She was no longer an innocent. Now she knew what the fluttery feeling in her stomach meant. And the dry hot taste in her mouth. And the bitter sweetness of longing. And she recognized the desire in Ben's eyes.

"We should be ashamed of ourselves," she whispered.

"I beg your pardon?"

He shouldn't look at her that way after just speaking of his late wife. Moreover, Juliette was a married woman. Neither of them should be thinking about long kisses and sweet caresses.

Rising quickly but cautiously, driven by conflicting wishes to escape what she saw in his gaze and to impress him, Juliette smiled at the first man to glance up and said, "Excuse me, please." When the man halted in surprise, she stepped in line in front of him, waved Ben forward, then politely thanked the man who had opened a space for them.

During the next forty-five minutes, a long empty stretch opened between Juliette and the man in front of her as her pace slackened. The line behind her slowed to a snail's crawl.

Finally, Zoe and Clara pulled her up the last four ice steps and into the wind and ground fog sweeping the summit. They held her upright until her legs stopped shaking and she could support her weight.

"I'm going to faint," she whispered, hanging on to them.

"You're tired and hungry and cold. The wretched wind cuts like a knife." Clara greeted Ben, then adjusted Juliette's scarf around her cold-stinging cheeks. "A pound of wood is fifty cents up here, it's an extravagant luxury. But Bear and Tom chipped in to buy enough wood for an hour's fire. We've been waiting for you and Mr. Dare."

"How did you know we'd be together?" Juliette asked.

Clara rolled her eyes, implying that of course she assumed Juliette and Ben would be together. Shock widened Juliette's eyes. Was her growing affection for him that obvious? And what did Clara and Zoe think about it? Did they consider her a fallen woman? Disreputable?

Brooding, she followed Clara and Zoe through hundreds of piles of goods and the drifting wisps of fog. Ben slipped an arm around Juliette's waist to support her, but she froze at his touch and then politely stepped away.

When Bear spotted them he grinned and gave a booming "Hoorah! You made it. Tom? Light the fire. I promised a certain lady a cup of hot coffee, and she's been waiting a while now."

Fully recovered from the exhausting climb, Clara laughed and made a remark about the ash and grease on Bear's face. Zoe brushed snow off a tree stump, then sat arguing with Tom over how best to arrange the precious wood for the hottest fire. Ben rifled through Bear's goods to find camp stools.

And suddenly tears blurred Juliette's vision. Because of these people, she had reached the summit.

She, who had never ventured more than half a mile from Linda Vista, was standing on top of Chilkoot Pass in Alaska. She, who disliked and feared new experiences, had just done something that few women would ever do. And that several men had failed to do.

Her swimming eyes widened with awe and wonder. Climbing Chilkoot Pass, succeeding, was a feat she would be proud of all of her life. But she couldn't have done it without Benjamin, Bear, Tom, and her husband's other wives.

She would have gone sentimental, let the tears fall, and gushed gratitude except she was a bit irked that none of them had congratulated her or applauded her success. They seemed to take it for granted that she had eventually reached the top, and didn't appear to think it remarkable.

On the other hand, she thought as she held her gloves to the heat of the fire, maybe the feat wasn't all that remarkable. She was no longer the person she had been. It seemed a lifetime ago that she had taken to bed in sick anxiety at the thought of moving to Oregon with Jean Jacques. She could no longer quite remember why moving to Oregon had frightened her so.

When everyone had coffee, Bear raised his cup in a salute. "Only six hundred and some miles to go," he said, laughing at the chorus of groans.

Juliette's bubble of self-congratulation burst abruptly.

"I know," Ben said, smiling down at her. "You think you can't do it."

She started to agree, then her chin came up. "Maybe I can."

The others laughed, but Ben nodded and said softly, "I know you can."

She wanted to kiss him for his faith in her. Wanted to kiss him because she dreamed about it night and day. But of course she didn't. From now on she would not let herself forget that she was married. She would try to regain Clara and Zoe's respect.

But she gazed into his eyes and felt his warm breath on her cheek, and oh, how she wished that she were free.

Chapter 12

One of the objectives for this trip had been to push himself physically, Ben reminded himself as he redistributed the weight of his backpack. He carried essentials, a twenty-pound arctic sleeping bag, matches, a canteen of coffee, beef jerky, and dried apples. An extra pair of dry socks and gloves, a pocketknife, and a candle stub were in the side flap.

Now that he was seasoned to the trail, his shoulders no longer felt as if they would fall off after a long day of toting his pack over terrain that would have been difficult in summer and was treacherous now that snow concealed loose rocks large and small. Still, he felt the strain and muscle fatigue at the end of the day in his shoulders and legs.

As he had hoped, a yearlong numbness was gradually giving way to the rigors of the journey and the beauty of the wilderness. Yesterday he'd observed a family of caribou near dusk, and this morning rabbits had scampered across the snow when he startled them by rolling out of his sleeping bag. It was impossible to ignore the biting cold air on his face and at the back of his throat. Impossible not to feel a satisfying exhaustion that led to a sound night's sleep.

The smell of coffee first thing in the morning was a pleasure he had forgotten. And after a long fatiguing day, he would have sworn his beans and bacon were the tastiest dinner he'd ever wolfed down. He was more aware of what happened around him; he even wondered if his hearing had improved.

Not all of the changes were positive. There were evenings when he pulled the sleeping bag up around his ears and suddenly realized he had not thought about Helen all day. The first time it happened, he'd stepped outside his tent, too upset to sleep. The second time he'd walked to keep warm and had struggled with feelings of guilt. How could he pass an entire day without thinking about her, without remembering that she was gone?

From there, he worried over questions that could never be answered. Had he found the best doctors and treatments for her? Had he made her last days as comfortable as possible? Done the right things, said the right things? Should he have left San Francisco or should he have remained near the cemetery?

And what would Helen have thought of Miss March? Would she have felt shocked and betrayed by his interest in Juliette? Would she believe a year of mourning wasn't enough? Would Helen have expected him to spend the rest of his life alone?

Juliette, he thought, frowning, forming her name in his mind as he searched for his cache of goods, brought to the camp by the Indian packers. Once he'd found it, he began to set up his small tent. Miss Juliette March was an intriguing, maddening enigma.

Since the day they'd climbed Chilkoot, Juliette had kept her distance, and when he did maneuver a moment alone, she behaved cordially, but erected a barrier of politeness between them. It was as if the startling incidents of closeness had never occurred. As if she had never wept in his arms. As if they had never sat on the side of a snowy mountain and stared at each other with growing desire. He felt certain he had not mistaken the signals sent by her parted lips and quickened breathing. And he well remembered his own rush of desire. It was the first time he had experienced a stirring since Helen was diagnosed.

Juliette's withdrawal baffled him. During the days of descending into a treeless valley he'd searched his memory for any offense he might have given. The only incident that came to mind was talking about Helen the day they climbed Chilkoot.

Listening to him speak about Helen hadn't seemed to upset Miss March at the time, but perhaps she had thought about it later and had taken offense. There were women who considered it insulting for a man to speak glowingly of another woman in their presence. If Miss March was such a woman, and this was the only reason he could think of to explain her behavior, he was glad he had discovered it now, because Helen would always be part of his life and memories.

If a few words about someone he had cared for was enough to drive Juliette away, then so be it. But it was disappointing.

The trail descended on a sharp incline past frozen waterfalls to the shore of Crater Lake. Within a month deep snow would conceal the huge stones and jagged rocks that were still visible and still difficult to climb over or around. Even Clara found the going hard.

"Did you hear about Mr. Coleman?" she inquired over a cold supper. The steep mountainsides no longer grew so much as a stick, and shrewd vendors charged a fortune for firewood. At her suggestion, they had decided to buy firewood only every other night. This was a no-fire night.

"Is it true he was killed?" Juliette asked, directing a tired frown down at her plate. Tonight's fare was canned corned beef, reconstituted dried cabbage, and cold dough cakes.

Clara had made the dough cakes yesterday when they had a fire. Mrs. Eddington, whom they'd met back at Sheep Camp, had told her how. You opened a sack of flour, tossed in some snow, salt, and baking powder, stirred it all together, then pulled off globs and fried the globs in bacon fat. Clara thought the result tasted like paste, but she had to admit the dough cakes were filling.

"Mr. Coleman is dead?" Zoe asked in surprise. "Isn't he the fellow who gave us each a piece of licorice a couple of days ago? He was a nice man."

Tilting her dough cake to the light of the lantern, Clara spread a teaspoon of berry jam over the top. The jam improved the taste a little. "He was about fifty yards below one of those idiots who are packing hundreds of pounds on a sled, even though there really isn't enough snow depth yet. The weight drives the runners through the snow and into the ground below."

"Tom told me about that," Zoe said. "The runners can hit rough ground, which often causes the sled to flip end over end and send it hurtling down the slope."

Juliette nodded. "Mrs. Eddington's husband insists there should be a rule allowing only the smooth-bottomed sleds instead of those with runners."

"But the flat-bottomed sleds are responsible for pressing down the snow and creating long dangerous stretches of glassy ice." Zoe shook her head. "Several people have fallen and broken bones in those sections. It almost happened to me."

"Do you want to hear about Mr. Coleman or not?" Clara asked irritably.

Zoe spread her hands. "He got hit by a fully packed runaway sled. What else could it be? I'm sorry to hear it."

They were beginning to recognize many of the other cheechakos and identify names with faces. What was making Clara irritable, however, was not meeting new people—that was interesting. Her irritation stemmed from not seeing much of the people she already knew. Namely Bernard T. Barrett.

"Does it seem to you that we haven't seen much of Mr. Barrett, Mr. Price, or Mr. Dare? It appears they've abandoned us," she added lightly, trying to make it sound like she'd only just noticed and didn't really care.

"I, for one, think it's good that we're not seeing as much of those gentlemen," Juliette said in the prissy voice that made Clara crazy. "When you implied that it was natural for Mr. Dare and me to be together, I realized I was spending entirely too much time with him. I am, after all, a married woman. And so are you."

Zoe finished her meal and scrubbed her plate with a handful of snow. "I think we should talk about that."

"I don't want to talk about Jean Jacques," Clara snapped. Thinking about that low-down no-good had given her the fury and the energy to climb Chilkoot Pass. She planned to cheer when Zoe shot him.

"I'd like to tell Tom the truth." Zoe held up a hand. "Just hear me out. Tom's a longtime family friend, and I don't feel right about misrepresenting myself to him. He asked outright if I was married, and I lied. That doesn't feel good. And there was," her face turned redder than could be accounted for by the frigid temperature, "something else that happened that wouldn't have happened if he'd known I was married."

Now that was interesting, Clara thought. And the incident wasn't difficult to figure out. Tom and Zoe must have kissed. Instant resentment stiffened her spine. Zoe had kissed another man. But she had not. And she had certainly wanted to. Well, damn. If she'd known the others were out there kissing men they were not married to . . .

"Have you kissed Ben?" she demanded, glaring at Juliette.

Juliette flashed as scarlet as Zoe. "Certainly not! Is that what you did, Zoe? You kissed Mr. Price? How could you! Even though Jean Jacques is a worthless scoundrel, he's still our legal husband. You're still one of his wives."

Zoe tossed her tin plate into the crate it had come out of. "I didn't say I'd kissed Tom. If I did—and I'm saying *if*—it would have been an accident. And that's my point. If I told him the truth, no further accidents would happen!"

Clara waved a hand at a thousand tents pitched along the lakeshore. "If you tell our story to Tom, how long do you think it will take for us to be laughingstocks? The gossip and scandal will run through this camp just like that." She snapped her fingers, the effect diluted by her gloves.

"I trust Tom not to tell anyone!"

"And maybe he wouldn't, but maybe he'd let it slip. I'd like to tell Bear the truth, too. I had an opportunity to admit I was married, and I didn't. That doesn't feel good to me either. But it would feel worse to admit I'd lied to him. And I don't want to risk everyone knowing our private business!"

"I'd like to tell Mr. Dare the truth, too," Juliette said slowly. "But I think I've inadvertently and completely innocently led him to mistakenly suspect that I might be a tiny bit interested in his company."

Clara sighed and sipped from a canteen of cold coffee.

"If he now discovered that I was married, what would he think of me? He'd think I was a promiscuous wife. He'd think I have the morals of a dog."

"Which wouldn't be true," Clara said after a minute, wondering if Bear would think that, too. "Jean Jacques had the morals of a dog, but we didn't and don't. And the truth is, we don't know our legal situation. We should have consulted an attorney, but we were in too much of a hurry to get up here and find that louse. My point is, it's possible that none of us are really married."

"We're really married. We went through the ceremony. And the wedding night." Juliette's cheeks flamed again.

"But was the marriage legal and binding? For all we know we might be free to marry again if we wished. We might be free to get on with our lives whether or not we run Jean Jacques to ground. For all we know, it's perfectly legal, permissible, and moral to spend time with Mr. Barrett. And Mr. Dare and Mr. Price," she added hastily.

"But maybe it's not," Zoe said. "Maybe Juliette's right, and enjoying another man's company makes us wicked women."

"I can't stand the thought," Juliette said, raising her gloves to her temples.

They fell silent for several minutes. Then Zoe jumped to her feet, swore, and kicked her cup into the night. "All right, I won't tell him. But I enjoy Tom's—friendship— and I'm going to spend time with him. I don't care what the two of you think." She glared at Juliette. "When we find Jean Jacques, you can tell him that I have the morals of a dog if you want to. I'd say he's in no position to cast stones on that score."

Juliette squared her shoulders. "When we find him, the only thing I'm going to say is 'I hate you.' Then I'm going to step aside and let you shoot him."

"After which one of us claims to be the widow. We go through his effects, and if he has any of our money left, we hire a lawyer to defend Zoe and we split whatever the lawyer doesn't take," Clara said in a tight voice. "As for this discussion, married women can have male friends. I've always thought so." Actually she'd always thought the opposite, but recent circumstances had changed her opinion.

Juliette closed her eyes and sighed. "I've lost the thread of this conversation. Have we decided anything?"

"We won't tell anyone how Jean Jacques married us all," Zoe said. "And we won't think less of each other for spending time with—our friends."

"We decided that?"

Clara nodded. "It's a sensible decision given our circumstances and our uncertain status."

Clara would have liked to jump to her feet, rush off to

find Bear, and plant a kiss on that man when she found him that would sink him to his knees. Her skin felt hot just thinking about grabbing him.

But she was reacting to her resentment that Zoe had kissed Tom and she hadn't kissed Bear. It wasn't right or proper for any of them to be kissing anyone. But at least she didn't have to feel guilty or wonder what Juliette and Zoe were thinking if they came upon her enjoying Bear's platonic company.

Still, if a kiss happened . . . Well, it was only fair since Zoe had done it. She couldn't wait to see him again.

Now that they'd discussed it, Juliette felt less self-conscious and guilty about spending time with Ben, although she hadn't seen him yet. She still wrestled with doing the right thing. And the right thing was by no means clear-cut. But she needed to know what it was, because every time she had ignored propriety and followed an impulse, she had either ruined part of her life or immersed herself in great difficulties.

But it did seem that she should be free to enjoy Ben's company. He was merely a friend, after all. Aside from a couple of thrillingly awkward moments, there was nothing romantic between them. No words or sentiments had been exchanged that she would be ashamed to hear repeated in a churchyard. She had conducted herself as a lady. And Ben might be only a prospector, but he knew how to act like a gentleman.

Pushing her gloved hands into her coat pockets, she kicked a stone and watched it skitter across the ice covering Crater Lake. None of the men she'd met on this journey were anywhere near what Aunt Kibble would consider a gentleman. Men of breeding and background did not pin their futures on discovering gold. A true gentleman traveled with a retinue and wouldn't dream of relinquishing his comforts to sleep in a small tent on frozen ground, eat the same monotonous beans and bacon every day, and wear himself out walking hundreds of miles to reach the Yukon.

She didn't know Ben Dare's background, but she reluctantly conceded that he wouldn't be here if he were a gentleman. On the other hand, he was liberal-minded and regarded women in a way that Juliette had not encountered before. Moreover, he made her feel interesting, and he made her suspect that she had potential to be more than she was. That frightened her a little, but it flattered her more.

She missed him. And she had no one to blame but herself. She had driven him away by bludgeoning him with inane politeness. It was disappointing that he'd given up so easily, but she had been the cause of their estrangement, if she could call it that.

Ben was heavy on her mind as she wandered out on the ice capping the lake. An inch of new snow covered the surface, but she felt the hidden smoothness beneath the soles of her boots, saw the tracks of animals in the snow. The strangeness of walking on frozen water interrupted her thoughts. If someone had told her a year ago that she would be walking on ice, she would have laughed and insisted they were dreaming.

A sharp cracking sound erased the smile from her lips. She didn't know exactly what the noise meant, but it sounded ominous, almost menacing. And now she noticed that she'd wandered beyond the animal tracks.

Panic stopped her heart when the ice seemed to give way beneath her feet, seemed to sink beneath her weight.

For an instant she couldn't move, couldn't think. Then she grabbed her skirts, fixed wide eyes on the shore, and dashed forward.

It happened fast. One minute the ice felt almost solid, the next second she dropped into water so cold that for an instant her brain and heart were shocked into paralysis.

Black icy water swallowed her whole, freezing against her face, penetrating her layers of clothing.

She had never learned to swim.

Thrashing wildly, the wet weight of her coat dragging at her arms, she tried to claw upward. The top of her hat banged against an ice ceiling, then broke through, and she gulped for air. She wasn't facing the shore, couldn't see if anyone had noticed her plunge through the ice. Throwing out her arms, she tried to lean on the surface with the idea of pulling herself out of the freezing water. But the ice broke, and she sank again. This time her toes touched a sandy bottom and she pushed off, but not hard enough. Her head didn't break water this time.

As her heavy clothing pulled her down, it occurred to Juliette that she was going to drown. In water shallow enough that a tall man could get his head above water to breathe.

She fought to bob up again, but her limbs were numb with cold and her effort feeble. In a second she wouldn't be able to help it, she would open her mouth and suck water into her lungs.

She was going to die. And not one person would shed a tear at her demise. It was a sad thought to have as her last. But there wasn't time to compose a thoughtful or eloquent last thought. The blackness closed over her and her water-heavy boots and clothing pulled her to the bottom.

Zoe couldn't believe her eyes. When she looked back at the snow-covered lake, Juliette had simply vanished. Then it struck her. Juliette was on the ice? The ice wasn't thick enough to walk on, and wouldn't be for at least another week.

"Oh, my God!" Wildly, she looked around for assistance. "She was on the ice!" Screaming to catch the attention of the men nearby, she ran to the shore and immediately spotted Juliette's footprints among those of a dozen small animals. "Help! Help me!"

"Get blankets and towels," Ben shouted, almost knocking her down as he ran past her and out onto the ice.

He'd taken only a few steps before he fell through. Swearing, he broke the ice ahead of him with his fists, leaving a jagged black path.

Horror paralyzed Zoe. Eyes wide, hands pressed to her mouth, she watched him struggling through the ice and water. The water reached his thighs, his waist, then his chest. Her heart pounded, each beat shouting hurry, hurry, hurry.

It wasn't until Mrs. Eddington tugged her arm and anxiously asked what had happened that Zoe came to her senses. "Bring blankets and towels," she ordered. "Go!" She saw Clara in the distance, preparing to launder a few things since it was a fire day, and she screamed Clara's name.

Now others came running, and another man plunged into the water, then another, struggling after Benjamin. Then Tom was suddenly on the shore, holding out his arms, stopping others from rushing into the icy lake.

"Too many people will confuse things. Give them room to work." He looked at Zoe. "Who?"

"Juliette. She can't swim."

Tom's expression turned grim. "Anderson! Bring enough wood for a bonfire. We'll worry about paying later. Move, man!"

One of the men who had gathered to watch scowled and spit on the sand and rocks. "What was the damned fool doing out on the ice? Everyone knows it isn't thick enough to walk on."

Clara paused in her rush toward the shoreline and pushed her face up close to his. "She's from California. She doesn't know about ice. So just shut your face." When she reached Zoe, she anxiously asked, "How long has she been under?"

"I don't know." Zoe twisted her hands together, wanting to plunge into the frigid water herself. But Tom was right. Too many people in the water would hamper the rescue effort.

Finally she noticed that Clara had snatched up blankets. And she realized Clara had guessed what had happened the minute Zoe screamed her name. Thank heaven their husband had married bright women.

Time slowed to a crawl. Out on the ice, heads broke the surface of the black water, gulped air, and vanished again. Zoe couldn't tell which of the heads belonged to Ben and which belonged to the other two men.

"I didn't treat Juliette very well," she said suddenly, staring at the lake. "I resented it that she was a real lady and that she'd had an easy life. I hated her for being Jean Jacques's first. And I hated her for paying Tom to pack us in."

"Her goody-goody ways made me want to smack her, and that prissy little holier-than-thou voice she spoke in sometimes." Clara also stared at the lake. "She doesn't know how to do anything useful."

"If she dies, I'll feel guilty all the rest of my life for the times I wished her dead or wished she would just disappear. Maybe God is punishing me by granting my wish. I can't stand it."

"I could have taught her more about cooking and laundry, but I didn't, even though she was willing to learn. It was more satisfying to criticize and sneer at her efforts."

"Oh, Lord! Ben's found her!"

He half swam, half pushed along the bottom, dragging Juliette by the collar behind him. When he could stand, he lifted her in his arms and stumbled toward the shore.

No one spoke. When Ben came out of the water, he turned Juliette in his arms, then went down on one knee and dropped her across the knee that was raised. A great gout of water shot from her mouth. But she wasn't breathing.

Zoe clung to Clara. "She's dead!"

When Zoe could bear to look again, Ben and Tom had placed Juliette on the ground, her head turned to one side, and Tom was pushing on her back. With each push, water gushed from her mouth. The other men who had participated in the rescue staggered out of the water and hurried to the fire Tom had ordered built on the shore. Mrs. Eddington was there, passing towels and blankets as the men stripped off their clothing. Ice had formed in their hair and mustaches.

Tom looked up and waved Zoe and Clara forward. "She's alive, but just barely. Get those wet clothes off her. Ben? You, too. Get out of those clothes before they freeze on you."

Clara pulled Juliette to a sitting position. Her face was as white as a corpse, her head lolled on her shoulders. With each weak cough, water and bile dribbled from the corner of her lips. She looked dazed and disoriented, but she was breathing.

A sob of relief caught in Zoe's throat, then she fumbled at Juliette's coat while Clara jerked off her boots and reached under her skirts to yank her stockings down and off.

Standing to one side, Tom helped Ben out of clothing that had begun to freeze and stiffen. Ben was shaking hard enough that bits of ice showered from his beard and hair. When he was near naked, Mrs. Eddington ran forward and pushed a towel and blanket into his hands, then hastily turned her back.

"*Mein Gott,*" Clara muttered, after she'd torn open Juliette's bodice because the buttons were frozen tight to the fabric. It would take too long to free and open them. "She's wearing a corset! I thought we all decided not to."

Wearing a corset into the Yukon was so like Juliette that Zoe would have laughed if she'd learned about it on another occasion. But Juliette was half-dead. Zoe didn't need a doctor to tell her Juliette's condition was very grave.

They were down to Juliette's chemise and knickers before Zoe sucked a breath between her teeth and stopped Clara before Clara ripped off the chemise. "Being naked in front of several hundred men would be her worst nightmare!"

Clara held her gaze a moment, then shouted to Tom and Mrs. Eddington to raise a blanket in front of Juliette for privacy. "Good idea," she muttered, tearing off the rest of Juliette's clothing.

Her body was mottled with cold and shook uncontrollably. Her teeth chattered in a staccato cadence. Zoe combed ice out of Juliette's streaming hair while Clara toweled her off.

"Can you stand?"

Juliette stared as if she had no recognition of knowing them. She didn't seem to understand what Clara had asked.

Stepping behind her, Clara grasped her under the arms and lifted. And suddenly Ben was there. A towel wrapped his waist, a thick blanket covered his head and body.

He opened the blanket and pulled Juliette against his naked chest, then closed his blanket around them both.

The only thing Zoe said was, "Are you warm enough yourself to warm her?"

Clara dropped a second blanket over Juliette's wet head. "Rub her arms and back."

Now Zoe became aware of the voices of the spectators. Later, when she remembered what happened next, she would recall several kind and gentlemanly comments. But right now, the only voices she heard were those making salacious and suggestive comments.

"What are they doing under them blankets?" Followed by laughter.

"I sure wouldn't mind being under there with a wet woman."

"I'd make her a lot wetter."

That was it for Zoe. Trembling with fury, she rushed toward the man who had made the last comment. His name was Jake Horvath, if she remembered correctly. "You're talking about a respectable woman, you swine!"

Her brothers had taught her not to make a fist around her thumb. If you didn't want to get your thumb broken, you tucked it tightly on the outside against the first and second knuckles.

She hauled back and drove her fist into the man's nose hard enough to feel something crack. Blood spurted from his nostrils, and he stared at her in shock.

"Good for you, little lady. He had it coming!"

"Oh yeah? He didn't say nothin' the rest of us weren't thinking."

A fistfight broke out on Zoe's right, then another to her left. In less than a minute, all hell broke loose. Three hundred people were shouting and fighting along the icy shore of Crater Lake.

Chapter 13

❦━━━━━━━❦

The hostile land and primitive living conditions strained tempers and frayed the nerves of weary men. Over the years Bear had seen brothers snap like twigs and try to kill each other. He'd watched two long-term partners saw a canoe in half so each had an equal share when they dissolved their partnership. He'd watched people go crazy and do crazy things along the trail. But he'd never seen anything like the scene that greeted his eyes when he returned from rabbit hunting.

Close to the shoreline two people appeared to be flapping their elbows under a mound of blankets, but no one paid any attention. And no one bothered to enjoy an expensive bonfire. But there was a hell of a lot of punching, kicking, gouging, stomping, swinging, and fighting going on. There must have been over three hundred men down there, fighting like an army in hand-to-hand combat. It was the biggest brawl Bear had ever seen. And he could hardly wait to throw himself right into the middle of it.

After tossing his rabbits and rifle and gloves to one of the spectators staying out of the fight, he waded into the melee looking for Jake Horvath and knowing that Jake would be looking for him. This was as good a time as any to settle their differences. But when he found Horvath, Horvath was sitting on the sidelines sopping up blood from a broken nose. Bear had to settle for a few of the men who had pissed him off by referring to him as a daisy-boy for letting a woman beat him at arm wrestling.

He'd happily flattened two men when he saw Zoe Wilder indiscriminately swinging a long piece of charred firewood, laying low anyone she managed to hit. Then he spotted Clara right in the thick of it, too. She had her skirts hiked up indecently high to give her room to kick. Any man who approached her got kicked between the legs. Five men lay at her feet, clutching their privates, groaning and throwing up.

Duty overcame Bear's pleasure in a good brawl. Someone had to get those women out of this before they got hurt. He tried shouting Clara's name, but the din was so loud his voice got lost in the noise. Throwing people out of his way, he fought toward her. By the time he reached her, she was facing away from him and another man lay writhing at her feet.

He tapped her shoulder and shouted her name.

Instantly, she turned. In the same fluid motion she stepped into him and brought her knee up hard between his legs. The ground shook beneath his body when he went down.

He saw her eyes widen and her hands fly to her mouth before pain exploded behind his eyes and between his legs. Damn it, she'd done it to him again.

Brooding, Bear sat hunched in front of his tent, staring at the flames of his campfire. Never in his life had he met a woman as magnificent as Clara Klaus. It was his profound bad luck that she was a respectable type. He had nothing to offer a respectable woman.

Even so, he couldn't get her out of his mind, couldn't stop watching her. Now that the days were considerably shorter, he'd developed a habit of standing in the darkness and observing as she and her companions ate their supper. He positioned himself so he could watch the firelight or lantern light flicker across her splendid skin. Now he knew that she preferred her own cooking, had learned that she constantly tucked a truant strand of hair behind her left ear. When she laughed, he smiled in the darkness. When she frowned or sighed, he wondered why and sometimes dared to hope that she sighed over him.

"We need to talk."

Well, speak of the devil and here she was. And she wore the hat he liked best, a winter green felt worn on top of a scarf that came down over her ears and tied beneath her chin. All he saw of her hair was a fringe of red curling on her forehead.

"Now why would I want to talk to you?" he said, as though he was still upset at her. But he waved her to a camp stool. Watched her fuss with the folds of a short walking skirt made out of brown duck. The color almost matched her coffee-and-cream eyes.

"I've come to offer my sincere apologies." The peachy tones in her cheeks were lost to flames of embarrassment. "I didn't know it was you. When you grabbed my shoulder, I reacted instinctively and I just . . ." She waved a mitten. "It's taken two days for me to find the nerve to come and speak to you."

He'd known she would. That's why he'd paid a king's ransom to get his hands on six bottles of German ale. He fetched two bottles out of his tent and brought them back to the fire.

"Apologies are drinking occasions."

"Thank you." Her eyebrows soared. "*Mein Gott!* Where on earth did you get this?"

He studied her, wishing he was more respectable or that she wasn't. Wishing he could forget her. Wishing he'd never seen those amazing breasts.

"For years I'm going to be hearing snickers about how you bested me at arm wrestling, then beat me up in a brawl."

"I am truly sorry."

"No man alive can claim to have beat me in anything."
Clara Klaus was the only person who had ever put his
arm on the table or his body on the ground. When he
thought about it, he didn't know whether to laugh or
swear or worship at her feet. But one thing was certain.
He'd have to whip every man in the Klondike to restore
his reputation.

But then, he could do that and he would enjoy it. So he
might as well forgive her. But not immediately.

"How is Miss March feeling?"

"She's stronger every day. Mortified that several hundred men might have glimpsed an inch of exposed flesh."
Clara smiled and shook her head. "She doesn't remember much about what happened. If Mrs. Eddington hadn't
told her, Juliette wouldn't have recalled that Mr. Dare
warmed her under the blankets with her completely naked,
and him mostly so. She won't see him. Won't come out of
the tent. But aside from some sniffling and sneezing and a
huge dose of humiliation, she'll be fine."

They drank the rest of the ale in silence, eyeing each
other and listening to the camp noises. Bear liked it that
she hadn't asked for a glass, but drank out of the bottle
like an ordinary person. She had some exemplary qualities for a respectable woman.

Still, she was nothing but trouble for a man like him.
That's why he'd been avoiding her and why he was mad
at himself for slipping around in the darkness to watch
her. He couldn't stay away from her.

"I need to say some things," he said at length. If she
kept gazing at him with those clear, steady eyes, and he
kept fantasizing over her ripe strawberry mouth, he would
do something he'd regret. Since he seemed to lack the willpower to forget about her, he'd have to make her take the
initiative and wash her hands of him. It was time for her
to understand that he was not husband material. There
was no future here.

"*Ja?* I'm listening."

Bits and parts of her reminded him of food. He didn't know what that meant. Her eyes were light coffee, her skin peachy, she smelled like apples. Her mouth made him think of strawberries. Her breasts were like melons. He wanted to taste every inch of her, wanted to nip and lick and suck and savor, wanted to make a meal out of this delectable woman. It would be a long time before he forgot about her.

"I keep thinking about you." He stared at her, every muscle tense and hard as stone. "In fact, I've been sneaking around in the dark just to look at you."

She blinked. "You are spying on me?"

"I guess I am. I didn't want you to know because you're no good for me, and I'm no good for you."

"Why do you think that?" She took a swig off the bottle, gazing hard at him as she swallowed.

"I own a saloon, Clara."

"I know. The Bare Bear. You won it from Jake Horvath."

"What would your father say about you keeping company with a saloon owner?" He knew the answer. Her father would object.

She surprised him by shrugging off the question. "Papa owned an inn. It was mine after he died. I imagine he'd see some similarities between your saloon and our inn."

"You own an inn?"

"I *used* to own an inn," she said, her chin coming up. A suspicious glare flickered in her eyes. Why, he couldn't guess. "I don't own anything now."

"What kind of an inn did you own?" The news didn't entirely startle him. He'd never been able to picture her sitting around wasting time with fancy needlework or china painting.

"One of the best of its kind. We didn't sell liquor, but we sold bed and board. We served the best food on the Oregon coast, I'm proud to say."

He drank the rest of his ale and thought a minute before his shoulders slumped. "It isn't the same. I don't guess you had nightly brawls at your inn. Or rinky-dink piano and cutthroat card games. I don't guess you had whores looking to make a buck off your customers," he added, watching her.

She was quiet, as he had expected she would be. Getting ready to jump up and march off in offense that he'd mentioned the whores who worked out of his saloon.

"I'm thinking. And I'm wondering—do the whores pay you part of what they earn?" she asked calmly, astonishing him.

"No," he answered when he could speak. "I charge them fifty cents a throw to use the rooms over the bar."

"How many—throws—does each whore have each night?"

He could not believe he was having this conversation with her. Or that she hadn't flounced away, never to speak to him again.

"It varies," he said finally. "With most of them, my take runs a dollar a night. Sadie usually pays six bits."

"Well, now. Let's see." Sucking in her cheeks, she looked up at a gray sky. "Adjusting for the Yukon's inflated prices, it probably costs you fifty cents per room for cleaning and laundry, would that be about right?"

Disbelief clouded his brain, and he didn't answer for a minute. "I suppose so."

"Bear," she said, lowering her head to look at him. "You have to stop renting rooms to the whores. You have to send them somewhere else."

"No, Clara," he said softly, almost sadly. It had taken her longer than he would have believed, but she'd reached the point of taking offense, as he'd known she would. "I'm a businessman in the business of owning a saloon. Whores are part of saloons. I don't expect a woman like you to understand, but I'd be foolish to close down a profitable side of the business."

"I understand perfectly because I'm a businessman, too." She pushed the ale bottle into the snow, then leaned forward. "But you're not making a profit. You're losing money."

"What? How do you figure that?" If she'd jumped to her feet and started dancing the cancan, he couldn't have been more surprised than he was at the turn this conversation had taken.

"Well, do the arithmetic. You're making fifty cents a night from everyone but Sadie. Sadie pays a bit more."

"No, I'm making a dollar a night from each whore."

"I'm talking after expenses. It costs you fifty cents a night to maintain each room. But if you turned them into regular hotel rooms, you could charge, I don't know, five or six dollars a night, maybe more, and your expenses would stay the same. You could earn four or five dollars a night for the same room."

His mouth fell open, and he stared at her. Then he sprang to his feet, paced, and swore steadily.

She was dead-on correct, and damn his hide, he'd never seen it, had never questioned an existing situation. Jake Horvath had made the deal with the girls, and Bear had simply continued Horvath's arrangement. The only flaw in Clara's argument was the price of a hotel room in Dawson City. He could get twelve dollars a night without changing a thing. If he spiffed up the decor, he could charge twenty bucks a night. Hell, the Grand Hotel two blocks from his saloon charged thirty-five bucks for a room. When the Grand opened, everybody in town had laughed and said no one in his right mind would pay thirty-five bucks for a place to sleep. Everybody in town had been wrong. The Grand Hotel filled to capacity every night of the week.

"I'll make a fortune with this idea," he said in a voice that turned husky when he gazed down at her. She was smiling and her eyes glowed with pleasure. My Lord, this was an amazing woman. "I could kiss you in gratitude," he said, giving her another opportunity to see his rough edges and stamp away.

Her smile widened, and she tilted her head in a manner that impressed him as almost coquettish. "I think you're too much of a gentleman to ruin my reputation by kissing me in public where everyone can watch."

Good Lord. His knees almost buckled. She wasn't stomping away, and she wasn't saying no. She was saying: Don't go kissing me in public.

Immediately his brain exploded in joy then feverishly began sorting through places in camp that might be private. And rejecting them all. Inside his tent was private, but the instant she stepped in there with him, the news would fly through camp, and her good name would be shot to smithereens. If he took her hiking, that, too, would be noticed, and besides, they could be seen on the barren mountainsides. He couldn't think of anyplace they could go that wouldn't compromise her.

Standing, she arched an eyebrow and gave him a long speculative look that made his chest tighten and his privates stiffen. What she could do with one lazy look ought to be outlawed. He wanted to grab her, jump on top of her, and roll around in the snow kissing her, among other things.

Finally she lowered her eyes, smiled, and walked away from his campfire without another word.

Some might have glanced at her and seen a ball of clothing with boots at the bottom and a green felt hat on top. But he saw an armful of woman with curves where there ought to be curves and muscle where there ought to be muscle. He saw the only woman who had ever made him feel less than invulnerable. She had bested him twice. That made her the most fascinating creature on earth.

Sinking down on his camp stool, his mind aflame, he studied the ale bottle she had pushed into the snow and thought about her mouth pursed around the lip of the bottle. Lord. Then he forced his thoughts to privacy. Where to find some.

Almost at once, his cabin at Lake Bennett sprang to mind. He made supply runs often enough that he'd built a cabin at the point where the Dyea and the Skagway trails converged. By the time he reached Lake Bennett, he was damned near desperate for a real bed instead of sleeping on the ground or on a camp cot that was too short and too narrow for a man his size.

His cabin would be very private. A wide grin curved his lower face, then he tilted his head back and shouted happily at the sky.

Now all he had to do was wait for Crater Lake to freeze solid, then hurry himself and Clara down to Long Lake and then Deep Lake, then Linderman Lake, and finally to the shore of Lake Bennett. Four weeks from now, five at the latest, he'd be licking strawberry syrup from those sweet lips.

"Has Ben come by recently?"

"You told us to tell him that you didn't want to see him," Zoe said, reaching deep for patience.

Juliette dropped back on her cot, her arms swinging off the sides. She stared up at the stovepipe exiting through the vent. "I need to express my gratitude, but I'm too embarrassed to see him. Do you think it would be unforgivably rude and improper if I just sent him a thank-you card? I sent the other two men a card. And there's a thank-you card on your cot and on Clara's."

Only Juliette would pack thank-you cards into the wilderness. "I don't claim to know the fine points of etiquette, but Ben did save your sorry life. And at great cost to his own. He could have drowned trying to rescue you, or he might have caught pneumonia afterward. It seems to me that he deserves something more personal than a thank-you card."

Actually the thank-you cards didn't surprise Zoe, not

after watching Juliette dispense little notes of appreciation to anyone who did her a favor or a courtesy. She had delivered thank-you cards to the late Mr. Coleman, who had given her a piece of licorice, to the man who let her cut in front of him during the climb up Chilkoot Pass, to Mrs. Eddington after Mrs. Eddington gave them the dough-cake recipe, and to the Chilkat responsible for transporting her outfit. The Chilkat couldn't even read.

"In my heart, I know it's proper to thank him in person," Juliette said unhappily. "But he saw me *naked*." She clapped a hand over her eyes. "How could you and Clara let that happen?"

"Oh, maybe because we were trying to save your life. Or maybe we took a walk, discussed it, and tried to decide what we could do to cause you the worst embarrassment of your life. And we concluded that we wouldn't let you freeze to death on the shore, but instead we'd tear off your icy clothing and let Ben Dare see you naked while he was trying to warm you and save you. If it's any comfort, I voted to let you freeze on the shore rather than cause you the tiniest bit of embarrassment." She made a face and sighed.

When she'd believed Juliette was dying, Zoe had vowed never again to treat her with impatience or bad temper. She'd already broken that vow a dozen times. To be fair, Clara irritated her, too, and there were signs that she annoyed both of them. Being cooped in the tent for almost a week might have something to do with everyone's short fuse. That's what her pa and brothers had called a quick temper—having a short fuse.

Sighing again and feeling a long way from home, she stirred the kettle of laundry on top of the camp stove, which they had moved inside the tent. Outside, a storm had pounded the Crater Lake area for almost a week, and the temperature had plummeted to a point well below zero—and that's where the thermometer stayed. Inside the tent, the camp stove radiated intense heat, forcing them to strip to their shimmies and knickers. Even then, they perspired. And suffered the boredom of confinement with nothing to do.

"I think the storm has ended." Juliette didn't sound as if she cared one way or the other. She'd been listless since nearly dying under the ice.

"The snow and wind ended sometime last night," Zoe agreed, stirring the kettle of laundry. Boiling laundry wasn't a problem. Drying laundry was the problem, so they didn't attempt to wash anything larger than hankies, stockings, and undies. They could hang these items on the cot frames to dry, but anything larger would have dragged on the ground and made it too humid and too crowded within the small tent.

"Zoe?" Clara shouted from outside, since they didn't open the flap unless they had to. "Tom's here. He wants you to go to the lake with him so he can show you how to drive a sled."

She stopped stirring and considered the effort involved in getting dressed in cramped quarters. With the stove inside, there was space for only one person to dress at a time, and you had to keep a sharp eye on hems so they didn't fall against the stove and catch fire. Four tents had burned in as many days.

"Go ahead and go," Juliette said, flinging an arm over her face. "I don't need tending anymore."

Zoe wasn't thinking about Juliette. She was thinking about Tom. They hadn't seen much of each other since the day they'd picnicked beside the glacier. In some ways, the day they kissed seemed a hundred years ago. In other ways, it was as immediate as last night's dream.

Feeling the back of her neck grow hot, Zoe frowned at the suds frothing on top of the laundry water. Tom was dangerous. He made her question long-held beliefs. He confused her. She couldn't sort out her feelings toward him. One minute he attracted her, the next he repelled her. And as hard as she tried, she couldn't forget the electric thrill of his lips or the hard length of his body pressed to hers.

"Tell him I'll be out as soon as I get dressed." Which wasn't at all what she wanted to say. Now she had to stand behind her words.

When she finally stepped outside, bundled up to the eyes, she noticed that Clara had swept loose snow away from the tent and she'd chipped the ice off one of the piles of goods so they could get to the foodstuffs. Today, Clara's energy and relentless good cheer annoyed Zoe half to death. And she didn't like the way Tom's eyes twinkled when he scanned the layers of clothing she wore. A heavy corduroy skirt over wool petticoats topped by a winter-weight shirtwaist and a thick sweater. A coat, a muffler, a pair of gloves beneath a pair of mittens, and a wool scarf that went over her hat and tied beneath her chin. She wore so much bulk that she couldn't see her boots.

"Are you laughing at me?" she said through her muffler.

"I'm not laughing." But she could see his lips twitching. He appealed to Clara. "Am I laughing?"

"No. I'm the one who's laughing." Her eyes crinkled above the scarf wrapping her throat and mouth. "We look like fat penguins, waddling along with our arms stuck out at the sides."

"What do you know about penguins?"

"In a bad mood, are we?" Tom asked, lifting an eyebrow. He'd pulled his scarf away from his mouth and she could see his smile.

"I'm either too hot or too cold. I've been stuck in that tent for a week. Juliette is driving me crazy. We're all starting to repeat ourselves. We've had no exercise. And I'm so sick of Alaskan strawberries and dough cakes that I could scream."

Alaskan strawberries was the name given to the pink half-cooked beans that everyone in camp joked about when they weren't complaining. No one had the energy to cook much else even if they could have found more interesting fare among the tumbled boxes of iced-over goods.

"When are we going to get out of here?" At least a hundred people had turned back. They might not have given up if it hadn't been so late in the year, if they could have sailed across the lakes and down the rivers. But the frigid temperatures and the long walk over ice had discouraged them. Zoe had watched them go with envy in her heart.

"A few folks left for Dawson today." Tom fell into step beside her, making walking on snowshoes look easy and graceful. "There's no reason our party can't depart tomorrow morning."

"Good." She wanted to get to Dawson, find Jean Jacques, do what she'd come to do, then go home if they didn't hang her as they probably would. She wanted to sit in Ma's snug kitchen, pour her heart out, and let her family comfort her. She wanted her life back the way it was before she met Jean Jacques and before she ran into Tom Price.

Jean Jacques had deceived her and ruined her, but he'd made her feel like a lady. Tom confused her and reminded her of a background she wanted to rise above. Good sense advised her to forget both of them.

Head down, she listened to the cold squeak of the snow beneath her boots, heard the rhythmic *schwoosh* of Tom's snowshoes. She couldn't think of a single thing to say to him.

When they reached the shore of the lake, Tom paused and pushed back the fur-lined hood of his coat. Mist gathered in front of his lips when he spoke. "That was some kind of fight you started last week," he said, shaking his head and grinning. "I never saw anything like it."

Zoe closed her eyes and cringed inside her layers of clothing. When she felt uncertain about her behavior, she asked herself: Would Juliette do this? Never in a hundred years would Juliette have punched a man in the nose and started a brawl. Only a low-bred person would do such a thing.

"I was proud of you, Zoe." Tom pushed his hands in his coat pockets and gazed down at her with soft eyes. "If you hadn't gotten to Horvath first, I would have flattened him."

She turned away, focusing on the men loading sleds out on the lake. "I'm ashamed of myself," she said in a low voice. How was she ever going to better herself if she couldn't control the Newcastle in her?

Tom took her by the shoulders and turned her to face him. "There's no reason to be ashamed of standing up for your friend."

Juliette was not her friend. They could barely tolerate each other. Although she'd thought about it at length, she didn't know why she'd flown at Jake Horvath like an avenging angel. It was nothing to her if some vulgar-mouthed man made scurrilous comments about Juliette. But at the time it happened, she had cared deeply, had cared enough to bust the man's nose. She still didn't understand what had come over her.

"Ladies don't get into fistfights."

"Is that what's bothering you?" His fingers tightened on her shoulders hard enough that she felt the pressure through all the layers. "The standards are different up here, Zoe. If you aren't a fighter, you won't succeed in the Yukon. And you might die. Qualities like toughness and loyalty are prized."

"Is that how you see me?" she asked, horrified. "As tough?"

"You bet I do. You're tough enough to go after what you want. Tough enough to fight for what you believe in. It takes strength to make your way in a big city like Seattle, and you've been doing it. It takes strength to set your sights on a place like Dawson City and endure what it takes to get there."

The praise made her feel a little better, and then a lot worse as she realized he praised her for the wrong things. There was nothing admirable about starting a brawl.

He grinned down at her. "You and Clara are becoming legends. There isn't a man on the trail who wants to get crossways with either of you. Everyone knows you can shoot that rifle you keep in the tent, and now they know you throw a mean right fist."

You could take the girl out of Newcastle, but you couldn't take Newcastle out of the girl. What a fool she had been to believe that Jean Jacques really thought she was genteel.

"I don't want to talk about this," she said, walking out onto the ice. Clara had reported that it was a foot thick now. Clara seemed to know everything, which was one of her annoying traits. "Tell me what we're supposed to do."

Tom followed, and she sensed that he watched her with a puzzled frown.

For the next hour, he worked with her on the sleds. Four of his clients had turned back midway to Crater Lake, therefore he had extra sleds and dogs.

"With fewer clients and goods to transport, we'll be able to move faster."

The plan was for the Chilkats to attach canvas sails to the extra sleds and let the wind blow the piles of goods across the lake. With any luck, the Indians would make such good time that camp would be set up by the time Zoe and her companions arrived. They would drive dog-powered sleds.

"So why do I need to know how to rig a sail?"

"Every survival skill you learn is like money in the bank."

That sounded reasonable. "Why do our sleds have wooden runners instead of metal like so many of the others," she asked, looking around.

"Metal runners stick to the ice in extreme cold."

He showed her how to water the wooden runners and

coat them with a sheath of ice. Then demonstrated how to hitch the dogs. Showed her where to stand, how to guide the animals. At the end of an hour, the information had begun to blur. The one thing that stuck in Zoe's memory was the warning that the sled driver did not add her weight to the load. The driver ran along behind, guiding the sled.

"There's not much to worry about. The dogs will follow the sled ahead of them. I'll drive the lead sled, and Bear Barrett has agreed to bring up the rear. Ben Dare will drive a sled behind Juliette to keep an eye on her. You and the ladies shouldn't run into any trouble."

She stared at him. "Let me make sure I understand. I'm going to *run* behind a sled all the way to Long Lake. Then *run* across Long Lake to Deep Lake. Then *run* across Deep Lake to Linderman Lake. Then *run* over Linderman Lake to Lake Bennett."

Laughing at her expression, he nodded. "The alternative is to camp here until the spring melt, then take a boat or a raft downriver."

"Neither possibility sounds appealing." But remembering her experience aboard the *Annasett* made running a hundred miles sound almost desirable. "You know, this really makes me mad." Her cheeks were fiery with cold, yet she was sweating inside her coat. The dogs frightened her a little. She didn't know if a foot of ice was thick enough. And she simply couldn't imagine running behind a sled for a hundred miles, except she expected it would be a grueling experience. "No one tells you about all this before you leave the States." She waved an arm at the lake. "I'll bet half of these people wouldn't be here if they'd known the truth about what to expect."

Tom tugged her muffler away from her mouth, bent, and kissed her quickly. "You're tough, remember?"

"You kissed me!" Startled and angry, she shoved him away and then glared. "In public!" After scrubbing her mitten across the tingle throbbing in her lips, she made a hissing sound. "How dare you compromise me like that!"

"I've thought about what you said up at the glaciers. And I've thought about fate bringing us together again. I want to be more than just a friend, Zoe. So I've decided to commence a courtship." His green eyes were clear and serious. "As for kissing you in public, that was deliberate. I'm staking my territory. I doubt I'm the only one who thinks you're a fine-looking woman with spunk and spirit. So I'm sending any rivals a signal that I won't tolerate anyone else courting you."

He had lost his senses. "I don't want to be courted!" she insisted, when she stopped sputtering. "I thought I made that clear."

"You did." He unhitched the dogs from the sled he'd used for demonstration and handed the trace lines to one of the Chilkats. "Changing your mind is one of my courtship objectives."

"*One* of your objectives?" She was still indignant and sputtering. Furious that he had compromised her in front of all the men on the ice. He'd treated her as if she were common and vulgar. "If I wasn't wearing gloves and mittens, I'd slap your face!"

He laughed. "Piss and vinegar. I like that in a woman."

Angry and exasperated, she started toward the shore, praying she wouldn't slip and ruin what she hoped was a dramatic exit by sprawling on the ice.

"Teach the others what I showed you today," he called after her. "And Zoe?" She refused to look back. "I've made up my mind. It's going to be you and me. You might as well accept it."

"Never!" she shouted over her shoulder.

She had made one disastrous mistake; she wasn't going to make another.

Chapter 14

In one of her beloved books, Juliette had read that a person's past flashed before her eyes while she was drowning. It hadn't happened that way for her. Her life had passed in review later, while she was recovering from deep racking chills and trying to cope with the shock of nearly dying.

What she examined was a safe sheltered life, predictable and monotonous. She had drifted through the years doing the same things day after day, week after week, with little variation. No challenges obstructed her path. Nothing alarming occurred, nothing exciting happened. She had sleepwalked through her boring routines, shying away from new experiences.

In retrospect, marrying in haste and impulse was more understandable than it had first appeared. Now she remembered the quiet desperation she'd felt as the years passed and she began to feel she was wasting her life. She remembered thinking that she had passed silently through the world and only Aunt Kibble would care when the end came. One of her pastimes had been to wonder what sort of epitaph would mark her tombstone.

Miss Juliette March never committed an improper act.

Here lies what's-her-name, gone but not forgotten.

She never went anywhere, never did anything.

In the end, marrying Jean Jacques, and all that had followed, had changed so much in her life, yet it had changed little.

She still fretted and worried about propriety and appearances. There was still no one who loved her or who would mourn her passing if she had drowned in Crater Lake. Yes, she had left Linda Vista. She was here in the Yukon, and she had climbed Chilkoot Pass, but not willingly, and she'd complained and resented every step. She had stepped out of monotony, but she'd lacked the sense to enjoy her new experiences.

Worse, once the confrontation with Jean Jacques lay behind her, she could so easily lapse into the same deadening routine she'd endured before her uncharacteristic break with convention.

She absolutely could not let that happen.

"Juliette? Come out of there so we can strike the tent. Everything else is packed."

She looked around the small wedge tent. The furnishings, such as they were, had been packed, but she could imagine the cots, the heavy stove made of Russian sheet iron, the piles of coats, hats, gloves. The camping equipment, their toiletries.

She hated sleeping in a bag atop a narrow cot, hated the cramped quarters, hated being too hot or too frozen. She detested wearing the same clothing day after day, loathed the awful beans and bacon and biscuits they lived on. Not being able to wash her hair and having to rely on spit baths was a hideous imposition. And most of the time Clara and Zoe rubbed her nerves raw.

However, if it hadn't been for the foregoing circumstances, traveling in the Yukon wouldn't have been too horrible. At least she could now say that she had been somewhere and had done something. She'd made a start at changing her life. But there was more to be done if she truly wanted to change.

"Juliette? Damn it, what are you doing in there?"

"I'm coming!"

She stepped into a pearlescent frozen world. A light shower of new snow had powdered last week's drifts.

The sky was the color of old silver. If one had to run across the ice behind a dog sled, this was as good a day as any to do it. Thinking about the ice made her heart stop until she ground her teeth and shook away the thought. Others had already left Crater Lake, traveling across the ice with no mishap. But most had decided to camp on the shore until spring. For a moment she wholeheartedly wished she could stay, too.

When she lifted her head and looked at Clara and Zoe she couldn't believe her eyes. "Good heavens! What have you done to yourselves?" They wore hideous gray masks.

"It's ash and bacon grease," Clara said. Before Juliette could protest, she'd rubbed the muck on Juliette's face. "We're going to be exposed to wind and raw temperatures out there on the ice. Tom gave us eyeglasses, too. To protect against glare."

Juliette stared at the blue-tinted glasses Zoe wore over the gunk on her face. Her face was framed by the fur trimming her sealskin hood, and she looked like a creature out of a nightmare. Now Juliette did, too. Her shoulders sagged.

To complete the indignity, here came Ben Dare, looking rugged and handsome in a fur-lined jacket and heavy boots that rose almost to his knees. She was going to have to speak to him. And she would have to thank him for saving her life. And she would do it looking like a demented monster in a bad dream.

He considered her, a twinkle of amusement softening his grim expression. "Before we leave, could you and I talk?"

Beneath the mask of ash and grease her cheeks burned hot. She didn't remember being naked in his arms, but she could imagine it. Had done nothing for a week but imagine it. Visualizing Ben pressing her naked breasts against his bare chest, and rubbing his hands on her shoulders and back and arms made her squirm and feel feverish and tingly all over her body. In a secret part of her mind, she resented being unable to recall the most shameful moment of her entire life. It seemed that fate ought to let her remember the two of them being naked together.

"Juliette," he said in a low voice. Behind him Clara and Zoe had begun to strike the tent while the Chilkats loaded their piles of goods onto sleds. "When I thought I'd lost you, too . . ." His gloved hands curled into fists at his sides. "We need to work this out. Helen was an important part of my life for eight years. I can't pretend the marriage didn't happen or that I didn't care for her."

Juliette's head came up, and she stared. She had spent countless hours trying to guess what they would say to each other. Not once had it entered her mind that he would talk about his late wife. She had supposed they would make an excruciatingly awkward attempt to discuss the day of her near drowning, and be swamped by embarrassment.

"Why are you talking about Mrs. Dare?" The words emerged in a blurted rush.

"I know you don't want to hear about her, but—"

"Ben, I enjoyed hearing about your late wife. She sounds like a remarkable woman. I just don't understand why you're talking about her now."

He tried to see her expression through the lenses of the blue-tinted glasses Clara had insisted she wear. "You were upset when I talked about Helen the day we climbed Chilkoot Pass."

"Why on earth would you think that? I felt nothing but admiration for Mrs. Dare, and envious of the life you had together." Envious? She hadn't fully realized it then, but that's exactly what she felt. Ben had loved his wife and had stood by her, unlike some husbands she could name.

Now he looked puzzled. "You've seemed distant since Chilkoot. I felt you preferred not to see me, and assumed it was because talking about Helen offended you in some way."

This was nearly as embarrassing as discussing their

nakedness would have been. She pressed her lips together and looked at the snowy ground. "I . . . thought we were spending too much time together. I felt that Clara and Zoe disapproved."

He tilted his head to stare at the sky. "Sometimes I'm an idiot. Of course you're concerned about appearances."

"I've lost someone, too. I understand wanting to talk about a loved one. And don't you remember? It was me who asked you to speak about Mrs. Dare."

His eyebrows came together in an expression of curiosity. "I didn't know you'd lost someone."

Their talk was edging toward dangerous territory. "He's been gone for a year now," she said uncomfortably.

"I'm sorry. Was it a brother? Your father?"

She could say that she'd lost her father, and it wouldn't exactly be a lie. But she cared too much to mislead him completely. "No," she answered, looking for an escape. "Oh, I see that Clara and Zoe are ready to leave."

Ben's frown deepened and his gaze narrowed, and she felt his jealousy. Amazement widened her eyes, and a tiny thrill made her shiver. Suddenly she felt like a femme fatale, an entirely new experience. And she profoundly wished that she could remember their naked moment on the shore. A femme fatale should remember such events.

Clara and Zoe gave the tent to the Chilkats and cast a pointed glance toward Crater Lake and then back at Juliette.

"Ben," she said, speaking rapidly. "Thank you for saving my life at the risk of your own." He could have bobbed up under the ice and drowned before breaking free. The frigid temperature could have paralyzed him and cost him his life. "I'm forever grateful. I . . . I was thinking about you right before I fell into the water." This new femme fatale persona was amazingly brazen and brave.

Her tinted glasses made his eyes flash cobalt blue, and he looked so handsome that he stopped her breath in her throat.

"I was thinking how foolish I'd been to worry about the impropriety of us seeing each other. We're friends, after all. At least I think—I hope we're friends," she added, feeling flustered. She was new at femme fatale assertiveness.

His hands opened and closed, and she had a sudden light-headed notion that he wanted to take her into his arms. "If I have my way, you and I are going to be more than friends," he said in a low, intimate voice that almost made her swoon.

"Ben? Juliette?" Clara called to them as she retied the scarf that held down her hat and protected her mouth and nose. "The others will be waiting."

Clara's intrusion reminded Juliette that she and Ben could never be more than just friends. "I'm content with your friendship," she murmured in a voice filled with regret. She wished they really could be more than friends. She loved his easy confident stance and the way his jacket emphasized the breadth of his shoulders. "I wonder how you'd look without that awful shaggy beard." Dismay rounded her lips. "I didn't mean . . . What I meant was . . ."

He laughed and then grinned at her. "If you don't like the beard, it's as good as gone."

"Oh, but I didn't say that. I just—"

Clara took one of her arms, and Zoe took the other. "We're going." Clara looked over her shoulder. "Ben Dare, do we have to drag you along, too?"

"I hope you ladies enjoyed a good night's sleep," Ben said, falling in behind them. "It's going to be a long, hard day."

The first time Zoe explained sledding, Juliette had listened in horror. The second time through, she had committed Zoe's instructions to memory. She had promised herself that running along behind a dogsled wouldn't be as awful as it sounded.

But it was. To begin with, she could barely see over

the four hundred pounds of goods piled on the sled she guided. Until she realized the dogs would follow the sleds ahead, she worried that she couldn't see well enough to guide them effectively, assuming that she could guide them at all. In rapid order she learned that a more important concern was keeping up with the others.

After the sled shot forward, pulling out of her grip, and she fell flat on the ice, Tom again showed her how to run. Not on her tiptoes, as she'd tried to do, but flat-footed in a rhythmic side-by-side, almost shuffling-forward motion. Once she practiced, she discovered she could maintain a pace that was faster than she would have believed herself capable of setting.

During the first hour her thoughts vacillated between worrying how thick the ice was to feeling self-conscious about Ben observing her waddling run.

In the second hour, she watched sleds with blankets rigged as sails zip past her, and envied the sailors because they could stand on the back runners and let the wind carry them.

When they stopped at noon for hot coffee, she asked Tom why they couldn't have sails, too.

"When the wind dies you'll see why the dogs are a better choice for the long run." Extending a paddle over the flames of a small hot fire, he toasted a slice of bread and cheese. "Without wind, the men will have to pull the sleds themselves."

"How are you little ladies doing?" Bear Barrett asked. His voice boomed across the lake, and a few people looked their way. "Are your legs holding up?"

Gentlemen didn't mention legs in the presence of ladies, but Juliette liked Bear just the same. Initially, his size and scarred face had frightened her, but now she thought of him as a cheerful and kind man. He made her think of a shaggy-haired Viking, golden and warlike in his zest for life, intensely loyal to those of his own tribe.

When Tom shouted and hallooed to another party, waving them toward the fire, Juliette's heart squeezed in her chest. The party was made up of men. They would have seen her naked on the shore or would certainly have heard about it.

Bear studied her expression before he dropped a huge hand on her shoulder. "No one is going to say one damned word about you falling through the ice," he said gently, with surprising tact.

Her lip trembled, and she spoke in a whisper. She would die of humiliation if anyone referred to her nakedness. "But what if they do make a comment?"

"Then Ben Dare is going to whup the innards out of them. Ben put out the word. If anyone upsets you, they'll answer with blood and bruises, by God. And me and Tom will be standing right behind Ben, ready to step in if he wants a little assistance."

"Ben did that?" Turning toward the sleds, she watched him tying a new set of burlap bags over the dog's feet to protect their paws from patches of jagged ice.

The party of men drawing up to the fire were additional clients of Tom's. Juliette caught them sliding glances in her direction, but as Bear had promised, none of them uttered an impolite word.

Learning that Ben was willing to fight any man who offended her cast him as more of a hero than she already believed he was. This turn of mind surprised her. Until this journey Juliette hadn't known the sort of men who engaged in violence and hadn't wanted to. She felt certain that Jean Jacques would never have joined the brawl on the shore.

But the men around her didn't shy from physical confrontation or disdain it. They were quick to punish insult or offense—and to protect their women. Juliette liked the way their hardness made her feel safe and cherished and respected in a way that good manners alone could not accomplish.

"I should be ashamed of myself," she muttered. Some of her new attitudes were not for the better.

"For what?" Zoe asked, looking unhappily down at her boots. "I think I'm getting a blister."

"For condoning violence."

Zoe waved a tin of coffee in one hand and a slice of toast and cheese in the other. "You? Condone violence? As I live and breathe. Is violence covered in the etiquette books?"

"Never mind. Where did you get the toasted cheese?"

"I fixed it for her," Tom called from the campfire.

"I didn't ask you to," Zoe snapped.

Tom smiled at Juliette. "Miss Wilder and I are courting. I'm showing her how thoughtful I am and how helpful I'd be around a house."

Juliette and Clara stepped backward and stared at Zoe.

Even the ash and grease could not hide Zoe's bright red flush of anger. "We are *not* courting! Do you hear me, Tom Price? We are *not*, as in never ever not possibly, courting!"

Juliette glanced toward Ben over by the dogs, and Clara shot a look at Bear, who was talking and laughing with the men in the second party. Both men had positioned themselves facing the women. As they always did, Juliette abruptly realized.

Tom smiled. "Would you like more toast and cheese, darlin'?"

Zoe sputtered, then shook her head fiercely and stomped away, heading toward Ben and the dogs.

"Fortunately I admire obstinate women, and God knows that woman is obstinate. But if she were easy to woo, she wouldn't be worth having." He winked at Juliette, then placed another slice of bread and cheese on his paddle and held it over the flames.

Clara blinked. "They're courting. When did this happen? Did Zoe suddenly get unmarried? I'd like to know how she did that."

Throughout the afternoon, Juliette thought about Zoe and Tom courting and, despite Zoe's protests, the long smoky glances between them. And clearly Clara and Bear were circling each other. The air fairly sizzled between those two. And then she thought about Ben Dare.

"I am *not* courting," Zoe continued to insist after they had eaten supper and retired to their tent to fall into their cots.

"I don't care what you do as long as you don't forget why we're here," Clara said, covering a yawn. Her long red woolen underwear clashed with her carroty hair, which had frizzed around her head like a halo. "As long as you remember to shoot our no-good weasel of a husband, you can court all you want to. Makes no never mind to me."

"What's the matter with you?" Zoe looked up from stabbing a needle at the blisters on her heel. "Juliette, give Clara the lecture about how we're married, about propriety, about not being free to get on with our lives. I'm too exhausted to do it."

Juliette turned her washrag between her fingers, frowning at the smears of ash and grease. The gunk had helped protect against the raw wind and cold, but her face still felt chapped and burned.

"Before I fell in the lake, I would have given the 'lecture' as you refer to it, but I'm not sure I believe it anymore."

Zoe and Clara stopped what they were doing and stared. Both looked faintly ridiculous in their shapeless long johns with hair streaming down their backs and the light of the lantern turning their faces as red and painful-looking as Juliette's.

"Now I'm thinking that people should grab hold of whatever happiness comes their way and do it while they can." She tossed the washrag toward their laundry bucket. "Tom's a good, decent man. He's honest, respected, a hard worker, and he's successful. The two of you have the same background, the same values, and the same way of looking at things. Now think about our husband. Not only has he vanished, he's a liar, a seducer, and a thief. But he wasn't from Newcastle," she added, looking hard at Zoe. "That's his only virtue."

"Juliette March! I don't believe you're saying these things!"

Clara sprinkled talc on her head and pulled a brush through her hair. The talc freshened her scalp and pulled oil from the tresses, but it also dried out her hair. Crackling noises sounded under the brush, and tendrils floated upward, snapping with static. "Any fool with eyes in her head can see that Tom loves you. He probably always has. If you weren't so stubborn, if you'd let it happen, you'd love him back."

Zoe jabbed the needle into her sewing kit. "You two have gone snow-mad. Have you forgotten that I intend to shoot Jean Jacques?" She patted the long lump of the rifle beneath her sleeping bag. "Then the Canadian Mounties will hang me or stand me up in front of a firing squad or whatever they do to execute murderers. I don't have a future."

"All the more reason to take whatever happiness you can while you still have time. I agree with Juliette."

"I couldn't possibly. Tom is from *Newcastle*!"

Juliette folded her hands across her red woolen lap. "Remember the story you told us about the Owner's Day Parade?" she asked softly. "And the people in the carriages who looked down their noses at you and your family?"

"I'm not likely to forget, am I?"

"Tell me, Zoe. How are you different from the people in the carriages?" Juliette watched Zoe's mouth drop and her eyes flare. "It sounds as if you, too, think the people in Newcastle are no better than dirt. It sounds like you also see your friends and neighbors as objects of scorn and denigration."

"My God!" Zoe stared and swallowed hard.

"If you and Tom are representative of the people in Newcastle, it seems to me that you'd be proud. Maybe the residents are poor, but they sound like good-hearted, hardworking people. Why are you ashamed of that? Why do you believe the carriage people's opinion instead of listening to your own heart?" She reached to Zoe's cot and pressed her shaking hand. "You don't have to ride in a carriage to be a snob," she said gently. "Please. Think about that when you see Tom tomorrow."

"I . . . I just . . . My God," Zoe whispered.

"Me, I am going to sleep," Clara said, yawning widely.

After Clara blew out the lantern, Juliette lay in the darkness, watching Zoe, who sat with her knees pulled up under her chin staring at the dying glow of the stove.

Had she been wrong to push Zoe toward Tom? She couldn't think so.

Her last thought before she'd lost consciousness under the ice had been: I'll never be with Ben. She had thought hard about that and had concluded that propriety killed spontaneity and robbed a person of joy and opportunity. Propriety was for the old, those who had lived their lives. Not for wronged wives.

"Listen to Juliette," Clara whispered from her cot.

Good heavens. Juliette almost sat up to stare at them.

They listened to her advice. Would wonders never cease?

Chapter 15

To cross the overland stretch between Crater Lake and Long Lake, Tom's Chilkat Indians removed the blanket sails and pulled their sleds by looping a rope over their chests or rigging a harness that fit across their foreheads. On a dare, Zoe tried to pull the load and was surprised to discover that the iced sled runners made it possible for her to move the sled forward.

"I can pull it," Zoe said, handing the ropes back to Tom, "but only for a few feet, and I'm glad I don't have to." The farther they traveled the less she resented Juliette's charity and the more grateful she felt, although she couldn't bring herself to say so out loud.

The snow was deep on the steep slopes enclosing Long Lake, covering rugged terrain. Yesterday Clara had walked into the woods to gather firewood, and she had dropped into the snow up to her shoulders. Bear pulled her out, but the incident had caused a commotion, and reminded everyone not to wander off the trail. Which Zoe and Tom had done without really being aware of how far from camp they'd meandered.

"What time is it?"

The November days were short, and they had to wait for daylight before starting the day's trek, had to halt and set up camp at about four o'clock. It was a relief not to endure long, exhausting days. On the other hand, their progress was frustratingly slow. At this rate they wouldn't reach Dawson City until early spring.

"It's about an hour until supper. Why? Are you bored?"

She smiled. Tom Price was the least boring person she knew. He told wonderful stories about grizzly bears and wildlife, about eccentric prospectors and the rowdy life in the boomtowns. He knew the names of the peaks and lakes and how to do just about everything. He had an opinion on every topic and encouraged her opinions, too.

"It's not that. I'm starting to become a little concerned. It's dark and the snow is filling in our tracks. Shouldn't we be heading back to camp?"

"I was about to mention that." Leaning against the sled's load, lantern light softening his face, he crossed his arms over his chest and grinned. "You're pretty, you're a great cook, and I'm sorry."

"What?" Just looking at this man made her mind wander into dangerous areas. If she had a nickel for every time she had relived his kiss, she would be a rich woman.

"My pa says the way to get along with women is to tell them every day that they're pretty, they're good cooks, and you're sorry for whatever you did even if you don't know what it was."

Zoe laughed and leaned against the fragrant trunk of a snowy pine. During the past few days she'd been seeing Tom in a new light and had concluded that he was everything Juliette had said. By dropping her armor, she recognized all the good things she admired in her pa and brothers. He was strong, dogmatic, honest, stubborn, and a leader with pride to spare. Tom was everything she had ever wanted in a man—except he was from Newcastle.

But that didn't matter anymore. It never should have mattered.

Juliette's stunning observation that Zoe was like the carriage people in the Owner's Day Parade had shocked her. And, as with all great revelations, she instantly recognized the bedrock truth. She had chosen to see through the eyes of the carriage people, and she'd been ashamed of her family, friends, and of herself. That shame had created a desperate need to shake off her background and the people in it like a bad dream. Worse (and to her everlasting regret), she'd worried that Jean Jacques's servants would laugh and dismiss her family as shanty trash.

That she had been ashamed of her family made her stomach cramp and ache. How could she have been so shallow and small? Even as a barefoot child with wild hair and mended clothing, she would never have denigrated someone because his circumstances were less than hers. She wouldn't have apologized for good people living a hard life. But that's what she had done as an adult.

Oh, she had shaken off Newcastle, all right. She had held herself high and told herself that she was better than the people she loved. She'd left town as soon as she could. She had taken classes to educate herself and speak well. And she had congratulated herself that she had finally risen above a background that shamed and embarrassed her.

"—do know the reason, and I'm truly sorry."

Giving her head a shake, she studied the lantern light sharpening the angles of Tom's strong face, her gaze settling on his mouth. "I'm sorry. I was woolgathering."

"I said we're lost."

"What?" Abruptly she straightened away from the tree trunk.

"Actually we're not completely lost; I have a fair idea where we are. But it would be foolish and dangerous to search for the trail with snow and darkness obscuring the landmarks."

The snow had thickened while Zoe let her thoughts drift, and now their tracks were obliterated. Snow had collected along Tom's hat brim and atop the goods stacked on the sled.

Her chest constricted and suddenly she felt the cold stinging her cheeks and chilling her feet. But she kept her voice level, not wanting to betray anxiety when Tom didn't. "What will we do?"

The sourdoughs loved to tell grisly tales of men lost in snowstorms, their bodies not found until the spring melt. Equally terrifying were the stories of frostbite and amputated limbs. She knew it could happen, because three days ago she'd seen a man whose nose had been lost to frostbite. His disfigurement had horrified her.

Tom stepped forward and clasped her shoulders, his expression reassuring. "I won't tell you the situation isn't serious. But I will tell you we should survive with no ill effects. It's just one night."

One night in the open. Fear dried her throat. She gripped the lapels of his coat and willed her heart to stop pounding so she could speak. "We'll freeze. They'll never find us." Lord, she sounded like Juliette.

Tom patted her back, his touch a caress. "We'll be fine, darlin'. Don't you worry."

His confidence assured and irritated her. Then she pulled her thoughts together and reminded herself that this was not Tom's first trek through the wilderness. He would know what to do. When she raised her head, her mouth almost met his, and she drew a quick tingling breath, then stepped away and dusted her gloves together.

"All right," she said, aware that he was looking at her as if he, too, remembered a kiss that had seared her. She hoped her voice sounded steadier to him than it did to her own ears. "What should we do? And how can I help?" It would be a cold and miserable night, the worst night of her life, but she would be with Tom, and she trusted him to get them through it.

"Let's see what we have to work with," he said, untying the ropes securing the boxes and crates on the sled. "It's one of my sleds. If we're lucky . . . excellent!" He hefted an ax in his hand, then found a hatchet and gave it to Zoe. "I'll build a lean-to while you cut some pine boughs. Don't wander too far."

First he located a relatively dry and protected site beneath two large pines, then began chopping smaller trees. Working in the light of the lantern he built a teepee-shaped structure and overlaid it with branches stripped from the poles. By the time Zoe had collected enough pine boughs to cushion the floor of his shelter, Tom had scraped back the snow, hacked a pit out of the frozen earth, and had a fire blazing.

"Warm yourself while I set up the stove."

"We have a stove?" Thank heaven they had the sled.

"And food. Once the stove is hot, I'll fry some caribou steaks." He handed her an armload of blankets and asked her to spread them over the pine boughs while he positioned the camp stove near the narrow opening of the lean-to.

"The others will be worried." Zoe hung one of the blankets across the lean-to's opening. "Will they search for us?"

"Not until daylight," Tom rummaged for a skillet and plates, brandishing them with a smile when the items were found. "Are you still worrying about spending the night in the open?"

She smiled uneasily. "A little. But it seems we have all the comforts of home." Home reminded her of earlier thoughts. "Do you remember what we talked about that day at the glaciers?" she asked softly, sitting on a log he had rolled near the fire.

"I remember every word and every moment of that day." Glancing up from the stove, his green eyes traveled from her mouth to her throat and back to her eyes. For a long moment their gazes locked, and Zoe almost forgot what she wanted to tell him.

"I've been wrong about so many things," she began. While Tom waited for the skillet to heat, she told him exactly how she had felt about Newcastle and its residents, not sparing herself.

"I'm sorry you feel that way," he said finally, dropping strips of meat into the skillet.

"I don't. Not anymore." She couldn't identify the moment when she had begun to align with the carriage people instead of with her own. But she would never forget the instant of revelation. She told Tom what Juliette had said and her shock of recognition.

"I'm devastated that I didn't see it myself." Anger and regret twisted her stomach. "If I could, I'd rush home right now and beg Ma's forgiveness." She blinked hard. "I've said and done so many hurtful things over the years. I'd watch the grabbing and big portions at supper and think, 'This isn't how refined people eat. This is Newcastle.' Pa teased me about putting on airs, but he and the others must have known that I was ashamed of them." It was hard to say these things. "All of us living in such a small house, and wearing mended shirts and petticoats. Never being rid of the damned coal dust." She lowered her head. "I judged everyone by their fingernails. If there was a line of coal dust, I didn't want anything to do with them. But if their nails were clean, the person could be a liar, a thief, and a seducer, and I thought he was gentry, finer and better than the people in Newcastle," she finished bitterly.

"Don't be too hard on yourself, darlin'." Tom sat back on his heels and studied her through the falling snow. "I guess everyone in Newcastle has had similar thoughts. Maybe it didn't take them as long as it's taken you to come around," he added with a smile, "but everyone hates the Owner's Day Parade. You have to ignore the swells and just enjoy the free beer and music and the candy for the kids. Rich people live in a different universe. We don't understand them, and they sure as hell don't understand us. They can't grasp that we don't want charity."

"I wanted to be one of them," she said in a low voice.

"Who wouldn't want to ride in a fancy carriage, wear fine clothes, and be attended by servants?" A shrug scattered snow off his wide shoulders. "There's no harm in dreaming. As long as we don't lose sight of the good things we already have."

"I wanted it so badly that I did something very stupid and foolish." She longed to tell him about Jean Jacques, and now was the time. The confession hovered on her tongue but died there. Pride stopped her from telling him that she had married a man because he had clean fingernails and was not from Newcastle. She didn't think Tom would be as forgiving if he knew how far her blindness had carried her.

She watched him flip the steaks. Caribou was a tender meat, best when turned often over a hot fire and eaten before the red was cooked out. Tom placed the steaks on plates and poured the cooking juices over the meat.

"I think I understand what you're saying," he said after handing her a knife and fork, "and why you're telling me this."

"You do?" She wasn't sure she understood herself.

"You're telling me that you've changed your mind about our courtship and you've accepted my suit."

She stared. And then laughed. "You're a persistent man."

"That is what you're saying, isn't it? That Newcastle isn't an obstacle between us?"

Sadness chased the laughter from her eyes. Courtship was out of the question. She had a husband and she had no future. Both situations put a cramp in any courtship plans. But Juliette and Clara were right. Surely she was entitled to a little happiness in what would be a brief life.

Setting aside her supper plate, she looked down at her clasped hands. "Courtship usually leads to marriage. But you need to understand that I can't marry you, Tom."

Her statement didn't ruffle his pleased smile. "Let's not put the cart before the horse. I'm not proposing marriage, only courtship. Courtship is when both parties get to know each other and decide if they want to proceed to an engagement."

"We already know each other." She narrowed her gaze. "I know you well enough to know that you don't start something you don't intend to finish."

His laugh crinkled his eyes and widened his mouth. "Could be I don't want to scare you away by rushing you."

"I have reasons . . ." She bit her lip. "There are things I can't tell you . . ."

"I know. I hope you'll confide in me when the time is right."

After she found Jean Jacques and shot him, Tom would learn the whole story. But she wasn't willing to put Jean Jacques between them just yet. Not tonight.

"As long as you accept that our courtship is a sham, and it absolutely won't lead to anything more . . ."

He shook his head. "I don't accept anything of the kind. Look at the progress we've already made, and we've just begun." His smile faded, replaced by a seriousness and intensity that made her catch a quick breath. "You and I were meant to be, Zoe. I guess I've always known it. If you hadn't come to the Yukon, I would have gone looking for you. I don't see it any other way."

"Oh, Tom." Juliette was right again. She could love this man so much. "Don't say that."

"I'm going to say it over and over, Zoe, because I love you. I always have."

They stared at each other across the flames dying in the fire pit. Joy, despair, surprise, regret—Zoe wondered if he could read those emotions in her expression. If so, what would he make of them?

"There's so much I want to say to you," she whispered, her mouth dry. "But I can't."

"Are you cold?" he asked when the silence between them had lengthened.

She had forgotten about the snow and sinking temperature. "A little."

"I'll clean up. You crawl into the lean-to and get warm."

"It will go faster if we both clean up." Glad for something to do, she washed her plate with snow. "I can't imagine the lean-to will be much warmer than out here."

"It will be."

After they repacked the plates and utensils in the box on the sled, Zoe entered the pine-scented lean-to, and Tom followed. He put down the lantern and then leaned out the doorway. With a long pair of tongs he lifted several rocks out of the fire pit and placed them inside the skillet he'd brought with him. At once the air felt warmer on Zoe's face.

Now she saw that he'd rearranged the blankets and pillows she had set out, moving them close together.

"For warmth," he said, taking off his hat and heavy coat. "You'll be more comfortable if you take off your hat and coat, too." When she looked doubtful, he smiled. "You can always put them back on."

Slowly she opened the scarf tied over her hat, then removed her hat pins and set her hat near his. Then she unbuttoned her coat and pulled off her gloves. Until now she hadn't allowed herself to wonder about sleeping with him in the lean-to. If Juliette thought her nakedness had created a scandal, wait until she and Clara realized that Zoe and Tom had spent the night together. The thought made her smile.

"You are so beautiful," Tom said in a husky voice.

"I'm too thin, and I'm tough as an old boot, remember?"

"But I happen to like tough, thin women, remember?" He smiled and patted the blanket next to him.

Suddenly Zoe was nervous. There was no more privacy in a prospector's camp than there had been in the home where she grew up. Being alone with a man—absolutely alone and with a man who made her nerves zing and her skin tingle—was an experience that was exciting and unnerving at the same time.

"Are you afraid of me?" he asked in a low, challenging voice.

She wet her lips and decided this was not the time for bravado. "You scare me to death."

"Good. That means I'm getting under your skin." Since she wouldn't come to him, he moved across the blankets to sit next to her. And suddenly the lean-to seemed hotter than the heated rocks could account for.

Zoe smoothed her skirt to cover a glimpse of woolen stockings. "There's going to be talk about us spending a night together."

"Do you care?" he asked, tucking a wisp of dark hair behind her ear.

She held her breath as his fingertips brushed her cheek. This was going to be a very long night. "A little," she whispered, thinking of Clara and Juliette.

"Nothing is going to happen unless you want it to," he murmured, turning her to face him. Lantern light glowed in his eyes, softening the color to a reminder of spring grass.

"Then you won't kiss me." Their breath mingled, and a tiny gasp caught in her throat. He smelled like snow and wood smoke, leather and soap.

"I wouldn't kiss you if you were the last woman on earth," he said, his lips grazing her forehead as he guided her into his arms.

There was nothing soft about this man. His arms were like iron bands closing around her, pressing her against the tight muscles of his chest. He pulled her onto his lap and beneath her skirt and petticoat, she felt thighs like cordwood.

"Oh, Tom," she said, closing her eyes on a moan. "I can't do this."

"You aren't doing anything. I'm the one who's doing something." His lips moved on her temples, kissed her eyelids.

"You said you wouldn't kiss me." She couldn't believe it. Her arms went around his neck, and she adjusted herself in his lap to make her lips more accessible.

"I'm not kissing you." Light kisses covered her face, the corners of her lips, the tip of her nose.

"Yes, you are."

"You must be dreaming."

If so, she had dreamed this dream before. Spreading her fingers on his cheeks, she gazed into his eyes, the lashes still damp with melting snow. Then she parted her lips and let him take her mouth.

Instantly she felt his arousal and the deep heat of her response. Her arms tightened around his neck, and she gave herself to a kiss that began almost chastely and ripened into a give-and-take that shook her to her core—where she had never been touched.

When they pulled apart, gasping and holding each other, Tom whispered, "Oh, God, Zoe. You don't know what you do to me."

He kissed her again, this time passionately, not holding back, kissing her as if he found heaven in her mouth and in her touch. She knew this because heaven was what she found in his arms. When his hand slid up to her breast, she gasped and rocked back on a wave of sensation.

"I'm sorry," he whispered, easing away to look into her eyes. "I only wanted to kiss you. I didn't intend to offend or take advantage."

A strangled sound midway between a laugh and a sob constricted her throat. "Oh, Tom." For a minute she couldn't say anything else.

It was possible they would never again have the luxury of hours of privacy together. Very likely, tonight would be her only chance to lie in his arms. And he loved her. Tears sparkled in her eyes. He had always loved her. If her circumstance had been different, if she had never met that bastard Jean Jacques Villette, she would have returned his love with all of her heart and soul.

And there was the answer to the question that had been circling her mind since she understood they would share the blankets she had spread over the boughs. She made her decision while gazing into his apologetic eyes. He had nothing to apologize for. She wanted him, needed him.

Lifting his hand, she placed a kiss in his palm, then gently curved his fingers around her breast, hearing his sharp intake of breath. Then her own shaking fingers rose to the row of tiny buttons running from her throat to her waist, and she opened them one by one.

"Zoe." His voice was hoarse with desire. "You don't know what you're doing." Swallowing hard, he dropped his gaze to the cleavage appearing beneath her fingers and a sound rumbled in his chest. "I was teasing earlier. I didn't mean things to go this far. Zoe, please." He caught her hand and looked into her eyes. "I would take a bullet in the heart rather than dishonor you."

"I know," she whispered, her eyes wet. "Tomorrow we both may regret this, but tonight . . . tonight I need you, Tom." She needed to know love from an honest man, a man whose words were true and whose body belonged to her alone. She wanted to know his touch as well as she knew his heart.

His arms went around her, and he crushed her so tightly to his chest that she felt his heart pounding against the accelerating rhythm of her own. His mouth claimed hers with hard, possessive passion, and she surrendered to the sunburst in her mind. Yes. Yes.

His trembling fingers finished opening her shirtwaist, and her fingers fumbled with the buttons on his shirt. Another time she might have laughed when they were both stripped to shapeless woolly long johns. But all she could think about now was the splendor of his long, hard body as he peeled away the last barrier.

"How beautiful you are," she whispered, staring at him in the lantern light. An arrow-shaped wedge of dark hair curled on his chest. Wide shoulders tapered to a narrow waist; his thighs were roped with hard muscle and sinew. She had never thought of men in terms of beauty, but he was so hard against her softness. So angular in contrast to curves. Only a master sculptor could have created a being so rawly magnificent.

He helped her out of her long johns and then stared at her with the same awe. "You're exquisitely perfect."

She had never seen a naked man in the light and had never let Jean Jacques see her naked with the light on. But she stood before Tom with no embarrassment and made no effort to cover herself from his gaze. There was nothing uncomfortable about nakedness between a man with love in his eyes and a woman who returned that love.

Gently, he guided her to her knees on the blankets and slowly withdrew the pins from her hair, catching long curls in his hands as they tumbled down her back and over her breasts. "I've wanted to draw out the pins since I first saw you." Closing his eyes, he rubbed a curl across his cheek and mouth.

Easing herself down on the blankets, Zoe held out her arms to him, and he came to her with a groan, covering her. The cold snowy night lay ahead of them—there was no need to rush. He kissed her again and again, his callused hands excitingly rough on her smooth body, exploring, caressing, bringing her up and up and up to a level of urgency and need that shook her body and left her panting and gasping his name. Her thighs were wet with readiness when he finally came to her, filling a deep emptiness she had not known she felt.

She knew he battled an urgency of desire as great as hers. She saw it in his eyes, saw that he wanted to be gentle with her. But their hunger was too powerful for quiet pleasures. They moved together in a tangle of fevered kisses and deep strong thrusts, gasped and whispered and clutched with flying hands.

Afterward, they collapsed in each other's arms, sated and happily quiet. Tom smoked, and Zoe lay nestled against his shoulder, listening to the odd silence of falling snow.

"Right now there is no place else I'd rather be," she murmured, her lips against his bare chest. It was snug and warm in the lean-to. The clean fragrance of pine mingled with the scents of their bodies and their lovemaking. Never again would she sniff a pinecone or step into a forest without remembering the joy of this night.

"I love you, Zoe." He stroked her hair, his touch so tender it was almost reverential. "And your secret doesn't matter."

She stiffened. Jean Jacques was the last person she wanted to think about right now. "You're wrong. It matters. Besides, you don't know what my secret is."

"I think I've put it together. I think you cared for a man you met in Seattle. Something happened, and you didn't get married. He went to Dawson City, and you're here looking for him."

Zoe sat up. His guess struck so close to the truth that goose bumps rose on her naked skin.

"There are two things I want to say." His green eyes were clear and steady. "I know you well enough to know that you decided a lot of things when you came to me tonight. You decided it's me you care about and not the other man. Your search for him is finished."

She couldn't speak, couldn't lie to him again. She knew she loved Tom, but her search for Jean Jacques had not ended.

"As for your secret—Zoe, it doesn't matter that I wasn't the first. People make mistakes. I know you're an honorable woman, and you must have believed you loved him. I don't want to know about him, don't want to know what happened between you. But I want you to understand that none of it matters. We start fresh from here. You and me."

He thought her secret was that she was not a virgin. Oh, Lord. And he believed she was an honorable woman.

Stricken, she lay down again and hid her face against his shoulder, blinking hard against the tears swimming in her eyes. She would have given ten years of her life if there had been no Jean Jacques Villette. She would have given another ten years if she were truly the honorable person he thought she was.

After a length of silence, Tom lifted her hand and kissed her fingers. Then he studied her wedding ring.

"This is an unusual ring. I've noticed that Clara and Juliette wear one like it. Is it club jewelry?"

"What?" Her voice was dulled and faint.

"I've wondered if you all belong to the same women's club."

"You could say that," she said bitterly, withdrawing her hand.

Long after Tom slept and the temperature began to drop in the lean-to, Zoe lay awake in the warmth of his arms, mentally flogging herself for the mess she had made of her life.

Tom believed they had made a commitment to each other tonight. And it should have been that way. It would have, if she hadn't been married. They would have found rapture in each other's arms, joy in declaring their love, and pleasure and excitement in planning a future that both their families would have heartily approved.

Instead, she had dishonored him, because she would have staked her life that Tom Price would never make love to a married woman. Just as he would stake his life that Zoe Wilder would never betray marriage vows.

And Tom would know what she had done when they reached Dawson City and ran into Jean Jacques, damn him.

Near morning, she reached for him and kissed him hungrily, needing him desperately for the brief time she could have him. Her selfishness dismayed her, but she needed this moment of happiness.

He touched her cheek in the darkness. "You're crying!"

"Just love me, Tom. Just for tonight." While they could. Before shooting Jean Jacques completed the ruin of her life.

This time they made love slowly, tenderly, their caresses lingering and long. They drank deep of each other, not knowing if there would be another chance for privacy.

She couldn't say the words aloud, but she said them silently. I love you. Oh, Tom, I love you with all of my heart.

Chapter 16

The group considered staying at Deep Lake for a few days because everyone was exhausted, but they voted to push on and spend Christmas at Linderman Lake, where a large camp had gathered around a collection of ramshackle buildings.

Stumbling with fatigue, Juliette ran behind her sled, tears cutting tracks through the ash and grease before freezing on her cheeks. She had never been this miserably bone-tired or this cold. Every morning she woke up shivering violently with her teeth chattering, unwilling to crawl out of her sleeping bag until Clara or Zoe had fired up the stove. On the mornings when it was her turn to start the coffee and breakfast, she cursed herself for ever leaving sunny California.

The frigid cold was unlike anything she could have imagined. No matter how many layers of clothing she wore, she was never warm, never comfortable. Icy talons of wind clawed through the layers and chilled her to the marrow, and then she had to worry about perspiration freezing on her skin and leading to frostbite. The first thing everyone did after the tents were set up at the end of the day was strip out of perspiration-damp clothing, towel themselves dry, then hasten into the next day's clothing, which they then slept in. Hovering next to the stove or a fire didn't help. The front of her warmed somewhat while the back of her froze.

In retrospect, she had taken so many things for granted.

Warmth. Clean clothing. Daily baths. Good food with plenty of variety. Once she would have laughed until her sides ached if anyone had suggested that she would or could run through snow behind a dogsled for mile after seemingly endless mile. Or that she'd go weeks with only spit baths to keep herself clean. Or that she would one day know what a blizzard was. Or that . . .

Ahead, the dogs began barking, which meant the forward sleds had halted. It must be time for the midday meal. Juliette wiped at the tears on her face, smearing ash and bacon grease on her glove. It didn't matter because her gloves were dirty anyway. She alternated two ensembles day after day and neither could be called clean or fresh.

But her spirits improved at the prospect of a rest. By the time she caught up, Tom and the Chilkats would have a fire blazing and soup and coffee bubbling on the camp stoves. And tonight they would pitch camp at Linderman Lake. Bear had told Clara there was actually a hotel at Linderman Lake, and Juliette intended to stay there. She'd been dreaming of it for days.

She ran her dogs up next to the other sleds and set the brake. Henry and Luc, two of the Chilkats, waved before they started changing her dog team's burlap shoes. Juliette flexed her shoulders and bent from side to side, working out the stiffness. It had been a long time since she had needed liniment, but her body felt the effects of hours of strenuous exercise.

Ben drove up behind her and gave his dogs to Henry. He'd shaved his beard the day after she wondered aloud how he'd look without it, but she couldn't judge the effect because he wore ashes and grease on his face like everyone else. At this point, Juliette was so used to seeing the gunk on everyone's face that she no longer felt self-conscious about it. But she wished she could see Ben's shaven chin.

"Did you notice the moose we passed about a mile

back?" he asked, falling into step beside her. As always, he scanned her thoroughly as if assuring himself that she was all right.

"I was thinking about the hotel at Linderman Lake and didn't notice much of anything." That was partly true, but as usual, she'd spent most of this morning's trek thinking about him. Sometimes she felt as if a piece of Ben Dare had crept into her mind to tease and torment her. She passed the hours behind the sled remembering every word of their conversation the evening before, wondering if he ever thought about holding her naked body in his arms, wondering what she would do if he tried to kiss her. She continually thought about kissing.

"Don't get your hopes up about the hotel," Ben advised after they had both poured cups of hot coffee and had swallowed their noonday dose of citric acid to ward off scurvy. "Bear says it doesn't amount to much. The men's side of one big room is separated from the women's side by a blanket, and the cots they rent aren't any better than what you have now. Lighting is provided by a candle stuck in a bottle on top of a flour barrel. As for the food . . ." He shrugged broad shoulders.

Crushing disappointment followed her shock. "That won't do," she said finally. It had to be the height of impropriety to sleep near a strange man with only a blanket separating them. "I was imagining a real hotel." Fiercely she told herself that she would not cry in front of him. "I'd hoped to sleep in a real bed and have a real sit-down meal at a table." She had imagined being warm all over at the same time, and a long bath in a real tub.

"This trip has been hard on you, hasn't it?" he asked softly.

Oh, Lord. Sympathy had a way of doing her in. Blinking hard, she tried to sound brave. "I'd just like a little break from all of this. Then I'll be ready to go again."

She was beginning to understand what Zoe meant when Zoe spoke of growing up without privacy. It was impossible to maintain modesty while sharing a tiny tent with two other women. She knew that Clara had a mole on her hip and knew that Zoe brushed her hair a hundred strokes every night. Clara snored, and Zoe muttered as she slept. Clara gargled with salt water; Zoe was fanatical about cleaning her fingernails. They left hair wound around the curling iron. Neither of them remembered to trim the wick in the lantern. Juliette had never known these small details about another woman, and she didn't especially like knowing them now. Was it too much to hope for one night alone?

"Maybe I can work something out. Let me think about it," Ben promised, giving her an oddly speculative look. At least she thought he did. It was hard to read his expression through his blue-tinted glasses and the ashy gunk on his face.

Clara joined her beside the stove, and they watched Ben walk toward the men. "So," Clara said, noisily sipping a cup of soup, "has he kissed you yet?"

"Do you have to make slurping noises when you eat? And no, he hasn't kissed me. I don't want him to."

"Liar. And yes, I have to make slurping noises. No one except you can drink soup without slurping." Clara made a face. "I didn't come over here to discuss soup etiquette. I'm worried about Zoe."

At least they could agree about Zoe. Juliette turned in a circle until she spotted Zoe talking to Tom. "Sometimes she seems happier than we've ever seen her, but I've heard her crying at night after she thinks we're asleep."

"It's Tom," Clara said flatly. "She loves him. I told her it was all right with me if she didn't want to shoot our husband. We could camp at Bennett Lake until spring, then go home. You and Zoe could tell your families that Jean Jacques died, and that's that. We start our lives over."

Juliette gazed across the snow at Ben, longing in her eyes. Clara painted a tempting picture. "But it won't work. What if we, say, remarried? That marriage would be based on a lie. And then, what if Jean Jacques showed up again? We'd have two husbands, both of them mad as wet hens, I'd imagine."

"*Ja,* that is what Zoe said." Clara heaved a sigh. "She said it's better if we know for sure the no-account snake is dead. I think she hates him enough that she's looking forward to shooting him."

"I never thought I would feel this way, but I hate him, too." Juliette gazed at Ben through a film of tears. "Things could be so wonderful if I wasn't married."

Clara shifted to look at Bear, who stared back at her. "You almost drowning and me falling in that hole in the snow made me think about things. Zoe is right to grab what happiness she can while she can." She squeezed Juliette's hand. "You should think about that, too, if you haven't already. Anyone can see that Ben Dare is pining for you."

"Exactly what are you saying?" Juliette asked slowly.

"You know what we wondered about when Zoe and Tom were caught in the storm?"

"I didn't wonder about any such thing!" Her lie and the subject matter made her cheeks burn under the grease.

"Of course you did. I did, too. Well, I hope they loved each other all night." Clara gave her a challenging stare. "If that makes me a floozy, then I'm a floozy. I've thought about it, and I don't think we should let Jean Jacques Villette ruin our lives more than he has already. We deserve to be loved and happy!"

"Clara Klaus!" Juliette stepped back, and her eyes widened. "You're planning to seduce Bear!" And it wouldn't take much to be successful. If ever Juliette had seen a man eager to be seduced, that man was Bear Barrett. He couldn't keep his eyes off Clara. It suddenly occurred to her the same could be said about Ben. She spun around to look at him. Sure enough, he was looking back at her. She wet her lips and swallowed.

"Maybe I do have plans," Clara said, raising her chin.

"And you know something? No one cares. Not up here. Up here the rules are different."

Juliette sniffed. "The proper rules for respectable ladies remain the same the world over."

"You're wrong, Juliette. Up here it's live and let live. No one cares what you do unless it affects them. When you fell into the lake there was talk, but—"

"See? I told you!"

Clara shook her head, shaking ice from the fur framing her face. "Not talk about you and Ben. Everyone understood stripping off your clothing to save your life. The speculation was about whatever possessed you to walk out on thin ice to begin with. And no one has made any scurrilous comments about Tom and Zoe being alone the night of the storm. It's taken me a while to understand all this, but now I think I do. And the freedom of it is exhilarating!" A wide smile curved her lips. "Think of it. Up here we can do whatever we want. We can be who we are. The only rules are those set by nature or by ourselves."

All afternoon, while running behind her sled, Juliette thought about Clara believing that Zoe loved Tom and about their being together, and she considered Clara's intention to seduce Bear. And self-pity swamped her. They were seizing some happiness for themselves and the devil take the hindmost. They weren't letting a little thing like a husband stand in their way. If indeed any of them had a legal husband at all. It was possible that none of the marriages counted. In which case, it didn't matter if they loved and let themselves be loved by another man. So why couldn't Juliette embrace this line of reasoning? Why couldn't she make her own rules, too?

Because it seemed improper to fall into the arms of one man while wearing another man's wedding ring.

Thinking about it gave her a headache. Did femme fatales worry themselves into a frenzy about these details? Was it laudable or truly stupid to cling to propriety? She knew how Aunt Kibble and her mother would answer that question. But Aunt Kibble had never seen Juliette as pretty or appealing enough to attract a man. A man could only be interested in her inheritance. It was easy to stand on firm notions of propriety regarding relationships between men and women when no man pursued the woman in question.

But Ben didn't know about her money. And he thought she was beautiful. She saw it in his eyes, and it thrilled her. Everything about him thrilled her. The way he moved and the way he spoke. The way he challenged himself and did some of his own packing even though he didn't have to. She loved his thoughtfulness and loved knowing he had run into the freezing lake without a moment's hesitation when she was drowning. She loved his loyalty to his late wife and how he placed no limits on women. She loved the look and touch and scent of him.

Oh, Lord. She loved him.

Suddenly Jean Jacques's ring pinched her finger and her conscience. The marriage hadn't meant anything to Jean Jacques, but it had meant everything to her. At least she'd thought it had. First pain and now fury had begun to blur her memories. She remembered Jean Jacques was handsome, but she could no longer recall his exact features. When she tried, her memory painted a portrait that looked remarkably like Ben Dare. In her memory, Jean Jacques spoke in Ben's voice. But the two could not have been more different. Ben was honest and loyal, whereas Jean Jacques was anything but.

She loved Ben.

Oh, Lord, what was she going to do?

The first two days at Linderman Lake passed in a rush of chores and renewing acquaintances. Mrs. Eddington brought them a molasses cake, and other ladies they had met stopped by to say hello and share their experiences on the trail.

Juliette helped Zoe and Clara melt snow in large pots

and boil their laundry, all of them weepy with gratitude for clean clothing and socks and undergarments. They aired their sleeping bags, blankets, and coats and scarves; they mended clothing and stockings. They took turns washing their hair and sitting next to the stove to dry.

Since they were settled for a while, they assembled their camp stove inside the tent and for the first time in a long time felt warm all over. To celebrate, Clara cooked one of the two-pound cans of corned beef and dried cabbage. Zoe made cornbread. And Juliette baked a dried apple pie that gave her a secret flash of pride. Three months ago she couldn't have made a pie if the fate of the world depended on it. They ate sitting on their cots, wearing clean woolen long johns, feeling better than they had since Chilkoot Pass.

"I tried to buy some butter for the cornbread," Zoe said, "and I actually found some. But the man wanted twenty dollars a pound. I decided we could eat it with grease and jam."

"It's wonderful. And so is the corned beef."

"Hurry up and finish. I want some of your pie, it smells so good. And you didn't burn the crust this time," Clara observed with a smile.

They looked toward the tent flap when someone called Juliette's name. She frowned in surprise. "It sounds like Luc. What could he want?" It wasn't usual for one of the Chilkats to come calling.

"Well, poke your head outside and find out," Clara said.

Juliette looked down at loose hair flowing over the top of her shapeless red long johns. "I can't answer the door looking like this!"

"Then you'll never know what he wanted, will you?"

"Damn." There she went again, showing the effects of keeping bad company. The bad company looked at her and laughed. "What do you want?" she called to the tent flap.

"I have a message for Miss Juliette March."

Her eyebrows lifted. "What is the message?"

"It's in an envelope, missy, and I can't read."

Itching with curiosity, Juliette stuck her arm through a crack in the opening. Instantly, icy wind raised goose bumps beneath the sleeve of her long johns. "Thank you," she called, pulling the envelope inside. Her name was written in a bold male hand. "Who could have sent this?"

"I can't imagine!" Zoe and Clara fell backward on their cots and rolled their eyes.

"Now who could it possibly be? Mrs. Eddington? That rat, Jake Horvath?"

"I know! Maybe the Queen is visiting Canada and wants to meet fellow royalty."

"That's not funny," Juliette said in the prissy voice that by now annoyed even her. She turned the envelope over and studied the initials stamped in red sealing wax. BJD.

"Ben sent it?" Clara fanned her face. "Well, knock me over. Who would have guessed?"

Zoe rolled around laughing. "So what does he say?"

"That is none of your business." But she couldn't resist reading it aloud. "Mr. Benjamin Dare requests the pleasure of Miss Juliette March's company at dinner on December eighteenth at seven o'clock. Twelve Main Street." She blinked. "He's inviting me to dinner. What shall I do?"

"More to the point, what will you wear?" Zoe sat up. "You can't wear the same clothes you've been wearing on the trail."

Clara nodded. "We'll have to rummage through the crates and find her other clothes." She narrowed her eyes at Juliette. "The ash and grease helped, but your face is still red and chapped. We have about twenty-four hours to work on you. Lard. There's nothing better than lard for softening skin."

"I'll grind some rice and make powder. And I can make a lemon rinse for her hair out of the citrus tablets."

"Miss March?" Luc was still out there. "I was instructed to request a reply."

"Just a minute, please." Flying up, she tore through her small overnight valise, digging for stationery. Frowning, she glanced at Zoe and Clara. "Do you think I should accept?"

They stared as if she had lost her senses, then continued discussing how she should dress her hair for the occasion.

Different rules, she reminded herself. There was no harm in having dinner with Ben. No one cared. After she found her pen and bottle of ink, she wrote: Miss Juliette March accepts with pleasure Mr. Benjamin Dare's kind invitation to dinner on December the eighteenth at seven o'clock.

My, how she had missed the small civilities of mannerly conduct. Receiving and responding to a proper invitation spread a satisfying warmth through her body. After she'd handed her reply through the tent flap, she sat back on her cot, half listening to Clara and Zoe, and she wondered where a prospector had learned to compose a proper invitation. She would have said that she knew Ben's character well, but there were gaps in her knowledge.

"Is number twelve Main Street the address of the hotel?" she asked, worried. Hoping that Bear had been mistaken, she had ventured a look. The hotel was worse than Bear had suggested. An out-of-tune piano assaulted the ears in the saloon on the ground floor. She had gathered her courage, stuck her head inside, and noticed gaps in the ceiling through which she could see cot legs. Knowing hotel guests could look between their shoes and see down into the noisy saloon was almost as disgusting as the overpowering stink of stale beer and tobacco juice.

She couldn't imagine having dinner in such primitive surroundings.

"Who knows? None of the buildings are numbered," Clara said, going back to her discussion with Zoe about what had to be done to pull Juliette together for her evening.

Juliette gazed at them with sudden startling affection. On her own, she might well have talked herself out of accepting Ben's invitation. It surprised her how much their approval meant, and how it settled her mind and affected her decisions.

Drawing a deep breath, she moved to sit on Zoe's cot. "Well, what would you two advise? Shall I wear my brilliants?"

Two hours later, while Zoe was giving her a manicure and they were nearing a consensus on her ensemble, Juliette realized how much she missed having sisters. And she hadn't even known it.

Luc called for her at a quarter to seven, assisted her into her snowshoes, and carried her small bag containing evening slippers, a second handkerchief, an evening fan, and various toiletries. An argument had ensued after she'd inspected the toiletries that Clara and Zoe had assembled.

"What is this?" she'd asked curiously, examining a pink ribbon attached to a ring-shaped collapsible object.

Zoe and Clara glanced at each other and then Clara whispered, "It's a pessary."

Shock made her drop the object and then stare at it with wide horrified eyes. Occasionally married women on the cusp of respectability whispered about such items, but decent women weren't supposed to know about contraception. "Where did you get this?"

"Mrs. Eddington helped." When Clara saw Juliette's face, she spread her hands. "Mrs. Eddington thinks it's for me."

"How dare you!" Anger and mortification made her

hands shake. She sputtered. "I have no need of this, none at all!"

Zoe touched her arm. "Very likely you're correct," she agreed soothingly. "But just in case . . ."

"There is no 'just in case.' Mr. Dare and I are having dinner together, and that is all!" Fire blazed in her cheeks and throat. "How could you believe that I . . . What kind of a woman do you think I am?"

"Despite what you'd like to believe, you're not a saint," Clara said briskly, tucking the pessary back into Juliette's bag. "None of us are."

Zoe's face turned almost as red as Juliette's. "If, and all I'm saying is *if*, things should, ah, move in a, say, direction you don't now anticipate, then you should—" She cast a helpless look at Clara.

"You should protect yourself," Clara finished firmly.

Zoe nodded. "I'm sure many a woman wishes she'd had the foresight to protect herself before circumstance placed her in a position that . . . that . . ." She pressed her palms against burning cheeks. "You know."

Juliette stared and understood positively that Zoe and Tom had been together. Clara also knew her suspicions had just become a certainty. Confirmation confused everything. If someone Juliette respected and considered an honorable woman could be with a man outside marriage, then . . .

"I see," she said slowly, uncertain how to proceed. "Well, thank you for thinking of me, but I won't need a . . . a . . ." She couldn't say the word. "And I don't need these items either." Frowning, she focused her attention on the other toiletries. A comb and extra hairpins, a washcloth, body powder, replacement buttons, for heaven's sake. Items one would need to reassemble oneself.

"Juliette." Clara gave her a hard-eyed stare. "Must you be a shortsighted idiot? If you don't need these items, fine. If you do need them—and that's your own business—then you'll have them." She closed Juliette's bag, snapping off conversation.

Now that she knew about Zoe and Tom, Juliette couldn't take the high road without sounding judgmental and thus embarrassing Zoe. After chewing her lips for a moment, she sighed. "I won't need these items, but thank you for being concerned about my welfare." Best to leave it at that. "How do I look?"

"Beautiful!" they said in unison.

Their answer made her smile. She'd never been beautiful, but tonight she thought she approached that happy state as closely as she ever had. They had brushed her hair until it shone glossy brown, then pulled it up and back with her brilliants, and they'd used the curling iron to create long fat curls that fell from her crown to her shoulders. Beneath her heavy trail coat, she wore a black cape, and beneath that she wore the only dress gown she'd packed, a smart combination of black velvet and cream-colored satin. The gown was lower necked and revealed more cleavage than she would have preferred for an evening alone with a man, but the puffy shoulder sleeves worried her more. A gap opened between her long gloves and the sleeves. She didn't think she was at her best when she was shivering and her teeth were clicking together with cold. On the positive side, she didn't have to concern herself about dragging the gown's train through slush and heaven knew what else. Zoe had put her needle to work and had shortened the train to walking length.

As Juliette and Luc traveled down Linderman Lake's noisy Main Street—such as it was—she eyed the tobacco-stained snow and whispered a silent thank-you to Zoe. She wasn't dragging a train through the slop. And thanks to Clara, her cheeks had a healthy glow, but the lard had softened and smoothed the chapped rough spots.

For several minutes Juliette believed Luc must have made a mistake as he led her past the last weathered building at the end of the street and they moved onto a sled track lit only by a half moon. Just as she was about to inquire, they entered a curve in the road, and she spotted the shimmer of light at windows.

Luc escorted her to a small log cabin and rapped his knuckles on the door. At once the door swung open, and Ben smiled at her.

For a stunning moment Juliette didn't recognize him. He looked years younger without the scruffy prospector's beard. It occurred to her that he was likely in his middle thirties; she had guessed him a full ten years older. And she seldom saw him without his fur hood or a hat. But tonight his hair was carefully parted in the middle and brushed back in dark wings. He wore a tailored three-piece black suit and the only starched collar and cuffs she had seen since leaving Seattle. For a full minute she could not breathe. This Ben Dare was a strikingly handsome stranger.

Suddenly feeling shy, she waited in silence while Ben took her bag before he thanked and dismissed Luc. "I won't need you any more this evening, Luc. Thank you," he said pleasantly. Then he turned those blue eyes on her, and her heart skipped a beat. "Let me help you out of your snowshoes."

He knelt before her, and she steadied herself by placing a hand on his shoulder. Beneath the expensive wool of his jacket, he was rock solid, the hard, honed Ben that she knew.

After placing her snowshoes just inside the door, he led her into the warm cabin. A colorful hooked rug covered the plank floor in front of a crackling fire—that's what she noticed first. She wouldn't have to worry about shivering through dinner.

"The windows!" Surprise widened her eyes.

"They're blocks of ice," he said, laughing.

Turning slowly, Juliette took in the cabin. The furnishings were sparse, but appeared comfortable. Someone had hung framed magazine covers on the walls, had assembled a collection of books in a low case. A small, minimally equipped kitchen was separated from a claw-foot table by a serving counter. Though small and plain, the cabin was snug and possessed a certain charm.

"Who owns this?" she asked, almost afraid to look at him. She didn't think she could without staring. Or without causing an odd fluttery eruption in her stomach.

"The cabin belongs to Bill Prather, who owns the general store. He agreed to let me rent his home for three days."

Juliette knew the price of things in this part of the world. "It must have cost a fortune!" If a pound of butter cost twenty dollars, what on earth had he paid to rent a whole cabin?

For three days. Suddenly her mouth went dry, and her hands began to tremble. Three days. And he had not asked Luc to return to escort her back to the tent.

"Ben . . ."

"The bedroom is through that door," he said, curving her fingers around her bag of toiletries. "If you'd care to freshen up."

They were alone together in a cabin with a bedroom. Which he had rented for three whole days. She licked her lips in indecision.

"A decent woman would remove herself from this compromising situation!" A tiny and indignant Aunt Kibble spoke from her left shoulder.

"At once!" Her tiny mother added from her right shoulder.

"When you return, we'll have sherry beside the fire," Ben said, interrupting the flow of admonitions. And then— and then he bent and lightly brushed his lips across hers.

Electricity seared through her body. For an instant, she could not move, could not think, could not function. It was as if lightning had struck and paralyzed her.

"Leave this very instant!" Aunt Kibble demanded, outraged.

"This man is no gentleman!" her mother's voice huffed. "He's only interested in your inheritance!"

"Shut. Up." Juliette stated the two words silently but with firm command. Throughout her lifetime too many evenings and too many situations had been spoiled as she did the right thing according to other people's notions of propriety. Tonight she was not going to be timid prissy little Juliette March.

Tonight, she was a modern woman, dashing and liberated from constraints better left to another life. Tonight, she would set her own rules of deportment.

After touching her lips, she lifted her head and walked toward the bedroom door.

Tonight she was a worldly woman with a pessary in her bag, by heaven. A femme fatale eagerly prepared for come what may.

Ben had kissed her. It was a different world now.

Chapter 17

Ben had thoughtfully lit a lantern atop the bureau so Juliette could see as she removed her heavy coat and mittens and her cape, laying them across a colorful bed quilt. The bedroom was a small jewel of a room with peeled log walls that still retained a faint scent of pine, and there was enough furniture to seem cozily crowded. But what caught her eye was a bathtub next to the interior wall, the first she had seen in months. It was old-fashioned, like Aunt Kibble's, and had to be filled with water heated in the kitchen, but it was a real bathtub, and she envied Ben for having the use of it for three days.

She imagined him lying naked in the tub, a cigar between his teeth, his eyes narrowed against the smoke. Suddenly she felt excessively warm. Spinning from the sight of the tub, she faced the mirror atop the bureau and frowned while she smoothed her hair, retied the black ribbon around her throat, and repuffed her shoulder sleeves. Then, leaning forward, she examined the hint of cleavage that showed at her low neckline.

For an instant, she regretted wearing an evening dress. On the other hand, tonight was a night fashioned for boldness and daring. She was a woman who had decided to make her own rules, who was having dinner alone with a man in his rented house. And he had launched the evening by kissing her. Oh, my heavens.

She pulled her fan from the bag and furiously fanned her face until she felt less overwrought by her own recklessness.

Then, while retrieving her evening heels from her bag, she withdrew the pessary and examined it in the light of the lantern. Her heart beat faster merely from touching and looking at such an item. Who would ever suppose that Juliette March knew about contraception, let alone would have a device in her possession. And might have need of it. Lordy. Pink flooded her cheeks.

Well, of course she would not have need of it. But how thrilling it would be to know she was modern and devil-may-care enough to wear a contraceptive device. That she, intrepid traveler as she had become, would be prepared for whatever wicked adventure wild destiny might fling her way. Oh, yes, there was more to Juliette March than anyone knew. She nodded wisely at her image in the mirror. Beneath her admittedly prissy little heart beat the pulse of a brazen hussy.

Or maybe she was just talking herself into something.

But tonight would never come again. Impulsively making the decision, she sat on the bed, flipped up her skirts, and after several failed attempts, managed to insert the pessary. The embarrassing immodesty of touching herself *there* was overshadowed by the guilty pleasure of having a thrilling secret.

Trembling at her daring, she pressed down her skirts, drew a deep breath, and then she twisted off Jean Jacques's wedding ring. Ben was not wearing the green scarf tonight. She could do no less. She dropped the ring into her bag, muttered good riddance, then lifted her head and returned to the living room. Wearing a pessary gave a woman flair and confidence.

Ben's reaction was all she had dreamed it might be. He inhaled sharply and stared, his eyes going smoky blue and hard. "Words fail me," he said in a husky voice. "It doesn't do justice merely to say that you are exquisite."

So was he. Anyone seeing him tonight would never have guessed that he was a prospector on his way to the gold fields in search of a fortune. He looked like a gentleman in every detail, from the gold watch fob crossing his waistcoat to the jet studs at his cuffs and shirtfront.

Taking her arm and pressing it to the side of his chest, he escorted her to facing chairs before the fire. After touching his sherry glass to hers, he leaned back and studied her with such obvious fascination that Juliette glanced down and blushed.

"May I ask a personal question?" After she nodded, he said, "You're such a lovely woman. I wonder why you've never married. I assume you chose not to?"

"There was someone. . . ." His question fairly quivered with underlying implications, but she didn't let herself think about them. Instead, she turned her face toward the fire in the grate and considered love and truth. She couldn't tell Ben about Jean Jacques, certainly not tonight, but Ben was too important to her not to come as close to the truth as possible.

"You see, I am an heiress," she confided after a brief hesitation. If she hadn't squelched the tiny Aunt Kibble on her shoulder, Aunt Kibble would have been having an apoplectic fit. The worst thing to tell a man seeking gold was that a fortune sat not three feet in front of him. "My aunt, who sought to protect me, was ever alert to fortune-hunters. And sadly, those were the men who wished to come courting."

Ben nodded. "I assumed it must be something like that."

"You did?" Her eyebrows lifted.

"I overheard Miss Wilder mention that you paid Tom to pack her and Miss Klaus to Dawson. She didn't sound happy about it," he added with a smile. "Only someone of means could afford such a generous gift." His gaze traveled slowly to her breast, waist, and then down the length of her gown. "And your clothing suggests a comfortable status."

"You knew all along!" The color drained from her face, and she forgot to deny that it was she who had paid Tom. She had believed Ben cared for her because she thought he knew nothing about her money. Now his attentions fell beneath a cloud of suspicion, and horror widened her eyes. She had done it again. She had fallen in love with a man who saw only her inheritance.

He laughed at her expression. "Dear Juliette. If you're thinking I'm interested in your money, I assure you I am not."

"That's what I'm thinking," she whispered.

He pulled his chair beside hers, took the sherry glass from her fingers, and held her hands. "I have a confession to make. I didn't guess your background from your attire or by overhearing Miss Wilder. I asked the hotel manager in Seattle who you were, and I recognized your name."

She was flabbergasted. "How could you possibly recognize my name? I'm positive we haven't met before."

"We haven't." His smile was almost a caress. "I know your name because the Bay City Bank in San Francisco manages your inheritance, and I own the Bay City Bank. You're not our largest investment account, but you're among the top fifty."

Her mouth rounded, and she stared. "Good heavens. I've heard my aunt mention you. She calls you 'the brawling banker.' "

He laughed. "Banking in the West isn't the gentleman's profession that it is back East."

"I thought you . . . I . . . ." She had never imagined that he was anyone other than who he appeared to be, a stampeder hoping to find salvation in the gold fields of the frozen north.

"Frankly, I was pleased that you didn't recognize my name. I didn't want my background known. Most of the prospectors we've met are desperate men. I doubt they'd look kindly on a competitor who doesn't care if he ever sees a gold nugget. And there was another reason I preferred not to mention that I'm your banker." He hesitated, and his expression sobered. "You have a substantial inheritance, Juliette, but . . ."

"But *your* fortune is far greater." It took a moment, but the significance sank into her mind. "My heavens! You feared if I knew the truth, I might be more interested in your wealth than in you!" She stared at him before bursting into laughter. "Oh, Ben."

After she'd caught her breath, Ben turned her hand and ran his thumb along her gloved palm. "The thought occurred to me, but not immediately. When I discovered you aboard the *Annasett*, I considered the coincidence remarkable. That the first woman who had caught my eye in a year kept crossing my path. But I didn't anticipate that you and I would . . ." He smiled and shrugged.

"But why did you come to the Yukon?"

"It was time to start living again," he said simply. "I wanted something outside the day-to-day routine, something physically demanding. I wanted an event to mark the end of one life and the beginning of another."

"Has that happened?" she asked, laying a hand on his arm.

"Oh, yes," he said, looking into her eyes. When she blushed bright pink, he released her hand and reached for his sherry. "Why did you come to the Yukon? You've never said."

This question would be difficult to answer truthfully. "I began the journey looking for someone. Now I know I don't want to find that person," she said in a whisper. Quickly she rushed past the enigmatic statement. "I was just . . . swept into this." She shook her head. "Clara first mentioned the Yukon," she explained carefully, "and Zoe insisted that we come."

"Are they looking for someone, too?"

"I'm truly sorry, Ben, but I can't explain further."

Curiosity curved along his raised eyebrow, but he nodded. "Someday I hope you'll feel comfortable enough with me to share your secrets."

A wobbly smile curved her mouth. "I wish I could confide in you, but other people are involved."

They finished their sherry in silence. Juliette imagined that Ben struggled with his disappointment in secretiveness while she fought to stamp down attitudes she had vowed to set aside for tonight. She absolutely would not think about Jean Jacques Villette—or the morality or propriety of being with Ben.

When he spoke again, Juliette understood with relief that she hadn't spoiled their evening. He wouldn't press about her secret, nor would he hold it against her.

"I considered asking one of Tom's Chilkats to serve tonight, but decided I didn't want anyone present but you and me. I hope you don't mind that we'll dine more casually than formally—I'll be setting the table and serving."

How considerate he was. The cabin was far enough from Main Street that no one had seen her enter and no one would see her depart. There would be no one present to gossip later about what they had said to each other.

"I'm willing to help. I'd be happy to set the table."

They both rose at the same moment and froze, aware they stood too close. Juliette inhaled the tangy scent of men's cologne and laundry starch and the sweetness of sherry on his breath. She sensed his strength and masculinity.

At the instant she thought the intensity of his gaze would make her swoon, he bent his head and kissed her again, as lightly as before, testing her response. And as before, his kiss set her mouth on fire and flashed a searing heat through her body. This time she experienced a pang of frustration. Suddenly she wanted him to really kiss her, hard and passionately.

He drew a finger down her cheek, trailing warmth. "You're my guest. I don't want you to do anything except enjoy the evening."

When she was certain her legs would perform without wobbling, she followed him to a round table separated from the kitchen by a counter and watched him shake out a snowy damask tablecloth. She loved damask, the elegant look, the sensual feel of it. He smoothed the cloth on the table and adjusted the overhang to precisely eighteen inches, exactly correct. When she raised her gaze, she discovered he was watching her eyes widen, aware that the cloth and its fit would please her.

Smiling, he placed a vase containing an arrangement of dried lupin, iris, and columbines in the center of the table and framed it between two tall white candles.

Juliette pressed a hand over her heart. The dried flower arrangement was low enough that they would see each other above it. Attention to these small details made the difference between a delightful dining experience and disappointment. Not to mention that she had not seen a centerpiece during the course of this journey. Inhaling a deep breath that was almost a sigh, she edged closer to the table.

"It must be beautiful up here in the spring and summer," he remarked, indicating the dried flowers.

"What? Oh, yes, I suppose it is," she murmured, surprised to discover that she sounded a little breathless.

But good heavens, a long time had passed since she had dressed for dinner and sat down to a properly clad table with candles and a centerpiece. The excitement of it trembled at the corners of her lips.

Watching her, Ben snapped open a napkin—and she knew at once that it was exactly 121 inches square. Oh, the joy of a proper napkin, the thrill of it. And then—then, in a move that made her stomach tighten in a shudder of bliss, he folded the napkins and placed them on the table to the left of where the forks would go. With the fold of the napkin facing out. Oh, my Lord.

Juliette drew a rapturous breath. "There's nothing as soul-satisfying as a properly laid table," she whispered. And nothing as incredibly seductive as watching a handsome man demonstrate his firm command of etiquette. It was utterly erotic. And who could help feeling aroused? The cloth overhang was exactly right. So was the size of the napkins. And he had placed them with the fold facing out.

Half swooning with emotion, she snapped open her fan and waved it at the heat pulsing in her face. For a full minute she and Ben gazed at each other across the centerpiece and candles, noting flushed faces and parted lips, quickened breath and the mounting tension of awareness.

"Would you be offended if I loosened my tie?" he asked in a husky voice.

"Please do." Her own voice had ripened with invitation.

Narrowing his eyes in a way that made her think of crumpled sheets and warm musky scents, he tossed aside his tie, reached behind, and brought forth two pewter service plates.

"Service plates!" Juliette gripped the edge of the table in the throes of near ecstasy. She hadn't seen service plates since the hotel in Seattle. A damp shine appeared in her eyes as she observed the sensual manner in which his long fingers slid across the pewter rims before he set down the plates. A shiver rippled down her spine.

"You have the most beautiful eyes," Ben said after he'd positioned the service plates on the table. "Occasionally the color reminds me of a stormy sky. Other times, like now, it's like gazing into a shimmer of silver."

"You look very handsome without the beard," she whispered. His smooth cheeks and square jaw invited exploration. She longed to stroke his face with her fingertips, wanted to press her nose to his skin and sniff the manly scent of his cologne.

The room suddenly felt so hot that she could have believed they dined in Linda Vista at the height of August. His eyes traveled over her face like twin suns, setting fire to her skin and igniting her heart. A trickle of moisture slipped between her breasts. Discreetly, she directed the fan toward her cleavage while trying desperately to steady herself. She wet her lips. "What comes next?" she murmured. Lord, she sounded like she was strangling.

"Crystal."

"Crystal? Oh!" Heaven help her and keep her on her feet. Not tin mugs, not thick everyday glass—crystal. She stared at his mouth, thinking of crystal touching his lips. Thinking about her touching his lips. And him touching hers. Crystal. The very word was carnal and evocative of lips and sliding fingertips. A tingle began at the base of her throat and spread throughout her body.

Teasing, shamelessly toying with her emotions, he held a water goblet in front of his chest and lightly tapped the rim. The clear ring of crystal sang between them, reverberating across Juliette's skin, electric and thrilling. No symphony had ever aroused her so. Gasping, she swayed and furiously fanned the sheen of perspiration appearing on her forehead. She noticed Ben's temples were also damp.

Not taking his eyes off her, he placed the water goblets above the service plates. After pinging the wineglasses and observing her sharp intake of breath, he carefully positioned them to the right of the water crystal.

"Forgive me, but may I remove my jacket?" He paused to blot his forehead and throat.

"Yes. Yes." She wished she could remove something, too. She was burning with an intensity of sensation. And her nerves burst into flame when he stood across the table in his waistcoat and shirtsleeves. In the world she usually inhabited, women seldom saw men without their jackets. Seeing him as he stood before her now was scandalously, excitingly, erotically intimate.

"Do the silver next," she whispered, her lips trembling.

He drew the moment out, sending a shiver of anticipation through her body. He slid his thumb and forefinger along the handle of a knife, extending the drama. This was where so many failed, placing the knife incorrectly. Finally, his eyes smoldering, he leaned forward and firmly positioned the knife with the sharp edge facing the service plate.

Juliette's heart gave a leap in her chest, and she thought

she might faint. It was perfect. Moisture flooded her secret places with liquid longing. He knew the language of the table. She could hardly stand it. By observing the knives, she read his signal that there would be a meat and a fish course. But his triumph lay in placing the sharp edge toward the service plate! She thought her heart would pound through her chest.

And now he was turning a soup spoon between his fingers. Knots ran up his jawline when he looked at her. His speculative gaze had grown bold, skimming her cleavage, searing her to the toes. And, my lord, this man had the most sensual mouth of any man she had ever met. Her heart raced, and her knees dissolved to the consistency of pudding. She didn't know if she could remain standing through the placement of the forks.

"The salad will come after the entrée," she murmured ecstatically as he positioned the soup spoon and finally the forks. They would not adopt the new style of serving the salad before the entrée. It was more than any woman could bear. She wanted him with a passion that steamed and boiled inside her mind and body.

When he saw her expression, his muscles hardened. "Juliette . . ." The tone of ragged desire undid her.

They flew around the table and into each other's arms. Locked in a passionate embrace, they kissed again and again, their hands flying, touching, stroking, caressing. Hot, fevered kisses rained over Juliette's eyes, lips, throat. And a sound like a sob choked her. "Yes, yes, yes," she whispered mindlessly. "Yes. Ben. Oh, yes, yes."

Scooping her into his arms, he carried her into the bedroom and gently stood her on her feet. "Are you very sure?" he asked in a voice rough with desire.

In answer she turned her back to him and lifted the weight of curls off her neck so he could unbutton her gown. "Hurry."

His fingers were sure and swift, familiar with the tabs and hooks and ties of feminine attire. In seconds, she stood before him, an hourglass clad in lace-edged shimmy and corset. He kissed her breasts, then tore off his shirt, sending jet studs skittering across the floor. He threw off his waistcoat and pushed away his trousers, kicked out of his shoes.

"Wait! Blow out the lantern!"

But it was too late. She stared at his body in awe, never having seen a naked man in the light before. How splendid he was. Tall and lean and wedge-shaped. He might have been one of the statues she had seen in a book on Greek sculpture. The absence of a fig leaf drew her attention, and her cheeks blazed. "Oh, my goodness!"

Drawing her to him, he kissed her hard, leaving her gasping, then sat her on the edge of the bed. Kneeling, he removed her evening slippers, then her garters, and he peeled down her stockings, his fingers hot on the curve of her legs. Rising to sit next to her, he turned her gently, and then his nimble fingers opened her laces, and her corset slid to the floor.

Her instinct was to beg him to extinguish the lantern. Then she remembered he had already seen her naked. And he wanted to see her again. After he smoothed down the short sleeves of her shimmy, she stood on shaking legs and let him lower the shimmy over her breasts, to her waist, and over her hips. The silky garment pooled at her feet, and she stood before him, eyes closed and cheeks on fire, listening to his ragged intake of breath. Every instinct demanded that she cover herself, but she made herself stand still.

"You are so beautiful! So small and perfect and beautiful!"

She didn't remember him pulling down the quilt and blankets, didn't recall climbing onto the bed. One minute she stood before him, the next minute they were wrapped in each other's arms, kissing and touching with building urgency. Not until she thought she would shake apart with longing did he rise above her.

And then it was so good. He was gentle and tender, kissing her as he moved, caressing her, whispering endearments. Because she was reckless and uninhibited, a woman willing to dare anything tonight, she let her fingers slide down his back, and she touched his bare buttocks, hoping the brazen move didn't shock him too badly.

If he was startled, he didn't reveal it, but continued kissing her, continued his gentle lovemaking. Emboldened, she opened her eyes a tiny bit and snatched a quick glance at him. He was watching her. Oh, my. She'd assumed that he, too, would have his eyes closed.

"Is something wrong?" he whispered when she stopped moving.

The light was dim but clear enough that she could see his tousled hair and the perspiration shining on his forehead. "Is it decent to have our eyes open?" she asked, also whispering.

"Dearest Juliette. Whatever gives two people pleasure is decent." Lifting on his elbows, he looked down at her and then kissed her in a way she had never been kissed before. His tongue parted her lips and tasted her mouth. Her eyes widened, then snapped shut, and she gave herself to the sensation.

"Do that again," she whispered. "If you're sure it's decent." It felt too exotic and too arousing to be proper, but she didn't give a damn. "Do it again."

The new way of kissing made her feel wild inside, strange and hot and urgent and then, and then, and then her body shuddered and the heavens exploded inside her mind. When the moment faded, she found herself shaking and drenched in perspiration.

"I don't know what happened," she said, peering up at him, "but it was wonderful. Did you make that happen?"

"I hope so," he said with a smile, brushing a damp tendril off her cheek.

"Did you? . . . What I mean is, I know that I . . . but, did you? . . ."

"It doesn't matter."

Oh, she loved him so much. "If you'd like to go on a bit longer, I wouldn't mind."

"Then I believe I will," he said, kissing her. She had an idea that he struggled not to laugh, but she couldn't imagine why he would laugh. She must be wrong.

Afterward, Ben pulled on his trousers, and she stepped back into her shimmy, and he insisted on serving the first course in bed. They sat shoulder to shoulder sipping dried mushroom soup, watching the lamplight reflect in the block of ice at the window. It was the most intimate moment of Juliette's life. And then she noticed that he was dipping the soup spoon away from him. And he didn't make a sound when he swallowed.

"Ben? . . ."

He recognized her expression at once, set aside their soup bowls, and reached for her. The second time was even more amazing than the first. This time he positioned her on top of him where she just sat, feeling confused, until he placed his hands on her hips and rocked her back and forth, up and down. At once she grasped what was expected, then discovered the delicious thrill of being in control. Best of all, she could peek at his face and read how much he liked this movement or that.

When they came together again between the fish course and the meat, Ben curved her fingers around him, and Juliette thought she would faint from the velvety feel of him and from her own bold daring.

Between the meat dish and salad, he bathed her in the tub, then toweled her dry, placed her back in bed, and kissed her all over. All over. She screamed in shock, then screamed with pleasure.

After wine and dessert, they made love lazily and slowly as if they were longtime lovers, then they wrapped themselves in blankets and ran outside to see the strange greenish blue lights flickering across the northern sky. Still wrapped in blankets, they warmed themselves before the living-room fire and sipped from snifters of brandy.

"I couldn't have imagined a night this amazing and remarkable," Juliette said, gazing at him with soft sated eyes. After her marriage, she had considered herself an experienced woman, uninhibited even. Now she knew her experience had barely scratched the surface of what was possible, and she hadn't had an inkling of what uninhibited really meant. Tonight had been astounding, splendid, unbelievable.

"I've imagined you a hundred times looking as you look now," Ben said with a smile.

Her hair streamed down her back, her face was rosy and happily drowsy, and the blanket revealed her pale shoulders and a small valley of cleavage.

"I love you, Juliette. You belong to me now."

Leaning forward, she kissed him and then covered a yawn, and he laughed.

"When we finish our brandies, I'll tuck you in bed, then I'll leave."

"*You'll* leave?"

He nodded. "Remember what you said about wanting privacy and solitude? The next two days are yours, my Christmas gift. Luc or Henry will come by several times a day. If you need anything, place your snowshoes outside the door, and they'll knock."

She clapped her hands. "The cabin is mine for two whole days?"

"Miss Klaus and Miss Wilder are aware of the surprise. They packed a bag for you. It's under the bed."

She threw her arms around him and kissed him soundly. "Ben, that's the nicest gift I've ever had! Thank you so much!" They kissed again at the door when he was ready to leave. "I don't know what to say about this evening," she said, pushing her face into the fur of the hood surrounding his face.

"You have the rest of our lives to think of something," he said, grinning.

The words stabbed her like an icicle. She was still standing stricken in the doorway when he turned on the road to wave good-bye.

Instead of going back to bed, she returned to the dying fire and blinked hard at the low flames. Ben was so perfect for her in every way. And she flattered herself that she could be so perfect for him.

Now she knew why Zoe cried into her pillow every night.

Her desire for solitude and privacy lasted as long as it took to sleep for a few hours and treat herself to another tub bath. Then the chaos of her thoughts against a backdrop of quiet began to scrape at her nerves. She kept thinking how much Clara and Zoe would enjoy a real tub and being warm and sitting down to a meal at a table. Sighing deeply, she set out her snowshoes and when Luc appeared, she asked him to fetch Clara and Zoe.

A swirl of falling snow followed them inside when they arrived, cold-cheeked and stamping snow off their feet.

"This is a palace!" Zoe marveled. "I can turn around without tripping over Clara's night case."

"Look at this stove!" Clara called from the kitchen. She lifted the lid off a bubbling pot and inhaled the steam. "Not bad, not too bad at all. You've made a good start. But this stew will be wonderful when I finish with it."

"I knew you'd say that." Laughing, Juliette took their coats and mittens and hung them on the hall tree. "The best is yet to come." Beckoning, she escorted them to the bedroom, made them cover their eyes, then said, "Look."

"A bathtub!" they cried in unison. And then, "I'm first!"

"There's plenty of time," Juliette said. "We have two whole days."

"Well, well." Bending, Clara picked an object off the

floor and held it to the light glowing through the ice block window. "A shirt stud. And here's another. Looks like it was raining shirt studs in here." Her eyebrow arched suggestively.

The smile vanished from Juliette's lips. "I . . ."

"You don't have to explain anything." Zoe glared at Clara and then studied Juliette's hot cheeks. She gave Juliette a hard embrace before she walked out of the bedroom. "I'll put on some water to heat for the tub."

Clara fell backward on the bed and flung out her arms. She stared at the ceiling. "It isn't fair. The two of you are carrying on, and I haven't even been kissed!" She threw the shirt studs at the ice block. "Damn!"

Juliette sank to the edge of the bed and folded her hands in the lap of the everyday dress they had packed for her. She lowered her head. "Ben loves me, Clara. And I love him. He left here believing that we belong to each other." A tear rolled down her cheek and dropped on her clasped hands. "He believes we'll spend the rest of our lives together."

Finally Clara sighed and gently patted her back. "I'm sorry. Maybe it will work out somehow."

"No, it won't," Zoe said quietly, returning to the doorway. "Even if Tom and Ben could forgive us for not telling them about Jean Jacques, they won't be able to forgive us for not being the honorable women they thought we were. Oh, Juliette. I understand what you're feeling, and I'm so, so sorry."

Zoe dropped down beside her, and they reached blindly for each other, bursting into tears.

Chapter 18

Two dozen men climbed through the deep snow covering the hills flanking Linderman Lake and brought back a Yule log and enough firewood to burn until midnight on Christmas Eve. It was a grand celebration, with singing around the Yule flames beneath a clear frozen night lit by a million points of distant star-fire.

On Christmas day, Bear and his team won the tug-of-war. Tom placed second in the sled races. Clara's chocolate cake won the baking contest, and Zoe took second with her apple bread pudding.

"You've all won prizes," Juliette called as everyone lined up for the couple's sack race. "Now it's our turn."

"We're going to win this one," Ben promised, grinning.

"Sorry, the victory will be ours," Tom shouted. But he and Zoe were already tangled in the burlap sack and Zoe's skirts, and laughing so hard it was doubtful they would hear the starter's gun.

"No one can beat me and this little gal," Bear boomed, slipping his arm around Clara's waist. He smiled down at her. "I like being tied to you."

"I like it, too," Clara said, a bit distracted.

She had spotted Jake Horvath's acne-pitted face in the crowd of spectators. Malice burned in his stare. Two days ago Clara had passed Horvath talking to a group of men as she was taking a loaf of Christmas bread to Mrs. Eddington. She'd overheard him swearing that he would get even with Bear if it was the last thing he did. When Horvath saw her, he'd stepped away from the men to spit near Clara's hem. Shock had widened her eyes. Apparently she was now included in his threats.

The starter raised his pistol. "On your mark, get set— go!" The gun fired and two dozen couples, their legs tied inside burlap sacks, hopped forward while cheers erupted from the sidelines.

Clara's mind was still on Horvath, and she didn't pay attention as she should have. Within five steps, her heel slipped on an ice patch and she fell, pulling Bear down with her. Laughing, they lay face-to-face on the snow-packed ground.

Instead of immediately struggling up, Clara placed her hands on his chest and gazed past the ash and grease and into his eyes. "Bear Barrett, are you ever going to kiss me?" She knew the shouts and cheers of the spectators drowned her question for any ears but his.

He stared at her mouth, his arm still loosely around her waist. "Oh, yes. I have plans for you, little lady," he said in a gruff tone. "We need some privacy, and I've figured it out."

Privacy was the cause of his delay? Clara rolled her eyes and decided that men could drive a woman crazy. The extended hours of darkness offered privacy to anyone seeking it. Every evening, Tom and Zoe and Ben and Juliette faded into the dark to steal some kisses. Clara wanted some stolen kisses, too.

Bear must have read something of her thoughts on her expression. "No, ma'am," he said, lying next to her on the ground, the warm vapor of his breath bathing her face, "I'm not going to sneak a quick kiss out behind your tent. The first kiss should be special. When I plant one on you, woman, I want you to remember it all the rest of your born days." He grinned. "I want us both looking good and smelling good. I want you gussied up in that outfit you wore to the arm-wrestling tournament. When I grab you, I want to feel woman, not just a bundle of coats and scarves and sweaters and whatever else you're wearing to stay warm."

They gazed into each other's eyes, not thinking about their scandalous position, lying on the snow without three inches separating them. Couples sprawled on the ground, laughing, from here to the finish line. It was only when Ben and Juliette came hopping past shouting, "We won!" that Clara regained her senses and sat up.

"It would be nice to know your plan and where you intend to find the privacy you have in mind." Leaning forward, Clara pulled open the sack and untied the twine binding their legs.

He blinked. "Didn't I tell you?"

Exasperation overwhelmed her. She smacked him on the chest, knocking him back on the snow. "No."

He grinned up at the sky. "I've thought about this so much I figured I must have told you."

"Well, tell me now, then I'll decide if I like your plan."

He sat up. "I don't remember if I mentioned it, but I own a cabin at Lake Bennett. My plan is to invite you to a private rematch at the cabin."

"And I'm supposed to show up looking good and smelling good," she said with a smile, pulling her leg out of the sack.

"I'm looking forward to that part. Then we arm-wrestle. I win. And afterward we have dinner."

"You win?" She narrowed her eyes.

"I know where I can get a chicken. It'll cost seventy-five dollars, but what the hell. I'll pay someone to fry it so we don't have to cook. Dinner will be ready whenever we want it."

"I can fry it."

"If you invite me to dinner, then you can cook," he said, kicking the burlap off his leg. "When I invite you, I'll make the arrangements. We'll have your favorite German ale, by the way, in case you need additional enticement."

She laughed. "I was wavering. But I can't resist the ale.

Since this is a detailed plan, what happens after dinner?"
She couldn't help thinking how Juliette's dinner evening
had ended.

"We sit by the fire and talk about everything and nothing, then right before I escort you back to your tent, I
take you in my arms—"

Clara stared into his brown-bear eyes and held her
breath.

"—and I pull you so close you can hardly breathe."

She wasn't breathing now.

"I tell you that you're the prettiest little thing I ever
saw—"

"Little." Clara fell back on the snow and smiled at
the sky.

"And then I kiss you until your knees buckle."

"Oh, Lord. I do like this plan."

She liked it so well that later in the day she cornered
Tom and demanded to know when he intended to depart
for Lake Bennett.

"As I just explained to Bear," he said with a smile of
amusement, "we'll leave tomorrow morning. I'll tell you
what I told him. We travel at the pace of the slowest person in the party. And no, you can't go on ahead of everyone. I'm responsible for you, so you stay with the group."

Sighing with frustration, she went in search of Juliette and found her packing in preparation for tomorrow's departure.

"How are you feeling?" Clara asked, sitting on her cot
and studying Juliette. Juliette was still pink-faced and ex-
cited from winning the sack race.

"I feel fine. Why?"

"Because it would mean a lot to me if you wouldn't
lollygag on this next leg of the journey."

"I don't lollygag! I go as fast as I can."

"Well, go faster. I'm in a hurry to reach Lake Bennett."

"Why is that?" Juliette paused in folding clean laundry, and her eyebrows rose. "What's at Lake Bennett?"

Clara smiled. "That's none of your business."

"Clara Klaus!" Juliette stared at her and then laughed. "I suppose the next question is, what are you going to wear?"

"I guess I can admit that I've been invited to dinner and it's been requested that I wear my arm-wrestling ensemble."

"I suspect that's an excellent choice." Juliette sat down beside her. "Clara, are you very sure?" she asked in a low voice. "I've never been so miserable as I am since Ben and I . . . since we . . ." Her cheeks flamed.

"But you've never been as happy either."

Juliette tilted her head back. "You know, sometimes I wonder if the three of us aren't bad influences on each other. I wonder if we don't somehow give each other permission to do things we wouldn't dream of doing on our own."

"I would dream of being with Bear whether or not you and Zoe were here." She'd been longing for that man from the day she bumped into him.

"And I would dream of being with Ben. But I don't know if I actually would have been brave enough to do it."

Clara took Juliette's hand. "I think you would. You're not the same person you were when we met. None of us are. This trip has changed all of us in ways we'll be discovering for years."

"Perhaps. But Clara, let me say one more thing." Juliette's gray eyes filled with sympathy. "You know that loving Bear can't end well."

"I didn't say I loved him."

"You don't have to."

Juliette was right. After all the weeks they had spent living together in a confined space, they knew each other's expressions, moods, emotions. Clara had known that Juliette and Zoe were in love probably before they had known it themselves. Now they were reading the signs in her.

The next day as she manhandled her sled down the treacherous frozen Linderman Rapids, she asked herself if she really did love Bear Barrett. She had, after all, been wrong before.

The answer came without hesitation. She loved him. She loved the big brawling size of him and his scarred beautiful face. The sound of his booming laughter made her smile. He would probably laugh now if she told him that he was chivalrous, but he was the type of man who turned gentle and protective toward women. She admired him for being a self-made man, appreciated that he wasn't too proud to talk business with her or take her advice. Best of all, he didn't see her as an asset sheet, he didn't want anything from her except her mind and body. Both of which, she decided, she was willing to give.

They would have to have a little talk about respectability when they had that fireside chat he'd mentioned.

Lake Bennett was the largest camp Clara had seen since leaving Dyea. Here the Skagway and the Chilkoot trails converged, spilling a tide of stampeders onto the shoreline. A layer of smoke overhung at least a thousand tents.

Some of the stampeders would push on to Dawson by sled, risking blizzards, frostbite, hungry wild animals, and getting lost. Most would rest on the frozen shore of the lake, using the time until spring to build rafts or boats. Many would drown in the Yukon River after the melt. It happened every year.

"We've been so fortunate that no one in our party has been killed," Clara said. Everyone had minor scrapes, bruises, and sprains, but no major injuries, thank heaven.

"Hold still," Juliette ordered, her mouth full of pins.

She was pinning Clara's dress at the waist and shoulders. It needed to be taken in. Clara had lost weight on the journey—they all had.

Both women looked at the tent flap as Zoe blew inside,

bringing a swirl of snowflakes along with her. "I got it," she said triumphantly. She started to remove her scarf, hat, mittens, coat, and two sweaters. The temperature had sunk to twenty below zero and remained there. "But I think your friendship with Mrs. Eddington is forever compromised. It was bad enough that you bought one pessary from her. She can't think why you'd need two."

"Why didn't you tell her it was for you?"

"Me?" Zoe placed a hand on her breast and fluttered her eyelashes. "I'm a married woman. Maybe I already own what's required."

Clara rolled her eyes. "No one knows you're married, but everyone knows you and Tom are carrying on. All they have to do is look at the two of you. So don't tell me about being married."

Juliette shifted to reach another part of Clara's waist. "Why does Mrs. Eddington have a seemingly endless supply of . . . those things? It's not decent."

"Mrs. Eddington is very shrewd. She brought pessaries to sell because she figured there would be trailside romances. She's made a tidy sum already."

Zoe and Juliette looked at her, fascinated. "Really?" Zoe asked. "Did she name the names of her clients?"

"Mrs. Eddington promises discretion. Let me see the pessary, will you? Uh-huh. Just as I thought. It's a pink ribbon." She started picking at the knot.

"What are you doing?" Juliette frowned. "You need the ribbon." She looked dismayed that she would know such a thing.

"I know, but not this ribbon. If I'm going to have a ribbon hanging out of . . . well, you know . . . I don't want it to be pink. I want a first-prize blue ribbon that says this is the best there is."

They stared at her, and then all of them burst into wild laughter. When they caught their breath, they sat on the cots, wiping their eyes.

And it occurred to Clara that she would miss these

women when their long journey ended. She would miss them badly.

Bear called for her the following evening. All Clara could see of him were his eyes peering at her between his hat brim and above a thick scarf that covered his mouth and nose. And that was all he could see of her. She was bundled against the cold like a bulky package.

He had equipped a dogsled for passenger use, padding the bed like a chaise longue. Once he had her settled and covered with wool blankets, he shouted at the tent flap that he would have her home before morning. Then he guided the sled through the camp, along the shore, and up an incline.

There was enough moonlight that Clara spotted his cabin the moment they rounded the last curve. The cabin appeared to float against a pine backdrop because the log structure sat on pilings that lifted the ground floor off the frozen ground. Light glowed at the windows, and chimney smoke curled gray against a black sky. He had shoveled a path to the steps and to the dog shelter.

"You go inside and get warm," Bear said after helping her out of the sled. "I'll see to the dogs and be there in a minute."

The door opened into a vaulted living room. A billiard table occupied the center of the room, surrounded by leather chairs. Animal heads hung on the walls: two grizzly bears, several elk and moose, caribou, a pair of wolves, and a wildcat depicted in full snarl. Almost as an afterthought, two or three photographs had been hung above small tables. One showed Bear standing outside the Bare Bear saloon with several men. To Bear's right was a snowdrift piled higher than his shoulders. Another showed him holding a rifle, his foot on the back of a bear. Presumably the fellow staring down from above the stone fireplace.

The place didn't have much of a kitchen. When Clara popped her head inside, she spotted the essentials, but no woman would have designed a kitchen with so little elbow room. In contrast, the bedroom was a comfortable size. From the doorway, she noticed shaving implements laid out atop the bureau, saw a row of boots neatly arranged beneath the hooks holding an array of clothing.

She liked it that he was tidy. She couldn't abide a slovenly man. Happily, she returned to the hall tree in the doorway just as Bear came inside.

"Allow me," he said, pulling down his scarf and smiling. He took her hat and scarf and mittens. Helped her out of her coat and heavy boots. Peeled her down to Juliette's black cape. Looking into her eyes, he drew a breath. "Shall I take your cape?"

Clara lifted her arms and fluffed the fountain of red curls exploding from the crown of her head. She wished he had a mirror near the hall tree so she could see how tousled she might be. Not that Bear would care. He stared at her as if she dazzled him.

She presented her back and let him lift the cape from her shoulders. Then she slowly turned.

"Oh, my Lord," he said softly, his eyes widening on her burgeoning cleavage. "I didn't dream you." He stood as still as a large rock, staring at her while melting snow ran off his coat into a puddle at his feet. "I never saw anything like you, honey girl," he said softly, gruffly. "You stop my heart."

Despite the ash and grease she wore on the trail, her cheeks were chapped and red, though recently softened with a liberal application of lard, so he probably didn't notice that she blushed with pleasure.

"And you smell like a beautiful woman ought to smell."

She was wearing her German cologne. And her bodice scooped so low that little was left to the imagination. Plus she wore Juliette's brilliants, Zoe's best purse, and the prizewinning blue ribbon.

"Can I help you out of those heavy wet things?" she

asked, reaching to unwind his scarf. Laughing, he allowed her to hang his coat and hat on the hall tree before he sat on a bench and changed out of his snowshoes into a pair of dress shoes.

When he stood, she saw that he'd chosen a dark wool suit and waistcoat for tonight. His shaggy gold hair had been trimmed and somewhat tamed. He smelled of bay rum and sweet cigars and the outdoors. He was one fine-looking man. So handsome that she couldn't take her eyes off him and didn't want to.

"Well," Clara said, realizing they were standing near the draft leaking around the door. "Shall we—?"

"Where are my manners! Come in, come in. Welcome to my Lake Bennett place. It's small, and I don't imagine you think much of the decor," he said, smiling. "I built it just for me. You're the only woman who's been inside."

"Then I'm flattered," she said, moving to the billiard table and running her palm across the green felt. "How in the world did you get this over the pass?"

"I had it brought in by the overland route. My Lord, you look beautiful! You make me think of peaches and honey. Good enough to eat with a spoon!"

Blushing again, she wandered toward the fire and tilted her face to examine the animal heads. "I imagine there's a story behind each of these trophies."

He followed, standing so close behind her that Clara felt his heat and massive size. "Not stories fit for the delicate ears of a lady."

Ja, they would have to have a talk.

"So. Are you ready for our rematch?"

Turning, she gazed into his brown-bear eyes. "I concede. We don't have to arm-wrestle. You win. I'd like to have some of that ale and talk for a few minutes."

Alarm flared in his gaze. "You're changing the plan!"

My heavens, he looked good. A golden giant. Clara studied him and genuinely could not imagine why every woman he met didn't throw herself at him. She especially liked the small scars on his face. They gave him character and distinction, and before tonight ended she hoped to know the stories behind them.

"I'm not changing the plan, except to dispense with the match, just rearranging it a bit. We can talk again after dinner like you intended."

Suddenly she understood his plan for what it was, a schedule that relieved his endearing anxiety about entertaining a lady. That he was nervous made her smile. Lifting on tiptoe, Clara brazenly brushed her lips across his clean-shaven cheek. Instantly, he went rigid and stared at her with narrowed eyes.

"You fetch us some ale, and I'll wait for you by the fire."

After touching his cheek, he gazed at the hills of peachy breasts rising above her bodice. Then he nodded and hurried toward the kitchen without a word.

Clara considered the distance between the chairs he'd placed before the fire, then moved them closer together. Exercising a woman's prerogative, she chose one of the small tables scattered about the room and set it near the chairs. Stepping back, she studied the arrangement. Much better. More intimate and cozy.

Bear noticed immediately. He looked at the chairs, then slid a glance at her before he placed the bottles of ale, and a glass for her, on the table she'd chosen.

"I thought you'd want a glass tonight," he said. Gripping the back of a chair, he started to slide it back.

"Why are you moving the chairs apart?"

"Honey girl, I can hardly keep my hands off you as it is." He gave her an apologetic look. "I want tonight to be perfect. I don't want a big uncouth lummox forgetting himself and doing something to offend you."

Clara tossed the fountain of curls and drew herself up with a glare. She flung out a hand and pointed to the chair. "Sit!"

"What?"

"Right now."

He hesitated, then sat. He reached for the ale bottle and took a long swig, watching her while he swallowed.

Clara sat on the edge of the facing chair and folded her hands in her lap. She hadn't worn a corset in so long that she had forgotten how uncomfortable they were and how they restricted relaxed movement. If she had leaned back in the chair, the steel bones would have pinched her waist.

"It's true that I am a respectable woman," she said finally.

"Oh, hell. If you feel you have to point that out, then I've already done something to offend you. I'm sorry." Leaning forward, he clasped his hands between his knees, the ale bottle dangling between two fingers.

"Bear, you haven't offended me. But we need to talk about this."

He didn't seem to hear. "There's something I planned to tell you later, after we'd enjoyed the evening. I should have told you long before now." Throwing his head back, he took another deep pull on the ale bottle and drained it before he placed it on the table and raised his head. "My mother was a whore, Clara. I don't know who my father was. I grew up in a Chicago brothel."

"Oh, Bear." Sympathy widened her eyes, but he waved it aside with a quick gesture. And suddenly she understood why she seemed to make him so uncomfortable at times.

"All in all I had a good childhood. My mother and her friends fussed over me, saw to it that I had everything I needed. When most children were tucked in bed, I was wandering the neighborhood, pitching pennies with other boys who were free to roam the night. I learned to fight, learned to take care of myself, learned a lot of things that aren't taught in books. It was a childhood most boys would envy."

"Bear—"

"Wait." He held up a big hand. "My mother and her friends were kind, generous, honest in their own way." His expression challenged her to disagree. When she said nothing, he continued. "But even as a boy I understood that most of the world didn't live like we did and didn't approve. I knew my mother and her friends were reviled, often by men who later came to the door. I won't say that I was ashamed of her. I wasn't. But I knew that she and I lived on the wrong side of life."

"Your mother—"

"My mother was everything you aren't. She perspired, swore, drank like a man, and made no apology for her pleasures. She wasn't a dainty person, cared little for proper manners. Her idea of culture was enjoying a bawdy melodrama at Basker's Lyceum."

Clara was beginning to understand. He believed respectable women were the direct opposite of his mother in every way. And he'd placed respectable women high on a pedestal.

"When I meet women like you, Clara, I lift my hat, nod, and walk on by. A lady isn't going to approve of where I came from or who I am. And she's right. As hard as I try not to, I'm still apt to swear or scratch or make an inappropriate remark. Look how many times I've offended you. And believe me, I've tried not to."

"If you don't feel a respectable woman could see anything admirable in you, then how do you explain me being here?" Clara asked softly.

He frowned. "You didn't know how I grew up."

"Whatever else your mother was, I applaud her for raising a fine son. You're ambitious, successful, honest, generous, and you have a zest for life. You try to be the best at everything you do, and you don't do anything halfway. You could be a bully, but you're not. With your background, you could have ended with a lot of unsavory qualities, but you didn't."

"You're different," he said finally. "You don't see things

the way most other women do. I didn't know that at first, so I tried to stay away from you. I figured there was no sense setting us both up for disappointment. But I couldn't stop coming around you, and you gave those little woman signs that said you didn't mind seeing me."

"I'm not different, Bear."

"Yes, you are. Everyone who meets you knows you're a respectable woman who's had a gentle upbringing." He smiled. "And then you show up at the tournament and win it. And you're right there in the middle of a brawl, laying men out all around you. You have amazing flashes of behaving like a real person."

She laughed. "A real person? Just what do you think a respectable lady is?"

He answered promptly. "She's led a sheltered, protected life. She's modest to a fault. She's always feminine and dainty. Her reputation is impeccable, and she doesn't associate with disreputable folks. She doesn't swear. Her morals are the highest in the land. She's a refined person with cultural tastes. She—"

"Bear, respectable women swear, sweat, work, argue, and lose their tempers just like anyone else. Just like your mother and her friends. There are good-natured respectable women and mean-spirited respectable women. Respectable women in business. Respectable women who drink straight from a bottle, who wouldn't know a fish fork if it stabbed them in the hand. Respectable women who wouldn't turn up their noses at a man like you."

"Clara . . ."

"Let me finish. Respectable women live by a code of conduct that is often constraining, restrictive, and artificial. Parts of the code are exemplary, good for the woman and good for society. But parts of the code are just plain silly. I mean, why should it be scandalous for an adult woman to travel unaccompanied? Why must we sew weights in our hems to prevent a glimpse of ankle? An ankle! Why should it be shocking for a woman to arm wrestle if she wants to? Or to own a business? Why should it be more respectable to marry a polished man who is a liar, a thief, and a womanizer than to marry a man who grew up in a brothel?"

He stared at her, listening to every word.

"I'm not different from other respectable women, Bear. Maybe it only seems so because you haven't known that many respectable women. We're just people with the same thoughts and feelings that everyone has. And Bear . . ." She leaned forward and gazed deeply into his eyes. "Respectable women have needs just like the women you grew up with."

He sucked in a quiet breath and the empty ale bottle slipped from his fingers. His gaze dropped like a rock to her impressive cleavage. Then he swallowed hard and jumped to his feet.

"I'll get us another bottle of ale."

Sighing, she watched him flee. Maybe he had accepted what she had said. More likely she'd put only a small dent in an idealistic way of thinking that had formed in his childhood.

She would have to take matters into her own hands.

Standing, she began to take off her clothes.

Chapter 19

Bear walked out of the kitchen carrying two bottles. "I think I know what you're saying, but—" Sucking in a sharp breath, he stopped in his tracks. The bottles dropped from his hands and spun on the planks, spewing foam and dark ale. "Oh, my God!"

She stood before the fire wearing nothing but dark stockings, white flannel drawers, and a lace-edged corset that propped up her generous breasts. Brilliants sparkled in her hair and at her ears. And she wore a sultry expression that no man alive could have mistaken.

Bear took another step into the room and then stopped as if his knees were too wobbly to proceed. "Oh, my God," he said again, his voice as ragged as sandpaper. Without taking his eyes off her, he slowly removed his jacket, exposing a white shirt that pulled tight across his large shoulders.

"I don't think you've really listened to what I've been saying, Bear Barrett. So it seems I'll have to show you that respectable women are made of flesh and blood."

His gaze traveled up her legs, curved around her hips, dipped to her waist, then rose to her breasts and stayed there. He cleared his throat with a hoarse sound. "Honey—show me."

"Get ready, because here I come. Brace yourself."

If he thought he was going to give her a kiss that she'd remember all her born days . . . well, *she* was going to give *him* a night he'd never forget if he lived three lives.

In for a penny, in for a pound. Clara had made up her mind that if she was going after Bear while married to the weasel, she wasn't going to let guilt inhibit her. If she cried in her pillow about this later, it wouldn't be because she had any regrets or because she hadn't given all she had.

She drew a deep, deliberate breath, letting her breasts swell. Then she focused on his mouth and raced across the room. At the last second she gathered herself, jumped up on him, wrapped her legs around his waist, and wound her arms around his neck.

Her momentum carried him backward, and he crashed against one of the small tables. The table splintered and shattered to the floor in pieces, and one of the photographs popped off the hook when Bear bumped the wall. Dimly, Clara was aware of breaking glass as the photograph hit the planks.

His big hands cupped her buttocks, the heat scorching her flesh through her flannel drawers. He swung her around and pressed her between his body and the wall, then his mouth came down on hers, hot and hungry and possessive. He kissed her like there was no tomorrow, and Clara dug her fingers into his hair and kissed him back like a sinner seeking salvation.

To her joy, her desire was intense and instantaneous, and so was his. She could feel her immediate future pressing against her drawers, and she almost swooned. She gripped him harder and kissed him again and again, nipping at his lips, sliding her tongue across his mouth, pulling his hair, stroking his jaw, unable to get enough of him.

"Lord, woman!" Gasping and wild-eyed, Bear raised his head and looked around, his gaze fixing on the billiard table. Carrying her to the table, he sat her on the side before a wave of his hand sent the billiard balls flying off the felt and rattling across the floor. Frantically, his eyes ravaging her, he tore at his clothing. His waistcoat sailed toward the kitchen. He ripped a sleeve while getting out of his shirt before hurling it aside.

Clara's heart leaped when she noticed the mat of fine golden hair glistening on his broad chest. He *was* a Viking. A shimmering gold giant of a man with flaring muscle and tight sinew. A man with no soft parts—except his heart.

Before he climbed up on the billiard table, she saw the golden hair on his calves and thighs. His manhood stood in a thick soft nest. She stared at that rampant manhood for a moment, and her eyes widened. "Oh, heavens," she breathed happily, fanning her face with her hand. "My, my, my."

Then Bear was on the table and lifting her up next to him. First he kissed her so hard and deep that she went limp with sensation. She was unable to move, unable to breathe. All she could do was feel. Feel her heart pounding against her ribs, feel the fire in her belly. Feel the heat and unyielding power of his big barrel chest hot against her body. Feel his thighs against hers, and feel his stiff length hard against her stomach.

Then she wrapped her arms around him and pressed against him as hard as she could while hot wild kisses rained over her face, her throat, the hills of her breasts. She rolled on top of him so she could shower kisses on him. Kisses on his shaggy flying hair. Kisses on the scar that tracked through his eyebrow. Kisses on his ears and the sweet corners of his mouth, kisses on his throat and the pulse throbbing at the dip of his collarbone. And oh, the taste of him. He tasted like salt and soap, an odd combination that drove her crazy with wanting him.

When her mouth and tongue had him groaning and gasping, he grabbed her, intending to roll on top of her. Locked together, they rolled across the billiard table and right off the edge, hitting the floor with a crash that jarred the whole cabin. A series of secondary thuds shook the planks.

"Are you all right?" Bear asked, blinking up at her.

"I landed on you. Are you all right?" Tomorrow they'd both have a few bruises from this fall, but that was the last thing on her mind.

He grinned. "Take off those drawers, and I'll show you how all right I am."

"What were those thuds?"

He lifted his head and peered through the legs of the billiard table. "The bear, two elk, and the wildcat fell off the wall."

"We've got a broken table, broken photograph, ale and billiard balls on the floor, and animal heads are falling off the walls. Should we—?"

"Never mind that, honey girl. We're busy." He rolled over her and kissed her hard and urgently again and again until they were both gasping for air, slick with sweat, and totally unaware of their surroundings.

When Clara thought she would die, would surely die if she didn't get her drawers off and jump on this man, when she thought she would shake apart, she was trembling so violently, he pulled her to her feet, scooped her into his arms, and carried her into his bedroom.

He placed her on the bed, and his big clumsy fingers fumbled at her laces, tugging and pulling until he'd loosened them enough for Clara to wiggle free.

"Honey girl," he said in a hoarse voice of wonder, "if you only knew how many times I've imagined this!" Sitting beside her, looking at her like she was a banquet, he drew his fingertips down the sides of her breasts, then gently rubbed his forefingers across the stiffening buds at the tips. He filled his hands, then bent his head and kissed and licked and nibbled and sucked until a half scream built in her throat.

Dropping back on the bed, she arched her body and whispered urgently. "The drawers. Help me with my drawers."

He tore them off and sent them flying over his shoulder. Then he just looked at her lying before him naked. "You are magnificent," he breathed, his brown-bear eyes soft. Almost reverently, he placed his hand over the triangle of curly red hair between her thighs. The heat of his hand sank deep into her, like a brand.

"Come here," she said in a throaty voice, opening her arms.

The hard, hot length of his body covered her, and he claimed her lips with his mouth, his fingers in the tangled fountain of curls. He kissed her breath away, kissed her senses away. And she loved the silky touch of his chest hair on her breasts, loved how their frantic heartbeats pounded as one and their legs wrapped together and their urgent hands found the right places.

Her fingers curled around him, and he dropped his head to the pillow with a low groan. "Clara, Clara."

Stroking and teasing, she turned her head and breathed in his ear until his member jumped in her hand and she felt him trembling.

Then he rose above her and gently guided her knees up. Leaning over her, he kissed her long and deep before he entered her. Slowly, carefully, watching her, he moved within her, and she sighed and arched to meet him. Joy lit his eyes, and he paused to clasp her in his arms. "My beautiful little Clara."

If there were no other reason, she would love him because he thought she was little. She grabbed his face and pulled his mouth down on hers, putting her heart and soul into a kiss that shook her to the center.

Passion exploded between them, a passion that demanded deep hard thrusts and the oil of sweat and cries of rapture. The powerful passion of gods coupling on Mount Olympus while lightning flashed and the heavens quaked.

At the height of their ecstasy, the ropes supporting the bouncing mattress broke with pinging snaps, one after another, and the mattress dropped to the floor, spilling them out on the rug. They scarcely noticed. Clara rolled on top of him, arched her throat, and rocked her body, feeling the burn of his hands on her hips and his mouth on her breasts.

Waves of dizzying sensation shivered through her. She couldn't see, couldn't think, could only soar and fall, soar and fall, mindlessly chanting his name. When her body slumped over him, he rolled her beneath him and thrust into her so fully, so fast and deep and hard that she thought the whole earth had slipped from its axis.

But it was the cabin. As Bear shouted her name and stiffened above her, the southern corner of the cabin rocked off its piling and smashed down on the frozen ground. An enormous crash sounded from the living room as the billiard table slid along the incline and then crashed against the south wall, bringing down the rest of the trophy heads. Tables and chairs followed, breaking apart as they smashed into the pile of debris.

The broken bed slid past them and slammed against the interior wall where the bureau had been. The bureau was now in the living room. They heard it crash and shatter against the billiard table.

Locked together, holding tight, Clara and Bear rolled downhill and hit the side slat of the broken bed.

As awareness slowly returned to Bear's gaze, he lifted his head and looked around. "My God," he breathed, staring down at her. "We wrecked my cabin!" Awe widened his eyes. "Good Lord, woman. You are the most magnificent creature who ever lived! I adore you. I worship the ground you walk on."

Laughing, Clara pushed the hair out of her eyes and struggled to sit up. "Give me one of your shirts, will you? We need to see what happened and make sure none of the lamps started a fire."

"I can see that I'm going to have to build us a house set in concrete! Never in my life have I had an experience that even came close to this! My house is wrecked, I'm covered with bruises. I don't think I could survive making love to you more than once a day." Grinning, he pulled himself off the floor and reached for the clothing swaying on the row of hooks. He tossed her a shirt and pulled on a pair of trousers. Then he did a double take and bent over her. "Is that a blue ribbon?"

"I believe it is," she said, trying to sound modest. When she extended her hand, he pulled her up, and she put on his shirt.

Laughing, he shook his head and then kissed her soundly. "Honey girl, if ever I saw a bottom that deserved a blue ribbon, yours is it."

"You were pretty spectacular yourself," Clara said, fluttering her eyelashes and giving him an admiring look. When he stepped toward her with that look in his eye, she placed a hand on his big muscled chest. "First, we better check out the damage."

He gave her a lingering kiss, then dug around in the corner of the bedroom until he found his rubber-soled boots that would grip the floor and help keep him from sliding down the sharp incline.

They made their way to the bedroom doorway and peered out. All the furniture was now a pile of broken rubble in the south corner. Fortunately, the fireplace was on the south wall, and the drop had not spilled out any flaming logs. But there was a small fire growing near the bedroom door.

While Bear beat out the flames with the bedroom rug, Clara crept toward the kitchen. The stove was wedged in the doorway. She called the news to Bear.

"Don't worry. It isn't hot. I'd planned a cold supper, a fried chicken picnic. Can we get to the food?"

"I've climbed Chilkoot Pass. I guess I can climb over a stove."

The kitchen was a god-awful mess of broken crockery, shattered jars, spilled flour and sugar. The smell of pickle brine filled her nostrils. But she came back to the living room carrying their picnic basket.

Bear was beating out another small fire at the edge of the rubble. Clara watched him, remembering that her clothes were under the pile of debris. Well, she'd worry about that problem when it was time to get dressed.

"The roof's cracked, and the chinking fell out of the walls. It's going to get cold in here. I think we have time enough to eat and then wreck the other end of the house before we start to freeze."

Returning his grin, Clara pulled herself up into the bedroom. She pushed the broken bed aside and arranged the mattress to curve up the interior wall. They could sit on one half and rest their backs against the half leaning on the wall.

Once she'd created a place for them, she took stock of herself. She'd rolled his shirtsleeves up to her wrists, and the shirttail fell past her knees. She was mostly covered, but already she felt a flow of icy wind streaming through the house. What she wanted most right now was a hairbrush. Wild tangled hair curled down her back and frizzed around her face. But there wasn't a hope of finding her hairpins in the mess of debris.

"Why are you laughing?" Bear asked, pulling himself through the bedroom door. He dropped down on the mattress beside her and opened the picnic basket.

"I'm imagining Zoe's and Juliette's expression when I come home disheveled and wearing a set of your clothes." She would never hear the end of it. "Are you going to tell people how your cabin got wrecked?"

He handed her a chicken breast and a boiled egg. "If I did, I've have to fight every man in the Yukon because every one of them would beat a path to your door," he said, laughing.

She arched an eyebrow. "Are you blaming me for destroying your house?"

"Hell, no," he said, still laughing. "I'm giving you the

credit." He bit into a chicken leg. "Clara girl, I can build another cabin. I'll build us a hundred of them, and if you wreck them all, I'll be a happy man."

And now came the moment that Zoe and Juliette had spoken of, a moment of pain so intense that Clara leaned forward and gasped, placing a hand on her side.

Bear blithely and happily assumed they had made a commitment tonight. This was the second time he had referred to building a house for them. Where they would live together happily ever after.

He stared at her with alarm. "Are you all right?"

"Yes," she said, blinking at sudden tears. "Oh, Bear. You've been open and honest with me, but I . . ." She halted. "Do you smell smoke?"

"Smoke?" Lowering the chicken leg, he raised his head and sniffed. "I'm sure I put out the fires."

"It's getting stronger."

"You're right. I smell it, too."

He'd just reached for a napkin when the far corner of the bedroom burst into flames. For a stunned moment, neither of them moved. They stared at the fire in shock.

"This isn't possible," Bear said, frowning. "There were no lamps in that corner."

Clara scrambled up. There was no hope of beating out this fire. It was too hot, and spreading with stunning speed. "We have to get out!" Frantically, she looked around for something to cover her bare feet.

"Here." Bear tossed her two mismatched boots, a pair of his trousers, and a vest. "Go directly to the door and get out. I'll come as soon as I find our coats in the rubble."

She glanced at the fire, then up at his face. The fire was sweeping across the ceiling. "If you don't find the coats, immediately—"

"I'll get out. Go!"

Clutching the boots and clothing to her chest, Clara stumbled to the bedroom door. "Bear! The smashed end is on fire, too!" Smoke curling in the corner burst into fire with a soft whooshing sound and flames crawled over the rubble.

"This simply isn't possible. I don't . . . Go, honey girl, move!"

Slipping and sliding, she inched upward toward the outside door, now at the highest point of the lopsided cabin. The doorway would be four or five feet above the ground, and she'd have to jump. That wasn't a problem. The frigid cold would be. She tried not to wonder how long they could survive without adequate clothing. Long enough to walk a mile back to the Lake Bennett camp? Not now, think about it later. Right now, all she had to do was get out.

At the steepest slant, her feet went out from under her, and she would have slid helplessly down the length of the living room and into the flames if Bear hadn't caught her. Gripping his shoulders, she watched the boots and extra clothing tumble toward the corner and disappear into the smoke and fire.

Her eyes widened, and she stared at him. She was going to jump out of the burning cabin wearing only a shirt. "One thing at a time," he said, understanding. "First we get out. Then, there should be some extra blankets in the kennel."

Nodding, she turned and half crawled, half climbed to the door. All she had to do was touch the latch and the door swung inward. Instantly a rush of numbing cold raised goose bumps on her bare legs and throat.

In front of her, the shadow of the house wavered across the snow, its outline framed in flickering red and orange. She had an absurd urge to hold her nose as she jumped out of the burning house as if she were jumping into water instead of snow. The instant she hit the snow, she rolled out of the way so Bear could jump after her.

She heard him hit the ground as she pushed to her feet, feeling first an icy cold on her toes and soles, then a burning sensation.

"Clara! I figured it out. This is an ambush! Get down!"

She heard a whack and stupidly stared at a flying chip gouged out of the cabin side. Then Bear was in front of her, his big hands pushing on her shoulders.

He stiffened, his fingers dug into her flesh, then he arched backward and fell in the snow, rolling to rest face-down. To her horror, she saw blood on his back. Lifting her head, confused and horrified, she peered toward the woods.

She heard the shot just as a burning punch struck her in the shoulder and spun her around. Before she fell, another bullet ripped through her side.

Chapter 20

A Canadian named Dilly Dame offered the use of his cabin for Clara's recuperation. Mrs. Eddington and her husband took Bear in with them. Clara and Bear were seriously but not critically wounded; both had lost a lot of blood and suffered minor frostbite before the men found them. Had the fire not been spotted leaping above the trees, and a group of men hadn't rushed up the mountainside to offer assistance, Clara and Bear would have frozen or bled to death.

Zoe leaned back in the chair beside Clara's bed and closed her eyes, wondering if there was anything she had overlooked. Tom had removed the bullet in Clara's shoulder. The bullet that struck Clara's side and the bullet in Bear's shoulder had both passed through, leaving ragged exit wounds. Those were the injuries that worried Zoe most.

Zoe had cleaned Clara's wounds with alcohol and packed them with surgeon's lint. She and Mrs. Eddington gave their patients regular doses of tincture of aconite to fight inflammation. They soaked the blistered frostbitten areas in kerosene oil. They insisted that their patients wear slings so as not to jostle healing shoulders. Zoe reminded herself that Clara and Bear were strong and healthy, and in fact, five days after the event, both were on the mend.

"I'm ready to be up and about," Clara stubbornly insisted. But less than a minute later she covered a yawn and her lashes fluttered sleepily.

Zoe helped her sit up and offered a tin cup of water. "Rest is what you need now."

"The fever's gone, and I'm fine. Just tired. How is Bear doing?"

"Very well," Zoe assured her. "But Mrs. Eddington says he's a terrible patient. She doesn't think she can keep him inside another day. She says she's wearing herself to a nub trotting over here four times a day, but if she doesn't get reports about you, Bear starts putting on his coat to come himself."

Clara eased back to her pillow, favoring the side where she'd been shot. "Now I know why you and Juliette cry at night," she said softly, closing her eyes. "Oh, Zoe, I love him so much, but it's hopeless. What are we going to do?"

Zoe asked herself the same question a dozen times a day. Every time Tom said something that indicated he assumed they would marry, she shriveled a little more inside, liked herself a little less. "I wish we'd told the truth from the beginning," she said finally. "Maybe we'd have become laughingstocks and a favorite target for gossip. And maybe Tom and Ben and Bear would not have come courting." She blinked hard at the log ceiling. "But we wouldn't feel deceitful and dishonest every time they look at us. Maybe we'd have a little self-respect." When she lowered her head, she discovered she was talking to herself. Clara had fallen asleep.

Clara was still sleeping when Juliette returned from checking on Bear and popped her head into the bedroom. She examined Clara, then beckoned to Zoe.

"We need to talk," Juliette said quietly, heading for Mr. Dame's small kitchen.

"It must be important if it can't wait until you take off your coat and mittens."

Making a face, Juliette tossed her hat and mittens on

the sideboard, then poured them each a cup of strong coffee before she removed her coat and sat at the table.

"First, Bear's still weak and mad as a wet hen about it. But he's sitting up most of the day now."

"Clara was up for several hours, too." She studied Juliette's angry gray eyes. "Now tell me what's troubling you."

"It's Jake Horvath. He's bragging all over camp that he brought down the mighty Bear Barrett and his whore." Juliette winced. "He says he shot Bear because he believes Bear cheated him out of the Bare Bear, and he shot Clara because he wanted Bear to know how it felt to lose something he valued."

Zoe frowned. "He's bragging?"

Juliette came to her feet and paced in front of the table. "That's not all. He swears he's going to finish the job. He's going to kill them both! Mr. Eddington heard him say this. I told Ben about the threats, but Ben already knew. He said they've sent someone to the Mounties' new headquarters at Fort Herchmer. But that's near Dawson, at least five weeks from here and five weeks back. Assuming the Mounties leave at once and encounter no bad weather, it will be close to three months before they come to arrest Horvath. If they come at all! And they may not." She looked at Zoe. "Ben says there are only about two hundred Mounties to police the entire Yukon territory, and they undoubtedly have more serious crimes to follow up than an ambush and attempted murder."

"Horvath threatened to 'finish the job'?" Zoe's heart sank. She'd wondered if Horvath would be satisfied with almost killing Bear and Clara or if he'd make another attempt.

Juliette nodded. Sitting down, she pounded a fist on the table. "And no one is doing anything to stop him!"

"Tom explained there's a group talking hard against vigilantism. They're saying no one was killed. They're saying this is between Bear and Horvath." She knew Tom felt pulled between going after Horvath and agreeing that vigilantism was wrong. The same conflict circled in her own mind.

"Zoe." Juliette cupped her hands around the coffee mug and leaned forward. "Horvath is going to kill Clara and Bear. And no one intends to do anything about it. We can't let that happen. Clara is . . . She's our sister. And Bear is our friend."

Bear was a better friend than Zoe had dreamed. Finally Tom had told her that it was Bear who had paid almost half of their passage to Dawson. Bear. She never would have guessed.

"On a different subject," she said, clearing her throat. "I know I've said this a dozen times in the last few days, but Juliette, I'm so sorry for the nasty things I said to you when I believed you'd paid the extra to pack us to Dawson. I'll always regret it. I've been so wrong about a lot of things."

Juliette waved the apology aside. "Zoe, please. If we don't do something, Clara and Bear are going to get killed."

Slowly, Zoe nodded. Juliette wasn't saying anything that Zoe hadn't already considered. "What would you suggest?"

"I think we should make a citizen's arrest and confine Jake Horvath to his tent until the Mounties get here. If no one else will do it, then you and I can take turns guarding him."

"Us? You and me?" She hadn't expected this sort of suggestion. Her impulse was to laugh, but Juliette's serious nod kept any smile from her lips. "What makes you think Horvath will allow us to confine him to his tent?"

"If he refuses, then you shoot him."

"What?"

"You came up here to shoot a man, didn't you? Well, shoot this one. Zoe, if Bear kills Horvath, then the Mounties will come after *him* because it would be a revenge killing. If we shoot Horvath, we can say that we had to do it because he resisted arrest. You know Bear won't try to arrest him. Bear will just walk up and kill him. He won't have a strong defense, but we will. Especially if Horvath threatens us."

"I think you can count on a few threats," Zoe said dryly. Then she narrowed her gaze. "You keep saying 'we.' Do you plan to shoot Horvath, too?"

"Of course not, I don't know how to shoot a gun. But I'm willing to be an accessory by coming along to support you. I don't care if I get arrested. It's better that you and I get arrested than that Clara gets killed. And Zoe, we don't know when Horvath will strike, but I believe we can agree it will be soon. If you were Horvath, would you wait until Bear is strong and well again?"

Zoe stared. Juliette's argument was making sense: the situation was dire.

"For all we know, Horvath is creeping around outside right now. He's probably planning to go after the easiest prey first, and that's Clara!"

Alarmed and worried, Zoe stood and peered out the ice-block window. The ice was so thick that all she could see was a smear of greens, whites, and browns.

"Before we go after Horvath, there are a couple of things we have to talk about." She drew a breath. "Suppose for a minute that Horvath won't agree to be arrested. Suppose he threatens us, and suppose I have to shoot him. Then suppose the Mounties arrive and arrest me for killing Horvath and they arrest you for being part of it."

"Yes?" Juliette drummed her fingers impatiently.

"Who's going to shoot Jean Jacques if I'm arrested?"

"That's easy. You give Clara your rifle, then she continues on to Dawson and she shoots him."

"She's like you. She's never shot a weapon."

"So she can learn. Or she can poison him. Or she can hire someone to do the deed." Juliette shrugged.

"Sometimes you amaze me." It was hard to believe

that she had once dismissed Juliette as a prissy simpering creature with no backbone.

"Clara will take care of Jean Jacques. She's resourceful, and she'll work it out. We don't have to worry about him."

"One more thing. I don't know what the Canadian Mounties do to murderesses. Maybe they'll hang us, or maybe they'll stand us in front of a firing squad. But Juliette, we can't kill a man in cold blood without paying serious consequences."

"What are you saying? We can't possibly walk up and shoot him in cold blood. That would be unforgivably rude! The polite thing would be to warn him first and explain why we have to kill him."

Zoe blinked. On the other hand, maybe Juliette hadn't changed as much as she had thought. "He's going to say, 'No, I won't let you arrest me,' and then you're going to say, 'Please stand right there because we're going to kill you, and by the way we're doing it because you're trying to murder our friends.' "

"That's the gist of it. But I'd better warn you. I'm too angry to be completely correct and polite. I can't agree to shoot him in cold blood, but I do predict rude words will be spoken."

"You know, on second thought it might be better if you stayed here with Clara while I take care of Horvath."

"That wouldn't be fair. I suggested this, and I should be arrested too if that's how it ends."

"It won't be just an arrest. Do you feel strongly enough about killing Horvath that you're willing to hang for it?"

They stared at each other across the tabletop.

Finally, Juliette frowned at her coffee cup. "None of us are going to have the future we want, Zoe. So what does it matter what happens to us?" She looked up. "I've thought about this. And I think it would be easier to hang than to live knowing I did nothing and let that crazy man kill two people I love. If we have to kill Horvath, then yes, I'm willing to pay the penalty. I believe Clara would do the same for us."

"Yes, she would." Zoe felt exactly as Juliette did. She turned her head to stare at the ice-block window. Had a shadow just crossed by? Juliette's most compelling argument was that Horvath would act soon. In her bones, Zoe agreed. "We'll have to find someone to sit with Clara."

"I don't think Mrs. Weber would mind."

Zoe pushed up from the table. "You fetch Mrs. Weber while I load my rifle." That son of a bitch was not going to kill Clara and Bear. She and Juliette would see that he didn't.

"Excuse me, sir. Where might we find Mr. Horvath?" Juliette inquired pleasantly.

Horvath's crony stood outside his tent, leaning on the handle of an ax. He looked the two women up and down, a smirk on his lips. "He'd be up yonder on the mountain," he said, jerking a thumb over his shoulder. "Working on the cabin he's building hisself. What you want with him?"

"Thank you, sir." Juliette nudged Zoe, and they walked down a snowpacked lane between rows and rows of tents.

Zoe was half disappointed that they wouldn't pass Tom's or Ben's tents. Part of her wanted someone to talk them out of this. She had no idea if she really could kill a man. But maybe she didn't have to. Maybe it would serve just to shoot Jake Horvath in the privates. Do enough damage to lay him low long enough for the Mounties to arrive and for the rest of them to continue on to Dawson. But the Mounties might not come, and then Horvath would eventually turn up in Dawson. He had publicly stated he would "finish the job." Either he followed through or he'd be labeled a coward and he'd never hear the end of it.

"Can you tell that I'm carrying a rifle under my coat?" she asked Juliette, speaking out of the side of her mouth.

"Just don't drop it, for heaven's sake." Juliette slid her a glance. "Are you nervous?"

"A little. I've never shot anything except a squirrel."

"This should be easy, then. Horvath is bigger and more loathsome."

"I think I see his cabin through the pines." As they climbed a steep snowy path, more of Horvath's place became visible. The walls were up, and a stone chimney chase, but no roof yet. Zoe heard sounds of a hammer and cursing, but no other voices. He was alone then. Good. "Let me do the talking." Carefully, they picked their way up the boulder-strewn path. "Mr. Horvath? Mr. Jake Horvath!"

He came out of the cabin and walked a few steps toward them before he halted. "Well, lookee what we got here."

Juliette drew herself up, angry enough that the frozen feather on her hat quivered. "We've come to arrest you for the dastardly deed of ambushing Mr. Bear Barrett and Miss Clara Klaus. Shame on you, Mr. Horvath!"

"I'll do the talking," Zoe snapped. Anticipating the worst, she looked around, then stepped behind a boulder that reached as high as her elbows. She could remove the rifle from her coat without being seen, and she could lean against the boulder to steady her aim.

"I know you two," Horvath stated, squinting at them. "You're the stupid skirt who walked out on the thin ice." His gaze swung to Zoe. "And you're the bitch who broke my nose."

"Juliette, fall back a couple of steps and get behind that big rock." She had the rifle out now, hidden from sight behind the boulder. "Mr. Horvath, this will go easier for everyone if you'll return with us to your tent. We intend to place you under house arrest until the Canadian Mounties arrive."

First he looked flabbergasted and then amused. "Now, why would I agree to let you two doxies arrest me?"

"Partly for your own protection," Zoe called. "You have to know that when Bear is strong enough he'll come gunning for you. He isn't going to let you burn down his cabin and shoot his lady without repercussions."

"I got reasons for what I done," Horvath snarled. He tightened his grip around the hammer in his hand. "That son of a bitch cheated me, and he's going to die for it."

"You can tell your reasons to the Mounties when they get here. Until then, it's best for everyone if you're confined."

To Zoe's surprise, none of her nervousness appeared in her voice. She sounded steady and sure of herself. It helped that she had a rifle and Horvath only had a hammer. And it helped that she'd been a fighter all her life. Men like Horvath, cowardly little men who blamed others for their own shortcomings and who shot people in the back, didn't scare her—at least not much.

"Well, ladies. I ain't gonna be arrested. And I ain't gonna confine myself to no tent. The Mounties ain't coming, and if they did, they'd recognize my right to punish the man who cheated me out of my saloon."

"You're the one who bet your saloon on a hand of cards, Mr. Horvath," Juliette called in tones of deep disapproval. "It's not honorable to blame another for your lapse of judgment. Or to accuse someone of cheating because the cards didn't fall your way. You are no gentleman, sir!"

Hatred blazed from his tiny raisin eyes. "You go on, now. Git. And you can tell Bear Barrett and his whore that next time no one will rescue them. Next time they're dead!"

Zoe narrowed her eyes and spoke with authority. "Drop the hammer, Mr. Horvath, and walk down this path."

"I ain't gonna do that. Ain't you listening?" He looked back and forth between them. "Now git."

Juliette stood tall behind her rock. "If you don't come

with us now, Mr. Horvath, then Miss Wilder will have to shoot you. We genuinely regret having to shoot you, I hope you understand that, and we apologize in advance. But since you've threatened to kill our friends, we have no choice." She nodded to Zoe. "I think you should fire a warning shot now."

Zoe wiped snow from the top of the boulder, then brought up the rifle and let him see it. She decided a small lie was in order. "I've killed dozens of men, Mr. Horvath, and I won't hesitate to kill you, too, if I must. But I'd prefer not to. So do as we ask and walk down the hill to your tent."

He glanced at the rifle and looked hard at Zoe. Then he pursed his lips and nodded. "Looks like you got me," he said finally. "Let me put away my tools and get my jacket, then we'll go."

The instant he stepped inside the cabin, Juliette called in a low voice. "It's going splendidly, don't you think?"

"Unless he went in the cabin to get a gun." Zoe chewed her lip and watched the unfinished doorway. Maybe this was a trick.

"Oh." Juliette considered. "Well, if you think he has a gun in there, why didn't you shoot him?"

"Because maybe he really is surrendering."

He wasn't. Horvath appeared in the doorway of the cabin with a pistol in each hand. Before Zoe could react to what she saw, a bullet glanced off her boulder, spraying up chips of granite. One of the chips hit her cheek, and she felt a trickle of blood as she ducked down.

"Things are really going our way now," Juliette called. Her voice came from low and behind her rock. "He's trying to kill us, so we can kill him back. I believe that's the law. No one will arrest us for killing someone who's trying to kill us. And he fired first." She shouted at Horvath. "It's extremely ungentlemanly to shoot at women, Mr. Horvath. Have you no shame? I demand that you cease and desist. This is your last chance."

In answer, bullets peppered the rocks in front of them.

"Well, there you are," Juliette called to Zoe. "The man has no concept of propriety. He's an incorrigible. We've warned him and we've explained. So why aren't you shooting at him?"

"I'd like to, damn it. But I have to see to fire, and I'm afraid he'll shoot off my head if I lift it above the rock."

"You didn't think of this before now? Really, Zoe."

Zoe ground her teeth together and wondered how many shots Horvath had fired. She'd lost count. But she did know that things had changed and now Horvath held the high cards. She and Juliette were pinned down, unable to retreat without exposing themselves. There wasn't a doubt in her mind that he would kill them both given half a chance.

Rising on her knees, facing the rock, she slid the rifle barrel up on top of the granite and squeezed off a blind shot. Ignoring Juliette's applause, she took a second shot. For all she could tell, the rifle barrel was resting on a bump and aimed at the sky. Or maybe she'd hit the cabin. The odds of actually hitting Horvath were slim, damn it.

A rain of bullets showered the rocks that protected them. When she heard Horvath laugh she knew she hadn't hit him.

"You bitches have to show yourselves sometime, and when you do, you're dead. You hear me? Dead."

"Did you hear that?" Juliette crowed. "He threatened us. We've got him now. But I wish you'd hurry up and shoot him. I'm getting cold."

"Well, I'm trying!"

Zoe managed a couple more shots and then took stock of their situation. As long as she continued to fire in Horvath's general direction, he wouldn't advance on them and come down the path. But she and Juliette couldn't withdraw without exposing themselves. And Zoe was getting cold, too.

"We're stuck," she said finally, calling to Juliette. "I

can't get a decent shot, and we can't retreat without Horvath killing us."

She had come to the Yukon with no illusions. She had planned to shoot and kill Jean Jacques Villette, and she had expected to hang for his murder. She had come to terms with Jean Jacques's death and with her own before she left Seattle.

But now, hunkered down behind the granite boulder while bullets whizzed over her head, she understood that everything had changed. She didn't want to die. Not by hanging, not by getting shot. She wanted to live happily ever after with Tom Price. She didn't even care if they ended in Newcastle as long as they were together.

"Somehow the tide has turned. I think we're in a bit of a pickle," Juliette said in a small voice. "I think we might get killed or badly wounded unless someone in camp hears the shots and comes to our rescue."

"Don't count on it. A hundred men are hunting in these hills every day. Shots are as common as tobacco juice."

"It's beginning to look like this isn't as positive a situation as it first appeared."

Zoe bit off a string of stinging comments about positive situations, because however annoying Juliette could be, she was, by God, a brave and loyal friend. She was here on the hillside getting shot at, and it had been her idea. Although Zoe had never believed she would have such a thought, she admitted that Juliette had many good qualities. And so did Clara. The two people she had hated most in the world had become her dearest friends.

Closing her eyes, she leaned back against the rock. The question now was how good a friend was Zoe Wilder? She had come here to save Clara, but she'd ended by placing Juliette in danger. Never mind whose idea it was. Zoe knew about weapons and fights, and she should have thought this through more thoroughly.

Juliette didn't deserve to die. After all, Zoe was the one

who had come to the Yukon to hang. And she reminded herself that it would never have ended well with Tom in any case.

"Juliette, listen." She drew a deep breath. Actually, getting shot didn't terrify her as much as being hanged. And she might even survive. Her hands were steady as she pushed bullets into the rifle's chamber. "When I stand up to shoot, you make a run for it. Don't use the path. Go through the trees. I know the snow is deep and it will be hard to move. But stay in the trees until the cabin is out of sight."

"I don't wish to be impolite, but . . . have you lost your mind? If you stand up, Horvath will kill you!"

"If we keep sitting here, we'll freeze."

"I've been thinking, Zoe. This was a bad idea, and I'm sorry." Juliette's voice cracked. "It's my fault that we're going to get killed."

"No, it's my fault. I acted on impulse instead of thinking this out more carefully." Zoe waved a hand, though Juliette couldn't see her. "Never mind that. Just get ready to run."

"Zoe? Whatever happens . . . I love you."

The air ran out of her chest. "I love you, too." She bit her lips. "Tell Tom . . . and tell Clara . . . Well, you'll know what to say. Make it sound nice."

"Oh, Zoe. Damn it."

"Get ready. On the count of three, I'll stand and you run." She sucked in a cold breath and pictured the cabin, the doorway. If Horvath hadn't overheard their loud whispers, she might get him first. It might happen that way. "One . . ." She turned to face the rock and gathered her feet beneath her. "Two . . ." The rifle was ready to fire and she was a good shot. "Three!"

Popping up, she fired into a hail of bullets. Bullets coming toward her, bullets flying past her. She could see Horvath, and he was shooting past her, at the path.

"Get down!" Tom's voice? But it couldn't be.

Completely confused, Zoe dropped behind the rock and peered down the path. At least a dozen men rushed toward her, with Bear in the lead and Tom and Ben right behind. All of them had weapons and fired steadily at Horvath's cabin. And none of them had the sense to seek cover, she noticed, her heart in her mouth.

Bear had one arm strapped to his chest, and his face was red with the exertion of climbing the path. But he was firing and roaring like a grizzly.

"You no-good, cowardly, worthless piece of garbage! First you shoot me in the back and try to kill my woman, now you're trying to kill my friends! Defenseless women!"

The mountainside reverberated with a fusillade of gunshots flying back and forth between the cabin and the men on the path, so many shots that no one could have kept count. Zoe covered her ears as the men rushed past her.

And then, finally, silence. Slowly, Zoe and Juliette stood behind their rocks. Horvath was dead, and the men stood in a circle around his body, quietly wondering whose bullets had found the mark. As she watched, Tom turned, and his eyes met hers. He and Ben walked away from the others and climbed down the path.

"Are you injured?" Tom asked in a clipped voice.

"No," she said as Ben passed, moving rapidly toward Juliette. "The cut on my cheek is just a scratch."

"Good. Miraculously, no one else is injured either. Now, what in the hell were you thinking of?" His fists came down on his hips, and his green eyes blazed. "God knows what might have happened if we hadn't had a couple of men up there on the hillside watching Horvath! You could have gotten yourself killed!"

She stared. "You have men watching him?"

"Of course!" Exasperation roughened his voice. "He threatened to go after Clara and Bear again. Do you think we were just going to let him do it?" Sweeping off his hat, he pushed his fingers through his hair. "Damn it, Zoe. If

Abner hadn't rushed down and sounded the alarm, Horvath would have killed you two!"

"We didn't think anyone was doing anything to stop him."

Bear came down the path. "Abner saw part of it, but Cal Rye heard and saw everything. These ladies tried to make a citizen's arrest. Horvath refused to be arrested." Bear rolled his eyes. "Horvath fired first." He glanced at Zoe's rifle. "Everything that happened from then on was self-defense or a rescue. There won't be any trouble with the Mounties. We've got a dozen men who will swear they saw Horvath firing at Zoe and Juliette."

Tom continued to stare at her. "I see the outlines of this. You thought you were going to save Clara and Bear, right? Was that your plan?"

"Yes." Her chin came up. "And I don't apologize for it."

"If you'd talked to me first, damn it, I could have told you that Horvath couldn't make a move without us knowing!"

"Well, damn all! That woman should be resting." Bear swore between his teeth and squinted down the path at Clara, who hurried toward them. She was hastily assembled, her hat askew, her arm in a sling over a coat that was buttoned wrong. They could all see her muffler dropped on the path behind her.

She threw herself on Juliette, almost knocking her to the ground. "Mrs. Weber finally told me where you two went and why. No one's ever done such a nice thing for me! I thank you from my heart, and I love you!"

Juliette emerged from the folds of Clara's coat, gasping for air, and Clara rushed on up the path and grabbed Zoe.

"Thank you," she said, squeezing the air out of Zoe's body with her good arm. "I love you both so much. I've never had friends like you and Juliette!" She gazed up at Bear. "I'm a lucky woman."

Bear dropped his free arm around Clara's shoulder, and Ben had his hand on Juliette's waist as they came up the path. But Tom still stood with his fists on his hips, staring at her.

"There are some puzzling things here." He tipped his hat toward the rifle leaning against the granite boulder. "I guess I understand why you came to confront Horvath. But I don't understand why you brought a rifle to the Yukon in the first place. And I sure as hell don't understand why you were apparently willing to die today."

He was angry and hurt that she would risk their future. She saw it in his expression. Saw the questions in his eyes. And she knew she could offer him an explanation that he might accept, but it wouldn't be the truth.

"Zoe, I've respected your privacy." He spoke to her as if he'd forgotten about the others. "But if you'd gotten yourself killed today, I would have punished myself for the rest of my life because I didn't insist on trying to help you with whatever problem made you pack a rifle and be so reckless with your life. Darlin', it's time for some answers."

Shoulders sagging, she pushed her palm against her forehead. "I am so sick of deception," she said in a low voice. Raising her lashes, she cast a beseeching glance at Clara and Juliette. "Please. I can't go on like this. I need to tell Tom the truth, and he needs to hear it."

Clara and Juliette returned her stare, then each slowly nodded. Clara edged away from Bear's arm. "*Ja*, the time has come," she said with a deep sigh.

Stepping away from Ben, Juliette turned her eyes down the path. Bright pink colored her cheeks. "I've dreaded this moment with all my heart. And I've longed to get it over with."

Frowning and puzzled, Tom stared at her. "Zoe?"

She drew her shoulders up and back. Her heart pounded so loudly that she was certain everyone could hear. After glancing toward the men standing around Horvath's unfinished cabin and hoping they wouldn't overhear, she met Tom's gaze.

"You know that I came here looking for someone. A man. His name is Jean Jacques Villette, and I came to kill him. That's why I brought the rifle."

No one said a word.

"Why do you want to kill Villette?" Tom asked finally.

Her lashes fluttered and then steadied. "You said you'd heard I was married, but I told you that I wasn't. I lied to you, Tom. Jean Jacques Villette is my husband."

"He's my husband, too," Clara admitted reluctantly, looking at her shoes.

Juliette kept her eyes fixed on the path. "And mine."

Chapter 21

It was time for explanations, but Horvath's cabin was not the place. They returned to Mr. Dame's and settled in the kitchen with the men ranged along one side of the table and the women along the other. They stared at one another with expressions of helplessness on one side and disbelief and anger on the other.

"So that's our story," Zoe finished, looking down at her hands pressed flat against the tabletop. "That's why we're traveling to Dawson, to confront and shoot Jean Jacques Villette for what he did to us."

"Punishing him doesn't seem as important now," Clara sighed, pushing a frizzy cloud of red hair back from her cheek.

"I know." Juliette glanced at Ben's stony face, then quickly looked away. "I don't care anymore why Jean Jacques married all of us. If he walked in here this minute, I wouldn't have anything to say to him."

"Villette isn't going to walk in the door, and you won't find him in Dawson either," Tom stated flatly. His green eyes didn't move from Zoe's face.

Zoe wet her lips. "How can you sound so certain?"

"Because I know where he is. That first day on the Dyea beach—if you had trusted an old friend who loved you—if you hadn't lied to me—I could have taken you right to Villette."

All three women sucked in a breath and leaned forward

to stare. "He was in Dyea?" Zoe asked, her heart in her throat.

"Villette hired my Indians to pack him to Chilkoot and over the pass. But he didn't climb Chilkoot, he returned to Dyea. That's where I met him. He wanted a partial refund since my people wouldn't have to haul his outfit up and over the pass. He said he was ill, and I sent him to old Doc Popov. Doc Popov thought Villette was suffering from consumption and advised him to return on the first steamer heading for the outside."

"I think I see where this story is leading," Ben said in a tight voice.

Bear nodded. "The son of a bitch sailed on the *Annasett*."

When Tom confirmed it, Zoe's face went white. She heard Clara and Juliette gasp.

"Jean Jacques was at Dyea when we arrived," she whispered. "Everything we've been through has been for nothing." Losing weight and worrying about scurvy, the cold food and frozen nights, Juliette almost drowning, Clara getting shot, being utterly exhausted, the continual range of bruises and bumps and never being warm, the fear of getting hurt, the continual anxiety—all of it. "And it's my fault."

"Because you didn't trust me," Tom agreed, nodding angrily. "Because you lied to me."

"You all lied," Ben said in a hard voice, his gaze narrowed on Juliette. "You let us believe you were unattached."

Ripples ran along Bear's big jaw. "I told you about myself and gave you the choice whether to accept who I am. I didn't hide from you." Clara lowered her head. "If you had given me the courtesy of truth, I would have tipped my hat and moved along. I've done things I'm not proud of, Clara, but until now I've never seduced a married woman." He looked disgusted.

Tom stood and gave Zoe an expressionless look. "We need a few minutes of privacy."

Nodding, Zoe led the way into the living room. After a brief hesitation, Clara stood and beckoned Bear toward the bedroom. Juliette and Ben remained in the kitchen.

Zoe turned to face him in front of the fire. "There were two reasons why I didn't tell you about Jean Jacques." Making fists so he wouldn't see her fingers shaking, she told him about not wanting her ma to learn the truth about Jean Jacques by hearing gossip at the company store.

Tom's eyebrows soared incredulously. "You didn't trust me enough to ask me not to reveal your business in a letter home? What did you think? That I'd agree to keep your confidence, then break it hours later? Do you think I'm the kind of man who doesn't stand by his promise?"

Every word he spoke knocked a piece out of her heart. "And I didn't want you to know how stupid I'd been. That's why I lied about being married. I didn't want you to know that I'd been taken in by a fairy tale and clean fingernails. That I'd be so foolish as to see only pretty lies and not the man telling them."

"What you saw was yourself riding through Newcastle in a carriage showing everyone that you were better than the rest of us," he snapped.

She winced and lowered her gaze. "I deserve that. Maybe that is what I thought I wanted." How could she ever have been so shallow and blind? She hated it. "And obviously Jean Jacques exploited my snobbery. But Tom, that was then, and this is now. Now I wouldn't give a man like Jean Jacques a second glance. Now I know it's the people who matter, not the place or the things."

"I don't care about that bastard or why you married him. I care about trust, Zoe. I thought you and I trusted each other because we were both from Newcastle and because we'd known each other for more years than I can remember." He looked at her as if he saw a stranger, and his expression broke her heart. "You trusted me with your life the night we were caught in the storm, but you can't trust me with your secret. If you don't trust me enough to confide something as important as the fact that you're married and gunning for your husband . . . then what did you and I ever have?"

"Oh, Tom." Tears strangled her, brimmed in her eyes.

Turning on his heels, he walked away from the fire. "I'm going out. I'll be back after I've had a chance to think about all of this."

Her knees collapsed, and she dropped into a chair facing the dying flames. She had known it wouldn't end well. She'd even known he would hate her more for not trusting him than for being married when she came into his arms.

Looking back, she no longer remembered why it had seemed reasonable to conceal the truth. When she'd tried to explain, her reasons had sounded trivial and insulting. Leaning forward, she buried her face in her hands. If only she could turn back the clock to that day on the Dyea beach. If only, if only.

"I don't want to know about him," Ben snapped. "The three of you should have contacted an attorney at once. But that's neither here nor there." He paused in pacing the small kitchen to stare at her. "Do you have any idea of the enormity of the scandal if it became known that the owner and president of the Bay City Bank seduced a married woman who is one of his investors and depositors?"

"Ben . . ."

"The public demands that bankers be circumspect. Even if the circumstances were known, this situation would be ruinous to me and to my bank."

"I wanted to tell you." Juliette blinked at tears and wrung her hands. "Surely you can understand why I couldn't."

"No, Juliette, I don't. Did you believe I would betray you? Who on earth did you suppose I would tell? Did you imagine that I'd distribute broadsides announcing that I was in love with the wife of a bigamist? For God's sake, if you can't trust your banker, who can you trust?"

Tears spilled down her cheeks and glistened on her lashes. "I love you, Ben. I thought if you knew about Jean Jacques, you'd ... you'd withdraw and ..." She covered her face with her handkerchief.

"Maybe I would have kept my distance. Maybe not. Considering how I felt about you, I think I would have thought it through and then said to hell with the possibility of scandal, you're more important. But the choice and the decision should have been mine to make."

She had no defense. He was right.

Ben studied her with eyes as unyielding as blue stones. "I would have wagered everything I own that deceit and deception were simply not in your character. I'll spend the rest of my life wondering how I could have been so wrong about you."

His words drove a dagger into her heart. "Please, Ben. I beg you." She didn't know what she was begging. Understanding? Another chance? She only knew that she felt sick inside. Even knowing this confrontation was inevitable hadn't prepared her for the anguish of seeing herself through his eyes and of knowing that she had lost him.

He stared at her with a flicker of bewilderment and loss. Then his shoulders pulled back, his expression hardened, and he nodded his head in a half-bow. "Good-bye, Mrs. Villette. We have nothing further to say."

Without a backward glance he walked out of the kitchen, out of the cabin, and out of her life.

Juliette crumpled to the floor like a broken doll. Blindly, she stared at the table legs and wished Horvath had shot her. A bullet would have been a thousand times less painful than what she was suffering now.

At another time Clara would have looked at Bear's sling and her own and would have teased about them being two wounded birds. But the ease of teasing had ended for them and wouldn't come again.

"I'm sorry," she said in a low voice, sitting on the edge of the bed. "I should have told you about Jean Jacques."

"I don't want to hear about some son of a bitch that you've been in bed with! But you sure as hell should have told me that you were married!"

"I don't know if I am. All three marriages can't be legal."

Bear paced to the ice-block window and glared out at the gathering darkness. "Damn it, Clara!" He struck the wall with his fist and the whole cabin shook. "I thought you were respectable. And I was so proud that a respectable woman wanted *me*! I kept telling you who I am, and it didn't scare you off." He pounded his chest. "And damned if something inside didn't start to feel better, something I can't name, but I've carried it all my life."

"Oh, Bear." She could name the weight in his chest. Shame. Of all the things he might have said, this would hurt the worst when she remembered it later. She had taken away the shame of his upbringing, and now she had flung it back on him.

"And don't tell me you're not married. You said the vows. You aren't divorced, and you aren't widowed. You have a living husband out there, and you came up here looking for him. Yet you went right on ahead and let me love you."

There was no way to deflect his words, nothing to say.

"Do you know why I've never married?" he asked suddenly.

"I can guess," she said in a whisper.

"A respectable woman wouldn't want a man with my background, and I don't want the other kind." For a minute his voice went soft. "Honey girl, I thought the sun rose and set on you. I thought you were the finest thing that ever came into my life."

Now the tears started, rolling silently down her cheeks.

"But you're no better than me."

"I was no better than you or anyone else even when you had me up on that pedestal, Bear." She raised her good arm and then let it fall back to her lap. "I'm sorry."

"I've never pretended to be what I'm not. I would have bet my life that you were the same way. I guessed from the first that the three of you had a secret. But I thought it was something like maybe you'd run off from your families seeking adventure. Or maybe you were all older or younger than you look. That kind of thing. If your secret was substantial, I figured you would have confided in me when I was confiding in you."

"I wanted to. You don't know how much I wish I had." The tears came faster. She detested it that his last memory would be of her crying, with her eyes red and puffy and her nose running.

"We might have worked this out, Clara, if you'd trusted me and if you'd been truthful. I don't know. Right now I'm mad, and I'm feeling like I've been had. I think you were correct up there on the mountainside when you said you were lucky. All Villette took was your money. I wish that's all you'd taken from me."

When she looked up again, he was gone. And her agony began.

No one slept that night. Eventually they sought the small comfort of warmth and company and gathered together before the fireplace. They wept until their eyes swelled and ached. Until their handkerchiefs soaked through and their bodies felt dry and boneless.

There was nothing compelling enough to rouse them until Tom returned near what passed for dawn in a Yukon winter. Then Clara and Juliette silently rose to offer Tom and Zoe privacy.

"There's no cause to go. Stay seated," Tom said gruffly. He directed his next remarks to a spot directly above Zoe's head. "When Villette returned to Dyea, he left his outfit at Chilkoot. My Indians decided it was more of a priority to pack our customers over the pass than to cause them delay by bringing back the outfit of someone giving up. Before Villette boarded the *Annasett* for Seattle, he directed me to ship his outfit to Loma Grande, California, on the next steamer out. Which I did."

"California," Juliette murmured with a sigh.

"How ill was he?" Clara inquired.

"I've seen men a whole lot sicker climb Chilkoot and go on to Dawson," Tom said in a flat voice. "But Doc Popov did diagnose consumption, and Doc did advise Villette to be on the next steamer out." He shrugged and pushed his hands into his coat pockets. "Frankly I don't care if Villette had a foot in the grave or if he exaggerated a cough as an excuse to go home."

Zoe turned her head toward the fire. Juliette touched her temples as if she had a headache. Clara cradled her sling next to her body.

"How soon do you want to leave?"

They all stiffened and stared at him with startled expressions.

"I guess there's no reason to continue on to Dawson," Clara said finally, breaking a lengthy silence.

Juliette raised shaking fingertips to her lips. "No reason at all."

"I suppose we can leave as soon as Clara's shoulder and side are fully healed and she's up to running behind a sled," Zoe said, speaking to the fire.

Tom stood before them, a handsome weathered man, tall with authority, his expression as hard as the ice on the lake.

"Since you won't be staying in Dawson, you don't need a year's worth of goods and foodstuffs. You can lighten the sleds considerably by selling off everything you won't need during a rough fast run for Dyea. If you lighten your outfits sufficiently, we can put Clara in one of the sleds. You could depart as early as tomorrow morning."

Zoe looked at the others, then gripped her hands in her lap. "I guess we could be ready by then." The others nodded. She gazed up at him, her heart in her eyes. "Will you take us back?"

"No. Luc will be in charge of getting you to Dyea and on board the next ship out." Tom's gaze locked to hers. "Good-bye, Zoe. When you see your brother Jack, give him my regards."

He hesitated as if there were more to say, then he muttered beneath his breath, nodded to Clara and Juliette, and tipped his hat on his head. The door closed softly behind him.

"We're going home," Zoe whispered when the silence became too much to bear. "Tomorrow." A tear hovered on her lashes and then zigzagged down her cheek.

Juliette pressed her handkerchief to her face. "I thought I couldn't cry anymore. I thought all the tears were gone."

Clara walked to the window and leaned forward as if she could see through the ice. "I'd hoped it wouldn't end like this. This is too abrupt, too . . . I don't know." Despair choked her voice. "One minute I am someone's sun, and an hour later I am his darkness. How can that happen so fast? How can I survive this?"

Clara was touched by the number of people who gathered to see them off and wish them well. Mrs. Eddington and her husband came, and most of the women on the trail. She recognized the men she had beaten in the arm-wrestling tournament, exchanged grins with a couple of men she had laid low during the infamous brawl. But the face she longed to see wasn't there.

She kept hoping Bear would appear until Luc locked the straps over the thick blankets covering her and shouted the order for the sleds to move out. Only then did she allow herself to admit that Bear wouldn't stop her from leaving.

Then, once they were under way, she hoped he would

come after her. Their pace was set by Juliette, the slowest member of their party. Bear could easily have caught up. But he didn't.

Her last hope was to find him waiting at their evening campsite, impatiently looking for the first sled, intending to surprise her.

"I know what you're hoping," Juliette said sadly after she'd arrived and inspected the site. "But they aren't coming."

"Look." Zoe's voice sounded peculiar. "The Chilkats are setting up our tent, and it appears that Henry is going to cook."

Overhearing the comment, Luc walked toward them with a smile. "Mr. Tom told us to take very good care of you ladies. Treat you like rich clients."

Zoe's face paled beneath the ash and grease, and she abruptly walked away.

"It isn't a reference to Jean Jacques," Clara insisted later when they were on their cots with their stove heating the cramped space inside the tent.

"Of course it is."

"No, Clara's right." Juliette lifted on an elbow. "Tom loves you, Zoe. He wants the trip back to be as comfortable as it can be, so he instructed his Indians to treat us like rich people. He used a phrase to help his Chilkats understand what he wants them to do. That's all."

"I don't want any favors from him," Zoe snapped. She flopped down on her cot and stared at the tent ceiling.

"Well, I do. I want every favor I can get," Clara said, covering a yawn. "I wonder if Bear paid the Chilkats for this portion of the trip, too."

Juliette cleared her throat. "I paid our way." Fire burned on her cheeks. "Tom didn't say anything about the cost of getting us back to Dyea. But I thought . . ." She shrugged. "By now Mrs. Eddington will have given him the envelope I left."

Zoe bolted up on her cot and swore. "Damn it, Juliette! I don't want your charity!"

"Just say thank you and shut up." Clara lifted her head and scowled.

"It won't kill you to accept a gift or a favor from Tom and me."

"Not only are you forcing charity on me, but you're talking in that prissy little voice! I don't know which I hate more!"

Juliette paused with her brush in her hair. "Did you hear a thank-you in any of that?" she asked Clara.

"I wasn't listening. I was thinking about the ship and putting up with her dying again." She sighed heavily. "Remember cleaning her up, and scrubbing vomit off the floor, and washing her nightgown in a basin the size of a thimble? Compared to saving her life, making this journey more endurable is hardly worth a thank-you. The way I see it, she'll never be out of our debt so we might as well continue to annoy her with gifts and favors."

"You're making me sound foolish and ungrateful!"

"Yes," they shouted in unison.

Zoe glared and then suddenly burst into laughter. "Oh, lordy, just listen to me. I'm angry at Juliette for paying Tom. I'm furious at Tom for making this awful trek a little easier. That *is* foolish." Jumping to Juliette's cot, she gave Juliette a fierce hug and then she embraced Clara, careful not to jostle her sling. "Thank you both."

Clara smiled. "I sure didn't think any of us would be laughing tonight."

"Or ever again," Juliette added.

"I wouldn't have laughed if it weren't for you two." Zoe fumbled for her handkerchief. "I'm such a mess. First I'm laughing, and now I'm crying. Is this how it's going to be?"

It seemed so. Every night for the next four weeks, they tumbled into their sleeping bags at night, exhausted from the day's labor and worn out by conflicting and quickly changing emotions. Sometimes they began conversations with, "Do you remember? . . ." and ended by laughing until their sides ached. Then someone would sigh, and the tears started.

At the beginning of their sixth week on the trail, Clara insisted on taking a turn running behind a sled and insisted that they rotate riding. As a consequence of a day of rest every third day, they weren't as bone-weary as they had been traveling in the other direction, and their pace improved on the days Juliette rode in the sled.

"Luc says we'll cut at least two weeks if the weather holds and we continue the present pace," Zoe remarked, lowering her face over a steaming cup of coffee. They stood near Henry's cookstove, stamping their feet occasionally to warm their toes. The long hours of darkness did nothing to dispel the frigid temperatures. At night the mercury dropped to thirty degrees below zero. The daytime high might rise to fifteen below.

Clara waved steam at her face. "I'll never forget how beautiful it is up here. The mountains, the snow . . . It takes my breath away. And the wildlife. Today I saw an eagle and a moose and a wolf."

"Spring must be lovely," Juliette said through her muffler. Her eyes rolled toward them. "What are we going to do when we get back to Seattle? Are we going to keep looking for Jean Jacques?"

"I don't have the stomach to kill him. Not now."

"I'd like to get my money back, but he probably doesn't have it anymore."

"I've thought about it, and I'm going to Loma Grande." Juliette nodded to herself. "I don't have anything else to do. So I'm going to find him, and I'm going to spit in his face."

"Well, *mein Gott!*" Clara stared. "If *you're* going to Loma Grande, then I'm going, too!" They looked at Zoe.

"You know," she said, "I'm getting mad again. Maybe I do have the stomach to shoot Jean Jacques. Because of him, the man I love turned and walked away. I know, I know. I lied to Tom. But I wouldn't have had to lie if it weren't for Jean Jacques." She threw her coffee on the snow. "Yes, I have a few things to say to that rotten bastard. And yes, I'm going with you to Loma Grande!"

"We'll line up, and we'll all spit on him," Juliette promised. "I can't believe I ever thought I loved that liar and cheat! I didn't know what love really is until Ben."

That's when they learned that crying outside was not a sensible act. At thirty degrees below zero, tears freeze on a woman's cheek.

Chapter 22

If anything, the voyage to the States was worse than the three Mmes Villette had dreaded it would be. The first steamer out of Dyea was the *White Star*, bound for San Francisco. They could leave immediately on the *White Star*, but Zoe would have to endure an additional week at sea to reach California, or they could wait a month in Dyea to catch a shorter voyage to Seattle. They opted to sail at once on the *White Star*, and Clara and Juliette dragged Zoe on board, where she became violently ill before the *White Star* weighed anchor.

The voyage was as much a nightmare as their first had been, with fierce winter weather tossed in for good measure. The *White Star* rode the waves like a cork bobbing on giant seas. They all believed Zoe hovered at death's door. Zoe hoped it was true and begged to die and end her torment. Clara and Juliette considered obliging her. They wore themselves to a frazzle tending a patient who cursed them, shouted at them, taxed their nerves, and threw up on their skirts.

All three wept with relief when the *White Star* dropped anchor in the San Francisco Bay. And when they set foot on the wharves they wept because they would far rather have been in the frozen Yukon instead of in California where the days were longer and the sun was full and warm. They had left their hearts in the icy north.

To allow Zoe time to recuperate, they spent a week at

the California Astor Hotel where Juliette insisted on taking a suite as a treat for everyone.

"This beauty cream isn't as effective as lard," Clara complained, examining her cheeks in the sitting-room mirror. "Look at my skin. It's as chapped and raw as if I just came in from seven hours behind a sled."

Juliette glanced up from the book she was trying to read. "Your skin is beautiful. And your new dress is definitely an improvement. Now if we could only persuade you to do something about those clunky shoes . . ."

Zoe edged Clara aside and examined her reflection with a critical eye. "I think my hair is starting to regain some luster. But I'm still too thin." She inspected Juliette in the mirror. "Your hair looks quite elegant today."

"Well, aren't we being nice and polite." Juliette set her book aside. "This might be a good time to request your advice." Frowning, she gazed at the scrolled tin ceiling. "Since I can't have the future I want, none of us can, I've been thinking about the future I can have."

Clara and Zoe took facing chairs and gave her their full attention. "Go on," Clara urged. "What future are you considering?"

"It's occurred to me that I've never enjoyed my inheritance or done anything useful with it. I'd like to change that. I've decided I won't return to Linda Vista because I don't want to deal with small-town gossip and because it would be too easy to fall into old habits and let Aunt Kibble make my decisions." She drew a breath. "I'm thinking of buying a home in a large city. Perhaps Seattle."

"Seattle? Why not here in San Francisco?" Zoe stopped. "Oh, Ben's bank."

"I want to get involved in important issues." As Ben's late wife had done. Juliette had thought a lot about Helen Dare's involvement in the world around her and had decided she, too, wanted to discover if she was courageous enough to face societal wrongs and fight to right them. Maybe she and her money could make a small difference for the better.

"What kind of issues?" Clara leaned forward, interested.

"I don't know yet. Now here's my question. Do you think it's scandalous for a single woman to live alone? And to get involved in issues and maybe travel a little?" She knew she would never marry again. If she couldn't have Ben, she didn't want any man.

"Not at all," Clara stated firmly. "Especially if you live alone in a big city where attitudes are freer, and especially if you donate enough money to worthy causes."

Zoe smiled. "After you've stood naked on a beach in front of several hundred men, I wouldn't think gossip or scandal would worry you ever again."

"You're right," Juliette said, laughing. "Still, there's that little voice on my shoulder. . . ." She returned Zoe's smile. "Have you thought about what you'll do after we confront Jean Jacques?"

They had talked about the confrontation almost nonstop this week, and they had decided that Zoe would not shoot Jean Jacques. Killing him wasn't worth the penalty Zoe would pay. But they had also decided they could not abandon a search that had now consumed nearly seven months of their lives. They had to see it through to the end. Each wanted Jean Jacques Villette to understand that he had ruined her life and any chance at happiness she might have had. They deserved to speak their piece and deserved to witness any remorse he might feel.

"This may surprise you," Zoe began. "But after we've found Jean Jacques and had our say, I want to go home to Newcastle. I want to stay with my parents for a few months and look at Newcastle through enlightened eyes. I want to renew my roots and enjoy knowing who I am."

"Are you hoping that Tom will eventually turn up in Newcastle?" Juliette asked gently.

"Maybe," Zoe whispered. "It's hard to accept that I can love this deeply and believe I was loved in return—but . . ."

"*Ja*, I know what you mean." Clara sighed heavily. "Me? If I could do what I wanted, I'd follow the gold rush and put up decent hotels that served good home-cooked food. I would make a fortune." She sighed again. "But if I returned to the Yukon, I would inevitably run into Bear, and that would break my heart. So maybe I'll buy a small hotel or a boardinghouse in Seattle."

Juliette leaned her curls against the back of the chair and closed her eyes. "It's such a shame. I would have made a perfect banker's wife. Zoe, you couldn't possibly find a man more suited to you than Tom. And Clara, you and Bear are so wonderful together, so right."

"We promised we wouldn't say these things," Zoe said in a choked voice. Standing abruptly, she smoothed down her skirts. "I need to finish packing. Didn't you say the carriage would call for us at seven A.M. tomorrow?" She leveled a forced smile on Juliette. "Thank you for this week in a suite, it was marvelous. And thank you for hiring a carriage to take us to Loma Grande. We'll be more comfortable than we would have been in a stage."

"You're quite welcome," Juliette said, smiling.

"Now, that wasn't so hard, was it?" Clara asked, her eyes twinkling.

"It's getting easier," Zoe admitted, speaking between her teeth.

Then they laughed, blinking back tears of affection. Their long journey together was nearing the end, and they knew they would never again share another woman's secrets or know her as intimately as they knew each other.

There was little about Loma Grande that could be considered *grande*. Like many California villages, Loma Grande had grown around a Catholic mission built years ago. It was a sleepy, leafy town, a town that roused itself for market day and then slumbered for another week in the pleasant California warmth.

"It reminds me a little of Linda Vista," Juliette mentioned, looking about after the driver handed her out of the carriage.

Mature shade trees overhung an unpaved main street. She spotted the post office, a Ladies Emporium, a feed and seed store. She imagined the rest of the town: A few large homes would occupy the streets on either side of Main. Behind them would stand more modest dwellings. Tucked in the low hills curving around Loma Grande would be the fruit and vegetable farms that provided the town a reason to exist.

Clara slapped down her skirts and considered Loma Grande's sole inn with a judgmental eye. "The veranda needs painting, but the flowers are bright and welcoming."

"Jean Jacques is here somewhere," Zoe said, wetting her lips. "It's strange to think about."

"Unless he's left again. Unless he recovered enough to wander off in search of more wives," Clara said sharply. Waving aside the carriage driver, she picked up her bag and strode toward the veranda. The door opened wide, and a tiny smiling woman bade them welcome.

"I'm Mrs. Wilson," she announced, stepping behind the lobby counter. "Will you ladies be staying long?" she asked, turning the registration book to face Zoe.

"We'll be here the rest of today and possibly tomorrow."

After Zoe and Juliette had signed the book, Clara stepped forward and accepted the pen. She gave Mrs. Wilson a comradely smile of one innkeep to another. "As we were driving into town, it occurred to us that we have an acquaintance who lives in this area. His name is Mr. Jean Jacques Villette. Perhaps you could direct us to his residence. We'd like to surprise him."

Mrs. Wilson's eyes rounded, and her gaze darted over them. "Oh, my, my."

Clara didn't know how to interpret Mrs. Wilson's drawn-out sigh, but it was clear the woman recognized Jean Jacques's name.

Suddenly flustered, Mrs. Wilson retrieved the registra-

tion book and studied their names. "I don't know anything about this affair, Miss Klaus—"

"I beg your pardon?"

"But I know someone who does. I'll send for Mr. Glascon at once." She banged her palm on top of a bell, and a
man appeared as if he'd been waiting in the wings for his
cue. Mrs. Wilson instructed him to take their luggage to
their rooms. Then she beamed with the most artificial
smile they had ever seen. "You'll have time to freshen
up." She waved a hand toward French doors opening off
the lobby. "Since dinner won't be served for several hours,
you're welcome to use the dining room to speak privately
with Mr. Glascon." After giving them another smile, this
one laden with sympathy, she lifted her skirts and fled
through a door behind the registration counter.

After a minute Clara frowned at Juliette. "You speak
the language of polite nonsense. Can you interpret what
she said?"

"I don't speak the language as well as I once did, but
I'd say Mrs. Wilson knows why we're here."

Zoe shook her head. "That isn't possible."

"Also, Mrs. Wilson has been instructed as to what she
should do and say if someone inquires about Mr. Villette.
She has performed as instructed and now wants nothing
more to do with us."

They followed the bellman up a flight of stairs and down
a corridor. "We can't be expected," Clara said flatly. "I
agree with Zoe. Jean Jacques had no idea that we'd chase
after him, so he would have no reason to instruct Mrs.
Wilson to do anything."

"And who is Mr. Glascon?" Zoe asked, before she followed her bags into a clean and pretty room.

"We'll find out soon," Juliette called from her doorway. "Shall we meet in the dining room in ten minutes?"

Clara and Zoe leaned into the corridor to stare. "You
are not in charge," Clara said. "You have never been in
charge."

"Haven't you noticed? I'm a new woman. I've traveled. I've climbed Chilkoot Pass. I don't like to be in charge, but I can be if I must," Juliette said, smiling. "Ten minutes."

Mrs. Wilson had laid out a coffee service on a table near a window that overlooked a warm, dusty valley.

"That's a vineyard, isn't it?" Clara asked.

Juliette nodded. "Someone tried and failed to grow grapes outside Linda Vista. Maybe the climate is better here."

Zoe poured from the silver pot and then glared. "How can you talk about scenery! Aren't you nervous? Before we finish drinking the coffee in that pot, Mr. Glascon, whoever he is, will have told us where Jean Jacques is." She held out her hands. "Look at me. I'm shaking."

Sunlight streamed through the window and gleamed along Zoe's silver heart ring. The one-of-a-kind heirloom ring. Juliette looked down at her own hand and the same ring. Sadness surged in her throat and behind her eyes. Once she had seen the ring as beautiful. Now it was merely a circle of tarnished metal.

The French doors opened, and a slightly breathless man hurried into the dining room, carrying a briefcase at his side. Juliette noticed he was tall, gray haired, distinguished. Kindness softened his gaze when he asked if he might join them.

"I am Henri Glascon. And you are Miss March." He nodded to Juliette as he sat at the table. "You must be Miss Klaus, and you will be Miss Wilder."

They stared.

"I'm not a magician. Mrs. Wilson gave me your names. Having previously heard each of you described, it isn't difficult to place names with faces."

And there it was. No one could have described them to this man except Jean Jacques Villette. They had finally found him.

"Where is he?" Clara demanded, breaking a lengthy silence.

Juliette drew a deep breath. "Am I correct to assume you are Mr. Villette's attorney, Mr. Glascon?"

"So, I think I understand," Zoe said angrily. "Jean Jacques has sent you to negotiate with us, hasn't he?" She waved a hand. "There is nothing that you or that bastard can offer that could possibly make amends for our ruination!"

"Ladies." Mr. Glascon's gaze swept their wedding rings. "I am indeed an attorney. And yes, I know who you are and why you're here." The kindness in his gaze deepened as if he understood their plight and personally regretted their circumstances. "Each of you married Mr. Villette believing you were his only wife. Somehow you encountered one another, recognized the rings, and you've come to Loma Grande to confront Mr. Villette."

"Yes!" They spoke in unison, their eyes fixed on his face.

"There can be no confrontation," he said gently. "Mr. Villette died shortly after he returned home from the Yukon."

The air ran out of Juliette's body. A soft sighing sound told her the same collapse had happened to Clara and Zoe.

"You won't see any tears here," Clara said finally.

Zoe agreed. "I feel cheated."

"How did you know about us? Did he make a death-bed confession?" Even to her own ears, Juliette sounded bitter.

"First, you'll want to know who he was." Mr. Glascon nodded toward the vineyard laid out in neat rows along the valley floor. "That is the Villette Winery." All heads turned to peer out the window. "The vines were planted by Luis Villette, Jean Jacques's father, about ten years ago, just before Luis died. The vineyard has never been successful." His shoulders lifted in a slight shrug. "Father and son believed California could produce quality wine. But it didn't happen in their lifetimes. Perhaps this is not the right part of California. Perhaps the vines are flawed.

It's impossible to say. But the man you knew as your husband came with his family from France to California to become a vintner."

Zoe covered her eyes. "Are any of our marriages legal?"

"I'm sorry—no."

Another sigh ran around the table, and then Clara spoke. "Why should we believe anything you say? How do we know that Jean Jacques isn't sitting on his porch, waiting for you to return and assure him that we swallowed a new set of lies?"

The question didn't seem to surprise Mr. Glascon. "I have a carriage waiting. In a moment, I'll drive you to the Loma Grande cemetery. Perhaps seeing Mr. Villette's headstone will help you cope with his loss."

"We're coping just fine, thank you," Juliette said. "But seeing his grave would assure us that he is indeed gone."

"Before we go . . ." Mr. Glascon lifted his briefcase to the table, opened it, and withdrew three thin envelopes. "Mr. Villette left these for you."

With a shock, Juliette recognized the handwriting flowing across the envelope. *To Mrs. Juliette March Villette.* But she wasn't certain that she wanted to read his last words.

"I didn't expect this," Clara murmured, her eyes wide and startled. "It's like a voice from the grave."

"How dare he! We should just tear up the letters and spit on the paper," Zoe said angrily.

"Mr. Glascon," Juliette said after drawing a deep breath, "exactly how many letters did Jean Jacques leave with you?"

A hint of a smile flitted across Mr. Glascon's expression, gone in an instant. "I'm not at liberty to answer that question."

"Which means there are several more letters," Zoe said.

"I can tell you that Jean Jacques Villette adored women.

He knew well an astonishing number of remarkable ladies, and I truly believe he genuinely loved all of you."

"He *ruined* all of us is what you mean," Zoe snapped.

They looked at each other. Then, as if they had discussed it beforehand, they twisted off their wedding rings and tossed the rings into Mr. Glascon's briefcase. Then they read their letters.

My dearest little Juliette,

No, darling, it was never just the money. Had it been only the money, I would have requested more, and generous heart that you are, you would have given it gladly. It was not the money, my beautiful Juliette, it was always you.

Your naïveté and the sameness of your days drew me and broke my heart. How I would have loved to sweep you away from Linda Vista and broaden your mind and your horizons. To stand by your side and watch your lovely shining eyes as you opened like a flower to your full potential. If you are reading this, love, then you have traveled beyond Linda Vista. You have begun a journey of discovery that I hope will never end. I envy the fortunate man who will travel by your side, for I know he will find you.

Thank you, my darling, for sharing yourself with me. I will love you always.

Your very own,
Jean Jacques Villette

My beautiful Clara,

I think of you so often. What a wonderful capacity for life you have, my dearest. How bright and quick and resourceful you are. By now you will have sold the inn, and marvelous new opportunities await you. Knowing you, you will make a success of whatever life brings you.

It was never the inn that interested me, love, it

was only you. It broke my heart that you believed you were but part of the inventory. No, my darling. The inn was merely a planet orbiting your sun. Somewhere, there is a man big enough to reflect your true image in his eyes and who will match the great love you have to give. In a better world, that man would have been me.

Thank you, my darling, for sharing yourself with me. I will love you always.

> *Your very own,*
> *Jean Jacques Villette*

Darling Zoe,

How much I regret that we had so little time together. I would have liked to know your family and tour Newcastle to meet the places and people that shaped the fine strong woman you became. It made my heart ache that you wished to shake off who you are. My love, the petty, forgettable people in the carriages should worship at your feet.

There is no disgrace in making a mistake, darling Zoe. Choosing a scoundrel for a husband doesn't diminish you or make you foolish. The disgrace would be to make the same mistake again, and that I think you will not do. Ah, beautiful Zoe with the flashing eyes and hair like midnight silk. Your next prince may or may not have gold in his pockets, but that fortunate man will find gold in you. As I did for all too brief a while.

Thank you, my darling, for sharing yourself with me. I will love you always.

> *Your very own,*
> *Jean Jacques Villette*

Chapter 23

They exchanged letters in the carriage, read them, and then sat in silence until Mr. Glascon turned the vehicle onto a shady road leading to the cemetery.

"Well, maybe he wasn't a complete scoundrel," Juliette said finally.

"I suppose we can admit that he had a few charms." Biting her lip, Clara stuffed her letter into her handbag.

Zoe sighed. "I never thought I'd say this, but maybe I'm glad I didn't shoot him."

"You know, in a way marrying Jean Jacques and his subsequent departure changed my life for the better," Juliette said in a musing tone. "If it hadn't been for him, I never would have left Linda Vista. I never would have climbed Chilkoot, something I'll be proud of all of my life. I never would have learned that I have a backbone, and I wouldn't have met Ben. I would never have met either of you."

Zoe clasped her hands and nodded. "I wouldn't have run into Tom again, and I might never have discovered who I am and who I want to be. I wouldn't have known the joy of sisters."

"If it wasn't for Jean Jacques, I would still own the inn. I might have married Hugo Bosch." Clara shuddered. "Now I've been somewhere and done something that few women will do. And I met a good man and two good women whom I will never forget."

"Jean Jacques did damage us," Juliette said slowly,

"but he gave us something, too. Perhaps he gave more than he took."

Clara nodded. "Who can understand the human heart? Maybe he did love us in his own way." She was first to alight at the cemetery, waving off Mr. Glascon's assistance.

Neat rows of headstones covered a grassy area that drew enough sun to seem peaceful and welcoming and enough of a breeze that visiting here would offer a pleasant respite on a hot day.

"This reminds me a bit of the Newcastle cemetery," Zoe said, falling into step behind Mr. Glascon. "Except we have more pines than shade trees."

They fell silent as they approached a white stone adorned with carved grapes and vines curling along the upper curve. Beneath Jean Jacques's name were his dates of birth and death. Below, an inscription read: SO MAY HE REST; HIS FAULTS LIE GENTLY ON HIM. WM. SHAKESPEARE.

"His faults lie gently," Juliette repeated. Closing her eyes, she lifted her face to the sunshine, and the anger drained out of her. It was over. The pain, the fury, the resentment.

When she opened her eyes, she saw that Zoe and Clara looked at peace. They, too, had said good-bye and released the anger.

At the sound of another carriage drawing to a halt, Mr. Glascon glanced back at the iron gates. His eyebrows rose, and his shoulders straightened. "My dears, I apologize for what is about to happen. But Loma Grande is a small town, and news travels quickly."

"What?"

"A lady has learned of your arrival and wishes to meet you."

"Who could possibly—?"

A woman dressed in widow's weeds stepped from the carriage and hurried toward them. Her face and form struck no familiar chord. But the four small boys who followed her were instantly recognizable. Juliette, Clara, and Zoe gazed in shock at four little Jean Jacqueses, the spitting image of their father.

Mr. Glascon managed a strained smile, then introduced Mrs. Jean Jacques Villette. The moment he mentioned Juliette's, Clara's, and Zoe's names, Marie Villette smiled, seemingly oblivious to their stunned expressions.

"I know each of you," she said in delight. She spoke in a charming French accent. "I know all of Jean Jacques's beautiful cousins. He spoke of you so fondly."

"Cousins," Clara repeated in a weak voice.

"*Oui*. Although I have not had the pleasure of meeting my husband's more distant relatives until recently, I feel I am acquainted with you all." Marie Villette's smile revealed dimples winking beside the corners of her mouth. If Clara had been asked to name which of Marie's pretty parts Jean Jacques most admired, she would have guessed that he fell in love with her dimples.

Or maybe it was the shining chestnut curls that bounced atop her shoulders when she pushed her boys forward and introduced them. Each of the boys had inherited Jean Jacques's straight, dark hair and his devilishly charming blue eyes. Little gentlemen all, they brought their cousins' fingertips to their lips and then politely stepped back. At a nod from their mother, they straightened the painted stones outlining their father's final resting place, pulled out weeds, and clipped the grass at the base of the stone.

"What?" Juliette wet her lips and tried to speak. "Forgive me, but I was admiring your sons and didn't hear."

"You're the heiress, and you love to read, Miss March. Miss Klaus, I believe you own and operate a wonderful inn on the Oregon coast. And Miss Wilder, you're the cousin with the large family. My husband spoke so highly of you all!"

Juliette stole a glance at Mr. Glascon, hoping he would step in and guide a shocking and unfortunate situation. But Mr. Glascon stood with his hands clasped behind his back, rocking backward on his heels, looking off into the distance. He would not intervene. If Jean Jacques's out-of-town wives wished to explain they were not cousins, if they wished to fully identify themselves and detail how egregiously Marie Villette had been deceived, he would not interfere.

"Please." Marie appealed to them with a smile. "Return with me to the vineyard. We'll have tea and a lovely chat."

Zoe jerked as if an invisible hand had tightened the strings holding her upright. "Ah, thank you, Mrs. . . . Mrs. Villette, but . . ." Helplessly, she sent a desperate signal to Clara.

Clara wet her lips. "We would love to know you better, but you see . . . well, we . . ." She turned pleading eyes on Juliette.

"We must decline with regret. We interrupted a rather urgent journey to pay our respects at our cousin's graveside," Juliette said smoothly. "Perhaps the next time we find ourselves in this lovely area, we can accept your kind invitation." It seemed a bit bizarre that they had come this far to end by protecting Jean Jacques. Or perhaps it was Marie and the little Jean Jacqueses they protected. But she knew it was absolutely the right thing to do. Moving as if in a dream, she stepped forward and clasped Marie Villette's gloved hands. "I'm very sorry for your loss, Mrs. Villette."

Clara and Zoe gaped at her, then swallowed hard and followed her lead. They stepped forward to express their condolences.

"He was a dear, good man," Marie Villette whispered, tears filling her eyes. "A good husband and a wonderful father."

"And I'm sure he was a generous provider," Clara said, her tone grim.

"Indeed. Mr. Villette left us in comfortable circumstances."

Before Clara could expand on Jean Jacques's methods of providing, Zoe elbowed her aside.

"You have my deepest sympathy," Zoe murmured. She meant it sincerely. She felt sorry for Marie Villette. No good woman should ever be married to a man with so many "cousins."

"Truly, I wish you would come to the vineyard. Couldn't you spare a few minutes? It would mean—"

"My, my, look at the time," Juliette said. "Mr. Glascon, we really must ... that is, if you wouldn't mind." Mr. Glascon nodded. Then came a flurry of pressed hands and pressed cheeks, good-byes and false promises to remain in touch. Finally Juliette, Clara, and Zoe climbed into the carriage, and Mr. Glascon stepped up to the driver's perch.

"Well," Juliette said in a dulled voice. "That's that."

Clara scowled. "I've changed my mind again. He was a no-good worthless snake in the grass! How could he treat her so badly? And us, too!"

"I wonder just how many cousins he had," Zoe said, speaking loudly enough that Mr. Glascon would hear. But Mr. Glascon didn't respond. They would never know how many women would appear in Loma Grande wearing the one-of-a-kind wedding ring.

"I feel almost as bad as I did when I realized Jean Jacques was not coming home." Juliette touched her gloved fingertips to her temples. "Maybe worse."

"You can't mean it!" Clara stared. "I cannot believe you hold an ounce of feeling for that miserable weasel."

"I don't. I'm missing Ben," she said simply. "If only we'd known that Jean Jacques had died. . . ."

They fell silent, and then Zoe whispered, "I'd give anything in the world to see Tom again. Even for one minute."

"Stop it, both of you, or I'm going to cry."

Mr. Glascon called to them over his shoulder. "Turn your faces, ladies. A group of horsemen are riding this way and kicking up a cloud of dust."

Zoe started to turn aside—then her head snapped

back and she blinked. "My Lord." Peering out the carriage window, she gasped. "I must be seeing things!"

"You sound—" Clara leaned over Zoe to look outside. "It's them! Good heavens, that's Bear! It's really them!"

"And Ben? Is Ben with them?" Juliette practically climbed over them to have a look. "Oh, my heavens!" She called to Mr. Glascon. "Stop the carriage, sir. We know these gentlemen."

Four men reined in close, as fine a sight as any female eyes ever looked upon. All had been freshly barbered and trimmed. They wore spanking new three-piece suits protected by tan dusters. They were armed to the teeth.

Clara didn't recognize the fourth gentleman, but it didn't matter. She treated her eyes to a brown-bear mirage before it disappeared.

"Is it really you?" she whispered.

"It took us a week, honey girl." Bear gave her a lopsided, sheepish smile. "Then Tom said, 'What the hell were we thinking of?' And Ben said, 'We've got to find them.' And I said, 'We'll solve this problem by killing the son of a bitch. Then they're widows and free to be courted.' "

Ben stared at Juliette, drinking in the sight of her. "Where is Villette?"

"Keep going along this road, then turn left at the tall iron gates."

Before they rode off in a swirl of dust, Tom blew Zoe a kiss. "You're pretty, you're a great cook, and damn, I'm sorry!"

The minute they rode off, Clara and Zoe turned on Juliette. "Why did you send them to the cemetery?"

"We need time to compose ourselves," Juliette said, sounding a hundred times more calm than she felt. "We need to decide if we intend to forgive them." She called to Mr. Glascon, "Drive on, please. We wish to return to the inn."

Clara gasped and clapped a hand over her heart. "*We* need to decide if *we* are going to forgive *them*?"

Zoe frowned. "Juliette, *we* are the ones in the wrong!"

"Well, I don't think so." She lifted her chin. "We confessed all, and they did not forgive us. It took them a whole week to realize they were wrong not to understand. They let us down."

"But they finally understood why we couldn't tell them about Jean Jacques, and here they are! I want to throw myself around Bear's neck!"

"And that's what you should do. But only *after* he begs your forgiveness and you decide to forgive him." She knew she was speaking in the prissy voice, but couldn't stop herself. "Aunt Kibble always said a person should begin as they mean to go on. It's excellent advice." She lifted an eyebrow. "Do you want to spend the rest of your lives always being the one who apologizes and hopes to be forgiven? Or would you prefer to be the one who is apologized to and who grants the forgiveness?"

Zoe nodded thoughtfully. "Clara, I believe Juliette has made a very good point."

"I see it, I see it. How long should it take to forgive them?" Clara hastily pinched color into her cheeks and pulled at the frizzy red tendrils curling on her forehead. "How do I look?"

"You look fine, wonderful." Zoe found a tiny vial of perfume in her handbag, touched the backs of her ears, then handed the vial to Juliette. "Hold out as long as you can, Clara, before you forgive him. Juliette, is my hair coming out of the pins?"

"There are a few loose tendrils, but it's charming." Juliette dabbed perfume at the base of her throat and then gave Clara the vial. "Tell me, does this look soulful?" She blinked her eyes and tried to look wounded but loving. "Do I look like a femme fatale?"

"Your expression will melt Ben to his knees."

They tumbled out of the carriage, called hasty good-byes to Mr. Glascon, then rushed into the inn's lobby.

"They have to be only minutes behind us."

"Damn. There's no time to freshen up!"

Clara stepped up to the startled Mrs. Wilson. "Some gentlemen will be arriving momentarily. We have need of the privacy of your dining room again." A clatter of hooves sounded outside.

Without waiting for Mrs. Wilson's approval, they lifted their skirts and dashed for the French doors as the inn's front door slammed open and men's boots sounded in the foyer.

Bear burst into the dining room and his gaze devoured Clara. "Of course you're respectable and better than me. That's how I want it, and that's the end of it." He talked as if picking up a conversation begun a minute ago. "As for the rest, I'm an idiot."

"I've held out as long as I can. You're forgiven!" Dashing across the room, Clara flung herself into his arms, and he swung her up and in a wide circle before he set her on her feet and wrapped his arms around her.

"I understand why you couldn't tell me. . . ." She smothered his words with kisses.

Ben swept off his hat in front of Juliette. "I was angry and I said it all wrong. I don't give a damn if some garbled story gets out and creates a scandal that rocks San Francisco. And I don't care about Villette. The only thing that matters in my world is you, Juliette. I love you and want to spend my life with you. Can you forgive me for not seeing the situation from your viewpoint?"

"Oh, Ben. I'll always forgive you, and I'll always love you." A joyous smile lit her expression, and she rushed into his arms. "I've missed you so much!"

Tom gazed down at Zoe. "I love you, and I believe you love me. We can work out everything else."

"I lied to you, Tom."

"I know it, and I don't like it. So don't do it again."

"I won't." She tilted her head and gazed up at him, loving the sharp handsome angles of his face, the twinkle in his green eyes. "It took you a week, huh?"

He laughed and pulled her against his body. "You never saw three more miserable men in your life. Lord, I've missed you, darlin'! Are you going to forgive me for not trusting that you had reasons for doing what you did?"

"I forgive you," she whispered as his lips came down hard on hers.

"Ladies? Gentlemen?" The man who had ridden with them cleared his throat and led a somewhat dazed Mrs. Wilson into the dining room. "Take your places, please."

"Who is that man?" Clara asked in a breathless voice. Her lips were swollen and her skin glowed.

"Maybe we're presuming a lot . . ." Bear said, anxiously examining her expression.

"He's Reverend Wainwright." Ben smiled down at Juliette. "We hired him to bury Villette and marry us."

Tom pressed his lips to Zoe's forehead. "Our plan was to ride in here, get rid of Villette, then marry you before you could say no. We're about to commence the marrying part."

Reverend Wainwright waved them forward. "Mrs. Wilson has agreed to act as witness. Will the brides stand here, please, and the grooms over here."

"I'm not certain we've discussed everything that happened in the detail it deserves," Juliette said. But her gray eyes flashed and danced.

"Darling, we have the rest of our lives to discuss anything you wish to discuss." Holding her arm to his side as if he would never let her go, Ben led her forward.

"Honey girl? Tell me you love me." Bear pressed Clara's hand against his big barrel chest. "I've waited all my life to hear a woman like you say those words."

"I love you," Clara said softly, gazing into his brownbear eyes. "I've loved you from the minute I saw you."

"There is going to be some house-wrecking tonight," he promised gruffly, gazing happily into her eyes before he led her forward.

"Zoe? I've wanted to marry you for half of my life." Tom clasped his hands behind her waist. "But you have to know—no matter where we end up, I'm Newcastle through and through. I'm not a prince promising you a rainbow."

"Oh, yes, you are," she said softly, blinking at tears of happiness. "I'm Newcastle, too, Tom. Nothing more and nothing less."

"That's all I ever wanted."

"Me, too. It just took me longer to know it. Oh, Tom. I love you so much!"

He kissed her deeply. Then, grinning broadly, he led her forward to join the others.

Reverend Wainwright smiled at three radiant brides and nodded to three impatient grooms.

"Dearly beloved, we are gathered here today in the presence of this witness to join . . ."

"Do you, Juliette March, take Benjamin James Dare to be your lawfully wedded husband?"

"I do!"

"Do you, Clara Klaus, take Bernard T. Barrett to be your lawfully wedded husband?"

"I do!"

"Do you, Zoe Wilder, take Thomas John Price to be your lawfully wedded husband?"

"I do!"

"If you like to hoot with laughter and
have your heartstrings twanged, don't miss . . .
Maggie Osborne."
—CATHERINE COULTER

SILVER LINING
by Maggie Osborne

As scruffy and rootless as the other prospectors searching for
gold in the Rockies, Low Down wanted nothing in return for
nursing a raggedy bunch through the pox. But when pressed
to reveal her heart's wish, she admits, "I want a baby." Not a
husband, not a forced marriage to the proud man who drew
the scratched marble and became honor bound to marry her.

To be sure, Max McCord was easy on the eyes, but he loved
another woman and dreamed of a different life. Yet they
agreed to a temporary marriage that could end only in disaster. But can this strange twist of fate lead to the silver lining
that both have been searching for?

Ask for SILVER LINING at your local bookstore.
Published by Ivy Books.

Coming in Fall 2001...

❧

BAND OF GOLD
by Maggie Osborne

Ten years ago Sam Holland had wanted Angie Ballard but couldn't have her. Now he's stuck with her, a wife he doesn't know and doesn't want. Angie has been waiting a long time for her life to begin, but first she must deal with Sam, his betrayal and a marriage that never should have happened.

Only Sam isn't the boy she loved and impetuously married. Now he's a man—rugged and handsome—with two children to care for. And soon their irresistible attraction blazes anew, and Sam and Angie are faced with a terrifying choice—can they risk making their ready-made family a reality after all?

Published by Ivy Books